A GIRL'S GUIDE
TO LANDING A
GREEK GOD

THE MYTHMAKERS TRILOGY

To my mother, Angie, and my father, Bill, for giving me the freedom to fly in my own direction.

A GIRL'S GUIDE TO LANDING A GREEK GOD

THE MYTHMAKERS TRILOGY

BILL FULLER

Jim & Michael,
Thanks for being two
great friends & fellow
readers who were kind
enough to buy my book.
Bill
Trix will love you forever!

MIDNIGHT INK
WOODBURY, MINNESOTA

FIRST EDITION
First Printing, 2016

Cover Illustration by Hugh D'Andrade/Jennifer Vaughn Artist Agent
Editing by Rosemary Wallner

Midnight Ink, an imprint of Llewellyn Worldwide Ltd.

Library of Congress Cataloging-in-Publication Data
Names: Fuller, Bill, 1956– author.
Title: A girl's guide to landing a Greek god / Bill Fuller.
Description: First edition. | Woodbury, Minnesota : Midnight Ink, 2016. |
  Series: The Mythmakers trilogy ; 1
Identifiers: LCCN 2015041013 (print) | LCCN 2015050905 (ebook) | ISBN
  9780738747774 | ISBN 9780738748160 ()
Subjects: LCSH: Gods, Greek--Fiction. | Goddesses, Greek--Fiction. |
  Mythology, Greek--Fiction. | GSAFD: Fantasy fiction. | Love stories.
Classification: LCC PS3606.U5 G57 2016 (print) | LCC PS3606.U5 (ebook) |
DDC
  813/.6—dc23
LC record available at http://lccn.loc.gov/2015041013

Midnight Ink
Llewellyn Worldwide Ltd.
2143 Wooddale Drive
Woodbury, MN 55125-2989
www.midnightinkbooks.com

Printed in the United States of America

ACKNOWLEDGMENTS

This novel was a labor of love—and sometimes just a labor—but ultimately one I'm proud of, if for no other reason because I finished it after throwing my hands up in defeat so many times. And when I say "I," I could just as well say "we," because there are many people without whose assistance I wouldn't have been able to pull this off.

First off, I'd like to thank my dear friend, veteran novelist Diana Dempsey. Writing alone has been an adjustment for me after having worked with a writing partner in television for so many years and coming to rely on the creative synergy of the scriptwriting process. As a result, I often find it daunting to sit down in front of a blank screen and create. Diana's assistance has been invaluable, both in the brainstorming and feedback process. It takes a special person to offer to read and critique a friend's rough draft, and an out-and-out saint to offer to do it a second time—Diana is a little of both. As terrified as I am of that mighty red pen of hers, her critical but supportive feedback has been vital to my growth as a writer. I'll never stop thanking her for it.

There are several other writers whose assistance has been essential to this book. My former writing partner Jim Pond gave me creative first aid along the way, lending a hand every time I wrote myself into a corner. His help was also invaluable when I decided to have Angie play an inning of major league baseball even though I know next to nothing about the game. Fellow novelists Gene Miller and Karen Kavner (*Unraveled*) provided support throughout the process and often commiserated with me over a glass of wine on the difficulty of writing a novel. Thanks, too, to Barbara Rabinowitz for her sage feedback and solid editing skills.

Dr. Nicole Miller, PhD in mythology, proved essential in helping me get the mythology right. She also showed the skills of the world's finest editor when she came prepared with fixes for most of the gaffes I'd made.

I also value the critique of my longtime friends, Carol Traeger and Sandy Mallory, who got their arms twisted into reading early drafts and helped me muddle through the mess. Special thanks goes to Melanie Nalepa for not only spotting errors I'd missed, but for providing vital information about horses and how to ride them. Eddie and Chrissie would not even begin to resemble living, breathing creatures if it weren't for Melanie's horse sense.

I'd like to thank my agent Scott Mendel for never losing faith in this book, even when I was ready to give up and conclude it would never sell. I'm indebted to my editor, Terri Bischoff, at Llewellyn Worldwide, not only for purchasing my debut novel but for her wisdom and patience as well. I'd also like to thank copy editor Rosemary Wallner for her keen eye at spotting typos, grammatical errors, and factual inconsistencies.

My late great golden retriever, Moker, was always there for me during the creative process, whether I needed to take her on a long walk to brainstorm a plot point or to simply see a smiling face when I was hopelessly stuck. My new golden, Tria, has also been supportive, despite her desire to eat the pages.

I'll always appreciate my sisters, Marilyn Rossi and Carol Masacek, for reminding me over and over that I've wanted to be a writer ever since I was a kid and that sometimes dreams come with a little sweat.

Finally, I owe a huge debt to my late parents, Angie and Bill Fuller. Although the world I wanted to inhabit was far from the world they were familiar with, they allowed me to follow my dreams. I hope there are books in the afterlife and that they're happily reading this one and not blushing too much.

ONE

As the ancient pipe organ at Saint Demetrios Greek Orthodox Church belched out the first few notes of "The Wedding March," Angie Costianes of Astoria, Queens, the daughter of a man who'd jumped off a bridge and a woman she often wished would follow suit, fought off a last-minute attack of the dry heaves and sashayed toward her destiny.

I'm doing the right thing. I know I am.

She was almost thirty, for godsakes. It was time. And it wasn't like she was settling. Nick was a damn good catch, with a full head of hair, a knowledge of baseball that rivaled her own, and a recession-proof job at FedEx. Not to mention he really, truly cared about her. Always had, ever since they were in the third grade and he'd flatten anybody on the playground who dared call her "Gi-*gan*-gie." So what if *he* was the one who had come up with that nickname. So what if his idea of the perfect evening was a bucket of hot wings and an Adam Sandler flick followed by ten minutes of welt-inducing sex on his corduroy couch. So what if he got a little stupid after two shots of ouzo and

1

developed a wandering eye after three. Seriously, what man in her little pocket of New York didn't?

And if she wasn't head-over-heels, weak-in-the-knees, heart-thumping-out-of-her-chest in love with him, she could honestly say she felt comfortable around him. Free to be herself, warts and all. That was enough to make a go of things, right? It wasn't like she was some starry-eyed teenager mooning over a Yankees player who happened to smile in her general direction. She was an adult, with miles of dating experience in her rearview. An adult who'd long since abandoned the notion that Prince Charming was out there somewhere, ready to come charging up in his white Porsche and sweep her off to a land of multiple orgasms and limitless credit cards. How did her mother put it? "Fairy tales are for children and the emotionally retarded. And the sooner you accept that, the sooner you'll be able to settle into a nice, ordinary life." Her mother said a lot of things that drove her nuts, but that one had a ring of reality to it.

So Angie slowed her sashay—*might as well give the people their money's worth of this gorgeous gown and killer 'do*—and worked up a homecoming queen smile. And just as she did, Nick turned and looked at her, his face so full of pride that she felt her eyes misting up.

Then he adjusted his crotch. And Angie Costianes did the only thing she could under the circumstances. She kept right on smiling.

———

Milos stood on the cliff, his bronzed feet clinging to the rocky outcropping above the tortured sea. And although the rain was pelting him from all directions, he didn't even feel it. His mind—and his heart—were half a world away.

She cannot be doing this thing, he thought. *It is beneath her.*

Nevertheless, there she was, marching that gloriously voluptuous body of hers down the aisle toward that imbecile. A man who wasn't fit to gaze at a single star in her constellation.

Oh, how I wish I could reach out and smite the little slug.

That, of course, was forbidden—a lesson he'd learned the hard way several years ago. But he'd do it again in an instant if it meant keeping her safe.

As she drew closer to her groom, a frightening thing happened. She smiled. Not hesitantly, but full-on with what appeared to be an abundance of joy. And although these images of his were never as clear as he wished them to be, there seemed to be no one in the vicinity training a firearm on her. She was doing this of her own free will.

A scorpion wriggled up to his big toe and playfully reached out a pincer, hoping to endear itself to him. Without a blink of hesitation, Milos crushed it under his foot, perceiving its almost childlike sense of bewilderment seconds before he felt its spirit soaring into the cosmos.

And when that act of dominion failed to bring him satisfaction, he zeroed in on another target—a cypress tree whose undulating dance seemed to be mocking him. At lightning speed, he bolted over to it, snapped it off at the roots and made quick work of the branches. Then he stepped up to the precipice, thrust his arm back, and heaved the thirty-foot trunk into the sea with the same warrior's cry his brethren had been making since their glory days. The sea received it, then retaliated with a towering wave that sent him flying backward onto the rocks, landing squarely on his butt.

As Milos stood up, smarting from the pain in his backside, he couldn't help but smile. The sea, his father's sea, had responded to his tirade by putting him in his place. And deservedly so.

Who in Hades do I think I am, the supreme ruler of the universe?

In truth, he'd always taken himself too seriously, a criticism that had been leveled at him since his first conclave. He'd also been warned repeatedly about this long-distance obsession. Despite his fiercest hopes, this was not the destiny that had been laid out for him.

He sighed. Maybe after countless years and untold yearning, it was time to close the book on this earthbound creature and embrace the chosen path.

But could he?

Sadly, this wasn't some passing infatuation. For nearly two decades, he'd ached for this woman, even though she wasn't even aware of his existence. She was the first thing he thought about when the sun greeted him in the morning and the last thing on his mind when the world fell into its blackest slumber. She was his alpha, his omega, his very reason for being. Would he ever be able to put her behind him and love another as deeply as he loved her? The answer to that question was in every tear that fell from his eyes.

He let out a groan. No doubt about it, love was … what was that expression his brother used? *A suckfest.* Indeed, love was a suckfest. And he was the biggest sucker of them all.

At that, Milos found himself laughing for the first time in days. Not just laughing, but chortling at the sheer lunacy of his predicament. So loudly, in fact, that a flock of seagulls flew off, presumably in search of saner harbor.

———

Who the hell was laughing? And right in the middle of her vows? She'd managed to write off the howl she'd heard earlier as an outburst from somebody's kid—probably her cousin Patsy's aggressively stupid eight-year-old. But this assault on the most spotlit moment of her life was impossible to ignore.

Angie whipped her head around and confronted the assembled. "Whoever's doing that, would you please knock it off?"

But there didn't seem to be a joker among them. Quite the contrary. Everybody was staring at her in confusion. Except her mother, whose steely glare seemed to be saying, *Get on with it before he changes his mind.*

"What's going on, Ang?" She felt Nick's hand on her shoulder and turned to find him regarding her with the same troubled look the congregation was giving her.

She bit her lip, puzzled. "You didn't hear it? The laughter?"

His eyebrow twitched for a moment, then settled into a dubious arch. "I didn't hear nothing, Babe. I think you're losing it."

Still not ready to buy into that theory, Angie turned to her maid of honor for support. But even Sylvie had an off-kilter look on her face, like she was witnessing her cousin having the stroke they'd always feared would get them due to all the pot they'd smoked as teenagers. Even her normally unruffled brother, Anthony, looked worried. In fact, the whole damn wedding party was a collection of cupped hands and suspicious whispers.

A wave of dizziness hit her. What in the world was happening? Was she so keyed up about her big day that her imagination was playing tricks on her? Was she having a bad reaction to the Xanax she'd popped this morning? Or was she out-and-out losing her mind, like everybody said her father did at the end?

Whatever was happening, it wasn't worth attracting further scrutiny. The last thing she needed on her special day was a crack from Nick about her mental state being brought on by PMS.

So she popped him on the shoulder and turned to Father Kontos. "Sorry about that, Father K. Nerves, I guess."

Father Kontos, who'd never met a plate of baklava he didn't like, nodded solicitously and picked up where he'd left off. "Nicholas, do you take Angelica to be your lawfully wedded wife? To have and to hold. For better or for worse. For richer or—"

And there it was again, that freakin' laugh! Even louder this time. Like a deranged banshee or one of those shrews from *Real Housewives*. And it went on and on, even as Nick said "I do."

Then all at once, it hit her. She knew exactly where the laughter was coming from. And it sent a shudder all the way to her toes.

My God, it's my conscience!

That was it. It had to be. All this time, she'd been putting up a brave front about marrying Nick. For her friends, who claimed to like him but always seemed to find an excuse to bow out after an hour in his presence. For her Ya-Ya, who'd never stopped believing her only granddaughter deserved the best of everything. For her mother, who'd been bugging her since forever to marry Nick and give her a grandchild, presumably so she'd have a brand-new ego to crush.

But mostly, she'd been putting up that front for herself. Because she'd really wanted to believe this was the right thing to do. That after all the humiliating blind dates and toxic relationships and sexual surrender, she could finally close the door on wishing and hoping and thinking and praying and start the next chapter of her life. That in a world of compromise, life with Nick was a reasonable proposition. And that growing old with *somebody,* even somebody less than ideal, was a helluva lot better than growing old alone.

But she'd been kidding herself, big time. She'd taken all her doubts, stuffed them in a trunk, and buried them deep inside herself, figuring they'd never find their way to the surface. But clearly, her conscience had had other ideas. First, through a scream, then through loud, nagging *are-you-kidding-me* laughter, it had awakened her to the cold, hard truth.

There was no way in the world she could marry Nick.

She wouldn't just be settling, she'd be raising the white flag of spiritual surrender. Starting that long march toward a fixer-upper in Long Island City and screwed-up kids and once-a-week appointment sex and hoping to God every Friday night he'd stay out super late at happy hour so she'd have a nice, long time to sit home with a bottle of wine and pretend she was still single and everything the world had to offer was still within her reach.

And as the laughter in her head ebbed away, she let out a whoosh of a sigh. *Who am I kidding? I still want it all. Dizzying sex, stellar companionship, and a man who sees heaven every time he looks in my eyes. I know it's out there somewhere. And I'll be damned if I'll let it go to some other girl because she held out longer than I did.*

Suddenly, Angie knew what she had to do.

She ran.

Off the altar and down the aisle, past a blur of friends and family. If anybody was calling out to her, she didn't hear them. If somebody grabbed her arm to try to stop her, she didn't feel it. She kept right on running. Out the door and down the steps and through the driving rain of the gloomy June afternoon. Straight into the street.

And a split second after the beer truck hit her, as she was somersaulting through the air, she saw a face. A man's face. Handsome and strong and chiseled and kind. With clear blue eyes and jet black hair and an impossibly dark tan. It was a face she'd never seen before, but felt she'd known all her life.

It was the most beautiful face she'd ever seen. And it was full of love. For *her*.

Then she hit the pavement. And the world went black.

TWO

As her eyes fluttered open, Angie took a long, bleary look around her. And shook her head in disbelief.

My God, is this really happening?

She did a couple of hard blinks to jog her eyes into focus. And when the images in front of her didn't disintegrate like some deceitful desert oasis, she let out a sigh. It was real, all right. Every last shred of it. Who in their wildest dreams would've imagined *this* was where she'd end up? Certainly not her.

"May I freshen your champagne, Mrs. Costianes?"

"Sure can." Angie extended her arms high above her head in a luxurious post-nap stretch. "And it's *Miss* Costianes. Oh hell, call me Angie."

"And you can call me Jace," the steward said with a frisky wink as he filled her champagne flute with Piper-Heidsieck. "Short for Jason."

Angie couldn't help smiling. Wasn't it just a few months ago she was swigging Two-Buck Chuck? Now here she was, sprawled out in a sleeper seat—in first class, no less—being pampered by Jace, a dishy specimen with puppy dog eyes, a swoosh of sandy brown hair, and a smile that had probably seduced countless men, a fair number of women, and the occasional too-tanked-to-care pilot. And for the next ten hours, he was *hers*, under contract by Delta to treat her like airborne royalty as she sopped up every ounce of extravagance this e-ticket ride had to offer.

And her destination? Well, that was the best part.

Athens.

As in the cradle of Western civilization, the birthplace of her ancestors, and—if the gods were game—the scene of some legendary adventures of her own. She'd been there three times before—twice with her family and once with her church group. But now she was en route as an emancipated bride, determined to take full advantage of the Land of the Three S's: sea, sun, and sex.

And for all this deliciousness, she had her Ya-Ya Georgia to thank. In a gesture that was both intuitive and generous, her grandmother had insisted on treating her to this Grecian getaway to help her put the past behind her. Angie had been hesitant at first, seeing as she'd lost her job at the bakery a month before the wedding and really needed to find a new one now that she was going to be swinging it alone. But Ya-Ya had offered to scour Craigslist and a few other job sites while she was away and put her up for anything that seemed remotely appropriate. So really, how could she argue with that?

As Jace walked his perfectly sculpted butt away to fetch her "some truly astonishing Mediterranean cheeses," Angie took a sip of bubbly and cast a mental glance back at the events of the past few months. And when it became evident that many of them were still too painful to revisit in any semblance of sobriety, she took a more therapeutic gulp.

The moments after the accident were still a bit of a blur, but there were a few images she'd never get out of her head. Faces, hundreds of them, staring at her as she lay on the rain-soaked pavement—a few ghoulish bastards even snapping pictures with their camera phones. Her beautiful Liv Harris wedding gown covered with gravel and bloodstains. Nick crouched over her, looking confused and scared, like a little boy with a five o'clock shadow. Father K sprinkling her with Holy Water, his face lit up like a pumpkin by the lights of the approaching ambulance. Her mother pacing around, wailing, "Why, God, why?!" while Ya-Ya stroked her hand, assuring her, "You'll be okay, my angel." Her brother offering an encouraging smile as he huddled with the groomsmen, swilling beers they'd lifted from the truck. And the driver, slumped on the curb, blubbering, "I'm cursed, is what I am. I hit a bride. I'll never marry!"

Then there were the surgeries. Six of them, to repair a multitude of shattered bones in her arms, legs, and hips. Lots of pain and lots of painkillers, some of them so strong she felt like she was floating above the bed—no mean feat for a plus-size girl. A revolving door of grim doctors speaking in hushed tones about the possibility that she'd never walk again. And when she asked one of them, an Asian orthopedist with enviably glossy hair, whether she'd be able to swing a bat, he stared at her with tombstones in his eyes before muttering, "In your next life, Miss."

But worse than that, and worse than the grueling physical therapy and horrific hospital food, were the questions. Thrust at her just about every day, by just about everybody.

"Why'd you do it, Angie?"

"Were you delusional? Depressed?"

"Was it my fault?"

How could she tell them about the laughter she'd heard that day without sounding like a lunatic? How could she make them understand that in spite of the relatively decent years she'd spent with Nick, she was still aching for a man who looked like he'd stepped off the cover of *Men's Fitness*? How could she explain, without coming off like a raging egomaniac, that she wanted a *bigger* life than the one that had been laid out for her? A life full of epic love and endless surprises and one grand adventure after another?

So, for a long time, she didn't open up to anybody—not her friends, her family, or even Nick, who, to her surprise, stopped by the hospital every day. She knew it was cruel to keep them in the dark, but she just wasn't ready to talk about it. Sure, she tossed out the occasional, "My memory's foggy" or "I'm too tired today," and in one instance faked a catheter emergency. But by and large, she kept the truth of her runaway bride moment to herself.

Eventually, they sicced a shrink on her, a perpetually smiling woman with a shock of spiky red hair and matching Dolce & Gabbana frames. In their first session, the woman produced a box of Crayolas and encouraged Angie to "color" her mood. Instead, she drew a picture of a Big Mac and fries and asked the doctor to put in her order for them. There would be no second session. No burger or fries, either.

All of this frustrated the hell out of her mother. To her credit, Connie was at her side every day, doing her blustery best to make sure her daughter received the best care Mount Sinai had to offer. And Angie loved her for it, she really did. And hated the fact that her hundred-yard dash out of the church had put her mother in an even deeper state of gloom than she was used to navigating.

Still, there were times when Angie wanted to throttle the woman. As anyone who'd ever met her mother might have predicted, she treated the whole thing as if it were her burden and hers alone. Poor Connie, who'd gotten herself knocked up by a beautiful loser who had a head full of dreams but barely eked out a living, then offed himself for no apparent reason. Poor Connie, who'd not only been cursed with twenty years of working her *kolos* off to support two kids, but now had to live with the fact that one of them had inherited a bucketful of bad genes. Poor Connie, whose dream of being surrounded by worshipful grandkids would never come to fruition. Poor Connie, who went to church twice a week and prayed till her knees blistered, but was clearly a joke to God and a failure as a mother—words she wore like a crown.

A tap on the shoulder rescued Angie from further musings about her mother.

"The feta has a nice vein of Kalamata running through it, but my personal fave is the mascarpone. So sweet and creamy you'll think you've died and gone to lactose heaven."

And there was Jace, hovering over her with a cheese platter and a shirt that looked a button or two poutier than it had earlier, revealing chiseled pecs and a nice little landing strip of chest hair.

After loading up a cracker for her, he set the platter down and gave her a long, appraising look. "Has anybody ever told you you look like Drea de Matteo?"

A few months ago, Angie would've done a breath check on anybody who suggested she resembled Drea, the sexy goombette from *The Sopranos*. But one of the miracles that had sprung from her surgeries and regimen of physical therapy was the shedding of twenty-six pounds. Granted, she was still what they used to call

Rubenesque and probably always would be, but she was finding it easier and easier to slip into her size fourteen skinny jeans.

So yes, when she and her curling iron won the rare battle with her pathologically kinky hair, when she chose the right shadow to bring out her pale green eyes, when she stationed herself under the most flattering light in the room and pinched her cheeks till they begged for mercy, she could possibly be mistaken for Drea.

And, indentured Delta servant or not, Jace had been a honey to point that out. Angie rewarded him with a pat on the hand. "Yeah, Jace, I get that all the time. Like you're probably sick of being compared to Matthew McConaughey."

"Sick to death of it," he said with mock sarcasm. "I just wish he weren't so narcissistic so I could throw him out of bed once in awhile."

As Jace crossed away, Angie couldn't help smiling. The man was not only hella fine, but witty to boot. If only she could bottle his looks and put them in a straight man with nesting aspirations ... heck, maybe she could. If these past few months had taught her anything, it was that anything was possible.

Case in point, the speed at which her mangled limbs had healed. She'd always been a scrapper, and despite the doctors' doomsday predictions, she'd tried to keep hope alive that she'd come through rehab with her mobility intact—not to mention her dignity. Seriously, the idea of trudging along on one of those walkers with the tennis ball feet and built-in handbag was too pathetic to imagine. So the minute she was able to wrestle herself out of bed, she devoted endless hours to getting back to some semblance of her old self.

But even her physical therapist was astounded by how well her body had repaired itself. Granted, Cornelius had worked her tail off in two-a-day sessions, six days a week. And she'd certainly been coaxed along by his exotic looks and Jamaican accent—so intoxicating that even his harshest commands were like aural chocolate.

But he swore up and down that he'd rehabbed professional athletes whose bones hadn't healed so seamlessly. "Angie, fluffy girl, you must be Superwoman," he said on the day she clocked a whopping thirty minutes on the treadmill.

And that wasn't the best of it. A mere eight weeks after her collision with the beer truck, Cornelius talked her into putting on a demonstration of her rebirth in a schoolyard near the hospital. Theoretically, it was designed to boost funding to the physical therapy wing, but Angie saw it as a chance to shove a big "I told you so" at her doctors. So, on a picture-perfect August afternoon, in the presence of friends, family, and physicians, she took to a makeshift baseball diamond, where she smacked a 70-mph fastball with her once-shattered arm, hurled a ball two hundred feet, and scooted after a grounder with barely a hitch in her step. After watching in awe, her doctors practically came to blows over who should get the lion's share of credit for her recovery. Even the orthopedist who'd gloomily predicted she'd never swing a bat again tried to claim it had been due to a masterful stroke of reverse psychology on his part.

Yet despite those victories, she still felt an occasional pang of doubt. And as much as she hated to admit it, she knew the source of that pang was … hell, she didn't want to think about it.

"By the way, if you want to talk about Nick, I'm a fabulous listener."

Angie whipped her head around to find Jace in the window seat next to her. How in the world had he managed to maneuver in there without her noticing? Picking up on her discomfort, he cupped a hand on her shoulder. "I totally understand if you don't want to talk about it. It's just that there was a lull in service, and I thought I'd kick back here instead of that nasty jump seat."

She stared at him, dumbfounded. "How'd you know about Nick?"

He flashed her a smile, displaying a set of choppers Tom Cruise would've killed for. "When I walked by a minute ago, you were asleep and kept repeating the name 'Nick.' Then earlier, you asked me to call you 'Miss.' I kinda put two and two together and figured you were taking what would've been your honeymoon, solo. Am I in the ballpark?"

She could've asked him how he'd landed on that theory instead of the more obvious one that she was freshly divorced. But why quibble with "right," especially when it was coming from a nice little nugget of eye candy?

So she gave him a nod and posed the most important question of the flight. "You wouldn't happen to have more of that—"

Once again, Jace proved to be a mind reader, whipping a bottle of champagne from under his seat and refilling her flute. Then he plucked another flute off the floor and poured some for himself. As Angie shook her head in amazement, Jace clinked his glass with hers. "*Stin* iyá *mas*."

"*Stin* iyá *mas*," she repeated, toasting his health in return. "Are you ... Greek?"

"In all the fun ways," he said with a wink. "But for the next few minutes, consider me your priest, your shrink—or if you prefer, your BFF."

After another sip, Angie did just that, filling him in on her relationship with Nick, from two misfit kids with a Jones for baseball to fractured couple at the altar. She explained how he'd helped her pick up the pieces after her father jumped off the Brooklyn Bridge. How even though Nick was only two months older than she was, she cast him in the role of protector, because that was what she needed. Protection from a world that could allow her sweet, loving father to take his life. Protection from the nagging fear that she hadn't been enough for him to stick around for.

Jace took all that in, then said, "So at the heart of it, Nick was more of a father figure than a boyfriend."

"You got me," Angie replied. Who *was* this man from Delta Airlines who seemed to know her so well? All she knew was that he couldn't have come along at a better time.

Expanding on Jace's observation, Angie explained how torn she'd been every time Nick came to the hospital. How wary she'd been of leading him on, but at the same time comforted by the fact that unlike everybody else, he never asked her to explain her exodus from church that day. How instead, he'd engage her in chit-chat about the Yankees or grouse about the indignities of urgent package delivery, in one instance tapping the FedEx logo on his shirt and saying, "Gimme one good reason why this uniform shouldn't be treated with the same respect as that of a cop."

After laughing along with her for a moment, Jace furrowed his brow. "So here's this guy whose ego had to've taken a hit when you ditched him. But he comes to see you day after day and doesn't ask you squat about why you did it. Why do you think that was?"

Although she had a feeling he knew the answer, she laid it out anyway. "Nick was a lot of things, but he was no dummy. Deep down inside, he knew why I ran away. He also knew that once it was out in the open, he'd lose me. But if he kept his mouth shut, maybe somewhere down the line the whole episode would be forgotten and things could go back to the way they'd always been."

She hesitated, wondering how much of her insecure self she should reveal to this virtual stranger. One look into his comforting blue eyes made the decision a no-brainer. "And maybe I was afraid of change, too. Sure, I'd made a bold move, but where had it gotten me? I was laid up in the hospital, worn down from all the surgeries and questions—"

"And you wanted to feel safe again."

Angie managed a smile, then looked away. Out the window and past the cloud tops and all the way back to her childhood, the last time she believed the world was a safe place.

As though to coax her back to the here and now, Jace waved a freshly cheesed cracker in front of her. "But you didn't give into that feeling, did you? Otherwise, you wouldn't be sitting here getting your flight attendant drunk."

"No, I didn't," she said, thankful for his intuitive ability to lighten the moment. "And one day I decided it was time to come clean and let the poor guy move on with his life. He strolled in after his shift, armed with my favorite candy in the world, caramel turtles. I scarfed five of 'em for courage, then said, 'Nick, we gotta talk.' Straight off, his face turned into a slab of determination. 'I know what you're gonna say, Ang. All that pressure, everybody looking at you ... you freaked. No worries. We all go a little third rail sometimes. But if you're worried about it happening again, how about I pay your way into some sort of ... crazy camp. You know, like that fat camp your Ma sent you to when you were a kid.'"

Jace shook his head. "And *there* went any doubts you had about dumping him."

"Actually, as oddball as it was, it touched me. I remember thinking, *God bless him, the man would still want me if I was strapped in a strait-jacket and fitted with a tongue depressor.* But that didn't stop me from telling him everything. About what was going through my mind before I ran out of the church, how those feelings hadn't changed and how it wouldn't be fair for him to be married to a woman who was forever looking over her shoulder for somebody who might be a better fit."

No doubt sensing how tough that must've been, Jace gave her a squeeze on the shoulder. "And how did he take it?"

"Like a pro. Didn't yell. Didn't beg. Didn't put a fist through the wall. Just sorta nodded to himself and kissed me on the cheek."

"Sweet."

Angie smiled. "Well, almost. Just before he left, he asked me if it'd be okay if he asked out my cousin Sylvie, who'd always had a thing for him. I said 'Sure,' and he headed out the door. And that, my friend, was the last time I saw him."

Angie sighed, cursing the tear that was trickling down her cheek. A tear that seemed to confirm that a small part of her heart would always beat for Nick.

Then she dabbed her eyes with the napkin Jace had slipped her and made a confession she never thought she'd have the guts to make. "And even though I know it's for the best, sometimes I wonder if it's gonna be like my mother said. Am I'm gonna end up the biggest old maid since Aunt Peggy and her pot-bellied pig on a leash? God, what I wouldn't do for some chocolate!"

At that moment, the other flight attendant passed by with a tray of hot towels and shot Jace a look. Jace tossed back the rest of his bubbly and undid his seatbelt. "I guess I should get back to the grind."

Angie reluctantly tucked her legs under the seat to let him pass. But he didn't get up just yet. He leaned toward her and said, "Angie, I've got a feeling about this trip you're on. Call it clairvoyance or a very intuitive gut, but I think you're gonna meet your soulmate. And you're gonna know it the minute you see him, like he's been out there all along waiting for you to claim him. And you're gonna invite me to your wedding, and we'll share a dance and make fools of our-selves. Okay, baby girl?"

"Okay," she said breathlessly.

He gave her a kiss on the cheek and stepped past her into the aisle. Then, with a wink, he reached down and dropped something into her hand. "Enjoy."

As he crossed away, Angie looked down at her hand and gasped. There were two caramel turtles in it.

She stared after Jace in astonishment. Where in the world had he gotten them? Had he had them all along, waiting for the perfect opening? But if they'd been in his hand, why weren't they warm to the touch? Melted, even? And how could he have even known she liked them, considering she'd only mentioned it a minute ago?

Then, just like that, she stopped wondering and allowed a smile to wash over her face. Clearly, there was magic in the air tonight. A whole planeload of it. Did she dare believe this magic was going to lead her to the adventure of a lifetime?

———

As Milos watched the 767 make its descent into Athens, with its mélange of the ancient and the modern, he wondered if their fates were to be similarly entwined. It was all so astounding. Just a few months ago, it looked as though she was lost to him forever. And now she was so close that he could practically smell the sweet perfume of her skin.

Before he knew it, he was smiling. After so many years and so much love invested in this faraway beauty, were the Fates finally conspiring to bring them together?

And then what? Milos asked himself, feeling the smile evaporate as quickly as it had come. *Will I still be forced to do the bidding of my elders? Or will I find the strength to express my wishes and walk away if they don't embrace them?*

One thing was certain. At long last, things were going to come to a head.

THREE

With one ginormous exception, the trip to Athens had been everything Angie hoped it would be.

First off, the accommodations were enough to make her feel like Kate Middleton, Cinderella, and Ariel all rolled into one queen-size princess. She'd stayed at the Hotel Grande Bretagne once before—but in a standard room, not the deluxe three-room suite her grandmother had treated her to this time around. Twice as large as any New York apartment she'd ever set foot in, the suite was jaw-dropping luxury at every turn, with sparkling chandeliers, antique furniture direct from Sotheby's, a marble bathtub with its own flat-screen TV, and floor-to-ceiling windows that offered killer views of the Parthenon—rivaled only by the suite's crowning feature: a sterling silver chocolate stand restocked daily with all kinds of sinful delicacies. Frankly, it was the kind of luxury nest a girl could feel guilty leaving every day, especially a girl whose own puny flat offered a rattling view of the F Train.

But leave it she had—morning, noon, and night—reacquainting herself with Athens in all its chaotic glory. She'd dined at the city's most delectable restaurants, enjoying fried codfish with garlic dip at Saita Bakaliaro and her childhood favorite, *pasticcio* or Greek lasagna, at Philippos. She'd shopped everywhere from designer boutiques to the famed Spiliopoulos, a free-for-all New York Stock Exchange of shoes, where she came away with a pair of discounted Manolos and a fistful of frosted blond hair from a pushy Czechoslovakian woman who dared try to steal them out of her cart. She'd gone topless on the beach at Voula, attracting a number of approving gawks as well as an offer of a hundred Euros from a silver-haired Italian lothario. *If you'd doubled it, I might have bitten*, she'd chuckled to herself as she politely waved him off. She'd bopped along to live jazz at the Half Note and danced till dawn at Café Bohème with a revolving roster of hotties. And while those dance floor couplings had led to a number of interesting propositions, she'd turned them all down. Content, for the time being, to keep things uncluttered.

Despite all that good clean fun, Angie had reason to sulk on her next-to-the-last day in Athens. She'd failed to come through on the one and only request Ya-Ya had made of her. A request that on the surface had seemed so simple.

It had come on the eve of her trip, during a bon voyage dinner at Ya-Ya's townhouse in Park Slope. Shortly after divvying up the last square of her famous moussaka, Ya-Ya had asked her other two guests if she could borrow Angie for a minute. Clearly not a problem, since her brother, Anthony, was embroiled in a text message squabble with his girlfriend, while her mother was scanning Ya-Ya's onscreen TV listings for a rumored *Keeping Up with the Kardashians* marathon. After sharing a chuckle with Angie over their eccentric kin, Ya-Ya plucked a bottle of Limoncello off the bar, asked her to grab two glasses, and led the way to Elysium.

As far as Angie was concerned, Ya-Ya couldn't have picked a better name for her rooftop deck. Part thriving garden and part outdoor living room, Elysium had always struck Angie as the perfect haven from the soul-numbing stress of life in the city. And on that evening, it seemed especially welcoming. A gentle breeze was blowing in off the East River, tickling the tomato vines and making the roses look like they were bopping along to some irresistible tune—which in a way they were, because Ya-Ya always had one of her favorite CDs spinning on the sound system. Tonight it was Simon & Garfunkel harmonizing about a girl named Kathy and a Greyhound bus, while the little waterfall in the corner accompanied with a percussive gurgle. And the sky was amazingly clear. As clear as any night Angie could remember, allowing spectacular views of the shimmering lights of Manhattan and the panorama of stars above them.

Staring up at the sky, Angie got a lump in her throat remembering all the wonderful times she'd had here as a child. How she'd play hide and seek with her father among the potted roses or lie beside him on a chaise lounge, being schooled on the constellations and the myths behind them. It was a time in her life that would end far too quickly, but she revisited the memories often enough to keep them fresh in her mind.

And thankfully, she still had Ya-Ya Georgia, who was not only her favorite relative, but also her best friend and closest confidante. In fact, sometimes it seemed a pity to even call her Ya-Ya, considering how little she had in common with the traditional Greek grandmothers, with their funereal attire and Old World attitudes. At the age of eighty-nine, Georgia Costianes had the vitality of a woman half her age and a windblown elegance that often had people comparing her to Olympia Dukakis. And although she'd been a widow most of her life, she never had a shortage of attractive, younger men on her arm.

And not just her arm. One winter evening a few years back, Angie stopped by Ya-Ya's townhouse unannounced and found herself smiling at the sound of fervent lovemaking coming from inside. "Take me to the sky, *agape mou!*" she heard her grandmother cry between dueling moans of pleasure. Then and there, Angie vowed that one day she'd find herself a man who could bring out the same kind of passion in her. And while it was a mission she was, sadly, still on, she had the example of her Ya-Ya's life to make her believe anything was possible.

And what a life it had been. Georgia Sophia Megalis came into the world on August 14, 1926, just as the steamship bringing her immigrant parents to America passed under the shadow of the Statue of Liberty. Years later, Ya-Ya was fond of saying, "Before I even saw my mother's face, I saw Lady Liberty smiling down on me, welcoming me to her playground." Georgia and her parents briefly bunked with relatives in Lower Manhattan before her father found work at a piano factory in Brooklyn and moved them into a two-room flat in nearby Astoria, Queens.

Those early years were, as Ya-Ya recalled, some of the best of her life, featuring boisterous gatherings with her extended family of Greek neighbors; the birth of a cherished baby brother; and rewarding hours spent at the Queens Library where, with the help of a sympathetic librarian, she learned to read and speak English at an early age, allowing her to enroll in a public school system that was open only to English-speaking children. She became so proficient in her second language that by the time she was eight, she was tutoring newly emigrated children at five cents a head per day, money she insisted on contributing to her family's kitty during the lean years of the Great Depression.

One summer evening, during a rare dinner out with her family to celebrate her sixteenth birthday, she caught the eye of their waiter, Zachary Costianes, whose parents were the owners of the thriving taverna. "He was a dapper fellow with a smile that outshone Gable's and the good sense to recognize a catch when he saw one," Ya-Ya used to say. With the wholehearted blessing of her father, Ya-Ya began dating the affluent young man, often ending their evenings dancing at some Manhattan nightspot. Within the year, they were married in a ceremony every Greek in Astoria would remember as the most lavish of their lives. Zachary's father even managed to coax budding soprano Maria Callas back from Athens to sing at the reception.

A few months later, when Zachary was drafted into military service in World War II, Georgia decided to enlist as a WAC. Soon, she was stationed at a base in England, doing everything from operating a radio to repairing rifles. It was in the summer of 1944 that they celebrated their first anniversary with a furlough weekend in Ireland, during which Angie's father, Tommy, was conceived.

But Zachary would never get to meet his son. Two weeks after their rendezvous, he was killed in the Battle of Normandy, leaving Ya-Ya an eighteen-year-old widow with a baby on the way. When Angie asked her how she'd gotten through such heartbreak, Ya-Ya confessed that she cried for a long time, cursing the cruel indifference of fate. But the first time she felt her baby kick inside her belly, everything changed. And as the grief washed away, she decided the best way to honor her fallen husband was to provide their son with the best life possible while living her own to the fullest.

Now, some sixty years later, Ya-Ya was still doing exactly that, and Angie couldn't imagine a world without her in it. In her prayers, Angie often asked God to make up for taking her father so early by keeping her grandmother alive and kicking till she was a hundred and ten. Angie knew there was a part of Ya-Ya that longed for the day she'd be reunited with Zachary and her son. But that day could wait, at least until she'd witnessed her granddaughter finally finding true love.

"Andromeda's really strutting her stuff tonight," Ya-Ya observed as she filled their glasses with the tart lemon liqueur.

Angie nodded eagerly. Indeed, her favorite constellation had never looked so vibrant. Almost as if the astral princess were giving her a grand send-off to her ancestral home.

Ya-Ya handed her a glass and extended her own in a toast. "To legendary adventures: past, present, and future."

"And to my wonderful Ya-Ya for making it possible," Angie replied, clinking glasses with her.

Ya-Ya took a sip, then leaned over and inhaled the delicate fragrance of her Queen Anne roses. When she stepped away, Angie noticed she had a faraway look in her eyes, as if she were caught up in some bittersweet memory.

Angie was just about to rush over and put her arms around her when Ya-Ya shook off the look and turned to her with a smile that glowed as brightly as the stars above. "Angie, do you believe that every once in a while, the universe opens its window of possibilities and allows us to be everything we've ever dreamed of?"

Angie couldn't help but smile. Over the years, Ya-Ya had inspired her in many ways. And while her style was usually endearingly direct, she occasionally dealt in riddles and vagaries, which were intriguing in their own way. She'd steadfastly refused to believe her son had committed suicide, offering instead that, "There are things in life we can't even hope to understand until the universe gives us the tools." And when Angie told her about the crazy laughter in her head that had prompted her to ditch her wedding, Ya-Ya hadn't seemed the least bit troubled. Instead, she'd shrugged and said, "Maybe it wasn't in your head at all, sweetie. Maybe you just have a very chippy guardian angel."

So whatever was behind this mysterious new question had Angie's full attention. "Ya-Ya, if *you* believe it, I'll go out on a limb and believe it, too."

Clearly, that was the opening Ya-Ya had been waiting for. With a burst of vigor, she marched over to Angie and clutched her hand with so much determination it hurt. "Sweetie, there's a day trip I'd like you to make while you're in Greece. A lovely little island just a hop, skip, and a jump from the seaport at Piraeus. Full of gorgeous vegetation, amazing food, and the most extraordinary people you'll ever come across."

Then she reached into the pocket of her apron and pulled out a scrap of paper that looked old enough to have been torn off the Declaration of Independence. Scrawled across it in Greek block letters were the words "Pier Four, Slip 1212," along with a crudely drawn map of a fishing harbor near the seaport.

As Angie looked over the map, Ya-Ya told her she should choose a morning when she was feeling "particularly audacious." Then she should take a taxi to the seaport and make her way to the slip, where she'd catch her first glimpse of the *Harmonia*, a unique little fishing boat in vibrant blues and greens. At that point, she should take a deep breath and prepare herself for Mathias, the grizzled skipper, who'd most likely regard her with a sour look as he puffed on a clay pipe.

"Tell him you're Georgia Costianes's granddaughter, and you just might get a grin out of the old bastard before he demands a few Euros to take you to the island," Ya-Ya said. "He'll probably order you to swab the decks, too."

Angie squinted in confusion. "Then ... he's expecting me?"

"I do believe he is," Ya-Ya replied, an odd twinkle in her eye.

Angie stared back at her grandmother, feeling for all the world like she'd been plopped into the middle of a J. K. Rowling novel. "Ya-Ya, what *is* this place? I've been to Greece with you twice and you've never even mentioned it. Now, all of a sudden, you bring it up as if it's your favorite place on Earth. When were you there?"

A smile spread across her grandmother's face, a smile that seemed to be as wistful as it was joyous. She started to speak twice, but each time swallowed her words, seemingly going deeper inside herself. Then she nodded decisively and cupped a caressing hand on Angie's shoulder. "That window of possibility I told you about? It opened for me a long time ago—right after your grandfather died. Something tells me it's *your* turn."

With that, Ya-Ya collapsed onto the love seat, as if the act of revisiting those memories had sapped her strength. Angie, on the other hand, felt like her head was about to burst from all the questions bouncing around in it. What was the point of this junket? Had Ya-Ya meant it to be one element of her trip to Greece, or was it the whole reason she was sending her there? And why? Although Ya-Ya had never expressly disapproved of Nick, she'd indicated in a million subtle ways she thought she could do better. "Sweetie, a princess needs a prince. Or at least someone who can pull off the epaulets."

And now, in the wake of the breakup, she was shipping her off to some remote island full of "extraordinary people." As in extraordinary men? Was that what this was, a transoceanic matchmaking scheme?

Angie sighed. *Only one way to find out.* She sat down next to her grandmother and summoned up her most probing look. "Fess up, Ya-Ya. Is this about a man?"

From the unflappable smile Ya-Ya gave her, it was clear she had no intention of fessing up. "Promise me one thing, dear. When you get there, you'll put all your preconceived notions aside and let the day take you wherever it's going to take you."

Then, as the lights of the stars and the city danced off her bright green eyes, Ya-Ya kissed her on the cheek and graced her with the smile that had always assured Angie she was loved. And somehow, in spite of all the unanswered questions, Angie bought into the mysterious voyage and its magical possibilities. And when Ya-Ya placed the yellowed map in her hand, she swore she felt a surge of electricity coursing through her veins.

But what did it matter now? With less than forty-eight hours to go before her return to New York, Angie hadn't set foot on the island. And the fact that it wasn't for lack of trying didn't make her feel any better. On her third morning in Athens, after an invigorating run on the treadmill followed by a three-course breakfast and a bubble bath, she'd decided there was no better day for audaciousness than that one. So she marched out of the hotel, climbed into the back of a cab, and asked the driver to take her to Piraeus. Fifteen minutes later, she paid the fare and stepped out into the hustle and bustle of the teeming port city.

Having toured Piraeus a few years earlier, Angie was aware it was not only home to hundreds of cargo and fishing operations, but also served as the largest passenger port in Europe. And indeed, as she made her way through the crowded harbor, she rubbed elbows with dozens of passengers rushing to and from cruise ships to the frequent accompaniment of whistle blasts. As she hurried through the commercial district, she managed to resist the intoxicating smells of fresh calamari frying at the tavernas and the come-on of street vendors hawking "designer purses at crazy-low prices." A few minutes later, in the port proper, she came face-to-face with a rowdy pack of Italian sailors, who made no secret of their intentions toward her, using colorful verbiage they no doubt assumed she wouldn't understand.

Fortunately, she'd been the star of her high school Italian class. "You naughty boys," she said, grinning impishly. "I understood every word."

At first, their faces dropped in shame. Then, one by one, they tipped their caps to her. She gave them a farewell wave and forged ahead, buoyed by her little victory.

Twenty minutes later, after several wrong turns and a dozen appeals for directions, Angie arrived at Pier Four, which was not only smaller and less frenzied than the three major piers, but considerably shabbier. As she made her way down the weather-beaten deck, she passed everything from ferries loading passengers for island-hopping tours to fishing boats whose nets were overflowing with crab and shrimp. When she caught sight of Slip 1205, she felt adrenalin building inside her. Slip 1212, her mysterious destination, was a mere seven slips away. Picking up the pace, she passed Slips 1206 and 1207. By now, her heart was in her throat. *What's going to happen to me on that island? Do I dare believe I'll find romance? Great sex? Both?* She paused at Slip 1209 to check her face out in a compact and run a brush through her hair. Then she took a fortifying breath, stepped toward Slip 1212 and found...

Nothing. Absolutely nothing.

It wasn't just that there was no boat in the slip. There was no Slip 1212. Period. The pier came to an end at Slip 1211. If there *were* a Slip 1212, it would have been three feet out in the ocean. Angie groaned in frustration. *It can't be. Ya-Ya's map made it so clear.* She pulled the map out of her purse and studied it for the thousandth time. No mistaking it. The object of her search was indeed Pier Four, Slip 1212. Twice, she retraced her steps, hoping that like many things in Greece, the numbering system was out of whack. But everything seemed to be in order.

Except that there was no Slip 1212.

By now, she wasn't just frustrated, she was pissed. How dare this portal to adventure elude her? Recalling a trio of Greek fisherman she'd passed a few minutes earlier unloading sardines while crooning, of all things, a Coldplay song, she made her way back to them and asked whether they were familiar with the *Harmonia* or its skipper, Mathias. All of them shook their heads. Then one of them, a shirt-less specimen with abs you could bounce a dime off of, introduced himself as Andreas and told her he could show her a far better time than some *malakas* named Mathias. Angie couldn't blame him for his candor—she did look pretty fetching in the hot pink sundress she'd picked up at the marketplace. And she loved the fact that men were so forward here, as opposed to New York, where they all seemed to be holding out for a runway model. But today, she was in pursuit of a more unique adventure than Andreas had in mind.

But how the hell am I supposed to find it when it's not where it's supposed to be? Unless...

The thought made her stop in her tracks, causing a young couple behind her to run smack-dab into her. After apologizing and reimbursing them for the ice cream cones they'd dropped, she approached the first official-looking person she spotted and asked him if he knew where the harbormaster's office was. Miraculously, he'd just been there himself and pointed out a modern four-story building about a hundred yards away.

As Angie wound her way through the crowd, she found herself skipping. *That's it. It has to be. The* Harmonia's *been moved to another slip.* By Ya-Ya's own admission, she'd been to the island a long time ago. And even though she still seemed to be in contact with Mathias, it was entirely possible he'd forgotten to tell her of the move.

With hope in her throat, Angie sprinted into the building and located an information center on the second floor, where a sympathetic clerk entered both the *Harmonia* and Mathias into the computer system. Unfortunately, he was unable to find a record of either one. At Angie's urging, he searched all the way back to the 1940s, when Ya-Ya had first come to Greece, but the result was the same. No record of either the boat or Mathias ever having existed.

Angie couldn't understand it. Her grandmother had always had an uncanny ability to recall the details of events that took place decades ago. And clearly, this boat, its skipper, and the adventure they'd inspired had made an indelible impression on her. It seemed inconceivable she could have their names wrong. There had to be another explanation.

Angie checked her watch. It was 2:30 in the afternoon in Athens, which meant it was early morning in New York. Most likely, Ya-Ya would be toiling in her garden to beat the afternoon heat. Ducking into a taverna, Angie ordered a glass of pinot grigio and a plate of garlic fries and rang her up. True to form, Ya-Ya was in the midst of pruning her roses and happy to take a break. After filling her in on her adventures since their last chat, Angie confessed she'd been unable to find the *Harmonia*—or any record of its existence.

"Oh, it exists," Ya-Ya replied in a no-nonsense tone, sounding almost peeved at the thought of her story being questioned.

"I'm sure it does, Ya-Ya, but I can't find it. There isn't a Slip 1212 out there. Are you sure it wasn't some other port? I know you've been to Olympia …"

"No, Angie, it's Piraeus, definitely Piraeus. You did offer to pay the man, didn't you?"

Angie rolled her eyes. "Ya-Ya, how am I supposed to pay him if I can't find him?"

Ya-Ya's only response was a perturbed sigh.

Angie was at a loss. This wasn't like her grandmother at all. Ya-Ya had always been such a calm, nurturing person. But now she was acting downright curmudgeonly. What *was* it about that island, and why was it so important to Ya-Ya that she get there? Angie waited for her to say something further, but there was only silence on the other end. Was her grandmother too irked to say anything? Or had Angie hurt her feelings by snapping at her?

All things considered, it was best to be proactive. "Ya-Ya, if I upset you, I'm sorry."

Finally, she responded, sounding like her old self again. "No, dear, I should be the one doing the apologizing. Lord knows I'm not angry with *you*. I'm just frustrated with the whole shebang. I really thought it was your time."

"My time? What do you mean?"

After another unsettling moment of silence, Ya-Ya let out a sigh. "Sweetie, I'm sorry. I misunderstood the signs. I'm afraid I'm just an old lady with a head full of confetti. Enjoy the rest of your trip."

But she couldn't. Despite Ya-Ya's apology, Angie couldn't help thinking she'd let her down. Maybe she hadn't searched hard enough. Or maybe she lacked some elusive quality that would've put her in the embrace of the boat, the skipper, and an island paradise.

And that made her even more determined to find it. What just a few days earlier had seemed like an intriguing diversion became the most important mission of her life. She returned to Piraeus three more times in search of the *Harmonia*. During the first two visits, she got to know every inch of Pier Four and queried everyone she encountered, describing the colorful boat as well as the pipe-smoking Mathias. And she'd spent the bulk of the current day combing all four piers, but once again came away empty-handed.

That evening, for the first time since arriving in Athens, Angie stayed in and ordered room service. And as she sat on her balcony, sipping a glass of wine, she told herself she was going to have to accept the fact that either her grandmother was slipping or that *she* didn't have what it took to find the *Harmonia*.

Either way, it looked like this grand adventure was simply not meant to be.

FOUR

Milos couldn't remember when he'd been so frustrated.

With a flick of my wrist, I can make a herd of stampeding buffalo stop dead in its tracks. But when it comes to bringing one woman to this island, I'm impotent.

A few days earlier, he'd been bursting with excitement as he watched Angie make her way through the harbor at Piraeus. And when she'd rebuffed those Italian sailors, he'd laughed so hard that he tumbled out of the tree he was perched in.

Too late, mortals, he'd mused as he massaged his separated shoulder back to health. *In a matter of hours, she'll be with me.*

Then, mere moments later, his hopes had been dashed. A crucial step had been missed. A step she couldn't possibly have known about. Truth be told, *he* hadn't even been aware of it. And however insignificant in his eyes, it was critical to her passage. Milos couldn't blame the old woman. It had been more than half a century since *her* journey, and unfortunately mortals didn't have the capacity to retain every nuance of memory, even extraordinary ones like ⟨ tianes. But sadly, without that link, the journey could n⟨

Earlier today, he'd taken the bold step of approachir cil. He'd virtually supplicated himself before them, bowing down like a toady and pledging centuries of dutiful service for the ability to affect change this one time. He'd even assured them he simply needed to bed this woman so he could move forward and embrace the grand plan that awaited him.

Whether they'd seen through his deceit, he'd never know. All that mattered was that amid their carousing and wagering over the death toll in some plane crash in the Andes, they'd rebuffed his offer. "It is no longer our way, Milos. Thus, it cannot be." And without another word, they'd dismissed him. He, who they'd vowed would one day lead them, was still a child in their eyes.

And it had only provided Milos a small measure of comfort when his elder cousin approached him later about it in private. Although Milos's cousin was a founding member of the Council, he was one of the few who'd never condemned Milos for his love of Angie. In fact, although he'd never said as much, there was reason to believe he supported it. He'd also been Milos's mentor since childhood, schooling him on everything from classical music to *episkyros,* the precursor to American football. So, naturally, when he appeared at Milos's door, Milos assumed he'd come to tell him he'd persuaded the other Council members to relent.

Instead, he put an arm around Milos and said, "If you really want to secure passage for her, you must find a way to work within this new system of ours—and at the same time, be its architect." Then he dissolved into thin air, leaving Milos confused and frustrated.

The bitch of it was, none of this insufferable passivity would have been necessary in earlier times. If Milos had wanted to cohabitate with a particular woman, he could've simply swept her out of her home and dragged her off to live with him. Or, if his desires were purely carnal, he could've assumed the identity of any man she cared about and made love to her. *She certainly wouldn't turn down that Jeter fellow.* But he and she and Jeter hadn't been born during those times. And frankly, Milos couldn't imagine treating the object of his affection so callously.

But it was all meaningless now. With the Millennium Conclave had come sweeping changes, and free will for mortals was the new maxim. And while it was, without a doubt, a more prudent way to go forward in these contemporary times, it meant his hands were tied.

As Milos sat there, on his favorite rock on the cliff, a flock of seagulls soared in from the Aegean and dropped their weekly offering of sea bass at his feet. When he indicated his approval with the usual palm to the sky, their leader swooped down and perched on his shoulder. And as Milos patted the old gull on the head, ensuring him another year of robust health, a scheme popped into his head. The question was, would his elders consider it a clever example of working the system or a forbidden foray into manipulation?

Yet if it achieved the desired effect, his angel might walk beside him in the morning. And for that, he'd gladly take the risk.

———

Angie awoke from a fitful sleep to find herself sprawled across the chaise lounge on the balcony.

Oh God, did I polish off that whole bottle of wine?

She looked over at the patio table and groaned. Indeed she had. And although she knew there'd be hell to pay in the morning—her last morning in Athens—she decided to go easy on herself. She really *had* needed to drown her sorrows over the *Harmonia* fiasco. And still did, for that matter. She wondered if it was too late to call room service and order another pot of that wicked chocolate fondue. She cast a bleary look at her watch. 11:06 p.m. Not a problem.

Wobbling to her feet, she caught a glimpse of something at the other end of the balcony. As she stepped forward to get a closer look, she let out a squeal.

A white seagull was perched on the railing, looking straight at her.

But this was no ordinary gull. He was huge—more than three feet tall with a wingspan at least twice that. And he wasn't just white, he was pure-as-the-driven-snow white. With a custard yellow beak and deep-set brown eyes that seemed kind, almost human. As Angie stared mesmerized at the majestic creature, he seemed to nod, as if he knew her.

Sweet Jesus, what is going on?

Then the obvious occurred to her. She was hallucinating. Had to be. Between trudging from pier to pier in the blistering heat and the insane quantities of wine and fondue she'd consumed, she was probably suffering from some combination of heatstroke, alcohol poisoning, and sugar shock. Surely, she figured, if she closed her eyes, the vision would disappear and she could crawl into bed, pull the covers over her head, and sleep it off.

But when Angie opened her eyes again, the gull was still there. In fact, he'd moved even closer, hovering in the air just a few feet away.

If you're a hallucination, you're a damn stubborn one. Probably from my mother's side of the family.

For the first time, Angie noticed he was holding something in his talon. A pouch of some sort. He seemed to follow her gaze, because at that moment he released it, sending it plunking to the ground. Then, with an oddly melodious squawk, he spread his wings and soared into the darkness.

Although she was shaking from head to toe, Angie managed to tiptoe over to the pouch and check it out. It was made of a rich maroon leather and engrained with a crest that featured the sun, the moon, and the stars shining down on a mountaintop. And it was heavy—at least five pounds and bulging with something that felt a lot like coins.

With the eagerness of a kid at Christmas, Angie rushed inside and dumped the contents onto the bed. Indeed, they *were* coins. Gold coins. Dozens of them. The first one she checked out was a five-drachma coin from 1943. And that made the whole thing even stranger. Although drachma had been the official currency of Greece for thousands of years, Angie knew they'd been phased out a decade ago when Greece joined the European Union and adopted the Euro.

As she examined more and more of them, she felt herself tingling with excitement. They were all various denominations of drachma. Ten drachma. Fifty drachma. Every single one from the 1940s or earlier. Where in the world had the gull gotten them? And had Angie gone completely bonkers, or had he intended them specifically for her? But why? Did she have some anonymous benefactor who wanted to see her cash in like a champion? Or could this be connected to the weirdness surrounding her search for the *Harmonia*?

Suddenly, Angie felt goose bumps popping up from head to toe. *Oh, that just isn't possible … is it?* She didn't care what time it was in New York. She had to call her grandmother.

One ring. Two rings.

"Yes, Angie. What is it?"

"When you paid Mathias for your trip to the island, what kind of currency did you use?"

"Why, drachma, dear. See, it was a good sixty-five years ago and ..."

Four thousand miles apart, grandmother and granddaughter uttered the words, "Oh my God!" at the same moment. Because both women had seized upon the thing that differentiated their respective quests to find the *Harmonia*. Forms of currency. Was that all that had kept Angie from her magical mystery tour? A finicky boatman who demanded to be paid in the currency he was accustomed to?

Not thirty minutes later, a sobered-up Angie was racing across Pier Four, clutching the coin purse in her hand. Now she really felt like a character in some spine-chilling novel. The pier was not only dark and deserted, but a murky fog cloaked the area, making it impossible to see more than a few feet ahead. She slowed down long enough to make out the sign for Slip 1207, then picked up the pace again, sprinting through the fog. Caution be damned. Either she was going to come face to face with the *Harmonia* or end up dogpaddling in the Aegean.

As spooky as the whole thing was, Angie couldn't help smiling at the irony of it. Three months earlier, she'd been running down the aisle of her church, away from a future that couldn't provide her with the romance she needed. Now she was running again, with the same hope that whatever was ahead, it had to be better than what she was leaving behind.

And then it happened. Her foot caught on a warped plank and she tumbled headlong onto the boardwalk, losing her grip on the purse. As she watched helplessly, it flew past her, hit the deck and spilled open, sending coins rolling forward into the foggy abyss. With a yelp, she leapt to her feet and raced after them. But it was too late. They were nowhere to be found. It was as if they'd been swallowed up by the fog itself.

As angry tears burned in her eyes, Angie shot a look toward the heavens. "I hope you know this sucks!"

Then she spotted the purse lying a few feet away, a lone drachma poking out. Figuring she might as well have a souvenir of this debacle, she dropped to her knees and picked it up.

Just as she was about to turn around and head back to Athens, she caught sight of a large blue object peeking through the fog. She looked to her left, where a shabby ferryboat was parked in Slip 1210. To her right was a lobster boat in Slip 1211. In her previous visits, this was where the pier had ended. But now it extended forward into the fog, where a patch of green was now visible along with the blue.

Although it was a sweltering night, Angie was shivering. She'd never thought of herself as a timid person, but this was creepy times ten. And she was all alone out here. Just the same, she knew if she turned back, she'd never stop kicking herself. So she sent a little shout-out to Saint Emily, the patron saint of single women, and ventured forward into the murk.

With each tentative step, she grew more and more confident that the pier wasn't suddenly going to end, sending her cannon-balling into the sea. She was also starting to make out more and more of the object looming before her.

And although it soon became apparent it was exactly what she'd been hoping it would be, she still gasped when she saw it, docked behind a faded sign that read Slip 1212.

"Freakin' unbelievable," she murmured. "There you are, lady."

There she was indeed, the *Harmonia*, in all her mystical glory. Although the little fishing boat appeared to be very old, she was scrubbed to perfection. Her wooden hull was about twenty feet long and painted a playful shade of blue that complemented her sea green cabin. Her twin masts reached boldly into the sky, and a crested flag hung at the end of the bow. Angie didn't even have to look down at her hand to confirm it was the same crest that was on the coin purse.

Then she caught sight of a man standing at the bow, nonchalantly puffing on a pipe. His face was so tanned and wrinkled that he called to mind those old apple-core dolls they used to sell at craft fairs. But in spite of his roughhewn features, he was dressed from head to toe in a crisp blue uniform, complete with a captain's hat.

If the whole thing weren't so bloody otherworldly, Angie would have found herself stifling a laugh. Instead, she stepped forward and offered him a respectful wave. "Evening, Mathias. I'm Angie Costianes, Georgia's granddaughter. I've gotta say, you're a hard man to find."

A smile flickered across his face, then evaporated inside that apple-core head of his. As he stepped out of the shadow of the cabin, Angie noticed he was holding something shiny in his cupped hands. It was a mound of coins. Coins she had no doubt were the drachma that had spilled into the fog when she dropped the purse. This was without a doubt, the most bizarre experience she'd ever had—and she'd grown up in Queens.

Nevertheless, she wasn't about to be deterred. She marched right up to him, displaying the coin purse. "So, I see my boat fare found its way to you."

He sifted the coins from hand to hand, then shrugged. "If you want to go to island, you are five drachma short."

Before Angie even opened the purse, she knew the denomination of her one remaining coin. And when she confirmed it was a five-drachma, she crossed to the lip of the boat and flipped it to him. He scowled at it for a moment, then dropped both handfuls of coins into a wooden chest that seemed to contain enough gold to buy and sell the world several times over.

Then, without so much as a "Welcome to the *Harmonia*," he cast a gnarled finger toward the dock. "You don't expect old man to cast off, do you?"

Angie couldn't help but chuckle. "Don't worry, skipper. I got your back."

Then she loosened the lines, tossed them onto the boat, and leapt aboard. A few minutes later, she and Mathias were sailing across the pitch black sea through a fog that seemed to grow more forbidding with every wave they crested. As Angie paced about the cabin, Mathias stood at the wheel like a statue, never looking at her and only occasionally responding to her questions. And she wasn't sure what smelled worse, the acrid tobacco in his pipe or his cologne, which was so sickly sweet it would make any woman gag if she came within a foot of him. Not that that was likely a problem. Angie pictured him living in a suspiciously neat lighthouse with a dozen menacing dogs that'd turn anyone into mincemeat if they dared try to get close to him. He was just as Ya-Ya had described. An old bastard.

Then it hit her. *Exactly how old a bastard?* According to Ya-Ya, Mathias had been old when *she'd* met him. And that had been over sixty-five years ago. Although the years probably hadn't been kind to him, he didn't look much older than eighty. But if her grandmother had been young then, didn't it stand to reason that *he* would've been as well?

"Mathias, when did you take my grandmother to the island?"

A prolonged pause, followed by a grunt. "Long time ago."

"Like say, sixty-some years ago?"

Angie wasn't sure whether his snort was supposed to mean "yes" or "no," so she took it a step further. "How old were you then?"

"Younger."

"How old are you now?"

"Older."

And that was how the journey went, plus or minus a grunt or two. She'd ask a question to try to glean some information about the island, her grandmother's experiences there, or what she should expect when she arrived, and Mathias would give her bupkis. Either he was the most aloof old fart in the world or he'd been trained by his superiors to play it close to the vest. But who were his superiors? Exactly who was Angie going to meet there? If it was a whole island of Mathiases, she'd leap into the water and drown herself. Dammit, why hadn't Ya-Ya told her more? Why had it been so bloody important to her that she arrive without an ounce of knowledge? And what self-respecting skipper would take on a paid passenger without providing so much as a bag of chips?

Before long, Angie abandoned all hope of getting anything out of him and plopped down on a chair in the rear of the cabin. Although it was a far cry from comfy, she found her eyes growing heavy from the excitement of the day. At first, she resisted falling asleep out of fear of what might happen to her if she did. *He'll probably have his way with me, then deliver me to the sharks.*

But eventually she got tired of pinching her cheeks to stay awake and fell into a deep slumber. When she awoke, the *Harmonia* was docking at the island in the midst of a downpour. But as Angie stepped off the boat, she noticed something odd. She wasn't getting wet. The raindrops were falling all around her, but not *on* her. And as she walked across a wide stretch of beach, she wasn't leaving any footprints—very unusual for a girl no one would describe as light on her feet.

As troubling as that was, it couldn't hold a candle to the sight of all the people emerging from the fog. Hundreds of them. Some she didn't recognize, while others were … well, it was just plain weird. There was Kurt Cobain walking alongside JFK, Jr., harmonizing on a Dylan song. And Geraldine Ferraro was strolling arm in arm with Telly Savalas as George Steinbrenner cavorted behind them, tossing rose petals in the air.

All at once, Angie realized she had to get out of there. But when she turned back toward the dock, she practically ran into a wall that had somehow been put up in the past few seconds. And there was no getting past it, because it stretched all the way to the sky.

"Where you goin', kiddo?"

At the sound of that voice, Angie gasped. It could only belong to one person.

Tommy Costianes. Her father.

She turned around to find him standing a few yards away, looking even handsomer than she remembered. His salt-and-pepper hair was endearingly unkempt, and his eyes were that brilliant shade of emerald she'd always wished she'd inherited. And as he strolled toward her, smiling that big, loving smile of his, she noticed he was holding a balloon that seemed to change color and shape every few seconds.

"Daddy, I've missed you so much!" She rushed up to him, holding her arms out for a hug.

But instead of hugging her back, he handed her the balloon, which suddenly looked an awful lot like Poovis, the golden retriever she'd had as a child. And then it *was* Poovis. The balloon string had turned into a leash and Poovis was at her feet, jumping up and down excitedly.

"We're sure glad you made it, Sugarplum," her father said, using the nickname he'd given her when she was seven and determined to dance *The Nutcracker Suite* regardless of her stupid teacher declaring she didn't have a prima ballerina body type.

As Angie stared back at her father, she felt tear after tear run down her cheek. Although he'd been gone for almost seventeen years, she'd never stopped wishing she could see him again and hear the sweet sound of his voice. And here he was—with her beloved Poovis.

And yet, she couldn't ignore the fact that something was wrong with this picture. Everyone she'd seen on this island was dead. Her father. Poovis. Kurt Cobain. What did it mean that she was walking among them?

"Daddy, what *is* this place?"

He rested a hand on her shoulder. "Come on, Angie. What did you think happened when you stepped off the end of that pier?"

It was raining harder now, but not on either one of them, and she was terribly confused. "But I didn't. I stepped onto a boat."

"The boat brings us all here, honey. The important thing is, we're together. Isn't that what you've always wanted?"

"Yes, but—"

Suddenly, Angie felt a bolt of pain and looked down at her feet to discover that Poovis had turned into a mangy rat who was gnawing on her ankle. She also discovered she wasn't on the beach anymore. She was on the Brooklyn Bridge.

She looked around for her father, but he was nowhere in sight. "Daddy, where are you?"

From somewhere far below her, she heard his voice. "Come on in, Sugarplum. The water's fine."

She looked over the edge of the railing and discovered he was floating in the East River, along with all the famous dead people. Then the rat took another chomp out of her ankle, and she shook her leg as hard as she could to knock him loose. But just as he went flying, Angie lost her balance and teetered on the edge of the bridge. Panicked, she tried to grab on to the railing, but her hand went right through it, and she began falling and falling...

...and woke up for real this time, trembling from the nightmare and totally disoriented. She shot a look around the cabin to find that Mathias was still at the wheel.

Bolting out of the chair, she called out to him. "Mathias, I just had the worst dream! Where are we?! Where are we going?!"

Without bothering to turn around, he muttered, "Almost there."

"There? Where?!" she yelled back, panic rising in her throat.

This time, he did turn around. And for the first time all night, his eyes seemed warm, like there was a genuinely decent person hiding under that leathery exterior. "Beautiful place," he said. "No dead people there."

She stared at him dumbfounded, wondering how he could've possibly known about her dream. Then, realizing she was living in a whole universe of "WTF?" moments, she decided to leave well enough alone. Why run the risk of spoiling this newfound state of détente she'd achieved with the prickly skipper?

As Mathias returned to his duties, Angie cleared the sleep out of her eyes and indulged in a long stretch, rotating her head from side to side to work the kinks out. When she finally felt semi-human again, she took another look out the window to find that dawn was breaking. And wonder of wonders, the fog was lifting, too, allowing her to make out the vague outline of a mound of land.

As the *Harmonia* drew closer to it, the object gradually took on the shape of an island. Not particularly large but hilly, like a lumpy pot roast floating in the middle of the sea. And it was alive with color. Bright greens and vivid blues and neon purples and saucy reds. It was as if some kid had gone nuts with a fistful of Day-Glo Crayolas.

And just like that, the tension of the past few days melted away. After all the false starts, there really *was* an island out here. And unlike the dismal island in her dream, this one looked idyllic. Add to that the fact that her dear Ya-Ya had sent her on this junket, and maybe she did have reason to believe good things were gonna happen to her.

As Angie stepped out onto the deck, the first thing she noticed was how perfect the climate was. Unlike Athens or New York, which would already be muggy at this hour, it was no more than 70 degrees without a trace of humidity. And there was an exhilarating scent in the air. Like jasmine and gardenias, with a hint of barbecued chicken thrown in for good measure.

A flock of seagulls flew past her, every one of them the same vivid white as the gull that'd perched on her balcony. Figuring he might be among their posse, Angie waved at them and was rewarded with a chorus of melodic squawks that managed to be in perfect harmony, like the string section of the Philharmonic. Then one of the seagulls plunged into the sea and emerged with a fish that was such an obscenely bright shade of orange it looked electric. The gull flew within inches of her, holding the flapping fish in his mouth, then did a circus-like toss that sent it back into the sea. It was impossible not to conclude he'd been putting on a show for her, and she pinched herself to make sure she was really awake and the gull wasn't going to morph into Michael Jackson.

Suddenly, she realized that while she'd been bird-watching, the *Harmonia* had reached the shore and Mathias was securing the lines. She leapt off the boat and rushed over to him. "Sorry, skipper. Lemme get that."

Instead, he shook his head. "You go now, Angie Costianes. You are expected."

He pointed to the end of the dock, a good thirty yards away, where a lone figure stood.

Although from such a distance, Angie couldn't tell if it was a man or a woman, she still felt a chill running down her spine. "Who…is…that?"

"I see you when you get back," was all he said. Then he returned to his docking duties, indicating she was on her own. She stared at him for a moment, then took a long, steadying breath and began the most extraordinary walk of her life.

Angie was familiar with the phrase "heart going a mile a minute," but up until that moment, she'd never experienced the sensation. Now, as she proceeded down the pier toward whoever was waiting for her, she was certain that he or she could not only hear her heart thumping, but could feel it as well. She was mildly relieved to find it wasn't causing the whole pier to shake.

Halfway down the pier, she realized her escort was a man. He was wearing a billowy white shirt, jeans, and sandals. His hair was black and silky and fell to his shoulders. And he was very tanned. She wasn't close enough to make out his features, but she was at least able to tell it wasn't her dear, departed father preparing to take her for a swim in the East River.

But who is he? A friend of Ya-Ya's? Some distant relative? God, I hope not.

Then she realized that without even knowing it, she'd picked up her pace and was on the verge of looking like one of those annoying power walkers who seemed to think the streets of New York were their own personal exercise course. She knew she was in danger of breaking out in a sweat, but she couldn't seem to slow down. It was as if a magnet were drawing her to this man, and she sent up a prayer that she wouldn't take a header and end up face first at his feet.

Half a dozen yards away, she finally got a good look at him. He was young, thirty maybe. About six feet tall, with broad shoulders and a build that just screamed masculine. And he was handsome. God, was he handsome! With piercing blue eyes, a commanding nose and a chiseled jawline, like something Michelangelo would've been proud to put his signature on. And when he opened his mouth, his teeth were as white as the seagulls and his smile was warm and tender …

… *and familiar.* Like she'd seen him somewhere before.

Although it seemed impossible, Angie couldn't shake the feeling. But where could she have seen this man before this amazing morning?

Then it hit her. Three months ago, just after the beer truck hit her and she was flying through the air. This was the face she'd seen smiling back at her.

And now he was here. In the flesh.

But how was that possible? What did it mean? What in the name of God was going on?

There was no time to consider any of those questions, because at that moment, he stepped forward and spoke his first words to her.

"Hello, Angie. My name is Milos. Welcome to Elysium."

FIVE

At that moment, Milos wanted to wrap Angie in his arms and kiss her till the sun went down and the stars came out and the sun rose again and the cycle went on for eternity. How long had he been waiting for this woman? Centuries, it seemed. And now, she was inches away, looking at him with what appeared to be wonder in her eyes. He was fairly certain she wouldn't protest. In fact, considering how relentlessly she'd pursued this adventure, she'd probably kiss him back with such urgency that his head would shoot off the top of his body and take out one of his seagulls.

But he knew it was crucial he take it slowly. There was so much to explain. So many mysteries to unravel for her. And if any of it wasn't handled just so, she was likely to panic and run away. And if that happened, well, he'd leap into an abyss and beg the earth to swallow him up.

But mercy, is she beautiful!

He'd only seen her in person one other time: on that dark day sixteen years ago when her world was shattered. But she'd barely been a teenager then, and now she was a woman in full bloom. Like a red rose on a spring morning when its petals have just opened and it's as vibrant and wondrous as it will ever be.

As he stood there, drinking in her beauty, those voluptuous lips parted and she spoke her first words to him. "Nice to meet you, Milos. Now please tell me who the hell you are."

———

The instant the words came out of her mouth, Angie wished she could take them back. *Dammit, why was I born without an edit function?* Granted, it was beyond strange to meet a man she'd first seen in a vision, but he seemed warm and friendly, and he certainly had that easy-on-the-eyes thing going for him. But now, thanks to her big mouth, he was staring at her in shock. And who could blame him? He probably wasn't used to such mouthy broads in this paradise of his.

"Sorry," she said, "that didn't come out right."

She smiled sheepishly, hoping he'd accept her apology and sweep her into his arms for a big welcoming hug. But he kept right on staring at her, the world's dishiest sphinx. Had she blown it already? Was her mystery man going to turn his back on her, forcing her to double back to Athens with a skipper who'd probably treat her even more dismissively because she'd failed her mission? Heck, maybe the old bastard would just sic the gulls on her and save himself the fuel.

Then Milos's mouth began to quiver. Was he about to say something … or was a smile taking shape? Sure enough, it was. A big, goofy-sexy smile that made his eyes twinkle and created adorable laugh lines. At that moment, he could say anything to her and she'd buy it.

Instead, he laughed. Long and loud and hearty. And although it was a wonderful laugh, it sent chills down Angie's spine. Because she'd heard it before. It had changed her life.

"You were at my wedding, weren't you?" she said. "You were the one laughing."

Now it was his turn to look stunned. "You … heard that?"

"Yeah, but nobody else did. Who *are* you, Milos?"

He averted his eyes for what felt like forever, seemingly weighing every permutation of his next move. Just as she was about to press him for a response, he nodded to himself and turned to her. "Angie, the fact that you were able to hear me that day amazes me. You see, I was not present at your wedding. I was watching it … from here."

She didn't know how to respond, other than to stare back at him in confusion. Then a theory popped into her head, something Ya-Ya had suggested. "Are you some sort of guardian angel?"

"No," he said, chuckling, "but I do have some astonishing things to tell you. That is, if you're willing to listen."

She considered his words, along with the hopeful expression that accompanied them. God bless him, this man she'd just met not only seemed to know her, but to care about her as well. Either he was a very smooth con man or a potential love connection.

Opting for the latter, Angie said the first thing that came to mind. "Shall we discuss it over a drink?"

Milos smiled. "I think that can be arranged."

A moment later, they were hiking along a trail toward a café he assured her would be glad to serve them at six in the morning. Although there were a hundred questions swimming through her head,

Angie couldn't help but get caught up in the beauty of the place. It seemed like everywhere she turned, there was a tour-de-force version of some everyday object of nature. She'd seen hundreds of cypress trees, but none with leaves so iridescent or branches that reached for the sky with such grace. She stared spellbound at a brook with cobalt blue water and a current that was so soothing and rhythmic she half-expected to see a jazz quartet floating along in its wake.

But nothing compared to the flowers. There had to be thousands of them, growing wild in the hillsides and rolling meadows. Violets, lilies, hyacinths, daffodils, roses—with nary a dead petal or withered leaf. And every last bloom was exploding with color. There were vibrant yellows, urgent reds, and pinks so hot they required sunglasses. And if that weren't enough to make a horticulturist do backflips, there were hybrids she'd never seen before. Lilies as blue as a summer sky and crimson roses with white daffodil bibs around them.

It was downright dizzying, and Angie considered herself lucky to be privy to a world that seemed to open its doors to so few. She shot Milos an approving look, but he was once again staring off into the distance, no doubt preoccupied with whatever he was about to tell her.

She considered letting him be, but some impish spirit in her just wouldn't allow it. "Milos, you ought to be ashamed of yourself, trying to seduce me with all this beauty."

All at once, his mood seemed to lighten, as if a pinprick of heavy air had been let out of his balloon. "Oh, I assure you, I've only just begun." His naughty smile sent a tingle through her body.

Then, after a deep inhale, he expelled a burst of air that was so powerful it caused a whole hillside's worth of flowers to sway. And that wasn't even the most astounding part. As Milos's breath passed over the flowers, they began changing colors. Reds faded to pink, then all the way to white before deepening back to red again. Pale yellows turned a brilliant shade of orange that gave way to green. Blues morphed into lavender and deep purple. And on and on, as if the meadow were some grand version of one of those fiber-optic Christmas trees.

Angie couldn't pull her eyes away, even after the manmade breeze died down and the flowers settled into their original spectrum of colors. What *was* this place, and more importantly, who was this man who seemed to have so much magic at the ready?

"How in the world did you do that?" she asked him.

"Nothing special about it. You can do it, too."

"Yeah, right."

He responded with a shrug, as if to say, "*Your* loss."

Figuring she had nothing to lose, Angie stepped up to the edge of the trail and sent a big puff of air toward the hillside. Although her breath didn't travel as far as his had, it managed to send a respectable ripple of color through the flowers near the path.

For a few seconds, she just stood there, gawking. Then she burst into laughter. "That is officially the coolest thing I've ever seen."

The look of delight on Milos's face seemed to suggest that watching her do it was one of the coolest things *he'd* ever seen. "So why stop now?" he said.

Why indeed? Angie sucked in her cheeks and inhaled as deeply as she could. When she was sure she'd never taken in so much oxygen, she blew out another breath, causing a dozen rosebushes to metamorphose into a kaleidoscope of colors. Then another breath and another and another, till she was giddy and wheezing.

After taking a moment to catch her breath, she turned back to Milos. "God, I hope my grandmother saw these when she was here during the war. She would've loved them."

"As I recall, she did," he said, smiling fondly.

She squinted at him, puzzled. "As you recall? How old are you, thirty? You couldn't have been alive then."

Once again, his face took on that stricken look that seemed to indicate he'd put his foot in it. But this time, she wasn't about to give him a chance to plot an answer. "Milos, if we're going to get along, you're going to have to be straight with me. When did you meet my grandmother?"

A bear with his leg caught in a trap couldn't have looked more cornered. "Seventy-two years ago."

Although math had never been her best subject, this one was a no-brainer. "But that would make you ... at least seventy-two."

He nodded hesitantly. "Yes, it would."

Suddenly, her head was swimming with questions. But one of them stood head and shoulders above the rest. "Milos, are you human?"

For the third time this morning, he looked away, no doubt seeking some verbal escape route. But this time, possibly reliving the sting of her last rebuke, he met her eyes. "No, Angie, I'm not."

"Then ... what are you?"

He took the deepest of breaths, seemingly sucking in every last ounce of air on the island. After slowly sending it back out, he uttered two words:

"A god."

Angie flinched. Had she heard him right? "Did you say 'a god'?"

Although he confirmed it with a nod, she couldn't bring herself to believe him. "Are you shitting me?"

"Trust me, Angie. I would never … shit you. And just in case I'm misinterpreting that colorful expression, let me reiterate that I am indeed a god."

"An actual god?" She was starting to feel dizzy now. "Like Zeus and Aphrodite?"

"As a matter of fact, they're my elders. They live on the island, too."

She studied his face for a long moment, searching for a flicker of playfulness. But she found only sincerity. His jaw was set. His eyes were clear, urging her to believe the unbelievable. But how could she? What he was suggesting was flat-out impossible. The Greek gods were nothing more than fiction, weren't they?

As though to challenge her belief in a rational world, a crush of otherwise inexplicable occurrences replayed in her head. A seagull dropping off a pouch of coins that had been out of circulation for years. A boat slip and a fishing boat that had suddenly appeared where nothing but sea had been before. A skipper who hadn't aged since her grandmother's day and was able to read her dreams. Flowers that changed color when you blew on them. The laugh she'd heard at her wedding and the adoring face that appeared to her later, both of which belonged to a man she'd only just met on the other side of the world.

And finally, Ya-Ya's words, as she'd toasted Angie's trip on her rooftop garden, which just happened to be named Elysium. "Angie, do you believe that every once in awhile, the universe opens its window of possibilities and allows us to be everything we've ever dreamed of?"

Angie felt the truth wash over her like a wave of crystal clear water. This wasn't just a window of possibilities, it was a whole skyscraper's worth. The universe, under the auspices of her grandmother, had sent her to some latter-day Olympus where the gods still frolicked. And what was supposed to happen to her here? What was the "everything you've ever dreamed of" part of the equation? Did she dare believe it had something to do with Milos?

At that moment, he cupped a hand on her shoulder. "Angie, are you all right?"

As she nodded back at him, a smile spread across her face. This altogether fascinating creature, whose hand was warming her shoulder and regions beyond, was a Greek god. Angie Costianes of Astoria, Queens, was having a flirtatious adventure with an honest-to-goodness Greek god.

She sent out a big thank-you to the universe.

Then she passed out.

SIX

Damn it all to Hades! He'd rehearsed this revelation so many times he had it memorized. His words, his tone, even his responses to questions Angie might ask. The plan called for him to ease into it gently, capitalizing on her knowledge of mythology as well as the open-mindedness he'd seen her demonstrate on so many occasions. And always, *always,* the revelation was to come after they'd spent an agreeable day together, during which he'd be able to gauge her feelings. If she seemed to be exhibiting a fondness for him, she'd be far more likely to accept such seismic information.

But one look into her eyes had sent the plan crashing down. One whiff of her sweet essence had turned him into a chowderhead. And when she'd playfully implied he was using the island's beauty to seduce her, what little gem had rolled off his tongue? *"Oh, I assure you, I've only just begun."* Bollocks! It was like he'd turned into his father or his uncles or any other deity who'd allowed their greed and lust to rule them and ultimately end their reign. For more than a century, with precious few exceptions, he'd exercised control in all his affairs.

But in the course of this one morning, he'd made a mess of things, sending the object of his affection sputtering into a faint.

Thankfully, Angie had recovered fully, setting a torrid pace all the way to the café known as The Ambrosia. But now, as they sat at an outdoor table, barely exchanging a word, Milos had to wonder, *Is that what love is? The unmanning of a man? The disintegration of a once-proud creature into a pile of flotsam? Is that what I want for myself?*

He ventured another look at her. She was still nursing her wine and staring out at the Aegean, apparently a more comforting sight than the dispirited being across from her. He steadied his gaze, virtually willing her to look his way. To say something. Anything. But he knew that unlike the mortals he'd encountered over the years, there'd be no glamouring her.

Finally, after what felt like an eternity, she favored him with a smile. "God, the water's blue."

"Yes. Blue," he replied, fumbling for the words.

Suddenly, her hands flew up to her mouth. "Milos, when I said 'God,' I didn't mean *you*. I meant, *that* God." She pointed to the sky. "Up *there*. Not that I'm comparing you to Him—if, in fact, you *are* ... God, this is awkward. There I go again!"

He probably should've said something reassuring. Instead, he burst into laughter. And kept right on laughing as she stared at him, slack-jawed. Although he knew it was inappropriate, he couldn't help it. Her words and her candor brought him so much joy. Aside from Zeus's wife, Hera, there were no females in his universe who spoke with such unfiltered honesty. They all chose their words carefully, with vast amounts of forethought, as if every conversation were a sporting event after which only one party could be crowned with the laurel. It was as wearying as this was revitalizing. Zounds, she was catnip to him!

Catnip which, at that moment, reached over and slapped him on the wrist. "Stop that."

Although he quickly said, "I'm sorry," he didn't feel sorry at all. Angie had touched him for the first time. And although her slap carried a sting, he still felt a surge of electricity coursing through his body. He could only imagine the sweet ecstasy he'd feel if she gently touched her hand to his face...

...which suddenly seemed far more likely than it had a moment earlier. Thanks to his mirth and the resulting slap, things seemed looser between them, less tentative. Not only was *he* more relaxed, but she was looking at him instead of the sea, with the beginnings of a smile on her face.

"Okay, funny man," she said, "just so I'm a hundred percent clear, I'd like to revisit the little chat we had down on the path. When you said you were a god, you meant..."

She paused, presumably waiting for him to complete the sentence. Which he did. "A god. Or if you prefer, a deity."

"And just so there's no confusion, no cultural barrier or anything, when you say you're a god, you mean..."

He shrugged. "A traditional Greek god. Just as you've read about in your mythology books and seen in your *Clash of the Titans* movies. Hollywood inaccuracies aside."

She took a more substantial sip, then uttered a single word. "Wow."

"Yes. Wow," he replied, for lack of anything wiser to say.

She shot him an admonishing look, no doubt mistaking his inarticulateness for ridicule. "Milos, you have to understand, this is hard for me. I've known guys with prison records. Fetishes. Heck, I once dated a cross-dresser who looked better in my lingerie than *I* did. But this one's got me freaked."

Although he found her discomfort a bit worrisome, he was pleased that she was expressing her concerns. Only through an open dialogue could she come to realize they could build a relationship, despite their differences. "Angie, I fully understand. And I'm happy to answer any questions you might have." *Well, almost every question.*

She seemed to consider the offer, then furrowed her brow. "You told me you met my grandmother back in the day. Was it ... romantic?"

"Not at all." After watching her let out what appeared to be a sigh of relief, he elaborated. "I met your lovely grandmother through an elder cousin of mine. She'd arrived on the island despondent over the loss of someone close to her. My cousin offered her comfort and conversation and helped her rediscover the fountain of strength inside her. In a very natural way, their friendship blossomed into a romance that endured for many years."

As Angie absorbed the revelation, a smile that seemed to be equal parts joy and sadness spread across her face. "Now I know why this island was so special to her," she said, her eyes brimming with tears. "She came here at the lowest point of her life. Widowed and pregnant at the age of eighteen. And in short order, she found love and magic and the will to go on."

"That she did," he replied.

She took a sip of wine, then settled back in her chair thoughtfully. A long moment later, she said, "So this cousin of yours ... I'm assuming he's a god, too."

"One of the twelve Olympians. You've heard of Apollo?"

Her eyes went as wide as saucers. "*The* Apollo? The guy who rides a chariot across the sky?"

Milos chuckled. "When he isn't playing the lyre."

Once again, she uttered that syllable he was growing to love. "Wow."

Unable to resist, Milos reached over and rested his hand on top of hers. "I'm hoping to introduce you to him while you're here."

"I'd love that." She squeezed his hand. "Do you think he'd let me snap a picture of him to take home to Ya-Ya?"

"I'm sure he'd be delighted." But not as delighted as *he* was, feeling the warmth of her touch. "So, do you have any other questions for me?"

"At the moment, just one. Where can I get my hands on a menu? If I have any more wine on an empty stomach, I'll end up doing another face-plant. And I've never passed out twice on the same date."

Milos smiled, delighted that Angie considered this a date. Perhaps there really was a way to undo the damage he'd done earlier. And considering her love of all things epicurean, the charms of The Ambrosia might be the perfect elixir.

As Milos might have predicted, their server, Alexis, arrived at that moment. Among the many gifts the gods had bestowed on the mortals who served them, the most beneficial was that of keen perception. Alexis would beg to differ, he imagined, considering she was ninety years old, but had the supple skin and youthful vitality of a woman in her twenties.

"May I interest you in something from our kitchen?" she asked them, her long, raven hair cavorting with the breeze.

"You bet," Angie replied. "What do you recommend?"

"Everything."

"Gotta love *that*. What do you serve?"

"Anything your heart desires," she said with an eager smile. Milos was well aware this was the wait staff's favorite duty: describing the café's unique bill of fare to the rare visitor to the island. Still, she gave him a deferential nod, wisely perceiving he'd take more pleasure in doing it himself.

After making a note to himself to ensure the old girl another decade of vigor, Milos turned his attention to Angie. "What she means is that if you have a favorite food—from any chef, any restaurant—they'll prepare it for you. Exactly the way you know it."

Angie raised an eyebrow. "Any restaurant? Anywhere in the world?"

"That's right," he said, enchanted at the prospect of enchanting her. "Or, perhaps there's a dish your grandmother used to make. Some special recipe?"

Another skeptical look. "You're serious."

"I've been told I'm *too* serious. But yes."

Angie sat back for a moment, no doubt trying to process the cornucopia of choices available to her. Then she nodded to herself and addressed Alexis. "I'd like a meatball from Angelo's in Little Italy. A slice of cheesecake from Mona Lisa's—with fresh strawberries. And a half-dozen wings from the Buena Vista, this little hole in the wall in my cousin's hometown that makes the best Greek fried chicken on the planet. But just for fun, I'm not gonna tell you where it is."

Alexis nodded, professional as always. "Thank you. And you, Milos?"

"I'll have the same."

As Alexis crossed away, Angie eyed him playfully. "You actually eat?"

"I'm not a vampire," he said, a bit more sternly than he'd intended. "We greatly enjoy food and wine. And immortality. Without the bloodlust."

She smiled faintly, then narrowed her eyes. "So you're like, thousands of years old?"

"Barely over a hundred. I'm the fifteen-hundred-and-ninth offspring of my father, Poseidon, and my mother, Carpathia."

"Sort of a change-of-life baby, were you?"

Once again, Milos burst out laughing, which apparently was infectious, because Angie got caught up in it, too. They kept on laughing for a good minute, each feeding off the other until they were practically convulsing with mirth. He couldn't decide when she was more beautiful—when she was full of joy, or when she was sober and thoughtful.

A few moments later, in a gesture perfectly timed to the waning of their laughter, Alexis arrived with their food. Milos watched, spellbound, as she set Angie's plate in front of her. The look of rapture on Angie's face was something he hoped he'd never forget.

"This looks ... wow!" she said, looking first at Alexis, then him.

Alexis smiled. "If there's anything else I can get you, please let me know."

As Alexis departed, Milos raised his bourbon in a toast. *"Kalí óreksi."*

"Kalí óreksi," Angie replied, clinking glasses with him. Then she began sampling the various items, no doubt comparing them to the originals. First, she broke a wing apart and took a nibble off the drumstick. Then she put a slice of meatball in her mouth and swirled it around a couple of times before swallowing it. Finally, she took a

forkful of cheesecake. And when one bite wasn't sufficient for her purposes, she took another.

At last, she set the fork down and rendered her verdict. "I've gotta tell you, Milos, they nailed every dish. Even the pinch of veal in the meatballs. How do you people do it?"

"Not to boast," he said, "but we have the sun, the moon, and the stars at our disposal. Acquiring a secret recipe or two is elementary."

She seemed to ponder his words for a moment, then returned to her meal, punctuating every bite with an "mmm" or an "ooh." For his part, he found the food quite appetizing, especially the little wings. He'd never had occasion to taste fried chicken before, but it was crisp and savory and far less greasy than he'd imagined. He could see himself ordering this delicacy again.

But mostly, he enjoyed watching Angie eat, delighting in the state of euphoria she seemed to be in. *Dear Angie, what I wouldn't give to be able to bring you pleasure every day.*

Finally, when her plate was clean, she graced him with another smile. "Thank you, Milos. This might've been the most unforgettable meal I've ever had."

"It doesn't have to be over yet. Is there anything else you'd like?"

Once again, she settled back in her seat. He watched her with amusement, wondering which of her other mainstays she was considering. Maybe one of those Big Mac things or that pepperoni-laden delivery pizza he'd seen her order on many occasions.

Then her expression clouded over and she seemed to go somewhere deep inside herself. Moments later, she looked at him and said, "There *is* one more thing."

Before Milos could raise a hand in the air, Alexis was at the table. "Yes, Miss?"

"A rack of ribs," Angie said. "The way my father used to make them."

As Alexis moved off, Milos studied Angie for any sign of sadness. Knowing how much she missed her father, he wondered if he'd erred in letting her know the café could duplicate recipes of favorite relatives.

But she seemed to be all smiles as she leaned in and explained her selection. "My father was a disaster in the kitchen. I mean, the man almost burned the house down one day making me a fried baloney sandwich. But when he got behind the grill, he turned into Superman. He made barbecued chicken that was juicy on the inside and charred just right on the outside. His steaks put Peter Luger's to shame, and that's saying a lot. But mostly, I remember his ribs. Meat so tender, you didn't need teeth. And the flavor? Not to be crude, but it was like an orgasm in your mouth. Sweet and sour and tangy and smoky. He never told us what he put in that marinade, but if he'd bottled it, he would've been a millionaire."

Milos wanted to say, *In my eyes, he* was *a millionaire, because he put you on the earth.* Instead, he simply said, "I can't wait to try them."

"Who says I'm gonna give you any?" she retorted, once again sending him into a fit of laughter. Had he ever laughed so much in such a short span of time?

A few moments later, Alexis arrived with a platter of ribs that looked as extraordinary as they smelled—an altogether intoxicating aroma Milos could imagine his brethren using to seduce mortals and deities alike. As to whether they captured the essence of Tommy Costianes's ribs, Angie's expression seemed to say it all. She was looking at them with a mixture of disbelief and wonderment, as if she were witnessing a beloved ghost come back to life.

"May I serve you some?" he asked her, earning an eager nod. He cut several off the rack and set the plate in front of her. She picked one up, closed her eyes and took a bite, giving every indication of relishing the flavor as well as the memories. Then she took another bite, and another, all the while keeping her eyes shut tightly, as if she were hoping that when she opened them, it would be twenty years earlier in a backyard in Queens.

When she finally opened them, a tear rolled down her cheek. Then, apparently noting the concern on his face, she smiled, but it was a sad smile. As another tear fell, Milos wondered whether there was something he could say to ease her pain. But what, exactly? How could a man who hadn't spoken to his own bastard of a father in over a decade relate to the loss of a father who was loving and kind? Then again, maybe words weren't the answer. Maybe what she needed right now was a comforting hand wrapped around hers.

He never got the opportunity to find out. At that moment, Angie bolted from the table. Milos watched her, stunned, for a second. Then he leapt out of his seat and followed her into the café.

At first, there was no sign of her. Then he heard a blur of voices coming from the kitchen and raced for the door.

Just as he was about to enter, Angie wandered out, looking like a lost little girl. "I'm sorry," she said, her voice barely a whisper, "I just thought … he might be in there."

Then she burst into tears.

This time, Milos didn't hesitate. He wrapped his arms around her. He held her that way for a long time, through tears and sobs and silence, hurting deeply for her, and at the same time experiencing the joy of finally embracing the woman he'd loved for so long, her body so close to his that he could feel her heart beating against his chest. They couldn't pry him away from her now if they used all their powers.

Eventually and all too soon, she pulled back and looked him in the eye. "Milos, I need to ask you something."

He took a deep breath, steeling himself for whatever was to come. "Anything, Angie."

"Why me?"

———

Angie realized her question was partly the product of the vulnerable place she was in. Those ribs hadn't just tasted like her father's; they *were* her father's—right down to the smoky maple flavor that came from those homemade briquettes of his. And with all the other miraculous things that had happened today, how could she *not* think he'd come back to her? So she'd raced to the kitchen so she could find him and hug him tighter than any daughter had ever hugged her father. And after she'd held him for an hour or so, just being his little girl again, she'd ask him the question that had been eating at her for sixteen years.

"Why did you leave me, Daddy?"

And he'd look her in the eye and tell her. And maybe then, she'd finally be able to believe that his leaving had nothing to do with her—that he really *had* loved her. Then she'd fix him with the sternest look she could muster and make him promise he'd never leave her again.

But of course, when she got to the kitchen, her father hadn't been there. The ribs were exactly what Milos said they were—godly razzle-dazzle. So she never got the answer she wanted so badly. And it was humiliating and heartbreaking a hundred times over.

But she knew that wasn't the only catalyst for her question. Truth be told, she was feeling a little outmatched. Sure, she considered herself a catch, regardless of society's narrow definitions of weight and beauty. But Milos was an actual god. In all likelihood, he'd had his pick of goddesses, wood nymphs, sirens, and supermodels, yet he was showing an interest in her. And she had to know why. She knew it was childish to be so insecure, but she really wanted to believe she measured up.

Then a troubling thought crept into her head. *What if I've misread the signs? What if he isn't interested in me at all?*

Indeed, for all she knew, Milos was some sort of godly matchmaker who was preparing to fix her up with one of his otherworldly clients. Sure, her grandmother had enjoyed a fling with Apollo, but who was to say *her* pickings were destined to be as lofty? Maybe at this very moment, her real hookup was waiting outside. For all she knew, Milos was about to trot out some minotaur to make her acquaintance. Not that someone like that didn't deserve love, too, but had she really traveled halfway around the world to find a pet? Then again, if the creature had witnessed her meltdown of a few moments ago, he just might turn tail on *her*.

All that speculation was rendered null and void by Milos's next three words. "Why *not* you?"

Angie stared back at him, wondering whether she'd heard him right. "What did you say?"

"I said, 'Why *not* you?' That's the question you should be asking yourself. You're beautiful, but not in a manufactured way. Yours is an unspoiled beauty that makes you equally stunning whether you're done up in a cocktail dress for a night on the town or clad in Yankees sweats at the batting cages. You're kind and generous, and not just to your family. You routinely hand out leftovers to the homeless and dollar bills to saxophone players in the subway, people everyone else in your world is terrified of looking at. You have a great sense of humor, but you're never cruel. And a thirst for knowledge that takes in everything from *The New York Times* to *TMZ*. You love to dance, and you do it with total abandon, closing your eyes and letting the music flow through your body. You turn strangers into friends wherever you go, because you take an interest in the minutiae of their lives. There are at least two dozen establishments where you know everyone by name, from customers to busboys. And there's a glow about you, Angie, a nurturing light I don't think you're even aware of. And anyone who's lucky enough to be bathed in the glow of that light feels better about themselves. I know *I* do."

For the second time this morning, Angie felt her eyes welling up with tears. God bless him, this stranger seemed to know her better than people she'd spent her whole life around. She couldn't deny there was something magical about it—like the storyline of a Kate Hudson movie.

So why were the hairs on the back of her neck standing up? "Milos, how do you know all those things?"

He took a deep breath, as if he realized his next few words could be troublesome. "Because I've been watching you, Angie. Most of your life."

Although that revelation might've worked for Kate Hudson, it made Angie even queasier. "Watching me? From where?"

"Here, mostly. We call it 'envisaging.' We simply focus our thoughts on something we wish to see: a person, an object, an event.

And it appears in front of us like one of your live news feeds, even if it's thousands of miles away."

At that moment, Angie knew two things. She'd never felt more violated in her life, and the café had gone deathly silent. She took a look around and discovered that every last soul in the place was listening in on their conversation. Even the chef had stepped out of the kitchen so he could hang on their every word. She motioned for Milos to follow her outside.

The second they were out of sight, she slapped him across the face. "All my life, you've been watching me?! Without my permission? What are you, a long-distance stalker?"

He seemed a little shell-shocked, but managed to sputter out a defense. "Of course not. My intentions are honorable."

"Really? How do I know you haven't been watching me when I'm in the shower? Or having sex? Ick! And trust me, I know my mythology. I know how you gods have always looked down on us mortals. What, do you get together on Saturday nights and pop us up on the big-screen so you can sit around making fun of our sad little lives?"

Milos shook his head. "Nothing could be further from the truth. Please allow me to explain."

But Angie was done listening. She threw her hands up in frustration and headed down the path. She didn't know where she was going. She didn't care, really. All she knew was that she needed some breathing room.

A whole island's worth.

SEVEN

Angie continued along the path, relieved that she wasn't hearing footsteps behind her. Good, maybe Milos was smart enough to give her some space. On the other hand, everything around her seemed more vibrant than it had earlier, as if he had enlisted the whole countryside to help bring her back to him. Sure enough, the colors were brighter, the breeze was friskier, and the roses more fragrant, tilting their pretty heads toward her, begging her to grace them with her CO_2.

Instead, she blew a big, fat raspberry—"Take *that,* magic flowers!" —which nevertheless sent a few blooms into a whirlwind of colors.

She wondered whether she should call Ya-Ya and demand some eleventh-hour enlightenment on her experiences here. There were so many things Angie wanted to ask her. How had Ya-Ya reacted when she found out she was in the presence of a real-life mythical creature? Had Apollo confessed he'd been spying on her for decades and knew her inside and out? Had she freaked out, too, and fled down this same path?

Unfortunately, the answers to those questions would have to wait. Angie's cell phone was no longer in her pocket. Then again, there probably wasn't a cell tower on the island anyway. Why would gods need cell phones when they could laugh in somebody's ear from half a world away or catch up on a person's most intimate moments by programming them into their heads?

"Ya-Ya, what the hell were you thinking when you sent me here?" Angie said aloud, half expecting some daylily to answer her.

Then it occurred to her that Ya-Ya *had* given her a heads-up, the night before her trip. In response to Angie's question about whether she'd find romance on the island, Ya-Ya had said, "Promise me one thing, dear. When you get there, you'll put all your preconceived notions aside and let the day take you wherever it's going to take you."

It had certainly started out that way, but now Angie was doing nothing of the sort. But how could she? The situation with Milos was beyond strange. Who *wouldn't* hit the road after a revelation like that?

Right?

Unless that was why Ya-Ya had urged her to make that promise in the first place. Because she knew her granddaughter well enough to know that left to her own devices, she'd make a snap judgment and miss out on something good. It had certainly been good for Ya-Ya. She'd come here drowning in grief and departed reborn and ready to face the world again. And seventy-two years later, when she'd witnessed her granddaughter going through her own brand of hell, she'd arranged for *her* passage to Elysium. Would Ya-Ya have done that if she had any doubt that the experience would be life-changing for Angie, too?

Angie slowed her retreat. Ya-Ya had never steered her wrong in her life. Through thirty years of ups and downs, Ya-Ya had been her champion, with nothing but her best interests at heart. Maybe it was once again time to take her advice. Maybe there was more to Milos and the whole voyeur thing than met the eye, so to speak.

Besides, this was one measly day out of her life. Would it really hurt her to put the big picture aside and go for it? What was the worst thing that could happen? That she'd have a fling with a Greek god? Hell, if he'd been watching *her* all these years, wasn't it her turn to check out the goods? Plus, there was no telling how amazing sex with a deity might be. Milos was gorgeous and sensitive, and he seemed to dig her. Factor in his superpowers and she might end up having an orgasm for the ages.

On that note, she declared herself officially back onboard. She'd head back to the café pronto and ask Milos what was next on the agenda. Whatever it was, short of wiping out mankind, she'd cheerfully embrace it.

As Angie started up the path, she caught sight of two horses grazing on a hillside. One was a chestnut stallion and the other a dark bay mare. And, like everything else on the island, they were spectacular. Tall and muscular and groomed so lovingly that their coats gave off a glow. But all that paled in comparison to their most distinctive feature.

They had wings.

Enormous, white feathered wings midway down their torsos that fluttered in the breeze as they grazed. As Angie crept closer, they regarded her with the same intelligent, soulful eyes she'd observed on the seagull. Then the mare nudged the stallion, sending him trotting over to her.

Although her adrenalin was pumping like mad, Angie didn't feel the least bit scared. Just thrilled to be in the presence of such mythical creatures. As the stallion drew near, he whinnied "hello" and lowered his huge head, presumably so she could pet him. But he was so tall that she had to stand up on her tiptoes so she could stroke him between the ears.

"You are one handsome fella. What's your name, boy? Pegasus?"

"Actually, his name is Eddie. And I call *her* Chrissie."

And there was Milos standing a few yards behind her, hands on his hips. So he *hadn't* let her go too far. Angie allowed a playful smile to slip out. "Eddie and Chrissie? Those are the most ungodly names I've ever heard."

"Not if you're familiar with the musical legends they're named after: Eddie Vedder and Chrissie Hynde. I've always appreciated tortured artists who manage to have a sense of humor about themselves."

Angie shook her head in disbelief. "You like rock and roll?"

"Don't be so surprised. If you've studied your mythology, you're aware my cousin Apollo is a pillar of the arts. As part of my education, he schooled me in all forms of music, from Gregorian chant to hip-hop. I just happen to have a special fondness for the genre that boasts a red guitar, three chords, and the truth."

Angie chuckled. "Quoting Bono now? Of course you'd know I love U2, considering all the times you must've watched me play air guitar in my room, singing 'Desire' at the top of my lungs."

Milos's cheeks turned a telltale shade of red. "I can explain everything, Angie. Then you'll be free to decide whether I'm an honorable individual who's smitten with you or an immortal pervert."

Angie didn't want to laugh, but she couldn't help herself. Milos was witty, ridiculously handsome, and crazy about her. She hoped to God he wasn't a freak.

Apparently satisfied that the threat of bodily harm had passed, he edged closer to her. "So where shall we start? What would you like to know?"

"For starters, how do you justify watching me like that?"

He only hesitated for a moment before smiling confidently. "If you were able to see yourself through my eyes, you'd realize how helpless I am. You're the rarest of treasures, Angie. A rose among a cosmos of thorns. You're as vital to my existence as water and oxygen are to yours."

Angie knew her blushing cheeks were on the verge of betraying her, but she was determined to stay on point. "Lovely speech, Milos. But can you honestly tell me you've never gotten a peek at me naked?"

He shook his head. "I'm afraid I can't."

She groaned. So much for giving Ya-Ya the benefit of the doubt.

But he wasn't done with his answer. "Unfortunately, this ability of ours doesn't send out warning signals. So yes, there were times when I summoned your image and saw more of you than I had any right to. But in every one of those cases, I closed the conduit. Even if I'd never been granted the privilege of meeting you face to face, I could never forgive myself if I disrespected you."

He stared straight at her, eyes open wide, seemingly challenging her to look into them and find a shred of deceit. She gazed back, long and hard. But all she could find was truth. And an almost boyish fear that warmed the cockles of her heart.

"One more question, Milos." She waved a hand toward Eddie and Chrissie. "Are these beauties just for show, or can we ride them?"

"It would be my pleasure. And theirs."

At that moment, it seemed like a great weight had been lifted off Milos. His shoulders, which had looked so tight a minute earlier, eased into their usual sturdy positions. His eyes rediscovered their sparkle, and his face blossomed in a wall-to-wall smile.

Angie smiled back at him, marveling at how flattering it was that this immortal being could have his confidence boosted by a reassuring word from the likes of her.

After calling Chrissie over to join them, Milos produced two carrots seemingly out of nowhere. He fed one to Chrissie and handed the other to her, indicating Eddie. "I think the two of you will get along well. He's calm and gentle. And he loves the ladies."

Angie placed the carrot in the palm of her hand and extended it toward Eddie. Despite his enormous teeth, he picked it up gently. Then, after polishing it off, he treated her cheek to a thank-you lick, prompting her to giggle. "You really are a ladies' man, aren't you, Eddie?"

Milos gave him a pat on the muzzle, then looked over at her. "I assume … actually, I *know* you've ridden bareback. Would you be agreeable to that today?"

"Absolutely." Angie couldn't help wondering at which point in her life Milos had seen her on horseback. As a girl, she'd spent many a Saturday afternoon at Prospect Park with her father, riding the rented horses. Despite her mother's shrill objections, he'd treated her to her first lesson when she was only eight. She took to riding so naturally that she was soon cantering alongside her father on the bridle paths, filling him in on school and boys, while he updated her on his money-making schemes. It was her favorite time with him because she didn't have to share him with anyone. And he never talked down to her. On the contrary, he confided in her as if she were his best friend, often beginning his updates with "Now, don't tell your mother about this, but …"

Even now, she went back to the park several times a year, alternating between the same two Arabians they'd ridden back in the day. Sometimes, when she and her horse were galloping through the woods, she could swear she could hear a familiar voice assuring her, *This is the one, Sugarplum. The little venture that's gonna make us rich.*

Another voice brought her back to the here and now. "Will you be needing a boost?"

She nodded at Milos. "Good idea."

Normally, she'd be comfortable mounting bareback, but Eddie was so tall that she was afraid she'd hurt him if she tried to lurch herself onboard. So Milos stepped over to her, put his arms around her waist and boosted her high enough to swing a leg across Eddie's back.

As she gently grabbed hold of the stallion's mane, Angie realized she was tingling from head to toe from the feeling of Milos's arms around her. The tingling continued as she watched him mount Chrissie, his butt looking eminently pinchable as he planted his hands, boosted himself up, and straddled the mare. Then he looked over at Angie. "Ready?"

"Ready," she eagerly replied.

He gave her a smile, then squeezed Chrissie's sides with his calves and started down the trail. After repeating the command with Eddie, Angie was soon trotting alongside the first man she'd ridden with since her father died. It was sad and happy and hopeful, all at the same time.

At first, Milos kept the pace slow, taking them through a rolling meadow at a moderate clip. But as soon as Angie felt her rhythm jibing with Eddie's, she coaxed him into a gallop that left Milos and Chrissie in the dust.

Angie turned around to see Milos staring after her in awe. *Take that, god!* she chuckled to herself.

Of course, it didn't take long for him to catch up. They spent the next half hour trading the lead as they raced through fields, up and down hills and along a grassy berm overlooking the sea.

Through it all, Angie had a smile on her face she figured was bright enough to illuminate the whole damn island. Flying across the countryside with the sun beaming down on her, the wind whipping through her hair and Milos at her side was the most exhilarating feeling she'd had in ages. She felt alive and invincible, as if nothing could stop her from getting the things she wanted. Regardless of how this day ended, she'd always hold it close to her heart.

And then it got better. After they crisscrossed the island a couple of times, Milos fixed her with a mischievous smile. "So, shall we take it to the next level?"

As Angie gazed at him, puzzled, Milos leaned forward and whispered something in Chrissie's ear. Suddenly, the mare began flapping her wings. Slowly at first, then gradually increasing speed until horse and rider were lifted off the ground.

As Angie watched them ascend into the sky, she felt little bells of excitement ringing all over her body. It was as graceful as a ballet, and she had to experience it for herself. Ironically, at that moment, Eddie tilted his head quizzically as if he'd been reading her mind.

"Go for it, sport," she urged him. "Take us to the sky."

Within moments, they were airborne, closing the distance on Milos and Chrissie. The feeling was so invigorating that Angie let out a little squeal, followed by a full-on "Wooooo!" Soon, she was flying alongside Milos, looking down on the very pastures they'd just ridden across. And the ride was impossibly smooth—totally free of turbulence—as if she were soaring through the air on a Sleep Number mattress set to "Mesmerize."

More than once, she looked over at Milos, intending to articulate her excitement. But each time, she got waylaid by an attack of the giggles. Finally, she managed to get the words out. "Freakin' fantastic!"

He chuckled, apparently getting a rise out of seeing her so giddy. "There's only one thing missing! The perfect soundtrack!"

With that, Milos closed his eyes, scrunched up his face, then opened them again. And suddenly, there was music in the air. Literally.

U2's "Beautiful Day," a song about choosing joy over despair, thundered out from all around them, as if there were a million invisible speakers floating in the air. And the sound was full-bodied and crystal clear, like no stereo Angie had ever heard.

"Where's it coming from?!" she shouted.

Milos smiled, looking quite proud of himself. "Another of those pesky abilities of ours. If there's a song we'd like to hear, any song ever written, we need only to focus on it and … *voilà!* A cerebral iPod, if you will."

"And you don't get any, uh … noise complaints?"

He shook his head. "No one can hear it but you and me."

As Bono and his mates continued their serenade, Angie and Milos flew through miles of clear blue sky on their winged rock-and-roll horses. After the first song ended, Milos called up a few more U2 songs that just "happened" to be Angie's favorites. Then, in a nod to Eddie and Chrissie, he dipped into the Pearl Jam and Pretenders catalogs.

The music seemed to energize the horses, spurring them to pick up speed without sacrificing a shred of grace. Halfway through "Mystery Achievement," Milos estimated they were going fifty miles an hour. "Would you be more comfortable if we slowed down?"

Angie shook her head. This was way too much fun. And even though she knew she could lose her balance and plummet to the ground at any time, she didn't feel an ounce of fear. It was as if she were born for this kind of exploit. She wondered if it was just Milos who was making her feel that way or if something had shifted inside her.

Eventually, Milos decided the horses needed a break. He pointed out a mesa about two hundred yards away and instructed her to give Eddie the "descend" command. Peering down at the ground from such an altitude while gently tugging on his mane, Angie felt like the pilot of her own living, breathing airplane. As Eddie gradually reduced his speed from a gallop to a canter and slowed the beating of his wings, Angie's ears popped and her upper body sloped forward until her chin was resting on the back of his head. They touched down moments later with barely a bump. Then Eddie tucked his wings to his sides, slowed to a walk and halted.

Before Angie could run a hand through her windblown mop of hair, Milos leapt off his horse and hurried over to help her dismount. But as it turned out, his assistance wasn't necessary. In a grand gesture of chivalry, Eddie lowered himself to the ground, allowing her to step off.

"You're a treasure, Eddie," she said, kissing him on the muzzle.

Milos shook his head in amazement. "In all these years, I've never seen him do that."

"Obviously, he knows how to treat a lady." She gave Milos a frisky pop on the shoulder. "Learn from him."

As the horses meandered over to a stream for a drink, Milos led Angie to the edge of the mesa and pointed out a housing development tucked into the neighboring hillside. There were at least three dozen mansions in a schizophrenic array of styles: Stately Victorians alongside rambling haciendas. Dutch Colonials coexisting with French chateaus. Contemporary glass and steel marvels in the shadow of medieval castles. And a gargantuan structure at the top of the hill that looked like the love child of Buckingham Palace and Tara. It was as if the Real Housewives had been given unlimited funds to build their dream houses, and each of them had been hellbent on having the most ostentatious.

"So what do you think?" Milos asked her.

She narrowed her eyes. "Don't tell me that's where you live."

"You were expecting a drafty colonnade? Trust me, no one cherishes luxury and comfort more than the gods. We are, after all, the original hedonists."

Considering everything she'd read about the gods and their appetites, Angie couldn't argue with that. But it did bring up another question. "What happened to Mount Olympus? Did you outgrow it, or did it get too crazy with all the tour buses?"

Milos laughed. "Mount Olympus was a suitable home for my ancestors when they were actively overseeing mankind. But when they took leave of those duties sixteen hundred years ago, they felt they needed a more remote location. To regroup and rethink. To take however much time was needed to devise the best plan for how to reign again."

Angie managed a casual nod, as though listening to a deity discussing world domination were the most normal thing in the world. "But *you've* lived here all your life, right?"

He nodded. "All one hundred and six years of it."

"Well, don't worry. You don't look a day over eighty."

Once again, Milos burst out laughing. Funny, Angie thought; when she'd first heard that laugh this morning, it had unnerved the hell out of her because she'd recognized it from her wedding. But in the course of the day, she'd grown to like it. And not just because of its earthy masculine timbre. Because of how it made Milos look, all boyish and breezy. And how it made her feel, all moist and tingly.

"So which one of these palaces is yours?" she asked him.

He pointed out a stately yellow house with black shutters. It was large, but not overly so, and reminded her of the country homes she'd seen during a trip to England. It looked to be the kind of place where there'd always be a fire in the fireplace, a sheepdog at your feet, and a snifter of brandy in your hand.

"Good choice, Milos. Classy, without tooting its horn."

He smiled. "Perhaps one day you'll come to know all its charms." He left that statement hanging in the air as he pointed out several other houses and their respective owners. His cousin Athena lived in a chateau surrounded by olive trees. Apollo made his home in a medieval castle that nevertheless had its own concert hall, screening room, and grotto-style swimming pool. And the Buckingham Palace/ Tara monstrosity belonged to Zeus and Hera and boasted seven hundred rooms, each of which featured a solid gold statue of Zeus.

As Milos finished matching homes to owners, it struck Angie that he'd left someone out. "Which one do your parents live in?"

At first, he didn't say anything. He stared off into the distance, his expression as dark as a storm cloud. Finally, he sat down under a fig tree and beckoned her to join him.

Then, in a voice tinged with sadness, he said, "My mother left the island when I was very young. As for my father, he had a falling out with the other senior deities some twenty years ago. It was about many things, really, but foremost among them was how to go forward in the new millennium. When it became obvious there was no compromise to be found, he left the island along with several others to form their own … community. I've barely heard from him since."

As Milos's voice wavered, Angie felt her heart breaking for him. It was hard enough to lose your father to an inexplicable death. But to have him alive but estranged from you had to be crippling.

She figured it might be wise to change the subject, but she couldn't resist asking him one more question. "Did he … ask you to go with him?"

"He did, but I turned him down. We were on opposite sides of the issue, as we'd been on just about everything throughout my life. He always considered me weak and easily swayed by emotions. A damn humanist, as he put it. I suppose in some way, he was right. But it won't stop me from going to war with him if the situation calls for it."

As Milos rose to pick up a boulder and hurl it into oblivion, Angie found herself wishing she'd kept her mouth shut. After all the ups and downs today, things had finally started gelling between them. He was growing more and more playful, and she was warming up to this man who already knew her dirty little secrets. But now, thanks to her inquiring mind, he was brimming with anger, and she was at a loss for what to say next. One thing was for sure, though. Despite the fact that they were two different species, they both had serious daddy issues.

A few seconds later, he rejoined her under the tree. "I'm sorry, Angie. It's just that after our quarrel, I promised myself I'd answer all your questions. No matter how difficult."

"Don't worry about it." She patted him on the shoulder. "I'm actually touched that you'd trust me with such heavy stuff."

He reached out and took her hand. "If we're going to have any chance at striking up a friendship, we have to trust each other, right?"

Although those were the words Milos spoke, Angie had no doubt he was saying something else as well. *I want to kiss you.* He said it with his hand, which was caressing her fingers. He said it with his shoulders, which had turned toward her purposefully. And he said it with his eyes, which were staring longingly into hers.

And yet, he remained a gentleman. "Angie, may I kiss you?"

She smiled. "Unless I beat you to it."

On that invitation, he wrapped his arms around her and pulled her so close that she could smell mint and ginger and an earthy musk that must've been his own particular scent. *Probably some sort of godly aphrodisiac,* she thought. *As if he needs one.*

As he lowered his lips toward hers, she felt a jittery anticipation she hadn't experienced since adolescence. She closed her eyes, then opened them again, determined not to miss a thing.

At first, his lips brushed against hers tentatively, as if he were once again seeking her approval. She indicated it by pulling him in closer and pressing her lips to his. Soon they were kissing with passion and urgency. And something else, too—an odd familiarity, as if they'd known each other forever and were reuniting after a long absence.

A few delicious moments later, Angie parted her lips, inviting him inside. And as her tongue touched his, she felt a surge of pleasure, the likes of which she'd never experienced before. It was as if something were being passed along to her from deep inside him, and it was nourishing and sensual. And as it slowly spread through her body, every nerve ending seemed to—

Suddenly, they were jarred out of their embrace by the roar of an approaching engine. It was coming from beyond the bend in the trail at breakneck speed, kicking up a dust storm as it rumbled closer. Angie looked to Milos for an explanation, but he merely groaned, looking more than a little annoyed. She couldn't say she blamed him. Whoever this fool was, he'd interrupted a kiss that had the potential to be downright historic.

A few seconds later, a motorcycle thundered around the bend, heading straight toward them. And it wasn't just any motorcycle. It was a classic Triumph Thunderbird in a sweet shade of blue. The kind of bike that guys like Nick would sell their souls for. And although it had to be fifty years old, it was in mint condition—all shiny and cocksure. There was no doubt in Angie's mind that a god was behind the handlebars.

Unfortunately, his identity would remain a mystery for the moment. Although he wasn't wearing a helmet, he sported a pair of wraparound sunglasses that obscured most of his face. What Angie *could* tell was that he was tanned and fit and looked positively wicked in his black leather bomber jacket, Levis, and engineer boots.

When he was just a few yards away, he reduced his speed and planted a foot in the dirt. Then he hit the throttle again, prompting the bike to spin around and around like a top gone mad, until he was swallowed up by the enormous cloud of dust he'd created. It was all so mysterious and surreal, and as Milos took her hand and led her toward him, Angie couldn't help wondering whether she was being presented for approval.

"Who is it?" she asked him. "Apollo? Zeus?"

There was no time for an answer. At that moment, the cyclist emerged from the dust cloud, ran a hand through his hair and offered her a cheeky smile. Then he whipped off his sunglasses, causing her jaw to hit the ground for the second time that day.

"Jace?"

"Glad you made it, baby girl. I hope this joker's been treating you right."

As thrilled as she was to see him, Angie couldn't imagine what Jace was doing on the island. And how was it possible he was aware of her association with Milos? In what universe was a flight attendant privy to the private lives of the gods? She looked back and forth between Jace and Milos, hoping one of them would enlighten her before she died of curiosity.

Finally, Milos let out a resigned sigh. "Angie, I believe you've met my brother."

EIGHT

COULD JASON HAVE PICKED a more inopportune time to make his entrance? For the life of him, Milos couldn't imagine how. Things with Angie had finally settled into a rhythm. He'd gotten over the hump of telling her he was a god and even made the prickly confession that he'd been watching her for years. And although she'd fainted once and run away twice, they'd worked through it each time, seemingly growing closer as they did. Certainly, some of the credit went to the enchantments of the island. But there was no denying that she felt something for him. How else to explain that kiss?

Mercy, that kiss! He'd been with goddesses whose sexuality was their birthright, but he'd never been overpowered by a simple kiss before. The sensation of Angie's lips pressed against his had not only made him feel blessed, but worthy—as if the darkest corners of his being had been bathed in a golden light of redemption. And how it had aroused him! For a moment, he'd worried that his member would poke through his jeans and make him look like a satyr. Then her tongue touched his and ignited something even deeper in him that erased all his fears and sent him soaring to heights he'd never dreamt possible ...

Until he heard the roar of that damned motorcycle.

And now, as he stood awkwardly by Angie's side, he felt it all slipping away. Because now, there would be more questions. And answers that could send her scurrying back to the boat. After all these years of worshipping her from afar—aching for her every minute of every day—to come *this* close and lose her forever would be a blow from which he'd never recover.

Yet there was Jace, leaning against his bike with that breezy nonchalance he assumed from dusk till dawn. What part of "Stay in the village till you hear from me" had he not understood? After all the conversations they'd had about the delicate nature of these first few hours with Angie, how could he come thundering in like a storm trooper? Moreover, how could two beings who'd sprung from the same womb, who'd been neglected by the same father, be so bloody different?

Insofar as he'd never have the answer to that question, Milos narrowed his eyes and silently asked Jace another one. *What in Hades are you doing here?*

Don't be a douche, Jace retorted. *I put my ass on the line to help you get her here.*

Milos scoffed. *And thanks to your ill-timed arrival, it could be all for naught.*

Jace rolled his eyes, no doubt expressing his long-held belief that his brother created hurricanes where there were only breezes. Milos wished that just once, the responsibility that had been laid on his own shoulders could be thrust upon Jace. How would he deal with the fact that the future of the Pantheon was riding on the way he conducted his life? Would he still be tooling around on motorcycles and acting like a horny teenager? Or would the crown hovering over his head engender an unease that would consume him like a cancer?

Milos's grumblings were interrupted by an impatient sigh from Angie. "Okay, guys. Who's gonna tell me what's going on? Or am I really supposed to believe that times are so tough for you gods that you're moonlighting as flight attendants?"

True to form, Jace laughed like a drunken hyena. Milos, on the other hand, could find no humor in Angie's question, just a growing dread in his belly. And the most maddening part of it was that the question wouldn't even have been on her lips if Jace had followed instructions and altered his appearance before boarding the plane. Then, if Angie had seen him here, it would have been as if she were meeting him for the first time. Instead, Jace's vanity had gotten the best of him and he'd remained in his own skin. And when Milos confronted him about it, how had he responded? "You're underestimating this girl, brother. She'll understand."

Easy for Jace to say. He'd never been in love, nor cared to be. In Jace's one-hundred-and-eleven years on Earth, he'd had as many conquests as some of the Olympians—and they'd been around for eons. Yet every one of his lovers—deity, demigod, or mortal—had remained in his thrall long after the liaison ended. To a one, they seemed content to remain his friend—or "on-call boink buddy" as Jace so delicately put it. Milos, on the other hand, had been with a handful of partners, all but one of whom had cursed him high and low when it finally sunk in that his heart could never be theirs. And the one who'd stuck by him wasn't in it for love, but power and glory. Hence, the predicament he found himself in today.

And now, as Milos stood close enough to Angie to tousle her rapturously curly hair, he knew the risk he was taking by answering her question honestly, not to mention the can of worms he was about to open. But what choice did he have? She'd already proven she could sniff out deception in him as if he reeked of sour milk.

He took a moment to gather his wits, then offered his best approximation of a reassuring smile. "Not to worry, Angie. Jace was only there as a precaution. To ensure your safe passage."

"Safe passage?" Her eyes darted between them. "Against who? Your father and his cohorts?"

Naturally, she'd hit it on the head, which Milos supposed was *his* fault for divulging such sensitive information. Or *hers,* for having the kind of face that made him want to pour out his soul. Regardless, how was he supposed to respond without scaring the stuffing out of her? He cast a withering look at his brother. *Dammit, Jason, how could you put me in this position?*

As if he'd been waiting for the invitation to swoop in and save the day, Jace waltzed up to Angie and kissed her on the cheek. "First off, baby girl, welcome to our little corner of the cosmos. I assume my brother's told you how long he's been waiting to meet you. And if he hasn't—well, shame on him. We'll find you a better god."

Angie smiled. "You mean like yourself?"

"No. Somebody who *doesn't* picture you with a hairy chest and a penis."

As Angie burst out laughing, Milos shook his head in disbelief. He was well aware of his brother's gift for charming members of both sexes. But he'd never expected it to work so quickly on Angie. While a few seconds earlier her face had been fraught with concern, she was now playfully punching Jace on the shoulder, her burden lighter.

"Actually, I've had a great time with Milos," she said. "A little horseback riding. A little U2. And a surprise around every corner."

"Well, I hope I'm one of the better surprises." Jace produced a handful of caramel turtles, which Angie eagerly accepted. Then, as she popped one in her mouth, he turned and gave Milos a reassuring wink. *Relax, brother. I got your back.*

Although Milos found Jace's use of slang a bit silly, he was heartened by the message. So much so that he didn't feel obliged to follow along when Jace led Angie a few feet away to the shade of the cypress tree. Better not to tamper with the flow he had going.

"Let's clear up some mysteries, shall we?" Jace said, plopping down next to Angie. "When my little brother found out you were finally coming our way, he freaked. 'What if something happens to her before she gets here, Jason? I'll never stop flogging myself.' I tried to reason with him, assuring him the chances were next to nil. But did he listen to his smarter, better-looking brother? Not a smidge. I guess when you worship somebody the way he does you, you go a little third rail, as dear Nick so eloquently put it. So I volunteered to be your flyboy into Athens."

Once again, Milos couldn't help marveling at how well Jace was handling things. Jace had managed to brush off the real danger Angie was in, implying it was largely the product of his brother's lovesick imagination. Now, would she move past it or challenge his veracity?

"My own personal flyboy," she said, squeezing Jace on the shoulder. "So who'd you have to seduce at Delta to get *that* gig? Or did Zeus pull some strings?"

Jace wagged a finger at Milos. "Shame on you, brother. Far too entranced by girlfriend's beauty to educate her in all things deity. Never fear, Angie. Jacie is here."

With the finesse of a schoolteacher, Jace offered her a rudimentary explanation of how for thousands of years, their brethren had been able to infiltrate hostile governments, military organizations, judicial bodies—even country clubs. All it took was a singular focus of will, and suddenly a previously unknown name materialized on an organizational chart; an office sprang up out of nowhere; and false memories took root in the minds of relevant individuals. It was a tactic that had fallen out of favor in these days of respecting the free will of mortals, but it was occasionally used for limited, less nefarious purposes.

Case in point, Jace told Angie, when he agreed to chaperone her on her flight to Athens, a schedule change took place under the noses of everyone at Delta. The assigned steward was shifted to another flight and replaced by one "Jason Carrington," whose personnel file showed he had fourteen years of experience and a spotless record. And anyone who'd have contact with him suddenly found themselves familiar with him. Even his fellow first-class flight attendant "remembered" serving with him on numerous New York to Athens jaunts.

"I suppose if I'd *really* been thinking," Jace said, "I'd have planted memories of a Dionysian fling into the mind of the pilot. Even after three martinis, that man was a tough nut to crack."

Angie burst out laughing. "That is flat-out the most incredible thing I've ever heard. I mean, you guys are like the CIA."

"Who do you think they were modeled after?" Jace replied with a wink.

Relieved that his brother had steered Angie past the immediate icebergs, Milos waded into the conversation. "Although it's not something I'm proud of, over the years kings have been beheaded, prophets crucified, regimes toppled. All because of the influence of a few well-placed outsiders."

"Dang, the things they don't teach us in Mythology 101," Angie quipped.

As Angie smiled at him with those sultry lips of hers, Milos felt his passion reigniting. The harsh light of the midday sun couldn't begin to diminish her beauty. If anything, it made her even more radiant. Her every asset kissed by the rays of Apollo.

Milos cast a glance at the motorcycle. Perhaps he could borrow it from Jace and take her on a tour of the island. How electrifying it would be to feel her arms wrapped around him as they cruised across the countryside. And to see her eyes light up as they took in the wonders of the great waterfall, which would be the perfect setting for a romantic—

His daydream was cut short by a slap on the shoulder from Jace. "What do you say we give Angie a taste of this sweet little skill of ours?"

Angie smiled. "Any sentence with the word 'taste' in it sounds good to me."

But Milos was already imagining Angie's arms around him on the motorcycle. "Actually, Jace, we should get going. Angie's just here for the day, and there's so much I want to show her."

"Come on, brother," Jace insisted. "It'll only take a minute." Then he privately added, *And it just might get you in the saddle.*

Not sure he could afford to dismiss that possibility, Milos shrugged. *Just don't go too crazy.*

Jace laughed deviously, then turned to Angie. "What do you say, baby girl? Is there a group you've always wanted to be part of? Congress? The Cabinet? Cast of *Dancing with the Stars?*

Milos didn't even have to guess.

"The Yankees," Angie said, proving him right.

Jace smiled. "The Yankees, it is. As what?"

Angie looked at him as if he were the most witless person on Earth. "Duh. A player."

Milos brightened. This little detour had the potential to be fun. Plus, if it enchanted Angie the way he suspected it would, his brother's prediction could well come true.

"Got it," Jace said, "A player." Then he cleared his throat dramatically to signal the beginning of his demonstration. "I'm going into my trance now. Needless to say, I require total silence. That means you, Milos."

As Milos swallowed a laugh, Jace closed his eyes and touched his fingers to his temples while humming like a Zen Master. Although Milos knew full well those gestures were only for show, he played along for the sake of Angie, who was enthralled.

An eternity later, Jace opened his eyes and graced her with a smile for the ages. "Congratulations, Miss Costianes. You are officially a member of the New York Yankees."

"Uh, thanks," she said, sounding confused. Then she took a long look around, presumably expecting Yankee Stadium to have popped up on the mesa. When she saw that it hadn't, she shrugged. "I don't get it."

Jace frowned. "What's not to get? You're a Yankee."

"Yeah, right. And this is September, smack dab in the middle of the season. So why am I here on this island and not playing in a game or going deep at batting practice? Huh, pretty boy?"

Jace emitted a stage gasp. "*Pretty boy?* Cripers, you do the girl a favor and she bites you in the ass. Are you sure about her, Milos?"

Milos couldn't help smiling. "Angie, it's not something I say often, but my brother speaks the truth. I'm sure we can find a way to confirm it."

"You mean like Googling it?" she retorted. "Yeah, that might have been a plan if my phone hadn't conveniently disappeared."

Recalling he'd slipped her phone in his pocket when she fled the café, Milos pulled it out and tossed it to her. "Google away."

"Trust me, I will." Then, as Milos and Jace exchanged expectant looks, Angie tapped the touch screen a couple of times and smiled. "Here it is, the official website of the New York Yankees. Let's do a little rundown of the roster, shall we?"

Angie tapped the screen again and began scrolling, her face set in a dubious smile. Suddenly she gasped. "Holy shit! *Angie Costianes! Birthplace: Astoria, Queens. Position: Second base. Batting average: .304.*"

"Dang, girl, you're an all-star," Jace said, patting her on the back.

She squeezed him on the thigh, prompting Milos to wish for that one moment he were his brother.

Then Angie tapped the screen again, squinted, and let out a squeal. "Oh my God, I'm in the team picture, too! Right there, between Ryan and Teixeira."

Milos leaned in for a look. Indeed, there she was in the second row, a Yankees cap on her head and a smile on her face. Seeing her in that environment, looking so happy and so at home, made his chest swell with pride. "I must say, you look dazzling."

Jace looked over his shoulder. "Yeah, girl, you *own* those pinstripes."

Tickled by his brother's quip, Milos started laughing. Soon Jace was laughing along with him. After a few more rounds of mirth, it occurred to Milos that he hadn't heard Angie laugh.

He turned to find her glaring at them. "I can't believe I fell for it."

He and Jace replied in tandem. "What do you mean?"

"Come on, you guys are scamming me." She tossed the phone at him. "So what'd you do to that thing? Add some app that popped me onto the roster? Photoshop me into the team picture? Fess up. This is how you two impress your groupies, isn't it?"

Although he found himself bristling at the accusation, Milos took a deep breath and spoke coolly. "First of all, Angie, although my brother may have a groupie or two, I assure you *I* don't. Secondly, you really are a member of the Yankees. And everyone in New York and much of the world knows it. But don't take my word for it. Feel free to call someone and confirm it."

She snatched the phone out of his hands, "As a matter of fact, I will. But not Ya-Ya. She's probably in on it. I'll call my brother. He wouldn't dare lie to me."

Once again, she began working the touch screen. Then she stopped, narrowing her eyes. "Hold up. If I really am a Yankee, I'd have Jeter's number, wouldn't I? He *is* helping out as a batting coach this season."

Milos shrugged. "You might."

The triumphant look on Angie's face indicated she was sure she'd found the chink in their armor. "Let's find out, shall we?" She began scrolling through her contacts, reading out names. "Zack Economos, Trish Galway, George Georgiades, Sandy Hatalsky..."

Then her face went as white as a cotton ball. "Oh. My. God. Derek Jeter."

"Told ya," Jace said in a sing-song manner.

Milos tapped his index finger on the phone. "Go ahead. Call him."

Angie stared at him for a moment, then tentatively lowered her finger to the pad, as if she were fearful of an electric shock. First, there was a loud beep, indicating she'd hit the speaker button. Then another beep for "SEND."

The phone rang once. Twice. Three times.

Then, a man's voice. Casual. Confident. "Hey, buddy."

From the thunderstruck look on Angie's face, Milos knew at once that she recognized the voice. She turned to him, then to Jace, her lip quivering with anticipation.

Then she took a deep breath and spoke haltingly, as if she were trying out her voice for the first time. "Hello … Derek. It's Angie. Costianes."

"Yeah, I saw the ID. What's up, Ang?"

She gleefully mouthed the word "Ang," then cupped her hands over her mouth and giggled like a ten-year-old. It took a pointed jab in the ribs from Jace to get her to compose herself. "Not much … Derek. How's it, uh, going with you?"

"I'm not gonna lie. We miss you."

Her eyes flew open. "You … do?"

"Hell, yeah. Sox killed us last week, as if you didn't know, and the Rangers are on a tear. When are you gonna get your ass rehabbed and back in the lineup?"

"Soon. Real soon."

"That's what I want to hear. Later."

For a good ten seconds after the call ended, Angie just stared at the phone. Then she looked up at them with a face full of wonder. "Derek Jeter just called me *buddy*."

Milos felt his spirits soaring. Angie was happy again, which meant things were back on track. And for the most part, he had his brother to thank. When he'd found himself incapable of explaining things to her, Jace had stepped in and taken care of business. Granted, it was Jace's unannounced arrival that had made it necessary, but the subject might have come up eventually, and Milos doubted he could've handled it better.

Feeling a rare rush of brotherly love, he reached out and patted Jace on the back. At first, Jace flinched from the alien touch. Then he warmed to it, fixing him with a grin. *Anything to help you get your swerve on, brother.*

Moved by their show of bonding, Angie gave them each a kiss on the cheek. "You guys are all right, you know that?"

As he sat there with his brother on one side and the woman he loved on the other, Milos felt a warmth spreading through his body. *There are moments in life that are rare and special. Without a doubt, this is one of them.*

Then just like that, the moment ended.

"So, baby girl," Jace said. "Before we break up this palaver, do you have any more questions for us? Ask away."

Milos felt every muscle in his body stiffen. *Really, Jason? Now?*

————

212-752-4362, 212-752-4362, 212-752-4362 ...

There was no way Angie was going to let herself forget that number. She had no doubt the man she'd spoken to was Derek Jeter. She'd heard him interviewed so many times that even the most skilled celebrity impersonator wouldn't be able to dupe her. But the spell would undoubtedly wear off, if it hadn't already, and those digits were her only proof that for one glorious moment, she really had been a member of her favorite ball club.

As mind-boggling as it was, it wasn't even the most amazing thing that had happened in the past hour. She'd come to find out that Jace, a guy she'd figured for nothing more than a charming flight attendant, was actually the brother of the god she was falling in serious *like* with. A god who'd been pining over her for years, despite having seen her at her bad-hair-day-bad-skin-day-overeating-overdrinking-feeling-sorry-for-herself worst. She couldn't believe it. Twenty-four hours ago, she'd been enjoying a fun, if chaste, vacation. Now, she was living a romantic adventure even Nora Roberts would consider too outlandish to write about.

But it wasn't without its dark shadings. Jace had been on that flight for one reason: to protect her from Poseidon. And although he'd done his best to assure her there was nothing to worry about, Angie wasn't convinced. She'd seen the uneasy looks that passed between him and Milos when she'd asked about it. Hell, she could've driven a truck through the awkward moment of silence that hung in the air before Jace sat her down and explained things.

But not everything. Case in point, why would Poseidon want to harm her? It wasn't like she was a sorceress with designs on Milos. She was an ordinary girl from Brooklyn who hadn't even known what she was getting into until she stepped off the boat this morning.

Why would the god of the sea give a shark's behind about who his estranged son was hooking up with?

She gazed over at Jace and Milos, who were watching her expectantly. Should she ask them about Poseidon? Get them to fess up about any real danger she might be in?

Then again, the vibe between Milos and her was light and playful again, and she could feel the heat growing, too. A tough question could send his spirits into a nosedive. And God, how she longed for another taste of those lips. In her experience, men who were good kissers were usually good in bed, too. Milos was a phenomenal kisser. She could only imagine how many times she'd be calling out his name in the throes of passion.

With that in mind, she decided to start out small, with a question that might shine a light in that direction. And depending on how it went, she'd either press forward or save it for later.

Summoning up her more carefree look, Angie leaned forward and smiled. "Actually, guys, I have one teensy question. Needless to say, you got me through the flight safe and sound. But I was in Athens for a week. Were there any other times when you were watching over me?"

Milos turned to Jace, then apparently thought better of it and tackled the question himself. "In fact, between the efforts of Jace and several other deities, you were never more than an arm's length away from a helping hand. Except when you were sleeping, of course."

Angie knew she shouldn't go there, but she couldn't help herself. "At which point *you* were watching over me."

Although Milos muttered, "No," his face betrayed him by turning a bright shade of red. Angie smiled. There was something comforting about knowing that the gods suffered the same humiliations as mortals. Embarrassment. Frustration. Anxiety. She couldn't imagine attempting a relationship with someone who was, for lack of a better word, Christ-like.

"And you, Jace," she said. "If you were keeping an eye on me in Athens, how come I never caught sight of your cute little self? Or were you in invisible-god mode?"

Jace looked downright gleeful. "It's way cooler than that. You've read your mythology. Are you familiar with all that shape-shifting stuff we do?"

"Sure," she replied. "Didn't Zeus get his jollies by impersonating husbands and having his way with their poor, oblivious wives?"

While Milos shifted uncomfortably, Jace kept on smiling. "Trust me, I've never done anything like that. Okay, once, but his fiancée was majorly neglecting him. But back to you, baby girl. Remember that sailor with the neck tattoo you boogied with at the Bohème? *Moi.* And that nasty Czech woman at the shoe store?"

Angie's jaw dropped. "No way."

In a flash, Jace morphed into the rotund Czechoslovakian woman who'd tangled with her over that last pair of Manolos, right down to the frosted blond hair, chartreuse pantsuit, and acid tongue. As he proceeded to cuss her out in an amazingly female timbre, Angie burst out laughing and kept right at it till tears were rolling down her cheeks. Milos got into it, too, and at one point, grabbed her hand in a fit of mirth. Or mirth-inspired lust. At any rate, it felt good.

And it helped blunt the impact of the thought that had popped into her head. *If they had people watching me all over Athens, there's a big problem.*

But for the moment, Angie decided not to press the issue. And it wasn't just because she was concerned about Milos's reaction. Truth be told, she was afraid it might scare the bejesus out of her, too. What if Milos told her his father hated him so much that he was determined to do away with anyone who made him happy? Would she accept the danger and let the romance unfold? Or would she hop the first flight home, lock the doors, and try to forget any of this had happened?

For the time being, all she wanted to do was enjoy this beautiful day on this beautiful island with these two beautiful men.

And do her damndest not to dwell on what might be lurking around the corner.

NINE

Was there a better remedy for your fears than the sight of two semi-naked men?

Okay, two buck-naked men, Angie thought. *But why get greedy?*

She was standing on a mountaintop, flanked by Milos and Jace, who were stripped to their undies. Milos was wearing white boxers, while Jace was rocking a pair of zebra print briefs. And when she wasn't stealing looks at their insanely chiseled torsos and six-pack abs, she was gazing at another wonder of nature—a gargantuan waterfall. The shimmering curtain of water fed off a cobalt blue river and plummeted hundreds of feet down a cliff to become a turbulent plunge basin before shaking itself off and continuing its journey to the sea.

And Milos and Jace were about to go over it. At Angie's request.

A few minutes earlier, she'd asked them how they'd gotten along when they were growing up. Considering they were only a few years apart, had they been close? Competitive? Heck, had they even *been* kids, or did gods pop out of the chute looking like fully formed adults?

"I can assure you that most of us come into the world just as you do, as bawling babies," Milos told her. "It's just that once we put away the diapers, we never have need for them again."

He explained that for the first thirty years of life, gods age much like mortals—with similar milestones in mental and physical growth. Even puberty. But then the aging process stops, and they spend eternity looking pretty much the same. No wrinkles. No hair loss. No diminishment of strength or sexual function. No senility.

"Sort of like Cher," Jace joked.

While the brothers were in agreement on that subject, they were miles apart as to how they'd related as kids. Milos maintained he'd been supportive, making every effort to help his big brother realize his potential, despite Jace's constant whining that nobody could tell him what to do. Jace took a sledgehammer to that notion, claiming Milos rarely supported him. In fact, when Milos wasn't ignoring him completely, he was criticizing everything he did, mostly out of jealousy.

"Jealousy?" Milos huffed. "What could I have possibly been jealous of? Your immaturity? Your recklessness? Your unerring ability to always be your own worst enemy?"

"How about the fact that I was better than you at everything? Without even trying."

As Milos gave Jace a shove, Angie struggled to keep a straight face. It was a kick to see these two deities behaving like any other brothers. Petty. Simmering with age-old hostilities. All told, acting more like teenagers than super-evolved beings who were roughly a hundred years old.

So she decided to fan the flames. "Tell me, guys. Was there one thing in particular you always kicked your brother's butt at?"

In unison, they said "The Falls." And in the midst of the bickering that followed, it didn't take much to convince them to head back to the waterfall and settle things once and for all. It hadn't even occurred to Angie that they'd have to remove most of their clothing to do it. Just an added perk for the lucky gal who'd be judging the competition.

But now, as she peered down at the swirling cauldron of water and jagged rocks at the base of the falls, Angie felt a shudder run through her. "Tell me you guys weren't terrified the first time you did this. That's a mother of a drop."

"Five hundred forty-two feet," Milos said proudly. "Three times the height of Niagara Falls. But really, there was never anything to fear. While gods experience small amounts of pain, it never lingers. And of course, we can't die."

"Don't let him get away with that," Jace said. "He was scared shitless the first time."

Milos laughed sarcastically. "You're right, Jason, I *was* scared. Petrified of the irreparable harm I'd do to your fragile ego when I beat you. And seeing as how you've turned out, I had reason to be scared."

This time, Angie didn't try to hide her amusement. She burst out laughing, prompting Milos to raise an eyebrow, no doubt concerned that his behavior might tarnish her opinion of him.

Don't worry about it, sweetie, she thought. *If anything, you're growing on me.*

A few seconds later, in a gesture Angie was becoming well-acquainted with, Jace pulled a pair of binoculars out of thin air and tossed them to her. "These puppies will give you a bird's-eye view of the race. So you can properly declare me the winner."

Angie held up the binoculars and aimed them at the falls. Close up, the waters appeared even more treacherous, and the drop looked to be perpendicular to the ground. She couldn't help thinking that if Milos and Jace weren't superhuman creatures, they'd break every bone in their hot little bods. Even so, the impact would have to hurt, wouldn't it?

But clearly, there'd be no talking them out of it

"Looks like fun, doesn't it, Angie?" Milos said.

"Sure, if you've got a death wish." She lowered the binoculars. "So … first one to the bottom wins?"

The brothers exchanged a look that seemed to carry some unspoken understanding, then broke out in the same mischievous smile.

"Just keep an eye on us," Milos said. "All the way."

"Yeah, baby girl. Let the coolness unfold," Jace added.

With that, Jace gave her a hug and headed toward the riverbank. Milos lingered a moment, looking like he was debating something. Angie offered him a curious smile, hoping to coax it out of him. Apparently, that was all the enticement he needed. He leaned over and kissed her lightly on the lips, leaving her in a state Ya-Ya would call "love-screwed."

Angie unscrewed herself long enough to wish them luck. They nodded their thanks and sprinted toward the river, looking like they should be on the cover of an Abercrombie & Fitch catalog.

Except for one thing. Milos had what appeared to be scars across the middle of his back. Long, jagged scars that looked like they'd been put there by a tiger or some other savage creature. Which didn't make sense. If gods didn't age or lose their hair, wouldn't it follow that they wouldn't retain any injuries? Vowing to broach the question when they were alone, Angie watched as the two of them stepped up to the edge of the riverbank and assumed diving positions.

And on her count of "Ready, Set, Go!" they were off, swimming furiously toward the falls. They were doing the butterfly, windmilling their arms over their heads and kicking their legs like dolphins, moving faster than any human swimmers she'd ever seen—aside from Michael Phelps, whom she wasn't convinced was human, either.

Pacing along beside them on the shore, Angie watched Jace take the early lead, outdistancing Milos by half a body length. But as the water grew more turbulent, Milos kicked it up a notch, inching ahead a few yards shy of the cliff. Then, as Angie held her breath, they hit the drop-off and began the fifty-story plunge.

At first, Angie couldn't see them at all. Then, with the help of the binoculars, she caught sight of two flesh-colored blurs flying headfirst down the falls like missiles on a suicide mission. As she watched with a mixture of wonderment and fear, their bodies kept ducking in and out of the churning column of water. Seconds later, they plunged into the basin a few feet from the falls, sending up a pair of surprisingly small splashes. She thought Jace might've touched down a split second before Milos, but it was too close to call.

For one scary moment, there was no sign of either of them. Just the swirling vortex of foam and water, taunting her with its roar. Then, to her relief, Milos popped to the surface, followed by Jace. As Angie shot them a thumbs-up, it occurred to her they'd never told her how they were going to meet up with her after the dive. Unless there was an elevator tucked into the mountain, there was no way they were going to get back to her, and she couldn't imagine any scenario that would have her taking the wild ride down to them.

After treading water for a moment, they started swimming again. First, they freestyled around the foamy plunge basin. Then, in a feat of eye-popping athleticism, they began fighting their way toward the falls—swimming against the rushing current like the world's most powerful salmon. And although the water bashed them back a couple of times, they kept inching their way forward. Closer and closer to the base of the falls. Then they went one better.

They started swimming up the waterfall.

Angie couldn't believe her eyes. Not only were they defying gravity, they were waging war with the crushing pressure of thousands of gallons of falling water. And winning. Slowly but surely, they were scaling the ferocious waterfall as if it were nothing more than a rope ladder.

Angie put the binoculars down to make sure it wasn't an optical trick. But even with the naked eye, she could make out two small objects rising up the falls. *Unfreaking believable. How many mind-blowing things can one girl witness in a day?*

She readjusted the focus so she could zero in on their tortured faces as the water pounded them. Every muscle in their bodies seemed to be cranked to full capacity. Taut. Bulging. Straining against the— for lack of a better word—Heraclean task. For a good five minutes, they were neck and neck. Then Milos dropped out of sight.

At first, Angie figured he'd simply disappeared behind the wall of water. Then she noticed Jace looking down for a second, then continuing his ascent. And was that a smile on his face?

"Damn you, Jace!" she shouted. Then, as it sunk in that she'd cursed a man she actually liked, she smiled. Could there be a better indication she was falling for his brother?

But where *was* Milos? Although Angie scanned every inch of the falls, she couldn't find a trace of him. Then she spotted something at the base of the falls and focused the binoculars on it. Sure enough it was Milos, once again beginning the climb, seemingly undeterred. If anything, he looked to be swimming faster, working his arms vigorously while moving his legs like pistons. Within seconds, he settled into a sturdy rhythm and began closing the gap between himself and Jace.

Over the years, Angie had attended hundreds of ballgames, but she'd never witnessed a moment as exciting as this one. Or rooted for an athlete quite as fiercely as she was rooting for Milos. *Sorry, Derek.* Her heart was pounding like a drum, her hands were clutching the binoculars like vices, and her toes were tapping out a staccato rhythm.

And even though she knew he couldn't hear her, she started cheering for him. "Go, Milos!"

To her delight, he drew within a few yards of his brother. Jace must've felt the heat of his pursuit, because he cast a glance over his shoulder, disrupting his momentum. Milos used that window of opportunity to pull within a body length. For the next few minutes, it was a battle for the ages. They traded the lead a half dozen times, all the while fighting the colossal forces of nature that were literally beating down on them.

Angie paced the sidelines watching them—anxious, out of breath, and buzzed from the adrenaline coursing through her veins. One thing was for sure. The minute she got home, she was going to call the IOC and insist they make waterfall climbing an Olympic sport.

Then, about twenty yards from the top, Milos started losing steam. The once furious pace of his stroke began to slacken, sending him drifting down the waterfall. Through the binoculars, Angie drew in a breath when she saw the exhausted look on his face. Meanwhile,

Jace was capitalizing on his lethargy, forging ahead by a body length, then another, as Milos appeared to be on the brink of defeat.

But Angie wasn't about to let him give up. Hoping against hope he was within hearing range, she screamed at the top of her lungs. "You can do it, Milos! Kick ass!!!"

He must have heard her, because at that moment, his face sprang back to life. Then he set his jaw and resumed his attack on the water-fall—modestly at first, but enough to help him reverse his slide. Then he shifted into overdrive, fighting his way up so vigorously that his limbs became a blur.

But would it be too late?

Although Milos was gaining ground, Jace was just a few yards from the top of the falls, the finish line. Angie continued screaming so bois-terously that her throat felt like it was lined with sandpaper. Milos seemed to feed off the encouragement, inching close enough to Jace to touch his feet. But Jace was getting a second wind of his own, moving ahead by two body lengths and almost ensuring himself a win.

Then out of nowhere, a flock of snow-white seagulls whooshed past the falls mere inches over the brothers' heads. Spooked, Jace whipped his head up to look at them, throwing off his stroke. Milos took full advantage, surging forward with a burst of speed that led him past his brother and over the top of the falls.

On the sidelines, Angie was beyond jubilant. Cheering, pumping her fists, even shedding tears of joy. She realized she should show some decorum on behalf of poor Jace, but she couldn't help herself. It was as if she'd witnessed Milos come back from the dead and was heralding his rebirth.

As Milos crawled out of the water and collapsed on the ground, Angie felt her legs carrying her over to him, moving her faster than she'd thought possible. And when she reached him, she didn't even hesitate. She dropped to her knees, threw her arms around him, and planted a kiss on his lips, which were cold and tasted like salt water but still felt like sacred fruit. Through his exhaustion, she felt him struggling to kiss her back—and doing a godly job of it.

After a moment, she figured she should let him catch his breath. So she raised herself up on her elbows and offered him a smile she'd hoped would convey the pride she was feeling. "You were a gladiator, you know that?"

Although his face had been battered raw by the pounding water, Milos managed to smile back at her. "It was your voice that carried me to victory."

Angie let out a sigh. It had been ages since a man's words had touched her so deeply. Then she put her arms around him and laid her head on his chest, feeling the heat of his skin on her cheek as her head rose and fell with the rhythm of his breathing. As romantic as the moment was, she couldn't help stealing a glance at the bulge in his soaking-wet drawers. That made her smile, too. Truly, this was a moment she could live in forever.

But sadly, it wasn't destined to last.

"Cheating bastard."

She looked up to see Jace looming over them, glowering at his brother.

Milos wrestled himself to a sitting position, displacing her from her sacred resting place. "You're delirious, Jason. I beat you fair and square."

"Bullshit. Those *were* your gulls, weren't they?"

"Yes. But no one told you to look at them."

Angie winced. Had Milos actually summoned the gulls? Had this god-man stooped to scheming to win a silly race? It did seem like a coincidence that they'd come along when they had.

A coincidence Jace wasn't buying. "You're a prick, you know that?"

"I'd say I did you a favor." Milos rose to his feet. "You've always been too easily distracted. Learn from this."

And there it was. Milos *had* cheated. How was that supposed to make her feel? Disappointed? Concerned that he'd try to pull one over on *her* someday? Concerned that he already had?

Angie's soul-searching was interrupted by the sound of Jace's fist connecting with Milos's chin. As she looked on, aghast, Milos staggered back a few steps, rubbing his jaw, then gave him the mother of all pitying looks. "My goodness, Jason. Can't you even lose like a man?"

"Not if you can't win like one," Jace retorted. "But let's get to the real. You're never gonna forgive me, are you?"

Milos's shoulders tensed. "I forgave you a long time ago, Jason. I just can't seem to forget."

Obviously, that stirred up something in both of them, because seconds later, they were brawling. Fists flying. Bones crunching. Contempt in their eyes. As much as Angie hated to see them pummel each other, it made her realize something. There was no reason to apply Milos's stunt with the seagulls to her relationship with him. It was a case of brothers being brothers. Royal pedigree aside, he and Jace harbored the same resentments as every pair of mortal siblings she knew. And they had a century's worth of misunderstandings under their belts, including the cryptically intriguing one that had gotten the fists flying just now.

But it didn't mean she wasn't tired of their skirmish. Plus, she figured, the testier things got between them, the harder it would be for Milos to cool down and ease into the kind of serenity they'd need for another smooch session. And she simply couldn't have that.

So she stepped between them, ducked to avoid an errant fist, then held her hands out for a ceasefire. "Okay, stop! I'm ready to declare a winner."

They stared at her dumbly, blood trickling down their chins.

"You guys did ask me to judge the race, didn't you?" she said.

This time, they managed to nod.

"Good, because I'm ready to call it. But first, I want you to shake hands."

That elicited groans loud enough to muffle the roar of the waterfall.

Milos spoke first. "Not to offend you, Angie, but a handshake isn't going to cure the bad blood between us. Plus, it's a silly mortal custom."

"Then humor the silly mortal," she replied.

At first, Milos and Jace just stood there, arms folded across heaving chests. But Angie held firm, clearing her throat pointedly to indicate she wasn't going to back down. Finally, Milos looked over at his brother, shrugged, and held out his hand. Jace shrugged back and held out his. And while it would never go down in history as one of the great détentes of all time, their hands met in the middle, shook for a millisecond, then retreated to their corners.

After rewarding them with a round of applause, Angie said, "And now, by the power vested in me, I declare the winner of the waterfall race to be Milos."

He pumped a fist in the air, then wrapped her in a hug that got the hormones hopping again.

"Figures you'd side with him," Jace grumbled. "You're sleeping with him. Or about to be."

"Jace!" Milos made out like he was offended, but there was a smile on his face.

Hers, too. "Guys, I wasn't finished. What I was going to say was that the winner is Milos—with a potentially unfair assist from the seagulls."

And there went Milos's smile. "Angie, how could you?"

"I'm doing you a favor, Milos. I'm sure you want to prove beyond a shadow of a doubt you would've beaten him regardless. So what do you say to a rematch? In say, ten minutes?"

Whether he was worn down by the exertions of the day or wanted to stay in her good graces, Milos nodded grudgingly. "Very well."

"I'm cool with that," Jace declared. "But could we put it off till tomorrow?"

Milos rolled his eyes. "I don't believe it, you're trying to buy time. What are you going to do? Work in a swimming lesson with Johnny Weissmuller?"

"Hadn't planned on it, but that's a sweet idea." Jace rested a hand on Milos's shoulder. "But actually, it's you I'm thinking about. You have a meeting with the Council in ten minutes."

"What?!" Milos looked like he'd been hit by a freight train.

"Yeppers. They're waiting for you in the Great Hall. Not sure what it's about. All I know is they asked me to deliver you and wait outside in case they want to talk to me afterward."

"Dammit, Jace, why didn't you tell me about this when you got here?"

"Because that would have ruined all the fun. Am I right, Angie?"

"Absolutely," she said, putting on a smile. But deep down inside, she couldn't help thinking this hastily called meeting had something to do with her.

TEN

As Angie made her way through Milos's house, checking out each and every room, one thought kept nagging at her.

It's too good to be true.

A few minutes earlier, he'd whisked her over here, poured her a glass of wine, and encouraged her to make herself at home while he went off to what he assured her was a very routine meeting with the Council—as if a powwow with Zeus and Apollo and their immortal brethren were the most mundane thing in the world. Then he gave her a brief but tingly kiss on the lips and scooted out the door, promising he'd be back as soon as he could. She polished off the wine in two nerve-steadying gulps, poured herself another one, and proceeded to take herself on a tour of the premises.

The house was large and splendiferous, like one of those old show-places in the Hamptons that a few of her friends had rented out for their weddings. High ceilings, oak paneling, moldings that looked like they'd been sculpted by Donatello himself, and floor-to-ceiling windows that looked out onto a lawn that was so green and manicured she half-expected to see a flag and a cup. Yet in spite of its scope, the home managed to be warm and inviting. Dare she say, *cozy.*

The starting point of Angie's tour was the kitchen. Although it was as big as any restaurant kitchen she'd ever been in, she could still picture herself kicking back with a slice of pizza or a bowl of ice cream. The cabinets were a soothing buttery maple with brushed pewter handles in an s-shape that managed to be both sophisticated and playful. There was a humongous center island finished in black granite with six burners, a Jenn-Air grill and an eating area with leather barstools. A second, more formal dining area held court in a half-open octagonal space off to one side and featured a round table with six blue chairs perched under a brushed pewter light fixture with six blue pendants. Whoever Milos's decorator was, he or she certainly had a thing for symmetry.

Of course, Angie couldn't help taking a peek inside the refrigerator. In her experience, you could tell a lot about a man by the way he stocked his fridge. During a brief breakup with Nick a few years back, she'd been set up with a friend of a friend whose refrigerator contained a red velvet cake, two splits of champagne, and a wheel of brie. Six months later, she got wind of his wedding to the waiter who'd been especially attentive to him during dinner.

So it was a relief to open Milos's fridge and discover a generous supply of guy-seeks-gal food, including two Porterhouse steaks, a carton of eggs, a spiral ham, and a six-pack of Sam Adams. She could almost hear Milos informing her, *Of course we eat, Angie; we're not vampires,* before giving her that stern, sexy look that made her knees wobble.

Before leaving the kitchen for territories unknown, Angie decided it was as good a time as any to confirm that thing from earlier today. She pulled out her phone and punched in the number she'd memorized. Two rings later, a harried male voice answered. "Yeah?"

She was so jazzed, she practically dropped the phone. "Derek, it's Angie."

"Who?"

"Angie Costianes. Your buddy."

"Who the hell is this? How'd you get this number?"

As Angie ended the call, it occurred to her that if those were the last words she ever heard from the man, they'd ring in her heart forever. For one glorious moment in time, they really had been buddies.

Then it was on with the tour. After topping off her glass, Angie ventured down the hall to the living room, where she let out a mother of a gasp at its sheer awesomeness. It was a full two stories high with a cathedral ceiling made entirely of glass and a sweeping grand staircase—like something Scarlett O'Hara might have glided down if she'd lived in Elysium instead of Georgia and was a goddess instead of a spoiled Southern belle who only thought of herself as a deity. There were also hardwood floors that looked like they'd been polished to within an inch of their lives and a sunken seating area that featured classy yet comfortable-looking sofas and chairs in several shades of blue, which she was beginning to suspect was Milos's favorite color.

But the most amazing feature of the room was a brook that ran through the center. An honest-to-goodness babbling brook about six feet wide and two feet below the level of the floor that flowed in from somewhere beyond the backyard and flowed out through the front of the house, presumably on its way to the sea. What made it even more wow-inducing was that it wasn't covered by Plexiglass or any other protective material. It was just there, as if it were as natural a touch as a throw rug.

And since it split the room in half, to get from one side to the other you had to make use of a wooden bow bridge. Or, Angie supposed, you could take off your shoes and wade through the crystal-clear water—maybe even bend down and touch one of the colorful fish that swam past you. Angie did just that, running her hand over an angelfish in a peppy shade of purple. The fish seemed to enjoy the attention, pausing briefly to bask before kicking up a splash of water she interpreted as a thank you.

Although the other rooms on the first floor didn't have anything as cool as the brook, they were all impressive. There was a screening room with several rows of seats and a widescreen that would be a worthy addition to any multiplex. A few doors down was a game room with a pool table and a wall of video games. While Angie couldn't picture Milos whiling away the hours playing *Call of Duty,* she could definitely see him tinkling the ivories of his grand piano in the adjacent music room. The domed chamber was also home to a harp, a drum set and a quartet of brass instruments that hung wire-free four feet in the air, as if a ghostly combo were due to materialize any minute and strike up "In the Mood."

Elsewhere were two bathrooms with the usual plumbing fixtures, prompting her to wonder whether they were solely for guests or if gods actually did things like shave, shower, and poop...

... which got her thinking about how—for lack of a better word—*un-deified* Milos's place was. Granted, the brook was a nifty touch, but nothing a wealthy mortal couldn't engineer into *his* dream home. Not that Angie was disappointed. It was just that she'd figured the home of a god would be more exotic. Full of ancient sculptures and long-lost treasures—like, say, the Ark of the Covenant. And either insanely expensive furniture or none at all. Just a collection of gizmos that didn't exist in the mortal world—things she wouldn't be able to put a name to if her life depended on it.

Instead, Milos's home was surprisingly human. The kind of place she could move into in a heartbeat and not feel compelled to change a thing. Well, she'd probably put Plexiglass over the brook for those occasional nights when she'd had one too many cocktails and her lack of coordination could land her facedown in the water. Otherwise, the place was perfect.

And that was what worried her.

Was it perfect because she and Milos were soulmates with cosmically similar ideas of comfort and style, or was there something insidious lurking behind the wainscoting? He'd already confessed he'd been watching her for years, which meant he probably had a handle on her tastes. So what *was* this place? A reflection of *his* tastes or a five-thousand-square-foot shrine to hers? Was every stick of furniture and every inch of wall covering part of a calculated effort to seduce her into believing they had more in common than they did? Heck, if she walked out the door right now, would the house metamorphose into a marble temple with hot-and-cold-running slave girls?

Ducking into the library, Angie decided to put her theory to the test. There had to be ten thousand books in there, resting on walnut shelves that spanned all four walls. But were they the kind of books Milos might favor or a deliberate nod to her tastes? She stepped up to the nearest shelf and put her eyes to work. Melville. Milton. Sir Thomas More. Clearly, Milos was a stickler for alphabetical order, but so far there were none of the mass-market titles that kept her burning the midnight oil.

She strolled across the room to another bookcase where she found titles by Nietzsche and Proust, but alas, no Jodi Picoult. There were even titles in French and Latin and what she was pretty sure was ancient Greek, but none by the likes of Stephen King, John Grisham or her most guilty of pleasures, Sophie Kinsella. Was it possible her theory was just plain wrong?

Still not ready to throw in the towel, Angie headed back to the first bookshelf she'd inspected and peered up at the highest shelf, a good twelve feet off the ground. Maybe Milos had tucked them away up there, figuring he'd move them to the lower shelves for her benefit when there was no threat of his cerebral peers spotting them. Angie had to squint mightily to make out titles by Henry James, Rudyard Kipling, and ... what was that?

Naw, it can't be. It's just my tired eyes playing tricks on me

But the more she stared at the spine of the book, the more convinced she was that she'd read it correctly. Knowing she wouldn't be able to rest till she'd confirmed it beyond a sliver of a doubt, she scanned the room for one of those handy rolling ladders that libraries always seemed to have, but she came up empty. Then again, she reasoned, why would a god need something as mundane as a ladder when he could probably *will* the book to sail down to him?

Angie took another look around the room and settled on an upholstered armchair. The damn thing weighed a ton, so she had to half-carry and half-walk it the short distance to the shelf, putting scuffmarks on the hardwood. Vowing to rub them out later, she kicked off her shoes, climbed up on the chair and took a closer look at the book in question.

Sure enough, it was *Beginning Algebra* by Margaret L. Lial. Although it had been years since Angie's freshman year in high school, there was no way she'd forget that book. Hell, she got a chill right now just thinking about it. But what was it doing in Milos's library? She couldn't imagine he'd need some third-rate textbook to enlighten him on the subject. Wasn't there some senior god who taught the young pups about math the way Apollo had schooled him in music?

Hoping there might be answers inside the book, Angie reached up to grab it, but couldn't even get her fingers close enough to reach the shelf. Even when she got up on her tiptoes and stretched her arm nearly out of the socket, the book was still a good six inches out of her grasp.

Cursing the short, stubby genes that ran in her family, she took another look around and came to the conclusion that the only thing taller was a gargantuan wooden table that would probably bring about the demise of half the discs in her back if she tried to move it. She let out a low grumble. It looked like she had no choice but to walk away from the challenge and ask Milos about it later.

So why did she feel a burning ball of determination in the pit of her stomach? Probably because along with their short, stubby genes, the Costianes family possessed a whole parcel of stubborn ones. Angie once again gazed up at the textbook, which seemed to be mocking her from its lofty perch. And just like that, another option popped into her head.

Hopping off the chair, she grabbed an armload of books off the shelf and stacked them on the seat, pushing them up against the chairback for maximum stay-power. She was about to give it a go when she noticed that the book on top was a collection of short stories by Edgar Allan Poe.

Okay, maybe I'm being paranoid, but do I really want to tick off the master of horror by stepping on him with my big Greek feet?

After replacing Poe with a seemingly safe title by Sylvia Plath, Angie took a deep breath and stepped onto the stack. After doing a quick stability test, she braced one hand on the bookshelf for support and used the other one to reach for the book. But damn if the elusive math text wasn't still a hair's breadth out of her grasp.

Reckoning she could reach farther if she had both hands working for her, she removed her support hand from the shelf and raised it up beside the other hand. Then, by stretching both hands till they smarted, she was able to touch the tips of her fingers to either side of the book. And by rocking it back and forth, she managed to work it forward enough to grab it and pull it toward her.

The plunge to the ground was sudden and wrenching.

"Damn you, Sylvia Plath!" she shouted as the stack spilled out from under her, sending her careening to the hardwood. Thankfully, she landed on her behind, which provided more padding than her head or hip would've, but it still felt like her butt cheek had been thwacked by a two by four. She'd also bitten her tongue, which could prove terribly inconvenient with Milos later.

Wrestling herself to a sitting position, Angie extended her limbs one by one and let out a sigh of relief when they all seemed to be in working order. Then she wobbled to her feet. Aside from the pain in her butt and the taste of blood in her mouth, she seemed to be intact. Which was a relief, considering she didn't know whether gods had the same healing powers as vampires, or whether Milos would even agree to heal her after she told him how the injury had come about.

She looked around the room for the algebra book, which had flown out of her hand during her tumble to the floor. Spotting it under the big wooden table, she hobbled over to it and picked it up, her behind protesting all the way. No doubt about it, this was the textbook she'd used in freshman algebra. Who could forget that cover? A photograph of a bunch of ducks splashing around on a lake. For the life of her, she'd never understood what waterfowl had to do with algebra. Then again, nothing about the subject had ever made sense to her.

Hoping the textbook would be more enlightening this time around, she cracked it open.

And felt the breath rush out of her body. Scrawled across the title page were the words: *Together we'll slay this beast, Sugarplum. I promise.*

It was the message her father had written to her to help her get through the dreaded class. Which would mean this wasn't just the same textbook she'd used, it was her actual textbook. But that was flat-out impossible. She'd hurled it off the roof on that terrible night sixteen years ago—from twenty stories up. It would've hit the ground and come apart in an explosion of unfathomable pages. But aside from a little wear and tear, this book was intact. Which meant it couldn't be hers...

... except for her father's unmistakable handwriting on the title page.

After a brisk walk around the room to fight off the chills she was getting, Angie carried the textbook over to the armchair, gingerly sat her butt down and began paging through it. Just as she'd expected, there were messages from her father on almost every page. And every last one was written in that bright green ink he always insisted on using, "Because green is the color of brilliant people, Angie, like you and me."

Feeling the sadness wrap around her like a shroud, Angie leaned forward on the seat cushion, rested her elbows on her knees, and covered her face with her hands. What in the world was going on? How did she come to be sitting here, in the home of a charming but increasingly confounding god, staring at a book she had every reason to believe she'd never see again? A book she'd hated, then cherished, then hated even more.

ELEVEN

SITTING THERE IN THE Great Hall, surrounded by the ancient and powerful, Milos was reminded of the peculiar tradition among mortals that grants a condemned man his favorite meal just before putting him to death.

"Is the music to your liking, young master?" Zeus asked him, cupping a thoughtful hand over his meticulously trimmed beard.

Milos nodded respectfully at the king of the gods. What he wished he could say was, "That's rather the point, isn't it? You've raided the Underworld to fête me with a group of musicians I've worshipped for decades. But at what price, old man? What price?"

And yet, if this *was* to be Milos's last concert, he'd be listening in style. Performing onstage was, without a doubt, the most remarkable band he'd ever seen assembled. Playing lead guitar was Jimi Hendrix, with John Entwistle of The Who on bass. Buddy Rich was keeping a dynamic beat on the drums, while jazz giants Louis Armstrong and John Coltrane were wailing on the trumpet and saxophone. And tinkling the ivories in a gold zoot suit was Wolfgang

Amadeus Mozart, whose relish for music written centuries after his passing never ceased to amaze Milos.

But the coup de grâce was the singer. None other than Billie Holiday.

She stood behind the microphone in a midnight blue dress, a white gardenia tucked behind her ear, gazing at Milos as if he were the only person in the world. Her voice was a soulful purr, as soothing as a swallow of cognac, and her demeanor playful and confident, free of the demons that had plagued her during her life. And Milos knew it was no accident she was singing "Them There Eyes," a jazzy gem about love at first sight. He'd treasured the song ever since he'd first heard her perform it at the Apollo Theatre some seventy years ago during a musical education outing with his mentor, who just happened to be the theatre's namesake.

But in spite of the song and the new life the ensemble was breathing into it, Milos wished he were anywhere but here. And it wasn't just because he was aching to be with Angie. A cloud of doom seemed to be hanging over every inch of the place. Usually, he was in awe of the cavernous hall, with its twelve Corinthian columns that had once graced the entrance to Mount Olympus. But today, it felt like they could come crashing down on him without warning.

Even the contemporary elements of the place had him on tenterhooks. The Swarovski chandeliers that dangled overhead. The towering speakers that stood on either end of the stage, shaking more and more with every thundering bass note. The floor-to-ceiling television screens that ran around the perimeter, which in a flash, could suck him into some netherworld from which he'd never return.

Milos frowned. He really was letting his imagination run away with him. He took a swig of bourbon to calm his jangled nerves. *Get ahold of yourself, man. You're far too valuable to them to be eliminated at this juncture.*

And yet, his every instinct told him that beneath the smiles they were wagging at him, the Council members were poised to unleash something deeply unpleasant. After all, it was rare that all twelve of them gathered together. But here they were, looking like the cast of some American television series about bed-hopping doctors: The five offspring of Cronus: Zeus; his wife and sister, Hera; their sisters, Hestia and Demeter; and their brother, Hades, who left his beloved Underworld so infrequently that Milos would be hard-pressed to pick him out of a crowd; Zeus and Hera's son, Ares; and Zeus's children by other women—Apollo, Artemis, Athena, and Aphrodite, along with Hermes and Dionysius, who'd been elevated to the Council eighteen years ago when Poseidon absconded, taking Hephaestus and several lesser gods with him.

To a one, they were dressed impeccably, in clothing custom-made by the world's foremost deceased designers. And they were drinking top-shelf liquor and nibbling on caviar, escargot, and tartares ranging from steak to Bengal tiger.

And the reason for their merriment? Milos himself, allegedly. When he'd arrived a few minutes earlier, Zeus had called him over and wrapped an Armani'ed arm around him, declaring the gathering to be a celebration in honor of "my favorite nephew."

"And why am I being celebrated, Your Sovereignty?" he'd asked him, feeling Zeus's fingers pinching into his shoulder like talons.

"Patience," Zeus had replied. "If I were to spoil the surprise at such an early juncture, what would we have to look forward to?" And while Zeus's charismatic smile hadn't wavered, there was a flash of something dark behind his eyes. A hint of that legendary temper.

At which point Hades had stepped up beside them, brandishing his sardonic sense of humor. "You speak the truth, my imperious brother," he'd declared, his ancient resentment of Zeus's higher station in the family little more than a simmering flame these days. "As one who's rarely been the guest of honor at anyone's table, I encourage our young stallion to sop up every drop of this love fest."

While the others chuckled, Milos fought off a powerful urge to take leave of the island and all the madness. He knew this was no love fest. It was the Council's twisted way of administering discipline—play mind games with an individual till he's his most vulnerable, then bring him to his knees with a stinging rebuke. Milos groaned. Why couldn't his superiors just express their anger and get it over with? Why did they always have to couch everything in glitter and subterfuge? Hadn't they gotten that out of their systems during all those centuries of toying with mortals?

Despite his frustrations, Milos knew he couldn't leave Elysium. For starters, they'd never let him. No matter how far he fled or what form he took to disguise himself, they'd find him, and the discipline would be swift and severe. Plus, he really did want to play a part in their return to power. Not only had he been preparing for it most of his life, he honestly believed he could help his family avoid the pitfalls that had doomed them in their first reign.

But there was an even more compelling reason for his decision to stay: Angie.

If he left, there was every reason to believe his superiors would get back at him by harming her. Their history was rife with tales of cruel retributions, warranted and otherwise. Athena had turned the beautiful Medusa into a monster simply because Poseidon had raped the innocent maiden in *her* temple. And as much as Milos admired the Hera of today, in ancient times she'd bewitched Heracles into slaughtering his wife and children to punish Zeus for bringing him into the world through an affair with a mortal. If anything happened to Angie, whether it be physical harm or the loss of even an ounce of that *joie de vivre*, Milos knew he'd never be able to live with himself. Which essentially meant he'd spend eternity in agony.

With that in mind, he'd ordered a double bourbon from a servant and allowed Zeus and Hades to escort him to the table, where he was greeted like a returning war hero.

And now, as he sat among them, trying to appear calm and jovial, one thought kept running through his head. *This meeting was called to castigate me about Angie.*

Otherwise, why would they have summoned him in the middle of her visit? *A visit they'd tried to prevent,* he reminded himself. Were they angry at him for outsmarting them and getting her here without violating the tenet of free will, or did the well of their discontent run deeper? It seemed reasonable to assume they'd been monitoring his interactions with her. Had they picked up on the fact that she had feelings for him, too? Feelings that could blossom into love and, to their way of thinking, jeopardize their plans for him? When were they going to realize that without Angie in his life, even the most glorious future held little appeal for him?

Suddenly, Milos felt a wave of longing for Angie that was so powerful it knocked the breath out of him. Every expectation he'd had for this day, everything he thought he'd feel when he was finally in her presence, had been eclipsed by the reality of the woman. She was more beautiful, more engaging, and more intoxicating than he ever could have imagined. And even though he'd been observing her from a distance for years, there were so many things about her he couldn't have anticipated. The way her hair sparkled in the sunlight, as if it had been sprinkled with flecks of gold. The devilish twinkle she got in those big green eyes of hers just before she ribbed him about something. The way she looked when she rode a horse across the sky, so graceful and self-assured, as if *she* were the one with the wings. The surge of desire that ran through him when she did something as mundane as dab her lips with a napkin.

And considering how passionately they'd been kissing earlier today before Jace interrupted, what manner of fireworks might they generate if left alone? He'd prepared one of the guest suites for her, but if he were a betting man, he'd wager that bed would never be slept in. A smile danced across his face. What would it be like, after all these years of fantasizing about it, to finally make love with her? To plant kisses on every inch of her body? To give her pleasure and take pleasure in *her* pleasure? To feel her arms around him, urging him on? He had a feeling that like everything else about her, the experience would exceed his wildest expectations.

But first, I have to get through this damned conclave. And find a way to convince them that my love for her is not only good for me, but for them as well.

But would he be able to do that? Would he even be allowed the opportunity?

TWELVE

For the first sixteen years of Angie's life, math was a thorn in her side, right up there on the dread-o-meter with acne and braces. Not only did she have trouble wrapping her head around the finicky formulas, but most of it seemed useless. Aside from learning enough of the basics to be able to work a calculator, what did you really need with it? At what point in your life would it make or break you to know that the logarithm of a thousand to base ten was three? Unfortunately, the New York Public School System didn't agree, so she was stuck taking the heinous subject every year till graduation...

Which almost didn't happen due to the trouble she had in freshman algebra, where she first laid eyes on the infamous splashing ducks textbook. It wasn't that Mr. Principi was a bad teacher. He was no better or worse than anybody else at PS 109. It was just that no matter how hard Angie tried to get a handle on the subject, the nuts and bolts of it eluded her. Two days into the semester, she failed her first pop quiz. Three quizzes later, she was barely clinging to a D.

The next day, Principi announced that, per district policy, he'd been compelled to start an after-school tutorial for "a select few mathematical misfits who insist on swallowing up what little free time I have." Angie couldn't help but notice his eyes were on her the whole time. And that pretty much remained the case throughout the twice-a-week sessions, even though the group included three football players, a wrestler with hygiene issues, and the biggest stoner in school. Despite Angie's best efforts, it seemed like everyone was catching on but her. She'd never felt dumber in her life. Or chunkier. The stoner turned out to be a really nice girl with a killer recipe for pot brownies, which were not only fattening in and of themselves, but gave her the mad munchies.

And not a hint of algebraic insight.

One Sunday, after arming herself with a bowl of popcorn and a Cherry Coke, Angie dug the textbook out of her backpack and settled in for an evening of torture. But when she opened the book, she discovered her father's whimsical message on the title page, pledging to help her slay the mathematical beast. That alone would have been enough to put a smile on her face. But as she flipped through the pages, she found dozens of handwritten phrases and mnemonic devices designed to make algebra not only easier, but fun. There was even a little ditty to the tune of "Don't Stop Believing" to help her remember the quadratic formula.

As touched as she was, she was also confused. All semester long, her father had been doing his best to help her with her homework. The trouble was, he knew less about algebra than she did. So every time he rolled up his sleeves and tried to solve a tricky equation, he ended up as frustrated as she was. But from what Angie could gather, the little sayings he'd written in the margins were accurate. How in the world had he managed to learn so much about the subject in such a short time?

She trotted out to the living room, where he was cursing his way through a Jets game, and parked herself between him and the television. "I'm glad you're sitting down, Daddy, because I have some disturbing news." She waved the textbook at him. "Some evil mathematician with a Jones for rock and roll has been forging your handwriting."

Always delightfully in tune with her, he let out a mother of a stage gasp and flipped through the book. "Damn those mathematicians! Is it any wonder the prisons are crawling with 'em?"

After sharing a laugh with her, her father gave her the skinny. He'd been feeling so guilty about passing his defective math genes down to her that he'd done some research and located a retired Columbia professor who was willing to accept a few bucks to give him a crash course in algebra. So every night for the past week, when he'd claimed to have been working late, he'd actually been at a brownstone in Tudor City, being whipped into mathematical shape by Dr. Elizabeth Christman, gifted tutor and tireless slave driver. In the end, she'd dubbed him her biggest come-from-behind victory in sixty years of teaching.

"Just don't tell your mother about her, Sugarplum," her father begged. "Even though Dr. Christman is eighty-two years old and has Parkinson's, she'll still accuse me of having an affair with her."

That night ended up being the turning point for Angie. Although algebra would never be her best subject, her father's *bon mots* in the margins along with the love he'd put into them inspired her to work harder than she ever had.

Two weeks later, Principi had a trace of a smile on his face when he handed back her midterm exam. "Methinks there's hope for you yet, Miss Costianes." His tone made it abundantly clear he'd never believed it before.

When Angie saw the "B minus" at the top of the page, she let out such a squeal that Principi reeled back in shock, sending test papers flying all over the room. She skipped her next two classes so she could rush home and reward her father with the biggest hug of his life. Thanks to his love and support, she was finally on the road to slaying the beast called algebra. She didn't think she'd ever loved him more than she did at that moment.

When Angie walked in the door, the first thing that struck her was how quiet the place was. Usually the little apartment was bustling with sounds: the TV blaring, her little brother's Nintendo games pinging, her father singing along with Springsteen on his headphones, her mother badgering him about the ever-growing pile of bills—which helped explain why he always seemed to be wearing headphones. But at that moment, the only thing Angie could hear was the ticking of the mantel clock—a sound she was barely acquainted with. And her father, usually the first one home, was nowhere to be seen.

Instead, lumped around the kitchen table like waxworks were her mother, Ya-Ya, and Father Kontos. Angie stared at them for a moment, wondering what the odd little gathering was about. But no one seemed to be in a hurry to tell her, even when she threw out a, "Hey, everybody. What's up?" If that wasn't bizarre enough, there was a bottle of Scotch on the table—something her mother never allowed in the middle of the day. In fact, she barely drank at all. But if the lipstick-smudged tumbler in front of her was any indication, she'd broken her rule in a big way.

As Angie took in the surreal scene, something occurred to her that sent her stomach into spasms. *Shit! Mom found the pot brownie I hid down in the toe of my UGGs.* She turned to her mother with a *you got me* shrug, silently urging her to get the fire and brimstone over with so she could go to her room and commence being grounded. But Connie didn't say a word. She just stared at her for twenty-two seconds, which the clock was kind enough to count out for her.

Now Angie was really getting nervous. This wasn't like her mother at all. Usually, when she was angry about something, Angie could hear her cussing her out before she got in the door. On a few occasions, Angie had even come up the subway stairs down the street to find her leaning out their twelfth floor window ranting about "my curse of a daughter." But today, she was giving her the silent treatment.

Angie sighed. "Um, Mom … what's going on?"

Still, her mother sat there like a sphinx. And Ya-Ya, who could always be counted on for information, was staring vacantly out the window.

Finally, Father K put a hand on her mother's shoulder. "If it's easier for you, *paidi mou,* I can tell her."

As if some stuck gear in her head had been nudged back to life, Angie's mother sat up in her seat and gazed purposefully at her. Still, when she spoke, her voice was so low and reedy that Angie could barely hear her. "Your father's gone."

Angie squinted at her, confused. "Gone? What do you mean?"

This time her mother's voice was stronger, with a self-pitying edge. "He left us, honey. Like I always knew he would."

Now Angie wasn't just confused; she was pissed. Her father would never take off like that. Granted, he wasn't exactly doing cartwheels over his marriage to Connie—and who could blame him? But even if he *were* thinking of leaving her, he'd never do it without talking it over with Angie. She was his confidante in everything he did—or as *he* put it, "my bestest buddy." So whatever sob story her mother was trying to peddle, Angie wasn't buying it.

Angie's attitude barely softened when her mother started crying. As much as Angie hated to see her cry, she'd come to accept it as part of her mother's compulsive need to always be considered the unluckiest person in the world.

Then Ya-Ya started crying, too. Not just crying, but weeping, in suffocating sobs. Angie could count on one hand the number of times she'd seen her grandmother cry—usually in the form of a few errant tears she dabbed away with a handkerchief and an apology. But today she was wailing like an old immigrant woman when her husband's casket was lowered into the ground.

Now Angie was really getting scared. Something bad had happened. And as terrified as she was of finding out what it was, the not knowing part was killing her. She slammed her palm on the table. "Will somebody please tell me what's going on?!"

Although they'd been jolted out of their crying jags, neither her mother nor Ya-Ya seemed to be able to get anything out.

It was Father K who delivered the words that changed her life forever. "Angie, I'm afraid your father has passed away."

She narrowed her eyes at him. Her father dead? Impossible. "You're lying."

Father K let out a pained sigh. "I wish I were, *mikroula*. I wish I were."

Angie looked across the table at Ya-Ya and her mother. Why weren't they shooting him down? They had to know this wasn't true. But all she saw on their faces was grim acceptance.

That was when Angie started shaking. "But I just saw him. This morning."

The next voice she heard was her mother's. "Honey ... he killed himself."

It was like being in an elevator that plunged a hundred stories into the basement. Angie felt nauseous. Disoriented. Unable to catch her breath. Before she knew it, she was on the floor, pounding her fists on the linoleum and screaming her lungs out.

She might have been down there a few seconds. Or maybe it was an hour. All she knew was that at some point, she felt a pair of hands around her shoulders, accompanied by the scent of Chanel No. 5, and she allowed Ya-Ya to help her to her feet. After steering her over to the table and sitting her down, Ya-Ya poured some Scotch and indicated she should drink it. Angie looked over at her mother, expecting her to balk. But when she blearily nodded her approval, Angie took the glass in her shaking hands and put it to her lips, feeling the whiskey burn its way down her throat the same way the sadness was burning through her heart.

Slightly sedated but still aching for answers, Angie set the glass down and turned to her grandmother. "What ... happened?"

Ya-Ya took a deep breath and spoke in a trembling voice. "A few hours ago, everything seemed fine. He met with a building inspector in the Bronx, then headed to Midtown to pick up a load of building supplies. Everybody at the lumberyard said he was his usual self. Smiling. Telling those dirty jokes he loves. He even collected twenty bucks on a football bet he'd made with one of the guys. And you know how happy that kind of thing makes him."

Ya-Ya paused for a moment to collect herself, looking like she'd aged twenty years since yesterday. "As soon as they got the truck loaded up, he said his goodbyes and headed for the bridge. And that's where it happened."

Angie stared at her numbly. "The Brooklyn Bridge?"

Ya-Ya nodded. "He was about halfway across, in the fast lane, when all of a sudden, he pulled over to the right and slammed on the brakes. It happened so fast that the car behind him ran right into him. Before the man could even get out of his car, your father leapt out of the truck, climbed all the way to the top of the bridge . . . and jumped."

An image of her father falling through the air, a haunted look on his face, burrowed its way into Angie's head, where it stayed, refusing to be blinked away. A moment later, she heard herself asking, "Just like that?"

Ya-Ya sighed. "Just like that."

"He didn't *say* anything?"

Ya-Ya shook her head. Then she poured herself a glass of scotch and drank it dry.

Angie could have sat there all day staring at her grandmother and the story still wouldn't have made sense. Not *her* father. Her sweet, loving father who seemed to find joy in every little thing life threw at him. Then a bubble of hope rose in her throat. "Wait. How do they know it was him? Maybe somebody else was driving."

Ya-Ya's eyes brightened, as if she were entertaining the notion. Then something shook her back to reality. "No, it was him. I'm afraid your mother and I had the terrible task of identifying his body. His *body*." Her voice broke. "My boy. My beautiful boy."

That sent all of them over the edge—even Father K, who started praying in Greek as he wept. As their sobs grew louder, Angie put her hands over her ears, wishing she were a thousand miles away. Or right here, yesterday, when the father she loved more than anyone in the world was still with her.

A few moments later, she felt Ya-Ya's hand on her shoulder and turned to find her gazing at her lovingly. "I'm so sorry, my angel. I wish I could say something to make you feel better. Just know that he loved you very much."

As Angie struggled to find comfort in that, her mother leaned across the table and spoke in a rare, tender voice. "He did love you, sweetie. Adored you. He loved your brother, too, but you were his favorite. Oh God, how am I gonna find the strength to tell *him*?"

Loved. The word pierced Angie's heart like an arrow. They were talking about her father in the past tense, because now he *was* in the past. Gone, just like that. She'd never see him or talk to him or feel his arms around her again. When just this morning, he was sitting at this table, eating the omelet she'd made for him, and serenading her with "Rosalita."

Right here. Full of love. And life.

And lies.

As the realization hit her, Angie felt the walls inching toward her. Even the floor and ceiling seemed to be conspiring to suffocate the life out of her. She knew she had to get out of here right away. She couldn't listen to it anymore. How her father had died. How normal he'd seemed that day. How sad and confused everybody was. How much he loved her.

Especially how much he loved her.

She shot out of the chair so fast that it toppled over and banged on the floor. Then she grabbed her book bag and raced out of the apartment, slamming the door on their questions. She bolted down the hallway into the stairwell, taking the steps two at a time, thinking about the promise he'd made this morning to take her to Coney Island, and the box seats he was going to get for a Yankees game next season and the help he was gonna give her with her fastball pitch.

Lies. All of them.

Eight stories and a hundred lies later, Angie shoved open the door at the top of the stairs and raced to the edge of the roof. Then, as the cold December wind pelted her with snowflakes she didn't feel, she took out the B-minus test paper she'd thought he'd be so proud of, crumpled it into a ball and hurled it off the roof. In its wake, she chucked out the charm bracelet he'd given her on her tenth birthday while promising to buy her a new charm every year for the rest of her life. Another damn lie.

Then, as the bracelet hit the pavement with a defeated jangle, Angie picked up the algebra book filled with her father's little sayings and opened it to get one last look at another broken promise. *Together we'll slay this beast, Sugarplum. I promise.*

Although the sight of his handwriting brought a lump to her throat, it didn't stop her from slamming the book shut and stepping up to the edge of the roof. Then, with a scream that drowned out the sirens and car stereos and every other sound that dared compete with her, she swung her arm back and heaved the textbook out of her life.

As she leaned over to watch it fall, the rooftop door banged open behind her, startling her so much that she lost her footing and fell forward off the edge of the roof. The next few seconds would never make sense to her, but for a moment she swore she was hovering facedown in the air, staring at the street below.

Just hanging there, two hundred feet in the air.

Then, in a blink, she was back on the edge of the roof, trying to get her bearings, as the three of them rushed toward her. And when she punched Father Kontos in the jaw when he tried to grab ahold of her, it wasn't *his* face she was seeing.

THIRTEEN

CLEARLY, THE MUSIC HAD passed muster with the Council, as several of them were taking their turns on the dance floor. Well, *above* the dance floor. As Milos watched from the shadow of his second bourbon, Zeus and Athena were jitterbugging twenty feet off the ground, swooshing through the air in perfect synch with the band's sizzling interpretation of "Let's Misbehave." A few yards away, Dionysius was doing a ferocious tango with Hera, promenading with such finesse that it appeared they were gliding across glass rather than navigating the air.

And yet, the magic was lost on Milos. Grumbling to himself, he checked the sun's position in the sky for the hundredth time since arriving. *As if they have nothing better to do. As if I have nothing better to do.*

He considered envisaging Angie to make sure she was all right, but decided to put a pin in it. He had, after all, promised to respect her privacy. Plus, he was concerned that the sight of her face, so frustratingly out of reach, would put him in an even deeper funk.

A tap on the shoulder from Apollo pulled him out of his head. "Your sour expression tells me you're not enjoying the entertainment."

Milos had no doubt the expression he was now wearing was one of disbelief. Did Apollo really think *that* was why he was unhappy? Still, Milos managed to inject some enthusiasm into his voice. "Of course I'm enjoying it, Maestro. You've made some splendid choices."

Apollo cast a proprietary glance at the band, then slapped him on the shoulder. "I toyed with the idea of adding your Eddie Vedder and Chrissie Hynde to the ensemble, but I suspected you'd be cross with me for having to kill them first."

Apollo laughed heartily, as did everyone at the table but Ares, who was sporting his usual above-it-all expression. Milos did his best to match their mirth, but his chuckle lost steam a few seconds out of the gate, prompting a raised eyebrow from Apollo.

Milos delivered a mental *I'm sorry,* but he had a feeling that it, too, would be perceived as perfunctory. Still, someone as intuitive as Apollo had to realize his cousin's state of mind had nothing to do with the band. And it wasn't just that Milos was missing Angie. The conversation he'd had with Apollo yesterday had led him to believe Apollo was finally ready to stand beside him in his quest to take Angie as his spouse. Not only had Apollo guided him toward the drachma solution, but later, when Milos told him she was en route to the island, the man actually had tears in his eyes.

But today had been another story. Other than that one comment about the band, Apollo had been as distant as the Andromeda Galaxy. Milos understood there were a thousand reasons why Apollo had to give the outward impression of being neutral about Angie, but couldn't he have found a way to tip Milos off about this gathering? Given him a few pointers on how to handle himself? How could Apollo be so blasé about something near and dear to both of them?

Aphrodite tapped a ruby-ringed hand on the table, indicating she had something important to say. Then again, when didn't she feel that way? "A splendid mélange of musicians, brother. With one shocking omission. There's not an artist, living or dead, who can hold a candle to Jim Morrison. A mesmerizing stage presence. Painterly lyrics brought to life by that whiskey-soaked voice. And the sensuality of that man … mercy! Those lips alone should have a temple erected to them."

As Aphrodite fanned herself, presumably to cool the fire that had been lit in her loins, Milos had to exercise every bit of self-control he had to keep from laughing. Although he was fond of his elder cousin, her habit of steering every conversation down an erotic road had always struck him as silly, considering she was almost five thousand years old. But Milos knew it wouldn't be prudent to make his feelings known. First off, she'd always been kind to him. Plus, she was one of the few Olympians who empathized with him about his love for Angie. So he gave her a simpatico smile, knowing that at some point, he might need her as an ally.

On the other hand, Artemis clearly felt no need to tiptoe around her half sister. The spunky fireplug erupted in a burst of laughter reminiscent of machine-gun fire, prompting a ferocious stare from Aphrodite. "And what is so funny?"

After catching her breath, Artemis said, "I was thinking those poor lips of Mr. Morrison's deserved a temple, considering how many times you plundered them."

Milos allowed the slightest of smiles to slip out. Hard as it was to believe, this antagonistic relationship had been going on for centuries.

Aphrodite, the patron of all things romantic, versus Artemis, who was so steeped in rational thought that she believed romantic entanglements distracted otherwise intelligent beings from reaching their potential. Which, sadly, put her squarely with the majority of the Council in terms of his relationship with Angie.

Aphrodite's painted lips quivered with disdain. "First off, Sis, kudos on that *de rigueur* sackcloth you're wearing," she said, indicating Artemis's rather mannish ensemble. "I'm sure it'll be all the rage at the Eunuchs' Convention. And allow me to assure you that when it came to Jim, there was no plundering. Our lovemaking was mutual, as was our pleasure."

For a moment, Aphrodite seemed lost in the memory. Then she let out a woebegone sigh and fluttered her hand in the direction of Ares. "But sadly, due to the indiscretions of a certain individual, I've been prohibited from further contact with Jim."

Ares groaned loud enough to be heard on the mainland. "For the love of Olympus, will you get over it? Throw a stone in Hades and you'll find a thousand just like him."

Aphrodite aimed her eyes at him like death rays. "Beautiful, brain-dead Ares. You're forgetting I'm not a rutting pig like you are."

"Right," he retorted. "You're a punishing shrew."

As the sniping heated up, Milos couldn't decide whether to check the sun's arc again or take a gulp of bourbon. So he did both. Normally, he could tolerate the animosity between Aphrodite and Ares, but today he found it tiresome. What made it especially frustrating was that the two half-siblings had once been the most passionate of lovers. Their torrid relationship had endured for centuries, despite the fact that Aphrodite was married for much of that time to Hera's hobbled son, Hephaestus. And while there had never been a consensus as to whether Aphrodite was truly in love with Ares or just enjoyed the attention, it was obvious to everyone that the God of War had fallen hard for her, declaring her the one true love of his life.

But Ares's volcanic temper and possessiveness took their toll on Aphrodite, and eventually she dropped him for good. After a brief period of mourning, he leapt headlong into hedonism, using his position and good looks to seduce thousands of women, living and dead, including the blond bombshell whose mistreatment had earned him Aphrodite's eternal wrath.

Ares began procuring Marilyn Monroe from the Underworld shortly after her fatal overdose. Like so many desperate souls before her, she fell hopelessly in love with him. But in his eyes, she was just another plaything to debauch and discard at his whim. Every time he summoned her to Elysium, she begged him to let her stay forever so she'd never have to return to the dark corner of the Underworld to which she'd been condemned. And every time, he agreed, until his needs were fulfilled. Then he sent her back down, kicking and screaming, seemingly enjoying disposing of her as much as he enjoyed ravaging her. Or maybe, as many suspected, what he really enjoyed was having power over a woman who was, in many ways, the embodiment of Aphrodite.

Whatever Ares's reasons, his misbehavior eventually attracted the attention of Hera, one of the few Olympians who refused to tolerate disrespect toward women. And when Ares scoffed at Hera's request to curb his behavior, she took her case to Zeus, insisting he put a stop to all serial liaisons between gods and deceased mortals. Ironically, while the mandate had crushed Aphrodite, who was forced to end her love affair with Jim Morrison, it only prompted

Ares to modify his appetites, carrying on one-time dalliances with an endless string of deceased vixens.

A week earlier, in fact, he'd invited Milos to join him in a *ménage à quattro* with the unique pairing of Cleopatra and Anna Nicole Smith. He'd politely declined. Not only was he uninterested in anyone but Angie, he also preferred to keep his association with Ares at arms' length. To get too close to the notoriously petulant god would only hurt him on that inevitable day when Ares turned against him on a whim. Besides, it was unlikely Ares would ever stand behind him in his quest to be with Angie. From what Milos had observed, Ares's bitterness toward Aphrodite had soured him on romance. Plus, Apollo had warned Milos that Ares resented him for getting more respect from Zeus than *he* ever had. Or would.

Back at the table, the bickering had grown so loud that Milos could no longer block it out with his thoughts. At the moment, Aphrodite was leaning across the table, waving a taunting finger in Ares's face. "Do you know what your problem is? You're not man enough to admit you don't have what it takes to satisfy me."

Ares smiled cruelly. "Fortunately, you have unlimited access to the horses in the stables."

Aphrodite raised a hand to slap him, but he grabbed her wrist and squeezed so hard that the bone snapped. Unfortunately, he wasn't fast enough to keep her other hand from soaring in and breaking his nose, raining blood all over the tablecloth. For a few tense seconds, they stared each other down like gunslingers, the only sound being their bones threading themselves back together.

Then Zeus's voice boomed out so powerfully that it scattered napkins and sent hair and clothes billowing. "When are you two going to grow up?! When you're ten thousand years old?!"

He swooped down from the air and stalked toward them, his body taut and purposeful. An instant later, he had them dangling three feet off the ground like puppets as he stared at them murderously. "I should banish you both to Tartarus. Perhaps a little fear and deprivation would knock some sense into you. Hades, is there room for two more down there?"

Hades chuckled. "Of course there is, brother. I'm sure Cronus would be thrilled at the prospect of meeting his grandchildren. And devouring them."

Whether driven by fear or vertigo, Aphrodite let out a resigned sigh. "I'm sorry, Daddy."

Ares had no such inclination. "As usual, Zeus, you're overreacting. It was just a little squabble, like you're so fond of having. Except no one ended up dead."

"Yet," Zeus seethed. Then, with a flick of his hand, he spun them around till they were hanging upside down, their faces growing flush from the blood flow.

Incensed at their predicament, Aphrodite punched Ares in the thigh. "Bastard!"

"Actually, unlike you, I'm not," he declared. "Wasn't your mother some sort of sea hag?"

As Aphrodite sent a foot flying at her brother, Zeus's anger reached a crescendo. He aimed his index fingers at them like pistols and shot out two beams of current that had them contorting in agony. "Do you know what really galls me?!" he shouted. "Your childish behavior is ruining this celebration for young Milos."

"I'm fine, really," Milos replied. In truth, he was furious with his cousins. Whatever Zeus's mood had been a moment earlier, it could only have grown darker as a result of their tiff. And how would that affect Zeus's treatment of *him* when the time came?

Thankfully, at that moment, Athena stepped up beside Zeus in full peacemaker mode. "Come on, Father, you know they can't help themselves. As long as there's so much sexual tension between them, they're always going to be at war."

She gently lowered Zeus's hands, disarming him. Then she reached up and took her siblings' hands in hers. "Aphrodite. Ares. Why don't you do us all a favor and resume that tawdry affair of yours? You'll feel better, I promise. And you'll be infinitely more pleasant to be around."

Athena's words may not have cooled things between her siblings, but they had an immediate effect on Zeus. He let out a booming laugh that shook the chandeliers, then raised a glass to his favorite child. "Hear, hear!" Wrapping an arm around Athena, he let the warring duo drop to the ground. "If all my children had this much backbone, we'd still be ruling the Earth."

Even though the remark raised some eyebrows, it wasn't long before everyone was following Zeus's lead and toasting the goddess of wisdom—even Milos, and not just because she'd calmed him down. In truth, Milos had always admired Athena's ability to cut through the artifice and get to the heart of the matter. Although he knew she was driven by intellect rather than emotion, he'd often wondered if she might endorse his relationship with Angie out of the knowledge that a fulfilled leader is a more effective one. And considering how much sway she held with her father, that could be critical to his future.

Onstage, the band switched gears—and eras—and launched into the pop standard "I Say a Little Prayer." Although it had been recorded by no less than Aretha Franklin, Milos marveled at how Billie made it her own, slowing the tempo and turning its sprightly sentiment into something akin to a plea. And she was gazing straight at him, as if she were delivering every word for his ears only.

Not surprisingly, it was another of Milos's favorite songs. Years ago, he'd watched a teenage Angie emerge from a movie theater with her arms around a pair of girlfriends, singing the song at the top of her lungs. It was a period in her life when he'd envisaged her daily, concerned for her well-being after the death of her father. How many nights had he watched her cry herself to sleep or mope around in a daze, wishing he could be there to comfort her and tell her the one thing she needed to hear? How many times had he turned the pages of that textbook, wishing her father had scribbled some vital message into the margins along with the math tips?

But when Milos witnessed Angie belting out that song, her eyes sparkling like diamonds, he knew she was on the mend. From that moment on, every time he heard the song, no matter what his mood, a smile found its way onto his face.

Even today, in spite of the circumstances. Which meant he owed a word of thanks to Apollo, the only being in the room he'd shared the story with. Despite Apollo's enigmatic behavior today, he deserved that much.

But when Milos turned back to the table, he discovered that the seat once occupied by Apollo had been taken by Hera, who offered him a breezy wave. As usual, she was decked out in a colorful array of scarves, skirts, and shawls, looking more like a free-spirited American actress from the 1970s than the Queen Mother of the Gods. But woe to the fool who underestimated her.

"My dear, you're positively glowing," she said, tipping her champagne flute.

Not at all sure what she was getting at, Milos delivered the safest response he could think of. "Well, it isn't every day a man gets serenaded by a musical legend."

I'm not talking about her, Hera playfully spoke into his head.

Although Milos was startled by Hera's candor, it didn't come as a total surprise. He'd always sensed that she was sympathetic to his plight, despite the fact that she'd never come out and said it. And he didn't just chalk it up to the fact that she was the goddess of marriage. Over the years, Hera had taken what seemed to be a sincere interest in his long-distance obsession with Angie, occasionally asking him how "that sweet little Greek girl" was doing. And Hera always seemed genuinely interested in his responses—wistful, even—which he imagined had something to do with her legendary troubles with Zeus and his wandering eye. But could Milos count on her to challenge her spouse and speak up on his behalf if things grew heated?

Above all else, could Milos really trust her? He didn't think she was testing him, but he couldn't dismiss the possibility either. Maybe she'd exacted some promise from Zeus in exchange for gaining his confidence—like say, a century of fidelity. Considering how fragile everything seemed to be at the moment, it didn't seem worth the risk.

So he smiled, figuring Hera could glean anything she wanted from it.

She looked at him for a studious moment, as if she were sifting through the contents of his heart. Which, he figured, was entirely possible considering how much cunning she packed into that five-foot, four-inch frame.

Then her face lit up in the kind of luminous glow that helped make her the most beautiful goddess of them all. *Milos, my dear, the girl who's lucky enough to see that smile every morning will live forever.*

The words were out of his mouth before he knew it. "Forever isn't long enough with a girl like Angie."

Hera squeezed his hand. "Then I wish you forever and a day."

At first, Milos thought the oohs and aahs that followed were the others' reactions to what Hera had just said to him. Then he realized they were looking at the bandstand. Microphone in hand, Billie was sauntering toward the table with her eyes trained on him. He tried not to blush as she caressed his shoulder while singing about a forever kind of love.

As the others looked on with varying degrees of amusement, Billie leaned over and whispered in his ear. "Keep me around, will ya, baby? We could have ourselves some fun."

Then she brushed her lips across his mouth and started back toward the stage. But after a few steps, she turned around and gave him a look that made his heart sink. A look that was as desperate as it was familiar.

Because Milos knew full well that it wasn't just lost souls like Marilyn Monroe who fought tooth and nail to stay on Elysium. No mortal who'd ever been summoned from Hades wanted to go back. It didn't matter whether they'd been brought up from the darkest bowels of the Underworld or the blissful Elysian Fields. Nor did it matter who they were. World leaders. Entertainers. Criminal masterminds. To a one, they begged to stay, offering everything from sexual favors to the souls of their living descendants.

Apparently nothing, not even paradise, compared with being alive again. To feel your lungs fill up with air and your heart pump blood through your veins. To gaze once again at the stars twinkling in the sky or the waves crashing on the beach. To be applauded by a worshipful audience or sought out for advice on your field of expertise.

And to know you were mere miles away from a place you'd cherished or a loved one you'd left behind.

And it frustrated Milos to no end. Because he wanted to reach out to Billie and the rest of them and tell them a new day was dawning. Not just for the living, but for the deceased as well. That after centuries of the Earth being ruled by deities who, by and large, lacked compassion for mankind, a new leader was about to step forward. A leader who felt their pain and hopelessness and would do everything in his power to hold his superiors true to their pledge to embrace a more benevolent approach to authority. To find room on Earth for those decedents whose gifts were too precious to be kept underground and hauled out only when the gods saw fit. To allow ordinary citizens of the Underworld to make the occasional pilgrimage to the Overworld to visit their homelands, see their loved ones, or handle precious unfinished business.

Like that of a father from Queens who was aching to tell his daughter the truth about his death.

But if even Milos had been able to summon the courage to step forward at that moment, he wouldn't have gotten a word out. With a thrust of his mighty arm, Zeus shot out a blinding beam of light that made Billie and her bandmates disappear.

Then he turned to Milos with a smile that managed to be both magnanimous and menacing.

"So, young master. Shall we talk about your future?"

FOURTEEN

In the months that followed her father's death, Angie's anger gradually gave way to a profound sadness she thought she'd never shake. Not only had she lost her best friend, she also had to live with the pain of not knowing why he'd left her. Nothing ever turned up. No hidden debts. No secret lover. No suspicious phone records. In all probability, she'd never have the answers she needed. Just the one cold hard truth that ate at her all the time.

He didn't love me enough.

Because if he did, whatever was bothering him wouldn't have sent him off that bridge. Because it would have meant losing her forever. And how could somebody who really loved you do something that would cause them to never see you again? Never see you go to prom or graduate from high school. Never walk you down the aisle. Never run around the maternity ward handing out cigars when you had your first baby, which you'd name after him even if it was a girl. Never be there for all the big moments—or the little ones, when you just needed a hug.

But that didn't stop Angie from missing him. Every single day.

Like right now, on an island on the other side of the world, as she paged through this doctored-up textbook that said so much about the kind of man her father was. And now that she was over the shock of discovering it, she had to admit it felt good to have it back.

Which meant she should be grateful to Milos. Somehow, he'd rescued it from certain destruction, reuniting her with another piece of her father. Another talisman she could call upon from time to time to bring him back to life.

So why wasn't she feeling a warm buzz of gratitude for her absent host? Why did it feel like there was an army of soldiers marching around in her stomach, poking her with their rifle butts, and sending up bubble after bubble of agitation?

Because he didn't do it for me.

Granted, she'd started nosing around the library because she'd suspected the whole house was a movie set created for her benefit. But even if that were true, this book couldn't possibly be part of it. It wasn't as if she'd stumbled upon her favorite snow globe in Milos's curio cabinet. This book was a deeply personal thing between her and her father that she'd had every reason to believe had been hurled out of existence. If Milos had an ounce of smarts, he'd have to know it would creep her out to find it here, which was probably why he'd tucked it away on the highest shelf.

Angie had a pretty good theory as to why Milos had taken the book. If he'd been spying on her that day, he'd have noticed how angry she was when she pitched it off the roof. And that would have made it a must-have in his quest to learn everything about her. By now, he probably had it memorized. But did it bother him in the least to know he'd violated her privacy? Doubtful.

After taking the edge off with a sip of wine, Angie gazed around the room. If she set her mind to it, how many more of her personal things would she find? Her first diary? The Snoopy doll her father had won her at a street fair? Would a search of Milos's bedside drawer turn up locks of her hair? Baby teeth? Panties?

You're doing it again, Angie.

Whoa, where was that voice coming from? Oh yeah, her conscience. That pesky alter ego of hers that always seemed to find the most upbeat explanation for everything. She supposed she could ignore it, but in her experience, her conscience didn't take kindly to the silent treatment.

"And what exactly am I doing?" she asked aloud.

You're turning Milos into a villain because it's too risky to believe a man like that might love you.

Angie swatted the thought away as if it were a housefly. All day, she'd been doing her damndest to give Milos the benefit of the doubt. But cumulatively speaking, this day had produced a mountain of doubt. What semi-together girl *wouldn't* question the sanity of a confessed voyeur who'd decided years ago, without even meeting her, that she was his soulmate? Granted, it was the stuff fairy tales were made of, but it was also the stuff of horror movies. Till the day she died, she'd never forget the image of that poor plus-size girl in *The Silence of the Lambs,* staring up out of a pit at the twisted psychopath who ordered her to put the lotion in the basket.

The sarcastic chortle came courtesy of her conscience. *Hold up. You're comparing Milos to a fictional killer with a skin-suit fetish?*

"No, I'm just saying a girl has to be on her guard," she snapped back. "Or should I ignore anything about him that seems suspicious?"

Of course not, her conscience replied, helping itself to her wine. *But when you find yourself arriving at the worst-case scenario every single time, you have to ask yourself if it's coincidence... or something deeper.*

Angie let the thought rattle around. On one hand, it was a hard theory to argue with. She *had* gone down the doomsday road a lot today. But in all fairness, this had been one weird-ass day. She'd hopped a previously nonexistent boat to an uncharted island where she'd met a smoking-hot god who fed her ribs that tasted like her father's and took her on a flying horseback ride and told her he was smitten with her and kissed her with so much passion that she wanted to believe it but couldn't, because where she came from, gorgeous non-serial-killing deities didn't fall for ordinary girls who had ordinary lives and ordinary looks...

Her conscience cut her off. *You mean* you. *They don't fall for* you.

"Yes, dammit!" she shouted loud enough to rattle the bookshelves. "They don't fall for me!"

There it was, the jugular of her doubts. In spite of all her positive thinking and the bravado she tossed around like confetti, she couldn't shake the feeling that there was something inside her that made her unworthy of the kind of swooning, soul-blazing love they wrote sonnets and romance novels and Taylor Swift songs about. And it pissed her off royally that she felt that way, but it had been engrained in her for a long time. Maybe all the way back to the day she'd hurled that algebra book off the roof. After all, if her own father hadn't loved her enough to stick around, what chance did she have at attracting Prince Charming?

And that brought her to the million-dollar question. Had she grown so stubborn in that belief that she was subconsciously finding the worst possible explanation for every questionable thing

Milos did? Was she so certain a good man couldn't possibly love her that she was turning a poster boy for happily ever after into a creepazoid out of *The Silence of the Lambs?*

She thought back to the last time she'd been in a situation like this. It was a year after her father's death, her sophomore year in high school. While she was heading for the M Train one day, Tony Hart, the star receiver on the football team, caught up with her and asked her to go to a party with him. She practically passed out right there on the sidewalk. Not only was Tony a senior with a full ride to Ohio State, he was also hella fine and charismatic and had every girl at school drooling over him.

Still, Angie was drowning in doubt. Why was Tony suddenly interested in her? Before that day, they'd never spoken, except in her dreams. Why wasn't he going after a cheerleader or a majorette? And although she sputtered out a, "Yeah … sure," she couldn't shake the feeling that something was wrong.

After tossing and turning all night, Angie decided there was only one thing to do. Tell Tony she couldn't go to the party because of a family obligation she'd forgotten about. And when Ya-Ya happened to call just before she left for school, Angie laid out the situation, figuring her grandmother would validate her decision.

But Ya-Ya couldn't have disagreed more. "Sweetie, you've got to start believing in yourself. You know what I think? The boy's finally wised up and graduated to a higher class of women. And you're gonna reward him by saying 'no'?"

While Ya-Ya's opinion didn't erase Angie's doubts, it helped persuade her that she owed it to herself to see the evening through. Maybe Tony really was interested in her. It didn't hurt that Ya-Ya insisted on taking her to Bloomie's to buy her a dress for the occasion.

Although her mother was less convinced of Tony's good intentions, even *she* was impressed when he showed up Saturday with a million-dollar smile and a box of chocolates for her—the good stuff, not some plasticy Whitman's sampler. A minute later, it was Angie's turn to be dazzled when Tony told her she looked "smokin'" in her turquoise halter dress—even though it didn't quite mesh with his 505s and Counting Crows T-shirt.

He was just as polite during the drive to the party, brushing aside questions about himself to ask about *her* dreams. And when he gallantly opened the door for her at his buddy George's house and escorted her in on his arm, she allowed herself to entertain the hope that maybe, just maybe, the gods of romance were smiling on her.

Angie's fantasy started to unravel the minute they set foot in the door. There were about a dozen guys there, all jocks of some persuasion, and an equal number of girls. But every single one of the girls was overweight—ranging from pleasingly plump to a morbidly obese specimen in a muumuu the size of a pup tent. The other thing the girls had in common was a deer-in-the-headlights expression, as if a dozen yearning fantasies about romance were about to be shattered.

And a moment later, they were. After ordering the DJ to cut the music, George stepped to the center of the room, hoisted his beer mug in the air and welcomed everybody to his party.

His *Bag a Fat Chick* party.

As a dozen double chins dropped, George explained that the guy who'd brought the heaviest date would be awarded three hundred bucks and a bottle of whiskey to share with her. Then he hauled out a scale and asked the girls to step up for their weigh-ins. But there were no takers. With reactions ranging from tears to fists through the wall, they stormed out in a tsunami of humiliation.

Except Angie, who decided she wasn't going to be the butt of anybody's joke, literally or figuratively. After fortifying herself with a sip of beer, she gave the guys a mild scolding and promised to forget the whole thing if they agreed to award her all the winnings, which they did. She spent the evening rotating between Tony and several other dance partners, teaching them the insane moves she'd picked up during her summer trip to Athens.

On the way home, Tony told her he was sorry for using her. He even offered to take her on a real date the following weekend at a restaurant of her choice. Angie told him it was sweet of him, but she'd have to check her schedule. When they pulled up to her building, she gave him a peck on the cheek and stepped out of the car. She kept right on smiling as she walked into the apartment, past her curious mother and into her bedroom...

... where she collapsed on the bed and cried her eyes out.

And that was where she stayed all night, ignoring her mother's pleas to open the door and tell her what happened. The next morning, Angie broke down and told her, a decision that was coaxed out of her by the scent of a fresh Cinnabon on the other side of the door. To her mother's credit, she listened to the whole story without interrupting or laying the blame on *her*. Her mother even took a moment to think it through before delivering the gospel according to Connie.

"Trust me, honey, this was a good thing. You learned a valuable lesson at a pretty low price. Those Kens and Barbies at your school might as well be a different species. You don't see dogs and cats humping on the side of the road. Stick with your own kind and save yourself a world of hurt."

As crude as that statement was, it pretty much jibed with what Angie was already coming to believe but had yet to make peace with.

Two weeks later, she let Nick kiss her for the first time and put his hand under her bra, a feel that launched a relationship that might still be limping along if Milos's laughter at her wedding hadn't rattled her into thinking she deserved better.

But did she?

Here she was, three months removed from that busted wedding, having all the old doubts again. And even if she did psych herself into believing there was a soulmate out there for her, was she prepared to get hurt all over again if Milos turned out to be another imposter?

She thought back on Tony and the *Bag a Fat Chick* experience. At first, it had hurt. So much so, that she stayed home from school for two days, scared to death of what people she didn't even care about might be saying about her. She even toyed with the idea of transferring. But slowly but surely, the pain diminished, thanks in part to Ya-Ya's support and some soul searching of her own. She went back with a who-gives-a-crap attitude and a fierce new perm, unaware that in her absence she'd developed a reputation as a girl who refused to take shit from anybody—a role model for the un-Barbies and un-Kens of PS 109. She also tracked down the other girls who'd attended the party and split her winnings with them.

And sure, if she'd had the choice, she'd have preferred that the whole thing had never happened. But it had. And life had gone on.

Now here she was, sixteen years later, being pursued by another man who seemed to have the makings of Mister Right. Hell, a hundred times more so than Tony, who was merely a god on the gridiron. Of course, she'd also been beaten down by other disappointments along the way. So while she was reasonably sure she could survive another romantic rug-pull, she couldn't imagine putting herself in this position again.

"Which means this is my last chance," she said aloud. "So why not go for it?"

And that earned her a standing ovation from her conscience.

Five minutes later, thanks to a coterie of beauty products Milos had laid out for her, Angie was stationed in front of the bathroom mirror, freshening her makeup and taming her tragically windblown hair. One way or another, she was gonna see it through. Put her doubts aside and allow herself to believe she was on the cusp of the kind of love the Taylor Swifts of the world wrote those insipidly catchy songs about.

Before she knew it, she was singing one of them. And then another.

She got so caught up in singing and primping that it took her till the third verse of the third song to notice the giant serpent that had slithered up behind her.

FIFTEEN

As Milos gazed at Zeus, wondering what fresh torment the next few minutes would bring, the table they were gathered around began creaking and groaning as though it were as anxious as he was. But Milos was well-acquainted with those sounds, as well as the physical changes that accompanied them. Sure enough, within seconds the table had sweated itself from an oval shape into the formal rectangle that had played host to hundreds of tribunals over the years. And Milos found himself alone at one end, with the twelve members of the Council gathered at the other, looking like the best-dressed firing squad in history.

It had begun.

Milos took a deep breath, cautioning himself to stay calm. Whatever they were about to demand of him—short of forbidding him to return to Angie—he could handle.

That bit of internal counseling seemed to do the trick. He felt his shoulders relax a bit and his fingers ease their death grip on the arms of the chair. And as he settled back, a smile found its way onto his face.

Until a troubling possibility occurred to him. What if they'd already sent Angie back to New York? What if this so-called celebration was their way of separating the two of them so they could carry out their plan without his interference? His smile wavered. A bead of sweat rose up on his forehead, trickled down his face, and dropped onto the tablecloth.

He had to find out. He had to envisage her. Now.

But he didn't get the chance. From his jewel-encrusted throne, formerly a garden-variety cocktail chair, Zeus took a long look around the table. Then he spoke slowly and solemnly, his words reverberating off the walls and ceiling, as if to ensure that even the heavens were listening. "One thousand, six hundred and twenty-two years. Nearly two thousand years' worth of war and famine and pestilence, perpetrated by a mankind that has grown more soulless with every passing year. And through it all, we've waited. Biding our time. Sometimes with patience, and sometimes with a burning desire to step in and right the wrongs we've witnessed. But with few exceptions, we've held back, paying heed to the Oracle as well as our own collective wisdom. Realizing that when our time came, we'd know it."

In spite of his trepidation, Milos found himself in the familiar position of being drawn in by Zeus's words. No doubt about it, His Sovereignty was an oratorical wizard. The timbre of his voice was soothing and mellifluous, and his tenor coolly seductive—rumored to have been perfected under the tutelage of Demosthenes himself. Milos only hoped Zeus couldn't hear his knees knocking at the other end of the table, lest the king of the gods be thrown off his rhythm and have another reason to be irritated with him.

As the others looked on, seemingly as caught up in the rhetoric as Milos was, Zeus rose to his feet and held out his arms in the kind of grand paternal gesture that all supreme beings seem to have in their wheelhouses. "Brethren, our time has come. I know it. You know it. And soon all of mankind will know it. And the righteous will rejoice at the prospect of their world being set back on its axis, while the wicked will cower in the shadows, knowing their death cries will soon fill the air. And the planet we ruled for thousands of years will once again be ours. For eternity!"

The cheers that rose up from the Council were so loud and hearty that the chandeliers swung even more vigorously than they had when the band was at full throttle. Milos ignored the churning in his stomach and cheered as boisterously as the rest of them, knowing his every move was being judged. And in truth, were it not for his trepidation about what they were up to today, he'd be as joyous as they were.

When the cheering died down, Zeus fixed his eyes on Milos, wearing a smile so bright it could compete with any number of stars in the galaxy. "As we prepare for this historic occasion, it seems appropriate that we take a moment to celebrate Milos. Obviously, he hasn't been waiting as long as we have. At a hundred and six, he's a mere pup. But he's spent much of his life preparing for it, as it was the sage declaration of the Oracle of Chaos that he be one of the twin faces of the family when we take those first steps back into the world. And although it is a role of unparalleled importance, I have no doubt he'll perform it with the kind of finesse and conviction we've come to expect from him."

Zeus paused, presumably to allow Milos to ponder whether those last few words were an endorsement or a warning. Then Zeus lofted his glass high in the air. "To the chosen one!"

Once again, the cheers rose to the rafters. But this time, Milos couldn't help noticing the veiled looks that passed among several Council members, Ares among them. Were they less than thrilled by the Oracle's decree, or were they bracing for the firestorm they knew was imminent?

Either way, Milos couldn't allow it to affect his performance. And it really was all about performance today. He knew it was imperative that he show them the Oracle had chosen well. That he was brilliant and courageous, every bit their equal. And an equal should have some say in who he was going to spend eternity beside, shouldn't he?

So he stepped over to Zeus and clinked glasses with him. "Your Sovereignty, members of the Council, I remain humbled by your endorsement. At the same time, I assure you the Oracle has spoken well. You have every reason to believe that when the time comes, I'll go forward with grace and confidence, utilizing all the lessons you've taught me during my brief but blessed life."

Another round of applause. And was that a tear running down Aphrodite's cheek? Milos cast a glance at Apollo, who was clapping earnestly enough, but his face remained as sphinx-like as it had all afternoon. And it made Milos sad to think that his mentor, who'd guided him for so many years, was prepared to leave him rudderless at such a critical moment.

A pat on the shoulder from Zeus shook him back to the here and now. "Well spoken, young master. By the way, how are you enjoying the girl's company?"

Blindsided by the abrupt change of subject, Milos sputtered for a moment before coaxing the words out. "Uh … very well. Thank you."

"Splendid. I believe I speak on behalf of the entire Council when I tell you we're pleased this liaison is working for you. You've certainly waited long enough for it."

Milos considered the words, wondering what might be hidden beneath them. But at the moment, there seemed to be no choice but to treat them as sincere. Besides, the fact that Zeus was referring to Angie in the present tense seemed to indicate they hadn't sent her back. Which meant there was hope—at least in the short term.

So Milos bowed graciously before the Council. "Thank you. Thank you all."

"No need for that." Zeus took him by the shoulder and hoisted him upright. "And if you require anything during her stay—anything at all—please don't hesitate to ask. A case of Château Lafite. Some of this fine caviar we're enjoying."

"Perhaps some Burmese opium," Hades volunteered.

The next offer came from a smirking Ares. "Or, seeing as how well-padded she is, we could slaughter some Tajima cattle and cook up a batch of steaks for her."

At that moment, Milos wanted to leap across the table and throttle his cousin. Ares had said some crass things about Angie before, but they'd never made his blood boil like this one had. Maybe it was because in the past few hours, she'd gone from being a long-distance fantasy to a flesh-and-blood creature who was well worthy of his love. And it frustrated Milos to no end to think decorum prevented him from beating the snot out of Ares.

Thankfully, none of the others laughed at the remark. On the contrary, Zeus was staring menacingly at his son, and for a magnificent moment, it looked like he was going to treat him to another jolt of electricity. Unfortunately, Zeus kept his anger in check. Hera, on the other hand, delivered a stinging slap to Ares's wrist, giving Milos another reason to like her.

"It was a joke, mother!" Ares declared. "Can't anyone take a joke around here?"

"*I* did, for hundreds of years," Aphrodite shot back. "But it was never funny and rarely satisfying."

As the room broke out in laughter, Zeus gave Ares a forbidding look, presumably to ensure he didn't retaliate against Aphrodite and reignite the fireworks between them.

A moment later, Zeus returned his attention to the god of the hour. "By the way, Milos, I'd be remiss if I didn't congratulate you on the way you managed to ferry your girl to the island without violating our tenets. Scaring up fifty drachma for her passage. Pressing that old gull into service. Genius!"

Once again, Milos felt a ripple of suspicion. Was Zeus giving him a sincere compliment or setting a trap? The way Zeus had been slinging the accolades today, he was either considering him for a position at his right hand or purposely building him up to make his fall that much steeper.

Still, Milos couldn't think of any alternative except to respond graciously. "Thank you, Your Sovereignty. I'm pleased to hear my behavior wasn't perceived as disrespectful. It certainly wasn't meant to be."

Zeus waved him off. "Please. It showed a crafty side of you we've witnessed far too infrequently. Speaks volumes about your fitness for the intricate duties ahead."

Before Milos could respond, Hades let out a chortle. "Do you know what it showed *me?* That the boy has balls as well as a brain. I was worried about you, kid."

Once again, the room erupted in laughter. Well, not quite. Milos couldn't help noticing Zeus wasn't caught up in the mirth. He was staring at him with a steely intensity, like a leopard about to make a meal of a rabbit. "All things considered, young master, you were fortunate your plan came off without a hitch. Goodness knows the tragedies that could have befallen the poor girl."

Milos felt a shudder pass through his body. Had the temperature in the room just dropped fifty degrees? "Misfortunes, Your Sovereignty?"

"Hundreds of them, really." Zeus's lower lip quivered with anticipation. "A tempest could have risen up during her passage and sunk the boat in the middle of the Aegean."

With a leisurely toss of his hand, Zeus turned on all twelve of the massive televisions that spanned the room. And every one of them was tuned to the same thing.

A frighteningly realistic "what if?" film that depicted Angie standing at the bow of the *Harmonia* as an enormous wall of water came out of nowhere, dwarfing the vessel. It was one of Zeus's most astounding powers—the ability to create a moving picture of something that had never happened, simply by imagining it into existence.

As Milos watched with dread, the onscreen Angie wrapped her arms around the railing and held on for dear life as the storm wave pelted her with an apocalyptic fury, tossing the boat around as if it were a bath toy. Her face was contorted in fear, her body drenched and shivering.

And things were about to get worse.

A bolt of lightning shot out of the sky and struck the cabin with a deafening crack, breaking the boat in half. Angie teetered on the rising bow for a moment, then tumbled overboard, hitting her head against the hull on the way down and disappearing beneath the sea.

It's not real, it's not real, Milos reminded himself. But his pounding heart didn't know the difference.

Seconds later, Angie bobbed to the surface, her face cut and bloodied. She treaded water for a moment, then spotted a piece of flotsam a few yards away and tried to swim to it. But she was no match for the powerful whitecaps. She was sucked under three times, but managed to claw her way to the surface each time, taking gulps of air and scanning the horizon hopefully.

But Milos knew that no one would come to her rescue. Clearly, the auteur of this film wasn't interested in happy endings. Indeed, moments later, another series of waves rolled in and thrashed Angie around, sapping her strength as well as her spirit. Soon, only her eyes and the top of her head were visible. She made a feeble attempt to fight back, but she was cold and weak and taking in water through her nose and mouth. A few tortured seconds later, she let out a watery whimper and gave up the fight.

But the sadistic film wasn't over yet. The point of view shifted underwater, tracking Angie's descent into the Aegean, presumably so Milos could witness her eyes lose their spark, then go blank with unconsciousness. As Angie sank deeper and deeper, her body suffered a series of convulsions before going rigid with death. Then and only then did the screens fade to black.

Milos let out a groan. Fictional or not, it was agonizing to watch the woman he loved die before his eyes and not be able to do a thing to save her.

He stole a look at Zeus to find him gazing at him with a look of manufactured sympathy, as if he'd merely stumbled upon the footage. "Heartbreaking, wasn't it?"

Realizing there was no safe or sane answer, Milos just shook his head.

Surprisingly, Zeus's fellow Council members were mostly silent. There were a few cryptic looks, an impressed smile or two, and what appeared to be a frown on Hera's face.

But only Hades felt compelled to speak out. "Bravo, brother! Such realism. But alas, no 3D?"

Zeus tilted his head. "I thought it would be too showy. No?"

"Well, you know *me*," Hades chuckled. "A sucker for the old razzle-dazzle."

Zeus seemed to take this under advisement, then cleared his throat and turned back to Milos. "But even if your girl's voyage had been as tranquil as a Disney Cruise, danger still might have been waiting for her. Imagine her walking down the pier toward you, her face aglow with anticipation. What if at that moment, a blood-lusting minotaur had come out of the wild?"

As Milos let out a low grumble, the screens sprang to life with a depiction of Angie's arrival this morning. This time, Milos himself was a character in the film, standing at the end of the pier, grinning eagerly, as she sauntered toward him in slow motion, her hair flowing in the breeze, her breasts bobbing. Then, as promised, one of the savage half-man, half-bull creatures leapt onto the pier a few yards behind her and barreled toward her on his nimble hind legs. At twelve feet tall, he was larger than any minotaur Milos had seen in real life, but he had the same muscle-bound body, protruding teeth and pointed horns. In other words, death on two legs.

Onscreen, Milos began racing toward her, calling out a warning about the predator behind her. But Angie didn't hear him. She kept strolling toward him, oblivious to the fact that her life was about to come down to a footrace between god and beast. For a moment, it looked like Milos might get to her first. But just as he reached out his arms to pull her to him, the minotaur took a flying leap and landed between them. Before Angie could so much as scream, the creature lowered his head and gored her in the midsection, spilling her blood all over the pier. Then he dove into the sea, leaving Milos to cradle his dying beauty.

Meanwhile, the real Milos was hunched forward in his seat, incapable of watching another frame. He was nauseous and shaken, not to mention pissed. How could Zeus claim to love him, yet put him through such a wrenching ordeal? Zeus would probably claim it was the way things had always been done, but by his own admission, those old ways were dying out.

Milos knew one thing for sure. The longer this spectacle went on, the harder it would be to stay calm and turn the other cheek. And then what?

Realizing the room had fallen silent, Milos raised his head and looked around the table. As he studied the faces of the Council members, he noticed that a few of them appeared to be less than enthusiastic about the entertainment, which gave him a small measure of relief. And Hera was staring at Zeus as though she were contemplating siccing a minotaur on *him*. Then she cleared her throat deliberately, as if to remind Zeus of some private promise he'd made to her.

Zeus stared back at her like a defiant ten-year-old, then returned his gaze to Milos. "So many agonizing possibilities. And dare I visit one more. Imagine that while the two of you were soaring through the air on horseback, as giddy as schoolchildren, the winds had whipped themselves into a frenzy. *You* might have been able to hang on, but what about her?"

On Zeus's command, the screens lit up with images of the sky-ride Milos and Angie had taken aboard Chrissie and Eddie. The two of them were playfully challenging each other for the lead, just as they'd done in reality. Even "Beautiful Day" was playing in the background, making it clear that Zeus had been watching them all day, plotting and planning his little film festival.

Moments later, Bono's soaring tenor was drowned out by the roar of the approaching windstorm. Before either of them could react, the winds began whipping around them, nearly knocking them off their mounts. They clung tighter to their horses and clamped their eyes shut, but the winds were so fierce that dust particles worked their way into their eyes and nostrils, causing them to choke and blink as tears coursed down their faces.

Sensing the horses couldn't take much more, Milos called out a "descend" command. Although the horses complied, the winds grew rougher the lower they went. And no matter their royal pedigree, the horses were getting more and more disoriented. Despite Milos's best attempts, Chrissie smashed into Eddie's flank, knocking Angie off him with a scream that grew more bloodcurdling as she began plunging toward the—

Suddenly, all twelve screens in the Great Hall exploded in a hail of flying glass that tore through the room like shrapnel, sending everyone diving for cover. Everyone but Zeus, who stood there trembling with rage as shard after shard pelted him, sending up blossoms of blood that ran down his face and sullied his suit. But it was unlikely he felt any of them. He was staring daggers at Hera, who climbed out from under the table wearing a triumphant smile that left no doubt as to who was responsible for the mayhem.

"You've made your point and danced on it, Zeus," she said, casually plucking a sliver of glass out of her cheek. "End this. Now."

But Zeus continued staring at her, and she at him, neither moving a muscle. As Milos watched the domestic chess match, he wondered how many silent invectives were being slung back and forth and how soon it would devolve into physical violence. Milos had never seen them fight, but Apollo once told him that centuries earlier, they'd gotten into a brawl over one of Zeus's infidelities that raged on for six brutal weeks until Hera claimed victory—albeit a hollow one, considering they'd broken every bone in each other's bodies and required weeks to mend.

Fortunately, after several tense minutes, Zeus gave Hera a conciliatory nod, followed by a smile that seemed grudging at first, then grew into something real and tender that seemed to pay homage to the centuries they'd shared and the storms they'd weathered. And when Hera smiled back at her husband and lovingly wiped the bloodstains off his face, Milos found himself not only relieved, but moved.

Those feelings went south the moment Zeus shifted focus back to him. "But none of those fates were suffered upon the girl, were they, Milos?"

"No, Your Sovereignty."

"And do you know why?"

Milos could only shake his head.

179

"Because we want you to get her out of your system. This obsession has gone on entirely too long. And we've tolerated it because up until now, it hasn't interfered with the duties that have been entrusted to you. And frankly, when we hold a mirror to ourselves, we can't deny that we, too, once dabbled in such foolishness. But with every second, the clock clicks closer to your destiny."

Zeus stepped over to Milos and clamped a hand so tightly on his shoulder that it was sure to leave a mark. "Go home and see this girl. Wrap your arms around her. Whisper sweet nothings in her ear. Then carry her to bed and ravish her in every conceivable position. Spoon with her, laugh with her, ask her every bloody question you've ever wanted to ask her. Then do it all again. Through the night and the dawn of the next day and the day after that. But know this. One week from today, your duties will begin in earnest."

Zeus was eye to eye with him now. "And then, this must end."

"One week?" Milos was flabbergasted. "Your Sovereignty, with all due respect, I was under the impression those duties weren't going to commence for months."

Zeus smiled pitilessly. "A last-minute adjustment to the schedule. You see, we can be crafty, too."

Milos felt like Zeus had reached into his chest, ripped his heart out, and stomped on it. It was bad enough that he'd forbidden him to see Angie in the future, though that he expected. But to move up his starting date was not only petty but cruel. In his grimmest imaginings, Milos had always figured he'd have a cushion of time after meeting Angie and romancing her to convince the Council their union was a better way to go forward into the world.

But one week? He'd have to be Hecate reborn to pull that off.

Milos looked across the table to see Athena studying him, her face tilted thoughtfully. After a moment, she turned to Zeus. "Father, allow me to take an opposing viewpoint," she said with the confidence of a daughter who knew she was the only one of his children who could get away with such treason. "Is it really necessary for Milos to expunge this woman from his life? Can't he just take her as a mistress? Bed her in New York twice a year?"

Zeus took a scant three seconds to mull it over. "Your concern for your cousin is admirable, Athena. But I truly believe the only way Milos can exorcise this girl from his heart is to cut her out entirely. Otherwise, she'll eat at him like a cancer till he's of no use to anyone."

The words were out of Milos's mouth before he knew it. "A cancer?! You're calling the woman I love a cancer?!"

Suddenly, Milos was jolted speechless by a voice that thundered through his head like a missile. *Dammit, Milos, shut up! Don't make things worse for yourself!*

Milos didn't have to look over at Apollo to know the warning had come from him. So his elder cousin *was* in his corner, looking out for him. On one level, it was comforting. If Milos was going to have any chance at changing Zeus's mind about Angie, he was going to need the support of his mentor. But did Apollo really expect him to sit back and accept the sentence that was being handed down? Didn't he realize Zeus's actions were petty and trifling, not to mention—

Are you even listening to me?! Do you want to live to see her tonight?! Do you want **her** *to live to see* **you** *tonight?*

Milos bit back his rage. Loathe as he was to admit it, Apollo was right. This was not the time to challenge Zeus. That time would come later.

The next voice he heard was Zeus's. "Do you dare finish your diatribe?"

Milos turned back to Zeus, whose face was so contorted there might as well have been smoke coming out of his ears, and knelt down before him. And when Milos's knees hit the floor, he leaned forward till his head was touching the ground and his arms were extended in front of him. Clearly, a moment as highly charged as this one required the most supplicating of gestures.

Then Milos took a fortifying breath and spoke. "Your Sovereignty, members of the Council, I apologize for my outburst. It was rude and disrespectful. I am young and still have much to learn. But I can promise you that nothing like this will ever happen again."

For a long moment, there was silence. No one spoke, at least not aloud. From his prostrate position, all Milos could see were Zeus's feet, wrapped in a pair of Ferragamos. Then one shoe began tapping. And when it stopped, the other began tapping. Over and over, until Milos wondered if he'd ever get the staccato rhythm out of his head.

Finally, Zeus spoke. "You selfish boy. Don't you realize there are events taking shape that are far more important than you and your puerile heart? You've been chosen for the opportunity of a thousand lifetimes. And yet you act as though it were an inconvenience. A roadblock to the middling life you seem to crave. Let me ask you something. Do you want the mission we've entrusted to you? Really, truly want it?"

"Yes."

"More than anything?"

Milos stiffened. But really, what could he do but lie? "Yes."

"Get up."

Milos rose to his feet to find Zeus regarding him like a father whose deadbeat son has shamed him for the last time. "Remember this moment, Milos. And don't let it happen again."

Milos braced himself for a jolt of electricity. But to his surprise, Zeus gave him a curt nod and returned to the table, where Hera gently squeezed his hand, presumably in praise of his restraint.

Milos stood there for a moment, wondering whether he'd been tacitly excused from the gathering. Was it over? Was he free to go home?

Then he felt something glance off his head. He looked down to discover a gold object spinning around on the floor. And when it stopped spinning and fell flat, his eyes went wide.

It was a drachma, possibly one of the very coins he'd sent to Athens with the seagull. A few seconds later, another one hit him in the shoulder, followed by another one that struck the bridge of his nose. Then another and another until he was literally being pelted by drachma.

Through it all, Zeus sat there, stone-faced.

What message is he trying to send me? Milos wondered. *What manner of retribution is this?* All Milos knew was that it was imperative he refrain from showing any sign of anger.

Finally, the deluge began to slow, then trickled to a halt. Milos glanced at the floor, where dozens of drachma glistened under the light of the chandelier. But still, not a word from Zeus.

Then a far heavier object hit him in the head and thudded to the ground. And when Milos saw what it was, it took every ounce of self-control he possessed not to cry out in anguish.

It was his seagull. His loyal friend of so many years and the means by which he'd gotten Angie to the island. The poor bird's neck was broken, and his dead eyes stared at him in dull resignation.

A moment later, Milos felt Zeus's breath on him. "Isn't it a pity, all the poor innocents who are sacrificed on the altar of our hubris?"

SIXTEEN

ANGIE LOWERED THE HAIRBRUSH and stared through the mirror at the creature looming behind her.

"Please God, don't let it be real," she said, her voice quivering with every syllable.

But even as Angie spoke those words, she knew that it was. She'd seen enough bizarre things on this island to change her view of reality forever. Up till now, though, every new discovery had been wondrous, as if she'd wandered into one of those old Disney movies where everything was supercalifragilisticexpialidocious.

But there was nothing remotely supercalifragilistic about this creature. Although he vaguely resembled a cobra that had risen up on its haunches, he had features that were unlike any serpent Angie had ever seen. First off, even with only a portion of his body in an upright position, he was at least ten feet high, with his head practically grazing the ceiling and his tail dangling off the balcony some twenty feet back. And the color of his scaly skin seemed to be changing all the time. When Angie first spotted him, he was a muddy green. But now, no more than thirty seconds later, he'd morphed into a shade of purple reminiscent of a fresh bruise.

Which is the least he'll do to me if he gets the chance, Angie thought, afraid to look at him, but even more afraid to take her eyes off him.

So far, he hadn't moved an inch, apparently preferring to size up his prey before lashing out. But if the size of his head was any indication of brainpower, he was plotting an attack for the ages. Perched atop his neck like an anvil, it was so oversized that it seemed to belong on one of those T-Rexes from the *Jurassic Park* movies. His eyes were just as intimidating: pitch-black slivers of menace that never shifted focus from Angie. His massive jaw hung wide open, showing off two rows of razor-sharp teeth coated with gore—remnants of the poor villager he had for lunch, Angie surmised. And dripping from his nostrils was a foul green pus that sizzled when it hit the carpet, leaving smoking holes in its wake.

And that was only the third most nauseating thing about him. Cloaked around his head like a hoodie was a semi-circle of skin Angie knew to be characteristic of cobras. What made it truly repulsive were the hundreds of glinting eyes inside it. And up and down his sides were flesh-colored arms that looked astonishingly human, all of them flailing and grasping at the air as if they were trying to escape the body they were born into.

But what was this horrifying creature doing here? Angie couldn't imagine he'd wandered into the house by accident. Why would the gods, who could control the sun, the moon, and the stars, allow some monster to slither around their island, indiscriminately laying waste to their houseguests? They wouldn't, which meant he'd been sent by somebody—some enemy of Milos's, no doubt. Which told

Angie two things: One, Milos must really care about her for his adversaries to know they could hurt him by hurting her. And two, since vindictive gods generally don't hesitate to kill mortals to make their point, it would behoove her to get her butt out of here pronto.

And unless she wanted to risk running past him and leaping off the balcony, there was only one way out: through the hallway. While holding the rest of her body as still as possible to avoid arousing his attention, Angie turned her head to the left. The door was about twenty feet away, and thankfully, she'd left it open. Estimating that the serpent was ten feet behind her in the opposite direction, she figured she'd have a slight head start.

But would it be enough? Angie was pretty sure most snakes weren't capable of outrunning people, but this guy clearly wasn't your garden-variety snake. Not only did he have the look of a mega-genetic hybrid, he'd also managed to hoist himself onto a second-story balcony. Probably by flapping those sick little arms.

Dammit, Milos, where are you?

Wherever Milos was, Angie prayed he was watching her—scoping her out in the middle of his powwow with the Council like somebody might sneak in an episode of *Empire* on their iPad during a boring class. The more Angie thought about how reluctant Milos had been to leave her, the more likely it seemed that he *was* watching her. Her spirits soared as she pictured him hauling ass over here, crashing through the skylight and slaying the beast like a clean-shaven Heracles.

Then, just as quickly, her hopes took a nosedive. Hadn't she made Milos promise he'd never envisage her again, right after she called him a voyeur and a pervert and threatened to take the next magic boat back to civilization? She groaned, disgusted with herself. *I hope you're proud of yourself, Angie. You scared the eaves-watcher right out of him. Not that there's gonna be anything left of you to watch if you don't get a move on.*

Angie risked another look at the door to the hallway, which suddenly seemed a hundred miles away. In such a mad scramble for freedom, there were probably a hundred ways to die. But what choice did she have? It wasn't like she could stand here all night hoping the creature would lose his appetite for voluptuous Greek girls. Eventually, he was going to pounce. And didn't a moving target stand a better chance than a sitting duck?

Figuring it was now or never, Angie started counting down from twenty, pausing long enough to send a prayer up to Saint Emily. Somewhere around *ten,* it occurred to her that the task ahead of her wasn't all that different from stealing home with a fireballing pitcher on the mound. And she'd done that a thousand times. By the time she got to *five,* she felt strong. Self-assured.

Then, somewhere between *three* and *two,* the creature let out a bone-chilling hiss that sent Angie's heartbeat into cardio workout mode. But that was nothing compared to what he did next. He sent his tongue shooting out of his mouth like a demented party horn all the way to the open door, then slammed it shut and rolled his tongue back in with a sickening slurp.

Angie stood there trembling with frustration. How the hell had he figured out her plan? Was he a mind reader? At any rate, her escape route was kaput. Even if she did manage to beat that tongue of his to the door, she'd lose any advantage she had in the time it would take to open it. And what if it were jammed? Milos would come home to an empty bedroom, aside from a pool of blood on the carpet and an earring or two strewn about, sans ears.

Angie felt the hope run out of her body like water down a drain. She was going to die. Right here in this beautiful house, on this so-called paradise of an island. At the whim of a savage monster who was, nevertheless, smarter than many of the people she knew. She felt small. And scared.

Then she felt something else. Pissed.

The bastard wasn't just going to steal her life. He was going to snuff out her chance to find out whether this thing between her and Milos could grow into love. And not just any old love. A love she'd been dreaming about since she was a kid. A love she'd ditched her wedding for. A love she'd survived a collision with a beer truck in the hopes of finding. A love she'd endured a bizarre midnight voyage to finally be face to face with.

Angie's fists clenched with fury. This scaly son of a bitch was quite possibly standing between her and the romance of a lifetime.

Suddenly, there was no room in her body for fear. She was going to kick some reptilian ass. Her heart rate dropped from that of a hummingbird to somewhere in the caffeinated-human range. Her hands stopped shaking. Her knees stopped knocking. And the sweat that had been running out of every pore slowed to a trickle.

Then, in a gesture aimed at showing her enemy she was ready for war, Angie turned away from the mirror and faced him dead-on for the first time.

And just about puked.

In the space of a few seconds, he'd slithered closer—close enough for Angie to smell his breath, which was so putrid it brought tears to her eyes and turned her stomach over like a cement mixer. He'd also turned a grotesque shade of brown, like something that might be found caking the inside of a public toilet.

But she wasn't going to let it break her stride. She swallowed hard a couple of times to keep the bile down and started breathing through her mouth to lessen the stench.

Then she narrowed her eyes at him and snarled, "I'm gonna end you, snake," landing every word like a hammer blow.

She half expected him to shoot that tongue out at her. Instead, he glared back at her, snorting and drooling, seemingly challenging her to turn away in fear. But she held her gaze. For thirty seconds. A minute. Not blinking. Not retching. Not scratching that pesky spot on her shoulder that wouldn't stop itching.

Unfreaking believable. I'm having a staring contest with a monster. And I'm holding my own.

But Angie knew this standoff couldn't last forever. Sooner or later, the sucker was going to make a move. In the annals of horror fiction, bloodthirsty monsters weren't exactly known for their patience. And despite the ballsiness Angie was feeling, she'd have to be crazy to think she could fight him off with her fists and fingernails. Sadly, he didn't have a groin she could knee him in.

What she needed was a weapon. Something that would give her a fighting chance of subduing him long enough to make an escape. Without turning around, she took an inventory of the items on the counter. Hairspray. Hairbrush. Blow dryer. Disposable razor. Perfume. Deodorant. Toothbrush. Moisturizer. Lit candles.

Angie sighed. Slim pickings. The Lady Schick would barely give him a paper cut. Unless he had super sensitive eyes, spraying Ralph Lauren's Romance on him would only rev up his anger engine. And if she hurled a candle at him, he'd probably dodge it and end up burning down the house, but not before fanging her to death and slithering off to safety.

Unless...

She'd seen it in a drive-in horror movie Nick dragged her to a few years back. His scheme was to get her so spooked that she'd end up with her head buried in his chest, at which point he'd coax her a little lower and satisfy his oral-sex-in-public fantasy. Unfortunately for Nick, the movie starred a young Channing Tatum, and Angie never took her eyes off the screen. Even now, she remembered the climax in all its titillating detail. As a bloodthirsty horde of zombies descended on a stripped-to-the-waist Channing and his forgettable girlfriend in the beauty salon they were holed up in, he sent them to hell with a makeshift weapon straight out of Chemistry 101.

But was it real or Hollywood real? Unfortunately, there was only one way to find out—and a ginormous price to pay if it fizzled. But, as the saying went: No guts, no glory.

Not daring to let the serpent out of her sight, Angie took several tentative steps backward till her butt hit the bathroom counter. Then she reached to her left, fumbled around till she had her hand wrapped around the perfume bottle and heaved it across the room as hard as she could. As the serpent instinctively turned his head to watch it fly past him and shatter against the wall, Angie whipped her head around and grabbed a lit candle in one hand and the hairspray in the other.

By the time the serpent turned back around, Angie was holding the candle a few inches in front of the hairspray, her finger on the trigger. As his eyes registered curiosity, she pressed down hard, sending a stream of liquid lacquer hissing toward the candle. The flame flickered for a second, causing her heart to skip a beat, then reacted to the combination of alcohol and butane by turning a pale shade of blue that shot forward under the force of the propellant.

A lousy six inches.

It didn't come close to the serpent. And even if it had, it wouldn't have done any damage, considering it was no bigger around than a toilet paper roll. As Angie cursed her fate to the skies, the serpent curled that mug of his into a sneer that seemed to say, *Is that all you got, bitch?*

For the first time since she'd turned away from the mirror to face him, Angie felt a shudder of doubt. Was she out of her mind to think she could kill such a powerful creature? Shouldn't she just accept the fate that had been handed to her, pray for a quick death, and hope the afterlife was one big fat Greek party after another?

"No!" she shouted. She was *not* going to give up. She was too young to die, and Milos was too hot to miss out on. She shook the can vigorously, then jammed her thumb down so hard on the nozzle that it cried out in pain.

This time, the spray shot out of the can a bit more powerfully, but the flame still petered out a foot shy of the serpent. Worst yet, he'd grown weary of this cat-and-mouse game. He began slithering toward her, his eyes twinkling with malice, his tongue dancing salaciously. Even those creepy arms appeared to have become a united front, extending toward her as if they were hoping to squeeze her to death.

As she watched him approach, Angie knew she should be scared out of her skull. In a few seconds, she was gonna be snake kibble. Instead, she was livid. Enraged at God or the gods or freaking Channing Tatum for letting her down.

She stared at her failed weaponry with rabid contempt and called out to any deity who might be listening. "Is that all you're gonna give me?! That pissy little flame?! Can't you do better than that?!"

Suddenly, the flame expanded to a hundred times its size and shot toward the serpent like a lightning bolt. Although Angie was startled by the power that was flowing from her hands, she managed to hang on to the makeshift flamethrower as a pillar of fire assaulted the beast. As his eyes flew open in shock, he skittered back toward the balcony, trying to escape the flames that were scorching him. But the fire kept coming, showing no mercy.

Just like the girl manning the weapon.

Seconds later, she had him fully engulfed in flames, sending him into frantic contortions. But no matter how violently he shook his body or tried to lick himself out with his tongue, he was no match for the inferno being leveled at him. His flesh blistered and blackened, his multi-eyed hood incinerated, his arms dropped off one by one, writhing on the ground like worms.

At one point, he tried to get relief by rolling his head over a puddle of perfume on the floor, apparently unaware that the alcohol content of perfume makes it highly flammable. As Angie watched impassively, a dark blue flame flared up over one side of his face, consuming an eye socket and half his mouth. He let out an agonized wail and tried to lunge toward her, but the column of fire that was blasting him kept him safely at bay and flailing around as if it were machine gun fire.

Through it all, Angie kept her thumb glued to the trigger. She wasn't thinking. She wasn't feeling. She was acting—in pure survival mode.

Eventually, a defeated shudder passed through the serpent's body and he dropped to the floor with a thud that seemed to shake the whole house. Through his one remaining eye, he stared up at Angie in disbelief. Then, after a final rattle of his tail, his eye flickered shut.

But Angie wasn't about to take any chances. She walked up to him and directed the flamethrower up and down his trunk. Over and over. From bow to smoldering stern. She could hear his body crackling, giving off a smell vaguely reminiscent of burnt chicken. But she didn't stop till the flow of hairspray sputtered to a trickle, then conked out. As she tossed the can aside, every last fire in the room went out, as if some master stoker realized his job was done.

As she stared down at the blackened remains of the serpent, Angie felt a surge of adrenalin unlike anything she'd ever experienced. She'd killed a monster. A real-life son-of-a-bitching monster. Angie Costianes of Astoria, Queens, had slain a beast far more powerful than the giant David slew in the Bible. And David had the benefit of a slingshot, an honest-to-goodness weapon. She'd had to make do with a beauty product and a sex candle.

I did it, Milos. For us.

Although her chest was swelling with pride, Angie felt a tear trickle down her cheek. Then another and another, as it dawned on her just how close she'd come to dying. In fact, had it not been for the memory of that zombie movie and some miraculous variable that kicked in at the last minute, *she'd* be the one on the ground. Or churning around in the serpent's stomach.

Then her mind went to an even darker place. She'd killed a living creature.

And not just killed it—like say, stepping on an ant. She'd taken a blowtorch to him and cooked him to death. Heard him cry out in pain. Watched him stare hopelessly into her eyes and heave his final breath. And although she knew intellectually it was a case of kill or be killed, she couldn't help feeling sick to her stomach over what she'd done. And how naturally it had come to her.

Her heart pounding, Angie rushed over to the sink and splashed water on her face. Then she planted her hands on the counter and stared into the mirror, willing herself to take deep breaths and picture herself sailing on a blue-green ocean, sipping a Piña Colada and playing a Jimmy Buffett song. But she couldn't get the image of the dying creature out of her head.

A few seconds later, she was slumped on the bathroom floor, sobbing like a baby.

SEVENTEEN

EVEN BEFORE MILOS TOUCHED down on the lawn astride Chrissie, he sensed that something was wrong. The house had a heavy look about it, as if it had weathered a cataclysm and was trying to build itself up again. He told himself it was just his dark imagination, fueled by the foul mood Zeus had put him in. Surely, when he walked in the door, he'd find Angie sprawled on the sofa sipping a glass of wine, looking so lovely it would take every ounce of self-control he possessed not to wrap her in a passionate embrace and see where the night took them.

Because there were things he needed to tell her. Straight away. Hard truths about the demands his superiors had placed on him and weren't likely to back off on anytime soon. He hoped she'd understand he was merely a pawn in their game, albeit a pawn who was going to devote every ounce of energy toward changing their minds. More than anything, he hoped she'd wait for him, but he knew that wasn't a fair thing to ask of her.

He also knew there was a possibility she wouldn't take it well. That she'd be hurt or angry and would insist on going back to New York. And if that happened—well, he'd find a way to live with it. What he couldn't live with another moment was keeping her in the dark about any aspect of his so-called life.

For at least the tenth time today, Milos wished he could make his own decisions. Be his own man, so to speak. He couldn't deny that he enjoyed immortality, along with the other perks that went along with being a god. And he truly believed he could make a difference in the world if he assumed the role they'd been grooming him for. But he'd trade it all in the flutter of a sparrow's wings for the gift of free will. To be able to do what he wanted, with whomever he wanted, and answer to no one but himself. He'd happily work a backbreaking job in a coal mine for the privilege of coming home every night to the woman he loved. And if that meant that one day his heart would stop beating and he'd take leave of the Earth, never to see her again—well, at least he'd have the satisfaction of knowing that every success and every failure, every joy and every disappointment, every precious moment, had been of his own making.

Chrissie smelled the smoke before he did.

As her hooves touched the ground, the mare began coughing so violently that Milos had to wrap his arms around her neck to keep from being thrown. Seconds later, he smelled it, too. And when he realized it was coming from his own house, he leapt off her mid-stride, somersaulted across the lawn a couple times, then clamored to his feet and raced toward the door.

The moment he stepped inside, Milos was hit by a fog of acrid smoke that stung his eyes and assaulted his throat. But he sucked it in anyway, picking up the smell of alcohol, several chemical compounds, and something that filled him with dread.

It was the stench of death. Someone had died in this house.

Realizing the smoke was coming from the second floor, he dashed over to the staircase and took the steps three at a time while screaming Angie's name as loudly as his throbbing lungs would allow. Every time she didn't answer, he felt the panic growing inside him. If anything had happened to her, he'd never forgive himself. Nor would he forgive his superiors for pulling him away for their asinine reprimand.

"Angie!" His voice echoed down the hallway. Dammit, why wasn't she answering? He tried to summon a vision of her, but the normally dependable sense failed him completely.

When he saw that the door to his bedroom was closed, he was hit by a wave of anxiety that caused him to lose his balance and stumble into the wall. What had happened in that room? Had she gone in there to take a nap and fallen victim to a fire? But how? He knew she wasn't a smoker. An electrical fire also seemed unlikely. The craftsmen under contract by the Olympians generally checked their work dozens of times out of fear of reprisal.

Then it hit him. He'd filled the room with candles this morning in the hopes of striking a romantic mood if he was lucky enough to bring her here. Had one of them tipped over while she was sleeping? The possibility unnerved him so much that he didn't even use the doorknob to get into the room. He broke the door down with his shoulder.

As Milos burst into what had once been an attractive bedchamber, his eyes flew open wide. Every inch of the room had been wracked by fire. The bed was a pile of springs. The drapes were tattered rags. The

Monet that hung over the dresser was a liquefied mess, its yellows, blues, greens, and vermilions running down the wall in sad little rivers. He couldn't imagine this devastation was the result of a tipped candle. It looked like a torpedo had ripped through the place.

And what was that smoldering object on the far side of the room? Milos rushed over to it and drew in a breath—and not just because of the foul stench it was giving off. It was a large carcass, reptilian in nature, with an exaggerated ribcage and an enormous skull. What *was* this thing? How had it gotten into his house? And under what circumstances had it ended up burnt to death?

Above all else, where was Angie?

He took another look around, settling on the open sliding door to the balcony. From observing Angie all these years, he knew her to be brave and resourceful. Had she jumped off the balcony to escape her attacker? Was she lying on the lawn, hurt but alive? He bounded toward the door, allowing himself to hope.

Then, a few inches from the door, he saw something that made his blood run cold.

A wrist bone, with five fingers. And it appeared to be human.

Milos didn't even feel himself dropping to the floor, but suddenly he was there. Sitting on his haunches with his head in his hands. Had the Fates really dealt him this hand? Had they conspired to take away the woman he loved, mere hours after finally granting his wish to meet her? If so, he thought, they damn well better grant him another wish: That he could become mortal and susceptible to hemlock.

Then, through his sobs, Milos thought he heard something. He sucked in a breath and listened intently. For a moment, all he heard was the crackling of a few embers. Then it came again. Either he was losing his mind or a woman was crying in the bathroom.

Leaping to his feet, he raced past the sink alcove into the bathroom. At first, the room appeared to be empty. Then he caught sight of a shadow moving on the other side of the closed shower door. With his heart in his throat, he rushed over and slid the door open.

And there was Angie, sitting in the bathtub with tears in her eyes and soot on her face, but alive and seemingly unscathed by fire or beast, right down to the two hands that were clutching her shoulders. Milos felt a surge of joy that would've lifted him to the sky if he'd let it. But why would he want to fly to the heavens when there was a celestial body right here that outshone them all?

"Angie," he said, never loving the sound of any word more.

But even though she was less than a foot away, she didn't answer. She didn't even look up. After calling her name again to no avail, Milos let out a sigh. Clearly, whatever nightmare she'd been through had sent her into shock. Never having faced such a situation, he had no idea how to proceed. Should he continue speaking to her in soothing tones? Remain silent and wait for her to come out of it? Turn on the bath water and toss in a batch of healing herbs?

Ultimately, he relied on instinct. He stepped over the edge of the tub, sat down beside her and gently rested a hand on top of hers. She flinched, but didn't pull away. So he kept his hand over hers and watched as a change came over her. Her body began to uncoil and relax. A blush of color returned to her cheeks. Her eyes blinked a couple of times and seemed to grow more alert. It was as if she were drawing nourishment from his touch.

Gently caressing her fingers, he whispered, "Angie, it's Milos. You're safe now."

His words seemed to resonate with her, because she raised her head and turned to him. And when she spoke, it seemed as if her voice was rising out of a deep, dark well. "Milos."

Then she smiled. Tentatively at first, then gradually spreading across her face like a sunrise on a cloudless morning. It was the most beautiful smile Milos had ever seen. Full of gratitude and joy and what appeared to be affection.

Milos smiled back at her, wider than he'd ever smiled in his life. *How many emotions have I experienced today that I've never felt in all my years of living? Or have I only begun living today?*

The spell was broken a moment later when she looked around her and winced. "Gotta get out of here."

She grabbed hold of his hand and tried to stand up, but her legs weren't cooperating. That was all the invitation Milos needed to wrap his arms around her and lift her out of the shower. He felt her clinging urgently to him, pressing her fingers into his back.

"Are you hurt?" he asked her, taming her hair with his fingers.

Although she shook her head bravely, he could feel her body trembling. What had happened to her in the bedroom? Was it tied to the warnings he'd received from the Council? And how had she managed to kill the creature? It certainly hadn't burned *itself* to death.

As eager as he was for answers, Milos knew that what Angie needed now was comfort and protection, which he was only too happy to provide. So he pulled her in tighter, reassuring her with the warmth of his body, as she sobbed and shivered and muttered things he couldn't make out. Through it all, she kept her face pressed gloriously against his chest, making him feel guilty that he was deriving pleasure from the wounded state she was in.

After what might have been a few minutes or a few hours, he felt her arms ease their grip on his body. Then she took a step back and gazed at him, smiling when he wiped the tears off her cheeks with his fingertips.

Finally, she spoke. "Admit it. You're pissed at me for trashing your bedroom."

He stared back at her, wondering if she was serious. She couldn't be … unless she was still in shock. Or maybe she'd suffered a concussion during the struggle.

Then she winked at him, and he realized she'd played him yet again.

Swallowing a chuckle, Milos regarded her with as straight a face as he could manage. "As a matter of fact, I am pissed. I'm afraid I'll have to charge you for the damages. Unless, of course, you'd like to take it out in trade."

"What did you have in mind?" She ran her hands up and down his chest in a manner that gave him an enticing glimpse into what she'd be like as a lover.

In a flash, his lips were on hers. Feeding off them. He slipped his tongue inside her mouth and felt a surge of ecstasy that enlivened every nerve ending. She responded by pulling him in so close that he could feel her nipples pressed against his chest. He wanted to take her, then and there, in the ravaged shell of his bedroom, and rechristen it with their passion.

Suddenly, the one segment of his brain that wasn't swimming in hormones snapped into action. *This is not the time, Milos. Or have you forgotten what you have to do?*

It took tremendous effort, but he managed to pull himself away from her. "Angie, as much as it pains me to say it, we can't do this now. There are things I need to tell you. Not to mention I'd be taking advantage of you."

She flinched, wounded but still sassy. "How do you know I'm not taking advantage of *you*?"

"But … after what you've been through. With that creature over there on the floor."

Although a shiver passed through her body, her eyes shone bright with determination. "That creature on the floor is dead. And we're alive."

As inspired as Milos was by her resilience, his curiosity could no longer be contained. "What was it, Angie? What happened to it?"

For a few seconds, she didn't say anything. She stared past him into the bedroom, deep inside herself, and Milos wondered if he'd erred in sending her back into the fray so quickly.

Then she nodded to herself and turned back to him. "It was a serpent. With human arms."

"Human arms?"

"There had to have been a dozen of them up and down his sides. All flailing and grabbing at the air. God, I'm gonna have nightmares about those suckers for years."

Milos cupped her shoulders reassuringly. Now he understood the source of the wrist bone that had sent him into torment a moment ago. But he knew of only one creature that had those characteristics. And it didn't seem possible Angie could have prevailed over him.

"What else do you remember?" he asked her. "What color was he?"

"You name it. He was like a damn chameleon. Green. Brown. Purple. And he had a freakishly long tongue. At one point, it shot out across the room and pushed the door shut. I was afraid he was gonna wrap it around me and strangle me with it."

Now it was Milos's turn to shudder. Angie had just described one of the deadliest creatures in the history of the Pantheon. And in so doing, left little doubt as to who had sent him.

"Gaileoñtos," he said, with a flutter of dread.

"Gaileoñtos?"

"Ancient Greek for 'ground lion.' A creature as powerful as the king of the jungle. But rather than swagger across the Earth in pursuit of his victims, he writhes across it, gathering strength from every element he passes over."

"Except Berber carpeting." Angie chuckled, indicating the floor.

Despite the anger growing inside him, Milos found himself laughing, too. Angie's wicked sense of humor was one of the qualities he treasured most about her—and wished he had more of himself.

When the laughter died down, Milos turned to her thoughtfully. "His fate tonight aside, Gaileoñtos is one of the most fearsome creatures in the animal kingdom. Thousands of years ago, Zeus and his siblings overthrew their father Cronus and sent him to the depths of Tartarus to be imprisoned for eternity. Gaileoñtos was one of several predators Zeus brought into being to keep him from escaping. From what I understand, there are legions of them standing guard outside the gates, their flailing arms a constant reminder of what Cronus did to incur the wrath of his children."

"I read about that," Angie said. "The old prick tried to eat them, didn't he?"

"And succeeded, for a time. He swallowed them whole when they were newborns to keep them from usurping his power when they grew older. All but Zeus, who escaped notice with the help of his mother and was spirited away. Years later, Zeus returned to his father in disguise, and after earning his trust, offered him a drink with which to toast his health. Unknown to Cronus, the drink contained a powerful emetic. Within minutes, he was vomiting up his children, who were not only alive but full grown, which no doubt made the disgorgement even more excruciating."

Angie blew out a puff of air. "Wow, you guys are the original *Game of Thrones*."

Although Milos knew she hadn't intended it, the remark left a bitter taste in his mouth. "Not exactly something to be proud of."

"Sorry." She rubbed his forearm. "Sometimes my mouth is a few steps ahead of my brain."

Milos waved it off. Truth be told, he'd gladly endure any aspersion Angie threw at him if it were followed by her touch.

A moment later, she furrowed her brow. "Okay, I totally get why the Gaileoñtos are needed down in Tartarus. But why do you keep them around here? To scare off the paparazzi?"

"To be honest, we usually don't. I've only seen one of them in my lifetime. Thirty years ago, Zeus unleashed a single Gaileoñtos on a group of villagers who'd betrayed our secrets to an Egyptian prince. The aftermath of the attack was so gruesome that even some Olympians were nauseated by the carnage."

Angie's face lit up in a smile. "Wow. I killed a real mother, didn't I?"

"To say the least. How in Hades did you do it?"

"With a sweet little weapon I put together. Courtesy of Channing Tatum."

Milos narrowed his eyes. "Someone was here with you?"

"Only in spirit. He's an American actor and all-around hottie. Not as easy on the eyes as you are, but in the ballpark. In one of his movies, I saw him incinerate a pack of zombies with a blowtorch he made out of a can of hairspray and a candle."

Milos's eyes went wide. "You killed a bloodthirsty predator with hairspray and a candle?"

"Pretty crazy, huh? What do you people put in the air around here?"

On one hand, Milos was amazed. He knew Angie was special, but what she'd done to that serpent exceeded his highest expectations. Not only was she beautiful and endlessly engaging, but she was a warrior, through and through. He knew of at least a dozen deities who wouldn't have exhibited a fraction of her bravery. And they didn't have to be concerned with the pesky possibility of death.

But would she be as fortunate if there were another attack? And sadly, Milos had a feeling there would be. In his experience, an aggressor who'd been humiliated as badly as this one tended to come back with even more firepower the second time around. Milos figured he'd have to be the most selfish being on the planet to risk putting Angie in that situation again.

So it was with the deepest of sighs that he took Angie's hand and led her out of the room.

She held on, knitting her fingers around his. "Where are you taking me, loverboy?"

"I need to get you off the island. Now."

Two steps into the hallway, Angie dug her heels into the carpet and stopped moving, sending Milos reeling back toward her. "Say what?"

"I thought you'd be safe here, Angie. Our enemies can't penetrate this island, just as we can't penetrate their stronghold."

"Or so you thought." She indicated the burned-out husk of a bedroom behind them.

He stared soberly at her. "I'm afraid the attack came from within."

Clearly, the statement took Angie by surprise, because she let out something akin to a gasp. "Wait a minute. Are you trying to tell me one of your own people tried to kill me?"

"I don't think that was their intent. More likely it was a reminder to me—to do their bidding or face the consequences. In all likelihood, they figured I'd come home to find the serpent menacing you. And after rescuing you, I'd get the message that they were not to be trifled with."

Even as he spoke those words, Milos found himself questioning them. Hadn't Zeus encouraged him to go home and enjoy his time with Angie until his duties began? Wouldn't he have been intuitive enough to know a Gaileoñtos attack was overkill that could alienate his young master? But if the attack hadn't come from Zeus, who was responsible for it? Had their enemies found a way to breach security? Or was the culprit right here? Sour grapes from Ares, maybe?

Whatever the source, Milos couldn't allow himself to keep Angie in this dangerous situation any longer. Once again, he took her hand and tried to lead her down the hallway. "Come on."

And once again, she refused to budge. "But it didn't happen that way, did it, Milos? I fought back. And I can do it again."

"You can't fight back every time."

She didn't even flinch. "Why not?"

"Angie, I will never stop seeking a way to spend eternity with you. But I can't guarantee your safety. I need to get you off this island as soon as possible so I can sit down with the appropriate parties and sort things out."

"I've got a better idea. How about *we* sort it out with them? Of course, I'll need a shower and … you wouldn't happen to have something by Stella McCartney lying around, would you?"

"Out of the question. I can't take you to them."

"Why not? Are you ashamed of me?" Her face was turning an angry shade of red that he nonetheless found attractive.

But not enough to change his mind. "Of course not. I'll explain it on the way to the boat." He reached for her hand. "Just let me summon the horses."

She swatted his hand away. "You may be a god, but you can't order me around."

Milos blew out a frustrated breath. "Angie, there are things I need to tell you about my duties and obligations. Things I should have told you hours ago."

She put her fingers to his lips, distracting him with their softness. "Right now, I just want to know one thing. Why did you bring me to this island?"

He supposed he could lie. Tell her he was only using her, like lustful gods had been using mortals for eons. And after slapping him a few dozen times, she'd probably storm back to the boat and, ultimately, to safety. But in his heart, he knew he couldn't do that. And even if he tried, she'd see right through him. If one thing had been made abundantly clear today, it was that the woman possessed all sorts of powers.

So he gazed back at her, clear-eyed. "Because I love you, Angie. More than anyone in the universe."

She let out a flutter of a sigh, then reached out and took his hand. "Milos, I don't know whether that creature was sent here to kill me or just scare the crap out of me. But when I was looking through the mirror at him, feeling like he could end me any second, do you know what made me buckle down and fight back?"

Milos shook his head, eager for the answer.

"You." She squeezed his hand. "All my life, I've been looking for my soulmate. I know, it's a stupid, girly word, but there's not another word in the English language that nails it better. That perfect fit of chemistry, intellect, and curb appeal. A guy who makes me feel complete when I'm with him and empty and aching when we're apart. Someone who loves me for everything I am and in spite of everything I am. Someone who wouldn't bat an eye at my obsession with Derek Jeter because he's secure enough to know *he's* the only one I'll ever share my heart with. And even though this mystery man has eluded me all my life, I've never stopped believing he was out there somewhere. Waiting for me, like I've been waiting for him."

Milos hung on to her words as if they were the lyrics to some new song that he loved at first listen and wanted to replay every day for the rest of his life.

"And now, here I am," she continued. "On an uncharted island in the Aegean with an honest-to-goodness god who says he's been waiting for me ever since I was a geeky teenager. And it's crazy, every bit of it. But you know what? The more I get to know you, the more I find myself believing you might be *him.* So when that serpent slithered his scaly butt in here, I decided there was no way I was gonna let him keep me from finding out. And now, thanks to my fascination with horror movies and Channing Tatum, I have the opportunity. And whatever risks there might be in spending this beautiful night with you, I'm willing to take them."

She paused for a moment, then gazed hopefully into his eyes. "How about you?"

Milos stared back at her, enthralled by her words, yet leery of them. Really, she was making all the sense in the world. He'd loved her for so long, from such an impossible distance. And now she was finally here, saying all the things he'd always hoped she'd say. And, considering the circumstances, this might be the only opportunity he'd have to make her realize he was indeed, all the things she described.

But was it worth risking her life to find out?

Before he could give it another thought, Angie put her hand around the back of his neck and pulled him in for a long, soulful kiss that was full of hope and promise. And every bit of logic in his head went sailing toward the full moon in the sky.

So he kissed her back with sixteen years worth of pent-up love.

And led her into a room with a bed that hadn't been incinerated.

At least not yet.

EIGHTEEN

Nothing that had happened today could have prepared Angie for the sheer bliss of the next few hours. Not the tenderness of Milos's touch. Not the connections they seemed to share on so many levels. Not the preview of his impossibly fine body she'd been treated to at the waterfall race. Not even the full-throttle passion of the kisses they'd shared.

None of those things compared with making love with him.

When Milos led her into the guest bedroom, which was almost as grand as the master suite had been before she'd torched it, the first thing he did was take her hands in his and gaze earnestly into her eyes. "Are you sure about this, Angie? We can always take it slow."

"Yes," she whispered.

He wrinkled his brow. "Yes, you're sure?"

"Yes, I'm sure. And yes, we should take it slow."

To illustrate her point, she reached up and undid the top button of his shirt, causing him to draw in a breath. Then she coaxed the next button open and parted the shirt to expose the sculpted curve of his pecs. After pausing to pay homage, she resumed her mission, enjoying each and every bit of flesh revealed. There was something deeply erotic about undressing a man, taking total control over him as he stood there, aiming to please. And if she had to guess from the look on his face, it was just as stimulating for him.

"I take it you've done this before," he said through flushed cheeks.

"Actually, I haven't. Up till now, I've practiced on store mannequins."

"No. Really?" The look on his face was priceless.

As was the look on hers when she said, "Psych."

Then came that infectious laugh of his, which was even more appealing because he was half naked. Time to take him all the way there.

After undoing the last button and unveiling his tight little navel, Angie proceeded to take off his shirt. Milos had to help a little, due to the fight those bulging biceps of his were putting up. But they were the only part of him that was even remotely putting up a fight. In fact, as Angie stood there admiring his fully exposed chest, proudly taking credit for the beads of sweat that had cropped up, he took her hand and placed it on the waistband of his trousers.

She smiled. "Gotta love a man who knows what he wants."

"Mmm-hmm," was all he could manage.

It took some doing, but eventually Angie unfastened that pesky metal button. Then she took the zipper between her thumb and forefinger and gently slid it over the bulge in his drawers, which seemed to be growing, thanks to the attention it was getting. She then took hold of the waistband and wriggled his pants down, taking enthusiastic note of the dense black hair on his thighs and legs. Donatello would have creamed to have had this guy as a model.

When she was at ground level, Angie raised her head to find Milos smiling eagerly, like an adolescent who knows he's about to have a sexual experience that'll catapult him into manhood. He then kicked off his shoes, pulled his socks off, and extended a hand to help her to her feet.

She took a deep breath as she placed her hands on the waistband of his boxers. *I'm about to see a Greek god naked. I'm the luckiest woman on the planet.*

Then she slowly pulled his boxers down, pausing at knee level to appreciate the prize that had been revealed. In its friendly state, it was as well-developed as the rest of his body and protruding from a playful patch of black hair. She was tempted to reach out and touch it, but based on the labored breaths he was taking, she figured it might be prudent to hold off.

After helping him step out of his boxers, Angie once again accepted his hand and stood up. "Hello, Milos," she said, drinking in every inch of his naked body.

"Hello, Angie," he replied, as if being gawked at by a fully clothed woman was the most natural thing in the world for him.

If that weren't enough of a turn-on, Milos wrapped his arms around her and pulled her in for a hug that graduated into a long, probing kiss. When she felt him pressed urgently against her thighs, she began rocking gently against him. He responded with a cadence of his own, and a moment later they were grinding against each other like drunken dancers in a honky-tonk. *How much better can things get?* Angie wondered. *Much better,* she suspected.

It was Milos who broke the kiss. Still holding her hands, he took a step back and fixed her with a naughty smile. "My turn."

Then he proceeded to undress her, taking time to celebrate every part of her body with his eyes. He pulled her blouse over her head, then stood there admiring her while her arms were still raised. After gently lowering them to her sides, he unhooked her bra with one deft move, pulled the straps over her shoulders and let it drop to the floor. Then he stood there staring at her. She'd received many compliments over the years about her voluptuous breasts, but the look of wonder in Milos's eyes put them all to shame.

"May I touch them?" he asked her.

Now it was her turn to go all breathy. "Uh-huh."

He cupped a hand under each breast, then slowly rotated his index fingers around her nipples. There was magic in those fingers of his, and Angie fell hopelessly under their spell. She was quivering and moaning and feeling herself grow moist.

Just as she was about to cry out in ecstasy, he stepped back, wrapped his fingers around her belt loops and lowered her jeans to the floor. Then he took off her shoes and caressed her feet. Up till now, she'd never thought of her arches as erogenous zones, but Milos proved her rapturously wrong. Then he rose to his feet, taking a moment to wipe a bead of sweat off his forehead.

Now there was only one more bit of clothing to remove and she'd be as naked as he was. He seemed to sense the significance of the moment, because he gazed into her eyes, searching for any sign of hesitation. And when he saw nothing but an enthusiastic green light, he placed his trembling hands under the elastic of her panties, sending a spasm of pleasure through her. The sensation of his warm skin against her belly was deeply sensual, better than most of the sex she'd had. Did this guy have aphrodisiacs oozing from every pore, or were the two of them cosmically matched?

Then Milos removed her panties—slowly, reverently—pausing once to stare wide-eyed at her. Angie knew her face was beet red, but at the same time, she was full of pride. And when Milos stepped back and took in her naked body, it was like watching a man stare at a work of art by some master sculptor, a work that was as erotic as it was accomplished.

"Beautiful," he said.

Suddenly, tears were running down her cheeks. She'd never felt more desirable in her life.

He was at her side in a second. "Are you all right?"

"Yeah. It's just that … Oh hell, make love to me, Milos."

That was all the encouragement he needed. After wiping her tears away, he took her by the hand and guided her toward the bed.

"Wait," she said, stopping him cold.

"Wait?"

"In my dreams, the handsome prince always carries me to bed."

He smiled. "The prince is happy to indulge the princess."

Milos took her in his arms and carried her to the bed as effortlessly as if she were one of those skinny waifs in *Vogue* magazine. Then he pulled back the comforter and gently laid her down so her head was resting on a pillow. For one silly moment, Angie felt a pang of insecurity, wondering whether she'd measure up to his expectations. After all, Milos was not only an immortal, but had almost a hundred years worth of sexual experience on his resume, with partners that probably included goddesses, sirens, and those freaky-deaky satyresses.

But those fears flew right out the window when he climbed onto the bed and gazed at her lovingly. "You have no idea how long I've waited for this moment."

What do you say to a man who's just said something so heartfelt? Nothing. You pull his body toward you and engage him in a kiss. Once again, Angie felt the pleasure of his skin rubbing against hers as their hands explored each other's bodies. At one point, her fingers slipped across those mysterious scars of his. He seemed to tense up for a moment, but the more she stroked them, the more he seemed to relax, as if her touch were healing them. And just as surely, he was healing her, too. Not just her body, but her heart, erasing any doubts she had about love and sex and how much ecstasy she deserved.

Finally, when she felt she couldn't hold out any longer, she reached down and guided him inside her, feeling him throb with anticipation. At first, he moved tentatively, seemingly encouraging her to pick up his rhythm. Before she knew it, she was doing just that, moving in tandem with him as if they'd been born with this erotic tango programmed into their hearts.

All the while, she was running her hands up and down his back, feeling his muscles ebb and flow, and cupping her hands around his glorious butt, begging him to take her deeper. And each time he did, she matched him thrust for thrust. She wanted to give him everything and take everything he had to give, over and over, until their bodies and souls were so completely intertwined that nothing could pull them apart.

As their rhythm intensified, she was kissing him, fondling him, inhaling him, with a sexual abandon she'd never experienced with any other lover. And just when she felt like she was going to explode from the pleasure of it all, she heard him draw in a breath and make one final thrust. And it seemed to her that they cried out at the same moment.

For a long time, they lay there together in silence, listening to each other breathe. She knew there were questions she needed to ask him. About those scars of his. About his meeting with the Council and what might have been said about her. About how he saw their future playing out beyond tonight. But for now, all she wanted to do was to lay here and luxuriate in the glow of being with him.

At least that was what she thought she wanted to do.

Five minutes later, they were making love again.

NINETEEN

When Angie woke up the next morning, sunlight was pouring through the window, bathing her in a warm, comfy glow. The sheets felt crisp and cool against her naked skin, in spite of the workout she and Milos had put them through.

And what a workout it was. Angie blushed at the memory of not one, but two orgasms, courtesy of her Olympian lover and a few gold medal touches of her own.

Stretching her arms high above her head, she let out a contented yawn, then rolled over to find that the other side of the bed was empty, but still warm. She listened for any telltale sounds from the bathroom, but the only thing she heard were the sparrows chirping outside.

Angie smiled. *They're probably comparing notes on all the wicked things they spied through the window last night.*

And it wasn't just the sex that was making her feel so right with the world. It was the tranquility she'd felt lying beside Milos all night long. The interest he seemed to show in every little thing about her. The feeling she had that the two of them belonged together, like two petals borne of the same rose. And apparently, he felt it, too. Several times during the night, she'd awakened to find him propped up on an elbow, smiling at her. She wasn't sure whether gods slept, but there was something comforting in knowing he was watching over her.

Although she was still sleep-deprived and her muscles ached from her nocturnal exertions, Angie wrestled herself over to the edge of the bed and teetered to her feet. She knew it was silly, but she just had to see him. And plant a kiss on his lips. And wrap her arms around his tight little body.

God, I'm falling hard for this guy. She decided it was perfectly fine to refer to a god as a guy. Probably not as a "dude," but definitely a guy.

After slipping into her clothes and doing a quick spruce-up, she headed out the door. As she made her way down the Scarlett O'Hara staircase, she felt lightheaded. Giddy. Almost as if she were drunk. And all of her senses seemed to be heightened. She could smell the salty sea air and sweet lilacs outside and hear the babbling brook in the living room as if she were already there.

If this is what total satisfaction feels like, I wholeheartedly endorse it.

Halfway down the stairs, she got a whiff of some cinnamony concoction coming from the kitchen and prayed this heightening of the senses would carry over to the taste of food.

"Milos?" she called out at the bottom of the stairs.

"I'll be back in a moment, darling," he replied. "I'm stepping outside to pick us some oranges."

Darling. Had anyone ever called her that before? Maybe, but coming from Milos, it sounded deliciously new and made her feel all warm and fuzzy.

I'm somebody's darling.

And not just any old somebody. Even setting aside the fact that Milos was a god, he was somebody smart and handsome and loving. The kind of man she'd always wished she could have, but never believed was due her. But here they were, the morning after the most passionate sex she'd ever had. And not only had he not hustled her out the door, he was cooking for her, too. Thank goodness she hadn't let her insecurities sabotage things.

"Hurry back, darling," she shouted. She felt those syllables roll off her tongue as if they'd been there all along, waiting for this moment. Someday, she figured, they'd have all sorts of pet names for each other. But she'd always remember the first time they'd called each other "darling."

She glanced down at the brook to find that it was just as lively as the day before, full of colorful fish of all shapes and sizes taking their morning swims. Slipping off her shoes, she waded in, feeling the warm water swirl around her toes. Then she leaned over and ran a hand along the fin of a blue and yellow angelfish with inquisitive eyes. And just like the fish she'd met yesterday, he swam around her in circles, basking in the attention.

Then oddly, he froze in place, as if distressed by something, and disappeared downstream in a burst of speed. Puzzled, Angie looked behind her to discover that the brook, which had been flowing along lazily, was growing more and more turbulent. Seconds later, the source of that turbulence came hurtling into view.

It was an enormous fish, easily five feet long, with orange tentacles that seemed to be undulating all around its head. And it was thrashing toward her so furiously that it was sending choppy waves spilling over the hardwood floor.

Her heart thumping out of her chest, Angie boosted herself out of the brook and started racing toward the kitchen, all the while hearing the splashes grow closer. Just as she was about to scream for Milos, the splashing stopped. She whipped her head around, terrified of what might be behind her. And gasped.

The creature in the brook wasn't a fish at all. It was a woman. A naked woman, who was rising out of the water a few feet away.

Although Angie realized this mystery woman could be just as dangerous as a sea monster, she kept right on staring at her as she climbed out of the brook and shook her head vigorously, raining a volley of droplets across the room. There was no doubt in Angie's mind she was a goddess. Even sopping wet without a stitch of makeup, she was drop-dead gorgeous. She had fierce green eyes, a graceful nose and full, pouty lips with sex written all over them. And her body was voluptuous, yet lean and toned. Like a Barbie doll with nipples and pubic hair—red, to match the flaming locks that swirled around her face like Medusa's snakes.

But she isn't Medusa, is she? No, this homegirl is way too beautiful.

But in many ways, she was just as unsettling as Medusa. Angie had been around the block long enough to be able to read another woman's expressions—from friendly to ready to rumble. Hell, at one time or another, she'd made every one of them herself. And this woman was staring at her with a look of sheer contempt, as if she were trying to burn a hole through her with her eyes. Which, considering the island they were on, just might be possible.

Who the hell is she? And why does she hate me so much?

Although Angie wished she could believe the woman was merely an overprotective friend of Milos, she seemed to be burning too hot for that. Could she be an ex-girlfriend? Or, God help Angie, a current girlfriend? Whoever she turned out to be, Angie had an uneasy feeling this day was about to go from blissful to blustery. So much for the fairytale high she'd been on.

After staring Angie up and down for a good twenty seconds, the woman smiled. But it was a bloodless smile. "Well, how about that?" she said, her every word dripping with venom. "Milos finally took my advice and hired some help."

At that moment, Angie knew two things. One, she hated this woman with a passion usually reserved for Red Sox players. And two, she'd kill to have a body like hers. But she wasn't about to give this red-haired vixen the satisfaction of knowing either of those things.

So she threw her head back and laughed, as if her best friend in the world had just zinged her. "Actually, we talked about it, but Milos hasn't agreed to my price." Then she extended her hand, hoping it wouldn't be bitten off. "I'm Angie, a friend of Milos's. And you are…?"

The woman blinked a couple of times, as if she'd been hit in the head with a tennis ball. But just as quickly, she recovered, extending her long, tapered fingers for a vice-like handshake. "Supremely embarrassed. I should've known you were the famous Angie. Milos has been blathering about you for what seems like forever. It's just that the way you were dressed and, well… *looked,* I assumed…"

Angie felt her right hand twitching with a need to slap the smirk off the woman's face. But realizing she probably wasn't going to win a catfight with a supernatural creature, Angie forced a smile instead. "Careful. You know what they say about people who assume."

"Yes, what's that tired expression? 'They make an ass out of you and me?'"

Angie smiled. "No. Just *you*."

Okay, maybe it wasn't as punishing as a right hook to the cheek, but it definitely landed. The woman's face turned an angry shade of red that rivaled the color of her hair. So why wasn't Angie feeling that familiar surge of adrenalin that usually came from a good ass-whupping?

Probably because deep down inside, she knew this woman was way more than a friend to Milos, and it was killing her. Because the woman was beautiful, and most likely immortal, the kind of woman who—on paper, at least—fit Milos to a T. And sure, he'd declared his love for *her* in a thousand ways since yesterday. But if he had to choose between them, could Angie honestly believe he'd pick an ordinary girl from Queens over one of his own kind? And it wasn't just her insecurities talking; it was thirty years of hard-earned experience.

So what should I do? Walk out the door right now and hold on to a shred of dignity? Talk myself into believing I was the one who did the rejecting?

Like she could ever make herself believe that.

Fact was, she was falling in love with Milos. Hell, she felt more for him after one day than she felt for Nick after fourteen years. Which meant she had to fight for him. Come what may.

And fighting meant surviving the wrath of Fish Woman, who'd gone from merely glowering at her to stalking toward her, nostrils flaring. "You silly girl. Do you have any idea who you're messing with?"

For a quick second, Angie reconsidered bolting for the door. But the scrapper in her wouldn't hear of it. After all, other than the fact that one of them could die and the other couldn't, this was no different from any other playground run-in. It was all about perception— which one of them appeared to have the bigger cajones.

Or so she hoped, because the woman had drawn so close that Angie could smell her perfume—Victoria's Secret Love Spell, which, ironically, was the preferred scent of the neighborhood skanks back home.

After swallowing a chuckle, Angie conjured up her most unfazed expression and pressed her trembling hands against her sides to quiet them. "Actually, I *don't* know who I'm messing with. You seem to know so much about me, but I don't even know your name. Care to enlighten me?"

Once again, the woman seemed taken aback by her spunk, narrowing her eyes in a manner that suggested no mortal had ever stood up to her that way. Then she smiled smugly and said, "Electra," as if it were the most important word in the universe.

Angie thanked her lucky stars her nemesis wasn't one of the heavy hitters like Athena or Aphrodite. Then she tilted her head, affecting a puzzled look. "Hmm. Never heard of a goddess named Electra. Are you sure you're a full-fledged member of the Pantheon?"

"Do you not have eyes?" she retorted, sweeping her hands across her body. "As a matter of fact, I happen to be the daughter of Hades."

Now Angie was sure she'd caught Electra in a lie. "Hold up, girlfriend. Hades doesn't have any children. The Underworld is a place of the dead, so there can't be any new life there."

Electra snickered disdainfully. "Sorry to burst your *Mythology for Dummies* bubble, but my father isn't a slave to the Underworld. I happen to be the product of a weekend he spent in Dresden in 1945. Apparently, watching it burn got him all hot and bothered."

For a moment, Electra's eyes grew distant, as if she were savoring the sick little tale of her conception. Then she shook it off and said, "But let's face it. That's not the most pressing thing on your mind.

So get to it, will you? Because frankly, all this beating around the bush is starting to irk me. And bad things happen when I get irked."

To punctuate her point, Electra aimed a finger at the brook, causing a bluefish to levitate out of the water, his gills heaving all the way. As Angie watched helplessly, Electra first sent him spinning in the air like a pinwheel. Then she floated him a few inches from Angie's face, close enough for Angie to see the terror in his eyes.

Unable to stomach the cruel stunt any longer, Angie reached out to rescue the bluefish. But just as she got her hands around him, he exploded in a torrent of blood and guts, as if a bomb had detonated inside him.

As Angie stood there covered in gore, she realized she was no longer even remotely afraid of Electra. If this was how her life was going to end—at the hands of a jealous deity—at least she'd go down fighting. Wiping the blood out of her eyes, she took a step toward Electra, every muscle primed for combat. "You heartless bitch."

Electra didn't even flinch. "You're calling *me* a bitch? I'm not the one who slept with another woman's fiancé."

Angie felt like she'd been punched in the stomach. "What?"

"You heard me. Milos and I are engaged."

As the declaration swirled around in her head, Angie stood there reeling, barely able to catch her breath. Was it possible that the man she'd just given her body to—as well as a big chunk of her heart— was engaged?! To this she-devil?

It couldn't be true. It had to be some sort of joke. But as she studied Electra's face, Angie saw something she hadn't seen there before.

Pain. Honest to goodness pain.

Angie, on the other hand, felt only numbness. Spreading through her body. Crippling her from head to toe. She opened her mouth to speak, not even sure what she wanted to say.

But Electra wasn't even looking at her anymore. She'd turned her attention toward the kitchen, apparently liking what she saw. "Good morning, dearest."

And there was Milos standing in the doorway. The look of shock on his face quickly turned to anger when he saw the blood on Angie's clothing.

But when he caught her eye, he looked away—a bad sign if there ever was one—and vented his rage on his so-called bride-to-be. "Electra, what have you done?!"

"Nothing at all," she said, as smooth as butter. "Your houseguest and I were having a lovely chat. Till one of your silly fish tried to steal the spotlight."

Grumbling to himself, Milos whipped off his shirt, revealing the bare chest Angie had nestled in just a few hours earlier. Then he walked over and handed it to her, still managing to avoid eye contact. "I'm sorry, Angie," he muttered, sounding a hundred miles away.

Angie wasn't sure what Milos expected her to do with the shirt—put it on over hers, probably. But at the moment, she wasn't feeling such an intimate gesture. So she used it to wipe the blood off her face, then flung it to the floor, fighting off an urge to stomp on it.

By the time Angie looked up again, Electra was strutting her naked body toward Milos, who appeared to be anything but aroused. "Dammit, Electra, why couldn't you stay away?!"

"Because I'm your fiancée," she replied, batting her impossibly long eyelashes. "As I just informed sweet little Angie. Forgive me, I misspoke. Sweet big Angie."

Then, with a malicious smile, Electra wrapped her arms around Milos and rubbed herself against him like a cheap stripper. As Angie stood there, hating herself for the jealous rage boiling inside her, Milos shoved Electra away.

"Not now!" he shouted. "I'm not interested in your games!"

Angie had to wonder if Milos was playing a game with her, too. "So is it true, Milos?! Are the two of you engaged?"

For a long moment, he looked down at his feet, as if he were hoping they'd run him far away from all this misery. Finally, as if it were the most agonizing task in the world, he raised his eyes to meet hers. "I'm sorry, Angie. I *am* supposed to marry her."

If Angie could have blown up the whole house with all three of them in it, she would have done it. She felt humiliated. Used. And sadder than she'd been since her father died. How could the best night of her life turn into such a vile morning? How could something that had seemed so real and passionate turn out to be such a crock?

And Electra was about to twist the knife. "Don't let him kid you, Angie. He's as excited as I am about this marriage. Although I must admit, there were times when I wondered if we were *ever* going to set the date. Men, you know. But just yesterday, we finally made it official: A week from today. I'm getting tingly just thinking about it."

Angie felt the bile rising in her throat. And even though the look on Milos's face seemed to confirm it, she had to hear it from him. "Really, Milos? You set your wedding date yesterday?"

"Yes, but ... Angie, you have to understand—"

She didn't let him finish the sentence. "Was that before or after you fucked me?"

Electra burst out laughing, then gave her what appeared to be a sisterly wink. As much as Angie hated Electra, she could at least understand why *she'd* treated her badly. Goddess or not, she was a woman scorned. Her fiancé had made love with another woman. And that actually made Angie feel sorry for her. But only a little. And it passed like gas.

But what possible justification did Milos have for his behavior, other than that he was a lying, heartless horndog? And the last thing Angie wanted was to let him see her cry, which she was dangerously close to doing. So she picked her shoes up off the floor and headed for the door. She had no idea how she was going to get back to Athens, but she'd swim all the way there if she had to.

Just as she reached for the doorknob, Milos appeared in front of her in a flash of motion that was part supernatural and part desperation. "Angie, wait. Perhaps I don't deserve to be forgiven for the mess I've made. But it's far from what it appears to be. And if you hear me out, you'll realize that hurting you was the last thing I intended."

Angie groaned. Did *every* man have that line in his repertoire? God, how she wanted to slap him. But since she couldn't bring herself to touch him, she hurled her shoes at him instead. One of them missed him completely, glancing off the doorframe, but the other one struck him square in the chest. Right where the bastard's heart would be if he had one.

Yet he remained squarely in the doorway, a stubborn block of granite.

Angie stared back at him, defiant, willing her tear ducts to stay dry. "Milos, I have no interest in whatever stupid apology you're going to concoct, which is probably about making *you* feel better. So do us both a favor and save it."

Still, he didn't move. "Angie, all I'm asking of you is a moment."

Before Angie could respond, Electra let out an exasperated sigh. "For pity's sake, Milos, you're as spineless as one of your jellyfish. Let her go!"

Angie was half hoping Milos would fly at Electra in a murderous rage, if only to free up the path to the door. Instead, he merely stared murderously at her while remaining in place. Clearly, it was time to find another escape route. Angie glanced at the brook, wondering whether he'd try to stop her if she jumped in and swam her way out. Just as she was about to chance it, she caught sight of something in her peripheral vision.

Her shoes. Floating in the air a few inches away. Electra was at it again.

Angie rolled her eyes. "What are you gonna do, Electra, impale me with them? Go ahead. Anything to get me out of here."

"No, silly. I want you to do us both a favor and throw them at his head this time."

Although Angie felt her fingers twitching, the last thing she wanted to do was take the fish goddess's bait. "Sorry. Not interested."

Electra snorted at her, disgusted. "Coward." Then she turned to Milos. "I'll be in the kitchen, laying waste to the Cristal. Feel free to join me when this pathetic melodrama is over."

With that, Electra sashayed away, displaying a perfectly rounded butt she had no right to have. Then, just as she got to the doorway, she turned to Angie with a smile designed to draw blood. "I do hope you'll come back for the wedding. I can always use an extra bridesmaid. Heck, you'd count as two."

Suddenly, Milos's voice thundered out—

"Get out of here, Electra!!!"

229

—so forcefully that it not only scared the crap out of Angie but rattled the windows, created storm waves in the brook and sent Electra staggering into the doorjamb.

For the first time, Electra actually seemed intimidated by him. Fearful, even. But all too soon, that bitchy smile found its way home. "Well, how about that, dearest. You *do* have a backbone."

Then she disappeared into the kitchen, leaving Angie alone with Milos for the first time since he'd left the bedroom this morning. How long ago and far away that seemed. Determined to distance herself even further from him, Angie plucked her shoes out of the air and knelt down to put them on. But just as she was tying the laces, something occurred to her. Something about this whole debacle didn't make sense. And she wasn't about to leave without wrangling an explanation out of him.

Rising to her full height, she said, "Tell me something, Milos. If all you wanted was a roll in the hay, there must've been millions of women who would've obliged, with a lot less trouble than it took to get me. So why'd you do it?"

He stared back at her, clear-eyed. "Because everything I've told you is true. I love you, Angie. I always have."

Choosing to ignore the pesky stirrings in her heart, Angie hit him with the obvious. "But you're marrying that she-fish in the kitchen."

Milos smiled briefly at her jab at Electra, then fixed her with a look that appeared to be both sincere and sorrowful. "Only because it's being forced upon me by my superiors."

Angie groaned. "Come on, Milos. Do you really expect me to believe that?"

"Yes, Angie, I do. And in my defense, it was what I was trying to tell you last night before you silenced me with that kiss."

"Well, maybe you should have tried a little harder."

"You're right, I should have. Suffice it to say it's tied to what we discussed yesterday about the future of the family. Much of it hinges on this union between Electra and me. Are you familiar with the Oracle?"

Angie almost asked Milos if she looked like an idiot to him. Instead, she recited the definition she'd memorized in childhood. "Oracle. A person or place through which the gods speak directly to mankind."

Despite the tension between them, Milos cracked a smile. "A noble effort, but only half true. Sometimes, the gods themselves pay heed to an Oracle, especially when it offers the wisdom of one of our primeval ancestors. For centuries, my superiors sought a definitive answer as to when they should return to their duty of overseeing mankind. Finally, two decades ago, a priestess with unimpeachable ties to Chaos, one of the first beings in the universe, delivered the historic message. According to Chaos, the sacred day of our return would come when the twelve hundredth generation of offspring by Poseidon and Hades had reached maturity. '*As the Twelve led them in the glory days, so shall the twelve hundredth lead them back to glory.*'"

Suddenly, Angie felt like her head weighed a hundred pounds. "Hold up. Are you saying you and Electra are gonna ... lead?"

"In a sense. The two of us have been designated as the vanguards—the face of the family as it moves forward. Zeus and Hera and the Council would, in many ways, still be in control. But we would serve as their liaisons with mankind."

Angie shook her head. "Unfreaking believable."

"I'm sure it *is* overwhelming. But I assure you I'm still the same man you met yesterday. Still in love with you. Still committed to—"

Angie practically bit his head off. "That's not what I'm talking about! I'm talking about the fact that you let me come here knowing it flies in the face of everything that's expected of you. No offense, Milos, but how stupid are you?"

Now it was Milos's turn to snap. "Dammit, Angie, I thought I could change their minds! They've amended Oracles before, and I believed I could convince them to do it again. I thought if they saw us together, and happy, they'd see how thoroughly *right* our relationship is, like every tale of true love they claim to have spun on Earth. But it only raised their hackles. Until yesterday, a date hadn't even been set for this infernal wedding. It was way off in the future. But suddenly, on the heels of your arrival, they decided it would be next week."

He took a moment to collect himself, then shook his head. "I may be a god, Angie. But in many ways, I'm as much their puppet as the mortals they've manipulated for eons."

Although she felt a pang of sympathy for Milos, Angie also found herself questioning his mental temperature. "Seriously, Milos, what loose screw in your head could've ever made you think they'd take *me* over Electra? She may be the bitch of the universe, but she's a full-fledged goddess, and I'm a mortal. It's like trying to talk them into drafting a junior college flunky when they have dibs on the number one draft pick in the country."

Once again, Milos failed to meet her eyes. Instead, his gaze settled on a cluster of sofa pillows. "Trust me. I have my reasons."

Which really sent Angie into a froth. Hadn't she cured him of that annoying habit? "'Trust me?!' Bullshit, Milos. Spell 'em out."

He let out a frustrated groan, then turned to face her. "Believe me, if I could tell you, I would. But I can't, Angie. My hands are tied. But I promise you this. I will never stop fighting until I find a way to be with you forever."

Somehow, that was harder to hear than the most callous of brush-offs. Because if Angie chose to believe it, it would mean Milos really *was* her soulmate. A soulmate who, despite his colossally bad judgment in failing to tell her about Electra, was loving and handsome and brought out a passion in her she'd never felt before. But it also meant that someone far more powerful than Milos was determined to keep them apart. So, in all likelihood, they'd never be able to be together. And what would be sadder than that?

Angie didn't know what to believe anymore. But since being pissed off felt better than being sad, she decided Milos was lying. Right through his pearly white teeth. Trying to pull another one over on the naïve little mortal from Queens. Which meant she should be even angrier with him than she was a few minutes earlier. Earrings off, fists up, ready to go twelve rounds.

So why was it taking so long for that anger to kick in? And why, in the meantime, were tears streaming down her face? And why was he reaching out to comfort her, touching his hand to her cheek? Why was she leaning into his hand, feeling the warmth of his caress, and wondering if maybe, just maybe, she closed her eyes and stopped breathing, everything that had happened in the past hour would go away and things would go back to—

"No!" She grabbed his hand and shoved it away.

He flinched, then held his hands up in a gesture of détente. "Angie, if you'd just listen..."

But there was no way she was going back to that needy place. "Save yourself a lot of grief, Milos, and stop fighting for me. I don't want to see you anymore."

He looked like he'd been slapped across the face. "You don't mean that."

"The hell I don't. Before I met you, I was fine. Free, unencumbered, and having a great time in Athens. But you ruined all that with your head games and fake declarations of love."

He took a tentative step toward her. "Angie, I'm sorry."

She waved him off, then pointed to the door, her hand trembling. "If you have any respect for me, you'll let me go home. Now!"

Milos looked at her for a long moment, seemingly studying her face for any sign of uncertainty. But through her tears, Angie stared back at him unwaveringly. Finally, shoulders slumped in defeat, he willed the doors open.

A blast of sunshine had the cheery nerve to hit her in the face, forcing her to shield her eyes as she walked past him toward an uncertain future. Now that she'd gotten out of the house, how was she going to get across the island and back to the dock?

The question was answered a few seconds later when Eddie fluttered down from the sky and landed on the lawn. As Angie made her way toward the stallion, he let out an affectionate whinny. Then, apparently taking note of her tears, he turned toward Milos, snorted with disgust, and lowered himself to the ground.

At least I've made one friend here, Angie thought.

As she was settling in astride Eddie, Milos called out to her. "When you arrive at the dock, the *Harmonia* will be waiting to ferry you to the mainland."

Without allowing him another look at her tear-streaked face, Angie nodded, hoping that would be the end of it. But as she beckoned Eddie into action with a tug on his mane, she heard Milos's voice again, strong and passionate. "You may never believe me, Angie, but I love you more than anyone on this Earth. And no matter what happens, I always will. For eternity."

She didn't look back at him, even though she could feel his eyes on her. Not then, and not a few moments later when Eddie began galloping away from the house.

And when the stallion rose into the air and flew her over the scenes of the unbelievable events of the past twenty-four hours, Angie didn't look down.

And later, when Mathias greeted her somberly and led her onto the boat, she didn't look back at the island. Not once, all the way to Athens. She prayed she'd be able to do the same thing all the way back to New York.

And keep it up for the rest of her life.

TWENTY

As Milos watched Angie disappear into the morning sky, he felt like the best of him was flying off with her. He was heartbroken and numb, as if his body had shut down in the absence of the thing that had been fueling it all these years. He was angry at himself, too. How had he managed to muck things up so badly? To have finally met her after all these years, spent a magical day with her, and enjoyed the most wondrous lovemaking he'd ever experienced, only to have her flee in a torrent of tears, hurt more deeply than anyone had ever hurt her.

If he had it to do all over again, he'd have sat her down the minute she arrived and laid it all out for her. *By the way, I'm a hundred-and-six-year-old immortal who's been obsessed with you for half your life despite never having met you. I've even watched you from afar without your knowledge, occasionally stumbling upon you at delicate times. Oh, and did I mention I'm being coerced into marrying a cold-blooded goddess, an obligation I may not be able to wriggle out of? So, care for a tour of the island?*

In all likelihood, Angie would have taken the next boat out. But at least she wouldn't have felt so betrayed, so bitterly convinced that the man she'd put her trust in wasn't at all who he'd claimed to be. And he himself wouldn't have come within a whisper of his dreams only to watch them fly away on the wings of an angry stallion.

What was it Tennyson had written? *Tis better to have loved and lost than never to have loved at all.* What a load of manure! Obviously, the fool had never met Angie. Otherwise, Tennyson would be standing alongside him on the edge of this cliff, contemplating the sweet release a leap to his death would bring him.

Sadly, Milos himself would never know such a release, which made him wonder what he was doing here at all. He'd left the house seconds after Angie departed, determined to avoid Electra at all costs. There was nothing she could say that would appease him. Granted, he should have told Angie about her before this morning, but what could have driven Electra to burst in like a bulldozer and lay waste to every good thing that had happened in the past twenty-four hours? It wasn't like she'd been blindsided by Angie's visit. She'd known about Angie for years and seemed comfortable enough with his feelings for her. He'd certainly been accepting of the revolving door of dalliances she'd been having. After all, hadn't they agreed theirs was to be a business relationship with occasional intimacy?

Then again, maybe her father had gotten to her. Hades was almost as fanatical as Electra was about her ascent to power. And if he'd led her to believe her position was in any way threatened by her fiancé's relationship with Angie, she'd blow up like Vesuvius.

Milos's thoughts were interrupted by a chorus of caws. His seagulls were gliding toward him, their wings shimmering in the breeze. When they got closer, they dropped a dozen sea bass at his feet. He raised a palm to the sky to thank them, then felt a pang of sorrow when he realized their leader wasn't going to fly down and perch on his shoulder, as had been their custom for decades.

Because their leader was dead. Killed by Zeus to drive home the point that his young master was to do his bidding or else.

Except that his young master didn't want to do his bidding anymore. Milos didn't want to be their vanguard. Didn't want to marry Electra. Didn't even want to see her again. Now that he knew how idyllic things could be with Angie, he wanted to be with her and her alone. But that was no longer possible. Sixteen years of loving her had come to a quick and ugly end.

So he jumped off the cliff.

And as he did, he sent up a plea to the Fates to make the plunge as agonizing as possible. He desperately needed to feel pain right now. Deserved to, really, for what he'd done to Angie. And if he was lucky, the physical pain would eclipse the emotional pain that was ripping at his heart.

Milos closed his eyes and let his body free fall through the air. After tumbling head over heels for several seconds, he hit an outcropping of rocks and felt the bones in his left leg crack in glorious fashion. Then he continued crashing down the mountain, fracturing his skull in an explosion of white light and breaking his foot so badly that it was pointing backward and shooting spasm after spasm of red-hot agony through his body. All the while, he was smiling.

But even before he hit the water, he felt the bones in his leg threading themselves together. And as he plummeted below the surface, the throbbing in his head began to dissipate, while his foot rotated into position with a click that was audible even underwater.

And yet he was laughing as he popped to the surface. What a melo-dramatic fool he was! Had he really expected his wish to be granted? The Fates were as indifferent to his plight as the gods who supposedly nurtured him. On the bright side, if any of his superiors had witnessed his leap, they'd declare him deranged and unfit for duty.

As the waves carried Milos to the shore, he caught sight of some-one on the beach. And when he drew close enough to see who it was, he groaned, causing him to swallow a mouthful of water.

"S'up, brotha?" Jace warbled, grinning like a Cheshire cat.

Irritated, among other things, by his brother's use of slang, Milos waded out of the water and scowled at him. "What do you want?"

"What do you think I want? I saw Angie fly off on the Eddie Ex-press a minute ago. And even from a distance, I could tell she wasn't a happy camper."

At the moment, neither was Milos. "It's none of your concern."

Jace marched toward him, berating him all the way. "Fine, don't unburden yourself. Just keep jumping off that cliff, hoping for a sick little miracle. Or, you could put a gun to your head and blow your brains out. But five minutes later, when the hole has healed and your brains are tucked back in, you'll still be brooding and joyless, which I guess isn't all that different from any other day in your life."

Milos felt his hands clench into fists. Would it be bad form to strike his brother right now? He settled for getting up in his face. "All right, dammit! Do you want to know what happened? Angie and I had a perfect evening, better than anything I could have imagined. She told me she cared for me and demonstrated it in a thousand ways. And you'll be pleased to know that for once in my brooding life, I was happy. But this morning, before I could tell her about the Oracle,

Electra stormed in and did it for me. And now she thinks I'm the biggest cad in the world."

The color drained out of Jace's face. "Cripers."

"Yes. Cripers," Milos deadpanned.

Jace cupped an unwanted hand on his shoulder. "Look Milos, I'm sure we can figure this out if we put our heads together. Come on, let me buy you a drink. How about some bourbon... on Bourbon Street? Or some port... in Portugal? Do you see where I'm going with this?"

"Straight down the toilet," Milos replied, slipping out from under his brother's grasp.

Jace burst out laughing. "How about that, you made a funny. And if a miracle like that can happen, it'll be a cakewalk to get Angie back. How about we catch her at the airport? I'll be your Cyrano. With your face and my words, she'll be eating out of our hands."

For a moment, Milos actually considered the offer. Then he came to his senses. "Forget it, Jace. Even if Angie *were* willing to take me back, it's better this way. Yesterday at the council meeting, Zeus moved the wedding up to next week. And he made it brutally clear that if I disobey his orders, the hammer will drop on Angie."

Jace winced. "Yeah, I kinda heard about that."

Jace punctuated his remark by popping him on the shoulder, which only served to remind Milos of all the times Angie had done the same silly thing in the course of their day together. And how each time, it had lit a fire inside him.

Seizing on his silence, Jace tried another approach. "Hey, I know everything feels like a suckfest right now. But there has to be a way to get the two of you back together and keep the peace with Zeus.

Maybe we can get Apollo to step up to the plate. It's not like he doesn't have a stake in this."

Milos waved him off. "I'll be fine."

"No, you won't. You've been driving me batshit about this girl for years. You love her, Milos. It's a sickness, I know, but by now it's spread to every cell in your body. Do you really think you can function without her?"

"I do," he lied. The next few words came to Milos as if they'd been written for this moment. "'Tis better to have loved and lost than never to have loved at all."

"That's it?!" Jace was practically frothing. "You're not gonna do anything?!"

What Milos wanted to do was take out his frustrations on Jace. Make him pay for having the poor sense to care about his train wreck of a life. Then it occurred to him there might be a way to do that and much more. "Jace. Brother. How about a game of episkyros?"

Jace's response was swift and sarcastic. "What? You haven't lost enough blood today?"

Twenty minutes later, they were on the ball field, stripping off their clothes alongside a rowdy horde of mortals they'd recruited from the village. Although episkyros was a favorite of the Olympians, Milos usually avoided it because of its brutality. In the course of the average game, teeth were broken, eyes were gouged, and bones were fractured, often in such gruesome fashion that even men with strong stomachs were known to part with their lunches.

But today, Milos felt like indulging all the way. Jace's pep talk had only made him feel worse about Angie. He loved her and always would. And no amount of logic, no rationalization about how she was safer this way, could take away the pain of knowing he'd never look into her eyes again and feel whole. So why not spread the pain around?

And it wasn't like anyone was here against his will. For every man present, there were five more who'd begged to participate. And they weren't just drawn by their love of the game. By Hera's decree, every major injury suffered by a mortal in a game of episkyros earned him an additional year of life. And while it troubled Milos to think men were salivating over the opportunity to suffer the most grievous of wounds, it was a far sight better than the old days, when the residents of the village were treated like chattel to be used and tossed out.

Twenty picks later, they were on the verge of a game.

"Lastly, but certainly not leastly, I pick Erasmus," Jace announced, rounding out his squad. "And not just because his flask is always full."

As if on cue, the old sot took a pull off his battered flask, stumbled over to Jace and handed it to him for a swig. Erasmus was eighty-six now and would live to be at least two hundred. But his body was a road map of scars, unevenly healed fractures and missing fingers and toes that catalogued his lifetime affair with the sport.

Milos motioned toward a thickset mortal in his twenties. "Which means you're with us, Dorian." Affable and hard-hitting, Dorian was nevertheless a fumble-fingers, which meant Milos would take great pains to ensure the man never touched the ball, but instead used that battering ram of a body to carve out a path for the rusher.

As the players ran through their warm-ups, Milos thought back to the days when he and Jace actually played on the same team. Although his big brother had a way of rankling him in every other aspect of their lives, it was a different story when they took to the field together. And it wasn't just because Jace was one of the best athletes on Elysium. The two of them had an uncanny mental short-hand that enabled them to anticipate the perfect moment to throw a block for the other or pass him the ball, even if they weren't in direct eye contact. And while they enjoyed taking each other on in feats like waterfall racing, there was a spirit of fun about it. As they often reminded each other, blood should celebrate blood.

But all that changed sixteen years ago. Milos still couldn't believe Jace had deserted him like that. And to what end? To court the love of someone who had no love to give? Although it hadn't taken Jace long to see the error of his ways and come crawling home, things between them hadn't been the same since. Even now, Milos felt a growl in the pit of his stomach every time he set eyes on his brother. And he hated himself for it, especially since Jace lived with that hostility every day but continued bending over backward to help him, no doubt hoping that one day he'd do something so monumental that things would finally be square between them. And in these moments of self-reflection, Milos wondered if he was any more evolved than their father.

But for the next few hours, he'd put all that out of his head. If his team prevailed, the victory would be even sweeter because he'd vanquished his brother and reminded him of his transgressions. And if Jace's team managed to win, it would fuel those hostilities, allowing them to live and breathe another day.

"Listen up, everybody," Jace called out. "Since I drew first, it's my privilege to dictate the rules of this skirmish. The first team to cross the opponent's goal ten times wins, either by carrying the ball, booting it, or heaving the ball carrier over. Punching, poking, slapping, scratching, spanking, elbowing, spitting, kicking, kneeing, biting, gumming, and gouging are strictly encouraged, and style points will be awarded for the most original bruise. Remember, good sportsmanship is for chumps and Catholics."

That provoked a wave of laughter from the players. It would be the last time they'd laugh as a group. The moment the game began, they'd be bitter enemies, inflicting unspeakable punishment on one another, often in the hope that their adversaries would return the favor. It was a sick, twisted game, and Milos couldn't wait to immerse himself in it.

And as usual, neither could Jace. In a display of exuberance that fell somewhere between cheerleader and hooligan, he slapped his hands together and shouted. "All right, miscreants! Are we ready to rumble?!"

"Yes!" they shouted back.

Jace made a face. "Hmph. Sounds more like you're ready to *rumba,* which I'm happy to do later this evening. But right now … ARE WE READY TO RUMBLE?!"

"YES!" They screamed boisterously enough to shake the portholes of passing ships.

"All right, then. *Kyklos!*"

With that, the two teams formed the traditional *kyklos* or circle at midfield, locking arms with their teammates, but leaving a space on each end. Then they sent up a guttural chant that grew louder when the referee stepped to the sidelines and hurled the ball high above them. Straight away, the violence began, with players pummeling each other in a struggle over possession. One young fellow who leapt in the air to grab it was rewarded with a paralyzing kick to the privates. When he collapsed to the turf in the fetal position, the ball rolled into the outstretched hands of Erasmus. But he only managed a few steps before a clout to the back of the head caused him to cough it up, along with a mouthful of blood.

"Slime of the Earth!" he croaked as he dropped to the ground, where he was trampled matter-of-factly by a mob of players lusting over the ball.

By this time, Milos's body was dappled with blood. And although none of it was his, it was feeding his desire to score the first goal. So when Jace's fleet-footed teammate, Petros, tried to bolt past him with the ball, Milos plugged him in the ribcage. But the son of a bitch not only held on, he sent Milos to the ground with a powerful shove.

Regardless, Milos was not to be denied. Taking full advantage of the "no rules" rule, he conjured up a brick wall directly in front of Petros. And when the hapless ball carrier slammed into it and crumpled to the turf, Milos plucked the ball out of his hands and deconjured the wall.

"Sorry, Petros!" he shouted back at him. "I'll see if I can get you an extra year for that!"

As Milos barreled downfield, he had to shake off a defender who'd sunk his teeth into his backside, juke to his right to avoid a patch of quicksand Jace had conjured up, and leap over two players who were rolling around throttling each other.

But it looked as though his efforts were going to pay off. The goal line was only a few yards away, and there was no one in front of him.

Unfortunately, Milos didn't have eyes in the back of his head. A pair of hands clamped around his left ankle from behind, threatening to bring him down inches from the goal. He tried to shake them off, but they held on like cast-iron fetters.

"You're going down, brother!" his unseen tormenter called out.

Which turned out to be Jace's undoing. Fortified by his animus, Milos channeled every ounce of energy inside him toward the top half of his body. Then he tucked the ball between his thighs and pressed his palms to the ground while swinging his legs above him with Jace still clinging to one of them. And when Jace lost his grip and careened over him, Milos tucked his body into a reverse somersault and spun over the goal line for the score. And even though he landed facedown on the hard earth and fractured his jaw, he knew the pain would pass. The important thing was that he'd scored first and set the momentum for the game.

So why wasn't he feeling the electric charge that always came from outsmarting his brother? Why instead was he wishing Angie were here so he could see the proud look on her face and feel her arms around him as she swept him into a hug?

As Milos was mulling that over, something else occurred to him. His teammates weren't cheering for him. Not a single hurrah. And Jace and his cronies weren't slinging the usual epithets about cheating and dumb luck. As Milos lay there on the ground, his jaw throbbing with pain, there was only silence … and then a wolf whistle. What in Hades was going on?

After wrenching his jaw back into place, Milos picked himself off the ground and followed the turned heads to the other side of the field, where a familiar figure stood, hands on hips, as if a bank of paparazzi were poised to take her picture.

"Hello, dearest," Electra said, as if the morning had never happened.

Milos stared venomously at her, never hating her flaming red hair more than he did at the moment. "I have nothing to say to you, Electra."

"Silly boy. I'm not here to talk. I'm here to play."

Milos regarded her with well-founded suspicion. "Why?"

"Does a girl need a reason to get in a scrum with a bunch of naked men?"

With that, Electra kicked off her stilettos and pulled her sleeveless mini-dress over her head. Then she stood there, as naked as they were, daring them not to ogle her. But of course, every man did. A few of them even became aroused, only one of whom bothered to cover his shame. And although Milos himself wasn't feeling anything remotely approaching lust, he couldn't deny that her body was a Botticelli come to life. Full, round breasts, a tapered waist, and hips that were so voluptuously sculpted they practically cried out to be straddled.

Still, she had no business being here, which Milos was only too happy to explain. "Sorry to disappoint you, Electra, but we're full up with players."

"Are you?" Electra pointed to Erasmus, who was lying nearby with a bone sticking out of his leg. "I don't think he's going to make it through the next minute, let alone another play."

To fortify her point, Electra marched over to the old man and stomped on the bone, causing him to cry out in pain.

"That should count, dammit!" Erasmus said through a grimace. "One more year!"

As Milos started toward Electra, prepared to dish out some pain of his own, Jace planted a hand on his shoulder. "What do you say, Milos? I *am* down one player. Or would you rather have your slim chance at victory tainted by the fact that you lost to an undermanned team."

Milos was about to cuss his brother out in a dozen languages when Jace spoke directly into his head. *Don't you realize what a gift this is? Can we say 'catharsis'?*

Milos blinked a couple of times. As much as he hated to admit it, Jace was right. It was the prospect of violence that had led him to propose this game. To provide himself a socially acceptable means of venting his frustrations over losing Angie. Could there be anything more satisfying than unleashing them on the harpy who'd set the whole thing in motion?

Milos gave Jace a shrug. "If you want her, she's yours." He almost added a mental "thank you," but decided not to build up his brother's ego at such a critical point in the game.

Jace locked eyes with him, smiled, then motioned toward Electra. "Welcome to the team, Lexie. Let's kick some fully exposed ass!"

This time, the referee's toss was followed by a melee so brutal that five men suffered game-ending injuries before the ball settled in anyone's hands. In Milos's eyes, much of that was due to Electra. Her presence seemed to have worked the other players into a hormonal frenzy. And she was playing more viciously than any of them, leading Milos to wonder whether she was exorcising demons of her own. Or one demonized fiancé in particular.

Eventually, Petros took possession of the ball, neutralized a pesky defender with a thumb to the eye, then heaved the ball downfield to Jace. Jace tore off a good twenty yards before meeting up with a wrecking ball by the name of Dorian who head-butted him into a stupor and stole the ball.

But Dorian would wish he never had. With a warrior's cry that cut through the air like a machete, Electra leapt onto his back and clawed his cheeks with her fingernails. And when that bit of bloodletting wasn't enough to take him out, she bit off a chunk of his ear.

As Dorian dropped to his knees screaming something about motherless bitches, Electra pried the ball out of his hands and whispered into his good ear. "For future reference, I do have a mother. But you got me on the bitch part."

Then Electra sprinted down the field, moving more like the off-spring of Achilles than Hades. As Milos barreled toward her from thirty yards back, he watched her take out every blocker who threatened her. She was closer to the goal now than Milos was to her, and under normal circumstances, he wouldn't have a prayer of catching her. But his anger was fueling him like a coal fire until he was moving so fast his feet barely touched the ground.

The twenty yards that separated them became ten. Then five. Four. Three.

Just as Milos was about to reach out and grab Electra, she did something stunningly unexpected.

She stopped in her tracks, turned around, and smiled.

Unable to halt his own momentum, Milos slammed into her, sending them both crashing to the ground. As he lay on top of her, confused and panting, she winked at him. "You just can't keep your hands off me, can you?"

Then she fluttered a hand through the air, rendering their twenty mortal witnesses deaf, dumb, and blind. As Milos watched, appalled and angry, the players stumbled around the field in confusion, banging into one another and letting out silent howls of fear. Only Jace remained untouched by the spell.

Milos whipped his head around to confront Electra. "What in blazes did you do that for?"

"Because we need a moment alone, dearest. Free from prying eyes. And if Jace knows what's good for him, he'll act as if he's been stricken, too."

Jace rolled his eyes and stalked a few yards away.

Milos stared disbelievingly at her. "You can't possibly think I want to kiss you right now."

"Goodness, no. I think you want to hit me. So go ahead. Flail away."

Milos had to give Electra credit. What she lacked in restraint, she made up for in intuition. Still, he hesitated, wondering whether the fact that she *wanted* him to punish her took away its appeal. Then he felt the rage that was still burning in his belly and realized he had his answer.

He was going to punch her, square in the mouth, and it was going to feel good. And why shouldn't it? This was the woman who'd exalted in hurting Angie. The punishing shrew who'd ruined the best day of his life, and in so doing, reminded him how little freedom he had.

Raising his shoulders off the ground, Milos squeezed his right hand into a fist, stared into Electra's taunting eyes, and swung with all his might . . .

. . . straight into the ground beside her, causing the Earth to shake so violently that several players were knocked to the turf, adding to their torment.

Milos rose to his feet, grumbling all the way. He hated himself for it, but he couldn't bring himself to strike her.

Electra was on her feet in a white-hot flash. "Dammit, Milos, hit me! I deserve it!"

"Why? For what you did to Angie?"

"Of course not. I'm still kicking myself for not eviscerating her when I had the chance." She fired the ball at him, striking him in the chest. "For falling in love with you, dammit!"

Milos responded with a dubious stare. "What kind of game are you playing, Electra?"

"I *wish* I were playing a game. At least I'd have control over that." Her voice collapsed into a whisper. "It's true, Milos. I'm in love with you. Hopelessly, stupidly, irretrievably in love with you. Emphasis on stupidly."

She gazed at him unblinkingly, challenging him to look into her eyes and see anything other than the truth. And when he didn't, a wave of unease hit him. "But ... how?"

She threw her arms up into the air. "How? What a stupid question. I don't know how. It was probably festering in there for years, feeding off every good thing you did for me. All I know is that yesterday, when I found out *she* was here, a rage rose up inside me I didn't think I could feel for anyone, least of all that cow. And when I watched you make love with her, I wanted to die."

"You watched us?!" Now Milos really wanted to hit her.

"Get off your high horse. You've been watching *her* for years. Yes, I watched you. It was written all over your face, and in every last thrust. You were lost inside her, in a way you've never been with me. And I'm the best lay in the world."

Electra planted her hands on her hips, as if she were daring him to contradict her. Milos gazed at her for a moment, then felt another pair of eyes on him. He looked to his right to discover Jace staring a hole in him, no doubt trying to get a read on where this revelation was going to lead.

Unable to enlighten him, Milos returned his attention to his fiancée. "I had no idea you felt that way, Electra. Otherwise, I would have sat you down and explained—"

"Don't patronize me! This is humiliating enough already. I hate you right now. And I hate *her*. But mostly, I hate myself. For being such a fool."

A single tear formed in Electra's eye, cleared her lower lid and trickled down her cheek. With a feral growl, she wiped it away and flung it to the ground as if it were a treacherous invader. Then she turned her back on him, possibly out of fear that her emotions would betray her again.

Milos struggled to hold on to his anger. He couldn't deny she'd done a terrible thing to Angie. But now that he knew what had driven her, he could no longer cast her as a scheming gorgon. She was a woman with a heart, which in and of itself was a revelation. And one day that heart had gone rogue and started beating for him, despite the fact that his own heart belonged to someone else. Under the circumstances, how could he not feel sorry for her?

But now that he knew how she felt, what was he going to do about it? Tell her to get over him because he'd never feel the same about her? All he knew was that he was seeing a side of Electra he'd never seen before. Raw. Vulnerable. Dare he say, human.

Milos kept his distance for as long as he could. Then he walked over to Electra and gently rested a hand on her shoulder.

She spun around defiantly. "You're a fool, Milos. For all your so-called intellect, you don't seem to understand how powerful a partner I can be for you. Or how dangerous an enemy."

Then, to his surprise, she wrapped her arms around his waist and pulled his body close to hers. For once, there was nothing sexual in it. It was as if she were a child who needed to feel the warmth of another soul to recover from the sting of a heartless world.

As Milos stood there, holding Electra almost as tightly as she held him, he heard Jace's voice in his head, delivering a message for his ears only. *This isn't what you want, and you know it.*

Maybe not, Milos silently replied. *But it might be what I deserve.*

Jace didn't say another word. But Milos had a sneaking suspicion his brother didn't consider the subject closed. Not by a long shot.

And that worried him.

TWENTY-ONE

"So … what? You wanna get back together? Is that what you're saying, Ang?"

"I don't know what I'm saying. I just want things to be the way they were, before … you know."

God, ten minutes with Nick and I'm already talking like him, Angie thought. *But it's okay. It really is.*

And really, it was. She was back home where she belonged. Among real people, not cartoon superheroes with killer looks and nothing under the hood. Real people who cared about her—some of whom actually loved her. And who'd never, ever hurt her the way a certain nobody had. A nobody who could rot in Hades for all she cared. Scratch that: rot in *hell.* More likely, he wouldn't have any friends there.

Had she thought about him over the past few days in between job interviews—and sometimes during them? Sure. But that was only natural. It *had* been a pretty over-the-top experience. And that was the problem. It was too over the top. Twenty-four hours crammed to the rafters with eerie, magical, terrifying, triumphant, passionate, painful moments. In a normal life, those kinds of extremes might be spread out over a decade or two. But they'd been hurled at her like a thousand fastballs out of a runaway pitching machine. It wasn't real. Life wasn't like that.

"How about I get the waiter over here?" Nick offered. "Maybe after a few meatballs and a shot of grappa, you'll clear the cobwebs out of that pretty head of yours."

Now *that* was a compliment. A real compliment from a real man. Not some starry-eyed declaration about the sun, moon, and stars shining out of your keister. Granted, some of Milos's fawning had gotten to her. But that was only because she'd been coming off such a low ebb in her life. And there was no denying the fact that the face behind those declarations had been nice to look at. What girl wouldn't want to buy such beautiful lies when they were coming from such a beautiful source? But she was a woman, not a girl. And a woman should know better. And if she doesn't, then she deserves to have the crap kicked out of her.

"Yo, buddy," Nick called out. "We're ready to order over here."

And so what if the sex had been great. Sex isn't everything in a relationship. Things like honesty and trust tend to carry a little weight, too. Heck, for all Angie knew, maybe the sex hadn't been good at all. Maybe the air on that island had heightened her senses. Or maybe there was an aphrodisiac in the wine or the food or those freaky color-shifting flowers. Or maybe—and this was very plausible—Milos had cast a spell on her to only make it seem like it was the best sex she'd ever had. He *was* a god, after all. They were notorious for that kind of trickeration. Maybe in reality, the sex had only lasted a minute and he was hung like a parakeet.

And the intimacy she'd felt with him afterward? The feeling that they just *fit* together, as if the whole thing had been plotted out while she was in the womb?

Nothing more than post-sex endorphins.

Meanwhile, here she was at her favorite restaurant in the world, Angelo's of Mulberry Street, about to indulge in her favorite food, rigatoni marinara with not one, but two mouthwatering meatballs. The real things, not those pale pretenders they served on the island. And truth be told, a good meatball trumps good sex every time. And it doesn't leave you feeling like a sucker.

"Wanna get the prosciutto and mozzarella to start?" Nick asked her.

"Sure, what the heck." It wasn't like she needed to watch her figure around Nick. He'd put on a good ten pounds since she'd last seen him. But it looked okay on him, although it probably wouldn't hurt him to go up a size in T-shirts. His belly button was cute, but not everybody in the place needed to see it.

"And what's that wine you like, Ang? Pinot gigolo?"

"Pinot *grigio*." Angie chuckled. Nick's malapropisms were legendary. When they were kids, he often talked about how much he liked to ride the "casserole" in Central Park. And for years, he swore the lyric of the old Elton John song was, "Hold me closer, Tony Danza."

"You know what, buddy?" Nick said to the waiter. "We'll take two pinots along with the grappa. I feel like expanding my horizons tonight."

"Good for you, sir." The waiter, whose name was Dante, had been working at Angelo's ever since Angie was a little girl and used to come in with her folks when they could afford it. In her eyes, Dante endured Nick like he endured everything life had thrown at him—with patience and grace. Plus, it didn't hurt that he knew she'd never let Nick give him anything short of a great tip.

As Dante started to walk away, Nick shouted to him. "Yo, I can switch it for a beer if I don't like it, right?"

"No problem, sir," he said with a charitable smile that was obviously meant for Angie.

"You're the best, Dante," she called out. "Oh, and say hello to Linda for me. I hope that new hip of hers finally figured out who's boss."

After Dante headed off, Nick turned to her with a constipated look on his face. And just stared, as if he thought the mysteries of the universe could be found in the pattern of her pores.

It didn't take her long to get antsy. "What?!"

"You look good, that's all."

Angie felt her cheeks flushing. "Really?"

"Hell, yeah. That tan you got in Greece makes you look, I don't know, tribal. And I like the way the sun streaked your hair up, like somebody went crazy with a paintbrush."

Somebody actually had, at a funky little salon in Athens. But Angie wasn't about to tell him that. She just allowed herself to bask in the glow of the compliments, something Nick had never been known for. Maybe things really were changing for the best.

She patted his hand. "Nice of you to say so, Nick. You've lost weight, haven't you?"

"You're the first one to notice," he said proudly.

For a moment, they just sat there smiling at each other, like the two kids who used to tear open their baseball card packs together and compare the treasures they found. And Angie got a lump in her throat thinking how comfortable it felt being with Nick. Like there was nothing to prove, or even aspire to.

Finally, Nick sat back in his chair, folded his arms across his chest and grinned. "So ... I guess you realized what a mistake you made, walking away from all this."

Angie had to laugh, and not just at the hollow sound Nick's belly made when he slapped it. God bless him, he'd read her mind. And as far as she knew, he didn't have superpowers like a certain nobody she'd once crossed paths with.

"Maybe so, Nick," she said. "But at the time, it felt like the right thing to do—for you *and* me. Call me crazy, but I thought I wanted more."

"More?" His face deflated like a lanced balloon.

"Different." She leaned in close. "You know me better than just about anybody. And I don't want to lose that. At the very least, I'd love it if we could hang out like this."

Nick's eyes lit up hopefully. "And at the very *most*?"

"How about we take it day by day?"

And when Nick nodded in agreement, Angie told him the thing that had been bugging her for months. "I promise you this. Whatever happens, I will never again put you in a position where you're watching me run off down the aisle. I'm so sorry about that."

He waved it off. "S'okay. But you better believe if we ever get to the altar again, I'm gonna have a Glock tucked into my waistband."

As crude as it was, Angie couldn't deny it was funny. Maybe it had something to do with what had happened to her on the island. When you've gone up against a vicious serpent and slowly burned him to death, the image of a little gun mayhem seems tame by comparison.

"Fair enough," she said, clinking her just-arrived shot glass with his. In truth, Angie didn't have a clue how far she wanted things to go with Nick. For now, she was content to let these ordinary moments wash over her and remind her that life doesn't have to be some grand Technicolor production with a sweeping score and a cast of glamorous characters. Sometimes black and white is just fine.

Not according to Ya-Ya, of course.

Naturally, Angie had gone to see her grandmother straight from the airport the other night, craving major doses of comfort and enlightenment.

The moment the cab pulled up to the door, Ya-Ya was down the steps, wrapping her in a hug. "Oh, sweetie, I've missed you so much."

"Lucy, you got some 'splainin' to do," Angie whispered in her ear, determined to start things off on a light note. But in a matter of seconds, she was blubbering all over Ya-Ya's silk kimono, releasing the tears she'd been holding inside all the way across the Atlantic. Ya-Ya held her for a moment, then led her up to her rooftop garden—which Angie couldn't imagine ever calling "Elysium" again. And there they sat, under the creamy light of a three-quarter moon, fortified by a pitcher of mojitos, a plate of lamb sliders, and pita chips with homemade tzatziki dip. Clearly, Ya-Ya had hauled out the big guns.

And although Angie had given Ya-Ya a brief post mortem from Athens, there were still so many things to say. So many questions to ask her.

Starting with, "Ya-Ya, did you know Milos was engaged?"

"Yes," she replied without hesitation.

Angie sighed. All the way to New York, she'd been praying the answer would be "no." Because that would absolve Ya-Ya of any responsibility for the anguish she'd been through. But in her heart of hearts, Angie knew her grandmother had been aware of it. Throughout the whole episode, Ya-Ya had been handing out information on a need-to-know basis, as if the trip were some sort of romantic scavenger hunt. But to have neglected to tell her that the gorgeous god who'd romance her on the island belonged to somebody else was downright inexcusable.

And before Angie knew it, she was yelling at her. "How could you do that to me, Ya-Ya? How could you send me there to get my heart broken?"

For a moment, Ya-Ya looked wounded and frail, and Angie wanted to crawl into a hole and die. But just as quickly, that wounded look turned into an admonishing stare. "Angie, I know you're exhausted, but I don't appreciate you taking that kind of tone with me."

"I'm sorry." Angie willed herself to take a deep breath and remember that Ya-Ya was her biggest cheerleader. "It's just been a really crappy couple of days."

Ya-Ya seemed to consider that for a moment, then asked her, "Was it all crappy, sweetie?"

Angie narrowed her eyes. What in the world had gotten into her grandmother? Where was her compassion? Her intuitive understanding that her granddaughter was hurting? Where was her *mea culpa*, for godsakes?

But clearly, there was little to be gained by alienating her with another outburst. "Of course not, Ya-Ya. The island was amazing. Like *Fantasia* come to life. I've never seen so many beautiful things in one place."

"And Milos?"

Angie smiled. Far be it from Ya-Ya to dance around the point. "Yes, he was one of them—at first. Handsome. Easy to talk to. Fun, once he loosened up. And full of wonderful things to say about me—like that he loved me and always had. And he really had me believing it. Thinking he might be the one I've been looking for all these years."

Angie let out a sigh. "I made love with him, Ya-Ya. Gave him my heart. And the next morning, I find out he's getting married. Who does that to somebody?"

Before the first tear ran down Angie's cheek, Ya-Ya had already placed a tissue in her hand. And for the second time since getting out of the cab, Angie let the waterworks flow, while promising herself this would be the last time she'd ever let a man get under her skin. She only let up when she heard Ya-Ya's voice.

"He does love you, Angie. Everything he told you is true."

Angie stared blearily at her grandmother. "And you know this, how?"

"Apollo told me years ago." She tossed out the name so casually she might as well have been saying Bill or Henry. "He was envisaging me one evening a long time ago when you and your parents were here. Milos happened to walk in on him in the midst of it, and Apollo allowed him to share the vision. And you were young, barely a teenager, entertaining us with that Madonna impersonation of yours. But Milos saw something in you that stayed in his heart forever."

Unfortunately, Angie couldn't summon the same mushy sentiment that was all over Ya-Ya's face. "And you don't think that's the least bit pervy? Watching somebody like that?"

"At first, maybe. But in time, I came to see it as reassuring. Like there was somebody out there who was always keeping me safe."

Ya-Ya gazed off dreamily into the distance, looking like one of those old prayer cards of Saint Emily when she was in the presence of God. At that moment, Angie knew beyond a doubt that the true love of Ya-Ya's life wasn't her late husband at all.

Despite her frustration, Angie felt a rush of emotions for her grandmother. The old girl had had a deeply romantic experience in Elysium, one that had stayed with her to this day. And in her wonderful, caring way, she'd sent *her* there years later hoping lightning would strike twice.

Inching her chair closer to Ya-Ya's, Angie put her arm around her and kissed her on the cheek. "He was very special to you, wasn't he?"

Ya-Ya's eyes were brimming with tears. "He saved my life, Angie. Changed me in more ways than I can count."

Now it was Angie's turn to take a tissue out of the box and pass it along. "Are you still seeing him?"

"We've kept in touch."

But there was something about the way Ya-Ya said it that set off Angie's radar. "Ya-Ya, what happened? Did they force him to marry some bitch-goddess, too?"

Ya-Ya took a deep, bracing breath, as if she were about to say something profound. Then apparently, she thought better of it. "Those sliders are going to get cold, you know."

Angie snatched one off the plate and downed it in one perturbed bite. Then she cleared her throat and gave Ya-Ya the full benefit of her probing green eyes.

And it worked, sort of. "I'll tell you all about it, I promise," Ya-Ya said. "But can we stick with you for a minute?"

"Fair enough," Angie replied in a "you asked for it" tone. "So why *didn't* you tell me Milos was getting married?"

"Would you have gone if you'd known that?"

"Of course not."

"See?"

"I also wouldn't have gotten my heart broken."

Ya-Ya smiled lovingly and brushed a stray curl out of Angie's eyes. "Sweetie, I know it must've hurt terribly. And I'm so sorry for that. But did you really get your heart broken, or did you have it opened up to a dazzling possibility?"

In Angie's mind, this line of questioning called for a liberal sip of mojito. So she took one, then set her glass down and stared intently at Ya-Ya. "What are you getting at, woman?"

"Do you love him?"

Angie groaned. "What difference does it make?"

"A great deal, actually. If you really, truly love him, there's a way. *I* believe it, and so does Apollo."

"Really?" Angie retorted. "Does he have some sort of magic scepter for me to use on Zeus? Couple of zaps to the cajones and he'll shrug off his grand plan? 'Sure, Milos, go ahead and marry that commoner. We can wait another thousand years to take over the world.'"

It was as if Ya-Ya hadn't even heard her. "You know, people think that if love is true, you don't have to work for it. It's just dropped into your lap, like a big, shiny prize. But most of the time, that isn't the case at all. Love is hard, Angie. Damn hard. And yes, sometimes you have to roll up your sleeves and fight for it."

Angie couldn't believe what she was hearing. "And that's what you expect me to do? Fight the king of the gods to get this guy? A guy who didn't even care enough to be up front with me about his situation? Why would I do that? Why would you want me to do that?"

Ya-Ya put her hands on Angie's shoulders and gazed into her eyes. "Because you and Milos are meant to be together."

Angie let out a frustrated sigh. "Well, I'm sorry. But I'm through getting hurt."

And although it felt like she was closing the door on something that had nourished her all her life, Angie gently removed Ya-Ya's hands from her shoulders and stood up.

"Thanks again for the trip, Ya-Ya. Good night."

"Angie, please."

Angie knew if she stayed another minute, she'd say something to hurt her grandmother more than she already had. So she kissed her on the forehead and began her retreat through the rose garden.

But Ya-Ya wasn't finished with her yet. "Believe me, Angie, I don't want you to get hurt either. But I also don't want you to miss out on something that could make you happy for the rest of your life. You deserve the best, sweetie. You have no idea how special you are."

Although every shred of reason inside Angie told her she should keep on walking, she couldn't let that remark pass without comment. She turned around to face her grandmother, who was now standing a few steps behind her. "You know, Ya-Ya, you've been saying that for as long as I can remember. Always telling me how special I am. That I was meant for great things. Well, guess what? I'm not special. I'm fat and I'm average and I'm okay with that. It's time for you to be, too."

Angie blew out an angry puff of air, which caused the roses around her to shift through an array of colors, from maroon to fuchsia to salmon and back to maroon again. Under the circumstances, it was anything but a magical sight. "These are from that damn island, aren't they?"

Ya-Ya pointed to the empty chairs behind them, indicating they should sit back down. "Angie, there are so many things I need to tell you."

"No," she said, holding out her arms for emphasis. "I love you, Ya-Ya, but I think I need some space."

With that, Angie turned around and walked out, her heart aching at the disappointment she knew she was leaving behind her.

That was two days ago, and she hadn't heard from Ya-Ya since. She'd half-expected Ya-Ya to show up at her door with a bottle of Limoncello and a plea for "five minutes of your time." Or barring that, a witty text message aimed at softening her up. But for now, it was better this way. Sure, she missed Ya-Ya, but the poor woman would only be wasting her breath if she tried to change her mind about Milos. And at her age, she didn't need that kind of stress.

In any case, Angie figured, she'd give it a week, then call her and ask her to lunch. With any luck, Ya-Ya would've already decided to hang up her matchmaking hat, and they could go back to the way things were before she'd ever heard the name, "Milos." And every day from there, the incident would grow dimmer and dimmer in their memories until it was no more than a blip. For Angie's part, it was already starting to feel like a bad dream she'd had after too many mai tai's.

Which reminded her she should order another glass of wine. She'd really been sucking them down tonight. But it was all in the spirit of celebration, wasn't it? She was patching things up with Nick and enjoying a festive bowl of pasta, which meant there was no better place in the world to be than this little table in Little Italy.

She only hoped Milos was watching her now. *Eat your heart out, god-man,* she thought. *I'm happy.* And she was determined to stay happy, no matter how much effort it took.

"Jumpin' Jesus, what do they put in these things?" Nick said through big bites of meatball.

"Pork, ground beef, veal, eggs, breadcrumbs, and a pinch of medicinal pot," Angie replied.

Nick practically dropped his fork. "Really?"

"Psych." It was always such a kick to mess with Nick. The poor guy could be so gullible, unlike a certain nobody back in Greece. Granted, she *had* punked Milos a couple of times, but who was to say his reactions were real? The bastard knew her so well from all the spying he'd done on her that his every move was probably calculated to reel her in.

But why was she wasting her time thinking about Milos? There were meatballs to conquer. And not just on *her* plate.

"Hey, isn't that Heidi Klum?" she said, pointing across the room.

Nick shot to attention—"Where?"—and whipped his head around, allowing Angie to snare half a meatball out of his bowl.

When Nick turned back to the table, it didn't take him long to spot the dent in his pasta where the meatball used to be. "I'm gonna get you for that."

"I hope so," Angie said with a wink.

Which didn't quite get the reaction she'd expected. Nick took a pull on his beer, then leaned in purposefully. "Listen, Ang. There's a little wrinkle in this taking-it-day-by-day-thing we're talking about. You know your cousin, Sylvie?"

"I hope so. We were practically raised together."

Nick let out a halfhearted chuckle. "Remember back at the hospital, when you gave me permission to ask her out? Well, I did, and we've kind of been seeing each other."

Naturally, Angie had heard all about it from her mother, her grandmother, and a large contingent of the greater Greek community. But what of it, really?

"And you want to know if it's okay to keep seeing her?"

Nick took her hands in his. "Don't get me wrong. She doesn't have half your personality and none of your brains. And you're better looking, especially with the tan and that streaky hair."

Suddenly, Angie knew where Nick was going with this, and she felt a rush of warmth for the big guy. "Aw, but you don't want to hurt her feelings, do you?"

"Yeah, that. And she's dynamite in the sack. So I thought, 'Hey, if Ang isn't sure where this is going, why put a cork in *that*?' Life is short, and if I've learned anything over the past few months, it's that nothing's guaranteed—even something as simple as a walk down the aisle with a girl you've been seeing since forever. Meanwhile, there's Sylvie. So perky and … gifted. I mean, she must be double-jointed 'cause—"

"Sure," Angie said, cutting him off before he could get into specifics about Sylvie's sexual technique. "No problem."

"Really?"

"Really."

Nick gave her a pop on the shoulder. "Thanks, Ang. That trip to Greece really matured you."

"Yeah, it did," Angie said, popping him back.

And damn if she didn't mean it. Sure, there was a small part of her that felt slighted. But she was the one who'd walked out on Nick.

She couldn't have expected him to live like a monk all this time, pining over her and praying she'd come crawling back. Besides, this would keep things at a healthy distance. They'd have a friendly relationship—with some intimacy, maybe—but as long as Sylvie was in the picture, nobody would be rushing things or insisting on saying those three dreaded words. It was all very modern.

And if it came down to it, Nick would never pick Sylvie over her. The poor girl was not only grotesquely top-heavy, but she was ditzy and spoiled and knew next to nothing about sports. Plus, her breath always stunk, like she had a jacked-up tooth in there. Nah, that dalliance would be over in no time. Nick was smarter than that.

Any further thoughts Angie might have had on the subject were cut short by the voice of their server. "Excuse me, folks. Dante had to bop on home, so I'll be filling in for him. Can I fetch you another round of drinks?"

"You bet," she said, looking up at him. When she saw his face, she almost fell out of her seat.

Their new server was Jace.

TWENTY-TWO

"You know, Central Park at midnight isn't exactly the safest place on Earth."

Angie's remark earned a deadpan stare from Jace. "Do you really think anybody's gonna mess with *me*, baby girl?"

And just like that, Angie was laughing. She hadn't planned on it, at least not this early in their rendezvous. Heck, she hadn't even planned on being here. The moment Jace popped up at the table, she figured he was in town for one reason and one reason only—to deliver an apology from Milos. And frankly, she didn't want to hear it. Not from him. Not from anybody.

So at the end of the meal, when Jace slipped a note under her cannoli that read, "Meet me at the Bethesda Fountain at midnight," Angie planned on standing him up. Sure, she liked him, but she'd kicked that chapter of her life to the curb and had no intention of revisiting it.

Besides, she had other plans for the wee hours. She was going to invite Nick back to her place and seduce his socks off. It had been months since they'd done the deed—two nights before the wedding, to be exact—and she missed sharing her bed with the big guy. Not that the sex was ever off the charts, but it was pleasant and predictable, and Nick didn't mind snuggling afterward. And she'd finally trained him to leave the bed if he had to fart, which would be a damn blessing after the meal they'd had.

Regular sex with a regular guy. Just what the doctor ordered.

So what had happened to that plan? Why, when they stepped out of the restaurant into the bustling swirl of Little Italy, didn't she ask Nick to come back to her place for a "wink-wink nightcap"? Why instead did she spin a tall tale about a watch she had to pick up for her mother at a repair shop in Tribeca? Why, when he offered to tag along, did she insist he head home? "Nick, that jeweler talks your ear off. And you know how queasy you get around the French." Why, after a quick, distracted kiss, did she watch him head down the subway stairs to the Q Train, then wait five minutes before taking the same stairs to the Uptown 6?

And now, as she stood here laughing with Jace, why couldn't she decide whether her mind and her legs had been hijacked by deities, or if it was only herself she had to blame for being here?

Whatever, it wasn't going to change anything. It wasn't like she was holding out hope for Milos and her. She was just being polite. She'd hear Jace out, wish him well, and give Nick a call. With any luck, he'd still be awake—and alone—and they could have their horizontal reunion.

One thing was for sure. In spite of the late hour and the presence of a few sketchy folks, Jace had picked the perfect spot for their talk. The Bethesda Fountain was one of Angie's favorite places in New York. Its crowning feature was a bronze statue of an angel with her wings unfurled as she touched down on the top tier, blessing the water that cascaded into a larger pool below it. According to legend, her blessing provided the water with healing powers, which probably explained why over the years, Angie had witnessed folks doing everything from dipping empty Tupperware containers into the pool to swimming in it.

But it wasn't just the mystique of the fountain that kept Angie coming back. It was where it was located. Just behind it was the park's glorious lake, framed against a lush growth of trees that marked the beginning of a woodland walk known as The Ramble. On either side were rolling hills and manicured lawns. And bordering it on the front was a two-story Gothic terrace that featured two grand staircases. If you'd been blindfolded and lowered onto the plaza from above, you might think you were on the grounds of some fabulous fairytale estate awaiting the arrival of your prince—which was exactly what Angie used to pretend when she was a girl. How ironic that she was here tonight to have the final word on a suitor who'd turned out to be anything but a prince.

Which led her to an amusing theory she just had to put out there. Pointing to the angel, she said, "I know why you picked this place, Jace. You heard about the spell she casts on the water and figured you'd toss me in and cure my homicidal feelings for your brother."

"You got me." Jace skimmed the pool and flicked a few droplets at her. "Actually, the fountain has sentimental value for me. It was the first place I saw outside Elysium."

"Really?"

He patted the bench that ran around the perimeter. "Sit."

Angie plopped down beside Jace, not at all minding the mist that came off the water and tickled her back as he enlightened her. "Milos may have had Apollo for a mentor, but I like to think I scored bigger: Aphrodite. Sweet, loopy, devil-may-care Aphrodite. When I came of age in the Roaring Twenties, she decided to kick off my earthly education by showing me her favorite city in the world. Starting with the sculpture she'd posed for back in the day."

Angie turned around and studied the angel. She was certainly beautiful, but in a noble, ethereal way. There was nothing about her that suggested the sensuous goddess of love. "You're shitting me," she said.

Jace laughed. "I shit you not, baby girl. Remember, this was sculpted in the stuffy old 1860s, and the artist had to make adjustments for the times—like toning down her boobies. But that's definitely my cuz. Check her out. Same cheekbones as me."

As Angie turned around a second time, the angel glimmered for a moment, as if she were lighting up from within, then transformed into a living, breathing person. If this was Aphrodite, she was the most resplendent creature Angie had ever seen, not at all the sex bomb she'd imagined. She had wavy blond hair, cut in a French bob; sapphire blue eyes; full red lips, alabaster skin; and yes, the same proud cheekbones as Jace. Her snow-white robe caught a breeze and fluttered playfully, along with the feathers on her majestic wings. And for just a second, she looked at Angie and smiled. Then, in a blink, she was a slab of bronze again.

Angie couldn't believe it. Five minutes with Jace and she was already shaking her head in amazement.

He chuckled. "Cool party trick, huh?"

"You said it. But how did Aphrodite know the sculptor? Did she have a love affair with him?"

"*Her*," Jace winked. "The sculptor was Emma Stebbins. Like all of us, Aphie has had paramours on both sides of the fence. Well, not *all* of us. A certain gloomy sibling of mine seems to be fixated on the opposite sex—and one sex kitten in particular."

Angie sighed. There it was, Jace's segue into a plea for her to take Milos back. Yep, that was what Jace was here for, and it was a shame. If he were anybody but Milos's brother, she could see the two of them becoming buds. Going on shopping sprees in SoHo. Hitting the theatre twice a week. Dancing the night away in Chelsea.

But since he clearly had an agenda, Angie figured she might as well save them both some time. "Jace, you're a good brother for stepping in for him, but give a girl a break. The man conveniently forgot to tell me he was marrying that red-haired succubus. How do I forgive him for that, let alone believe anything else he told me?"

Jace gazed back at her, giving her the full benefit of those puppy dog eyes. "Oh, I'm not here to change your mind, baby girl. To be honest, my brother thinks the best thing that could happen to you would be to never see his sorry mug again."

As much as Angie wanted to scoff, there was nothing in Jace's expression that suggested he was lying. "Milos said that?"

"Well, he didn't use the words, 'sorry mug,' but that was the gist of it."

For one scary moment, Angie thought she felt a pang of disappointment. Then she decided it was nothing more than indigestion. "So why *are* you here?"

But Jace wasn't looking at her anymore. He was focused on a young brunette in a Columbia sweatshirt as she closed her eyes and tossed a quarter into the fountain. As the girl started to walk away, he called out to her. "Don't worry, Kaitlyn. You're gonna ace it."

Angie was confused. Was Kaitlyn a friend of Jace's?

Apparently not, judging from her spooked reaction. "Do I know you?"

"Chemistry midterm, right?"

Kaitlyn looked over at Angie, apparently hoping for enlightenment, but all Angie could do was shrug. A pensive moment later, the girl turned back to Jace. "Right."

"Well, don't worry about it, kid," he said. "You got it in the bag."

Whether it was the infectiousness of Jace's smile or the fact that he was telling her exactly what she wanted to hear, Kaitlyn seemed to buy into it. The wary look on her face warmed into a full-blown grin. "Thanks. I hope you're right."

Angie waited till Kaitlyn was halfway across the plaza, then poked Jace in the ribs. "What was that all about?"

He chuckled. "Yet another thing that makes me the life of the party. I have this radar thingie that allows me to read peoples' thoughts in objects they've handled, even if I don't touch them myself. Like when somebody makes a wish, there's a moment when the coin is hanging in the air that I can suss out who they are and what they're wishing for. In Kaitlyn's case, it was to kick ass on her chemistry midterm so there'd be no danger of losing her scholarship. She got a C on the last one, but she seems like a smart kid. I think she's got a shot at it, don't you?"

Angie couldn't help laughing. Between Jace and Milos, it felt like she was becoming personally acquainted with the X-Men and all their peculiar powers. She pointed at her jacket. "So this button I've been fumbling with. Can you read it?"

"Child's play."

Jace blinked a couple of times, then eyeballed it with comic intensity, much like he'd done on the island when he'd hocus-pocused her onto the Yankees roster. A few seconds later, he nodded to himself. "Okay, there's the X-Men thing. Your initial confusion about how I knew Kaitlyn. Oh, and you're dying to know how I feel about what happened between you and Milos, but you're afraid if you ask me, I'll think you're still interested in him."

Angie shook her head adamantly. "No! I was *not* thinking that."

"Really?"

"Really. Not once since we've been here."

And she hadn't. So what if he'd been spot-on about the other things? He'd probably made it up to see if he could get a dialogue going...

...unless he had access to her subconscious, which would mean she was in denial. Whatever, she wasn't about to start a dialogue about how he felt about her and Milos...

...except she really did want to know how he felt. And when she realized she'd been fumbling with her button again, she shrugged in surrender.

Jace gave her a consoling rub on the shoulder, then cracked his knuckles in what she interpreted to be a warm-up exercise for the emotions he was about to lay bare. "For years, I thought my brother was the biggest dipstick on the planet. Hung up on some chick he'd never met. Every time I thought about all the fun he was missing out on as he sat around, pining over this long-distance obsession, I wanted to throttle him. So a few weeks back, when he told me he was finally, maybe, gonna meet you, I said to myself, 'Thank the Fates! At last, he's going to get her out of his system. Or maybe she won't like *him*.' Either way, I figured, this stupid saga was on the verge of extinction. Then, surprise of surprises, when I met you, I actually liked you. And I thought, 'Okay, he's still certifiable, but at least the guy has taste.'"

Angie chuckled, giving Jace a natural story break. He reached into his jacket and pulled out a pewter flask. "A little something-something to warm you up?"

Without even asking what it was, Angie took a swig. It was Scotch. Smooth and woodsy and oh, that burn.

When she handed it back to Jace, he took a rip and continued. "Of course, when you got to the island, I couldn't resist motoring out to see how things were going. And even though Milos was pissed at me for showing up, I saw something else in him. He was happy. And trust me, the man is never happy. Most of the time, he just broods and tells me what a suffocating disappointment I am. But there he was, glowing like a kid who'd just learned to ride a two-wheeler. And I could see from the look in your eyes that you were up in the clouds, too."

Angie couldn't deny it. She had been in the clouds that day. Feeling like love was there for the taking, as easy as picking an apple off a tree. Why couldn't she have lived that day over and over for the rest of her life? From the moment she met Milos at the pier till that first ray of sunlight hit the bed in the morning. Why had reality insisted on poking a hole in her perfect canvas?

When she looked over at Jace, he seemed to be as glum as she was. "Then all of a sudden, you were gone. And it made me sad. Not just for my brother. For you, too. I wished I'd been there to give you a hug and tell you how sorry I was to've had a part in something that ended up hurting you so badly. So ... here I am."

"Yes, here you are." Angie wiped a tear away. "I hope you're still good for that hug."

Jace wrapped his arms around her and pulled her in. And as she hugged him back, it occurred to her that her trip hadn't been a total waste. Out of that heart-wrenching experience, she'd managed to land a friend, proving there was at least one good god out there. *One good god.* She chuckled over how silly that sounded, piquing Jace's curiosity.

"Am I tickling you?"

"I'm just glad you came, that's all."

"So am I, baby girl. So am I."

As they sat there hugging, a light rain began to fall. And even though Angie knew her makeup was going to run and her hair would turn into a raging nest of curls, she didn't mind. Because she knew that in life, there are few things as rare and satisfying as a true-blue hug.

The spell was broken when a man in a cashmere overcoat walked up next to them. He was thirtiesh and handsome in a masters-of-the-universe kind of way, and his Burberry umbrella kept him dry and kempt. But there was a heaviness about him, as if he were carrying Sisyphus's boulder in his briefcase. After contemplating the fountain for a moment, he took a silver dollar out of a coin purse and flung it into the water. Then, with a sigh that could be heard all the way to Jersey, he trudged off.

Before Angie could get the question off her lips, Jace was answering it. "He's a broker at Cantor-Fitzgerald, and he made a major boo-boo today. He was supposed to buy ten thousand shares of IBM for a client, but he accidentally typed in a *hundred* thousand. By the time he realized it and sold the extra shares, they'd dropped in value, and now his firm is out a half million bucks. He's hoping to find a way to make up the difference before anybody finds out."

Even though Angie didn't know the man, she felt sorry for him. "And will he?"

A deadpan stare. "What am I, a fortune-teller?"

For at least the third time this evening, Angie burst out laughing. How comfortable she felt around Jace. But not the stay-at-home-in-your-sweats-watching-ESPN kind of comfortable she felt around Nick. The kind of comfortable that emboldens people. That makes them look up at a tightrope and ask, *Why* not *me?*

And just like that, she was asking him, "Do you really think he loves me?"

Jace pointed at the broker across the plaza. "Nah, I'm pretty sure he's into Asian chicks."

That earned Jace a swat on the shoulder. He chuckled for a second, then took Angie's hand and squeezed it. "He really, really loves you. Always has, always will."

Somehow, the satisfaction Angie was hoping to feel didn't materialize. Instead, she was pissed, because maybe if Milos had told her about Electra right away, before she'd gotten invested in him, she wouldn't have felt such a sense of betrayal. Which begged another question.

Jace cleared his throat. "You're wondering how a man who really loves a woman can set her up for such a fall."

Angie's theory that Jace had read her mind again was dashed when she looked down at her hands and realized they'd been nowhere near her coat button. "How'd you do that?"

"It's the kind of thing I'd be asking myself. And since you and I seem simpatico, I figured it was where *you* were, too."

"So, what's your answer?"

"Simple. He was afraid of losing you."

Angie winced. Milos had claimed the same thing back on the island. But in the heat of the moment, she hadn't wanted to believe him. Better to think of him as a womanizing deity who was treating her the way his ancestors had treated mortals for centuries. But now, coming from Jace, it was a little harder to brush off.

"Well, he *did* lose me," was all she could bring herself to say.

"I know. And I'm not here to defend him, but I know where he was coming from. He'd spent all those years mooning over you like a lovesick teenager. Then all of a sudden, you were right there beside him, and he wanted to hold on to that bliss as long as he could. So he put it off and put it off until Electra took care of it in her own special way."

"But wouldn't he have figured that might happen? The girl's not exactly a wallflower."

Jace smiled, but there was a sadness about it. "We may be gods, Angie, with killer looks and bitchin' superpowers. But when it comes to relationships, we're as screwed up as you are."

An unwelcome emotion bubbled to the surface. Angie was beginning to empathize with Milos. To understand why he'd done what he'd done. And if forgiving him was the next step, what came after that? Feeling something for him again? If so, it was a place she didn't want to go. Among other things, it was a dead end.

So she took a look around the plaza and spotted an elderly woman tottering toward the fountain, wearing a saggy overcoat and a once-proud cloche hat. A few labored steps later, the woman took a coin out of her pocketbook, made the sign of the cross, and pitched it into the water.

Angie pointed her out to Jace. "So what's *her* wish, Kreskin? A callback on her Rockettes audition?"

Jace gave the joke a perfunctory chuckle. "Her name is Camilla Liberatore. A month ago, her husband died. Prostate cancer. They were together for sixty-two years, from the time they were kids playing stickball in Bensonhurst. And she's consumed with missing him. Takes the subway here every night and begs her God to take her, too. And she just might get her wish, seeing as she's pretty much stopped eating."

Angie took a long look at the woman and felt a numbing kinship with her. "God, to love somebody so much, then get up one morning and know you're never gonna see them again."

"The thing is, she had herself convinced she *didn't* love him. Not that he was a bad man, but he could be a real son of a bitch when he wanted to. She even wished him dead a few times, and that was before the cancer made him *really* hard to live with. So when he died, she felt relieved. Finally free of him. Then a week later, she was frying up a pork chop and didn't hear that craggy voice that used to say, 'Don't overcook it, woman, or I'll throw it atcha.' The next thing she knew, she was sobbing into a potholder."

"All because of a pork chop," Angie murmured.

Jace smiled. "Sometimes all it takes is one little thing to break down the walls you've built around yourself and make you realize you really do love the son of a bitch."

Angie looked over at Camilla, who was slowly making her way across the plaza, and wished she'd never asked about her. Because now the old woman wasn't a stranger anymore, but a living, breathing person who was hurting, and Angie felt powerless to help her.

Just as Angie was about to express that to Jace, he surprised her by leaping to his feet and heading across the plaza. "Camilla, may I speak with you?"

The old woman squinted at him. "Do I know you?"

"I have a message from Joseph. He says he knows why you keep making that wish."

Camilla took a shaky step back. "Who are you?"

Jace responded with a smile that was as comforting as a summer breeze. "Think of me as someone who cares."

Whatever it was about that smile, it seemed to have the same effect on Camilla as it had on the coed. Her fear seemed to vanish, replaced by a look of serene acceptance. And when she spoke, her voice was no longer feeble, but clear and strong. "Tell me what he said."

As Angie watched the drama unfold, her stomach was in knots. What was Jace going to tell the poor woman, and how would she handle it?

As if to reassure Angie, Jace looked over at her and smiled, then returned his gaze to Camilla. "He said he knows you miss him, but that's not why you keep making that wish. It's so you can find him in the afterlife and beg him to forgive you for all the nasty things you said to him over the years."

Although Camilla didn't say a word, it was obvious from the stricken look on her face that Jace had hit a nerve. After a moment, she looked into his eyes. "Did he say anything else?"

Jace put a hand on her shoulder. "There *is* one more thing. But it's not pretty."

Angie cleared her throat loudly, hoping to get a sign from Jace that he knew where he was going with this. But his eyes remained fixed on Camilla, who nodded for him to continue.

"He said you should get over yourself. He forgives you, just like he knows you forgive *him* for all the nasty things he said to you. And he means no offense, but he's not all that eager to see you just yet.

Don't get me wrong. He loves you. But eternity is a long time to spend with somebody, and you shouldn't be in such a hurry to jump-start it."

For a moment, Camilla just stood there, as still as the angel on the fountain, and Angie wondered if Jace had botched things. Then she tilted her head back and laughed, long and hearty, giving Angie a glimpse of the girl she'd been all those years ago in Bensonhurst. And when the old woman finally caught her breath, she said, "He always was a son of a bitch."

As Angie headed toward them, her eyes welling up with tears, Camilla reached out a bony hand and touched Jace on the cheek. "Who are you? Really?"

He kissed her on the forehead. "Would you believe me if I said I was God?"

Camilla studied Jace for a moment, not quite believing him, but not ready to write him off either. Then she looked at Angie, eyebrows raised hopefully.

Angie shrugged. "Technically, he is."

That seemed to satisfy Camilla. For a moment. "I'm hungry," she groused.

Jace pulled out a wad of bills. "Take yourself out to dinner, Camilla. On God."

It took Camilla exactly three seconds to snatch the money out of Jace's hand and stuff it into her pocketbook. Then she gave them a pert little wave and hobbled away, still slowly, but with a newfound verve.

Angie watched her navigate the stairwell, then turned to Jace, beaming. "That was the most beautiful thing I've ever seen. You saved her life, Jace."

He harrumphed. "There's a rumor going around that I have a heart. Don't feed it."

"It'll be our little secret." She hugged him. "But how'd you know how her husband felt about her? Did you ... communicate with him?"

Jace shook his head. "Just took what I got from her and improvised. If I'm wrong, so be it. Why saddle her with the old son of a bitch before it's necessary?"

As they shared a chuckle, Jace wrapped his arm around the small of Angie's back and spun her around and around until she was dizzy and giggling and feeling seventeen years old.

Which gave her an idea. "Do you know what would be a kick?"

Twenty minutes later, they were tearing up the floor at Splash as Nicki Minaj called out over the sound system, urging everybody to pound the alarm. Other than a few champagne breaks, they spent the next three hours dancing. As Angie might have figured, Jace was a master at it, and at first she felt like a spaz. But whether it was the bubbly or his gentle coaching, it wasn't long before she was matching him step for step. At one point, it was just the two of them on the floor as a throng of revelers surrounded them in a love circle, like something out of *Step Up*. It was the most fun she'd had on her feet in months—the perfect antidote to the gloom of the past few days.

By the time they rambled up to the door of her building, it was three in the morning. But even though Angie was exhausted, she wasn't ready for the night to end. "There's an all-night coffee shop down the street," she offered. "Can I treat you to a cappuccino?"

Jace shook his head. "Actually, there's a gentleman I promised I'd meet up with. I see him every time I'm in town."

"Well, I hope he appreciates you."

"Hey, a few hours of fun is all I'm asking, right?"

For just a second, Jace's smile flickered, and Angie saw something in him she'd never seen before. A sense that maybe he wasn't all that happy being a perpetual party boy.

Before Angie could press it further, Jace reached into the pocket of his sport coat and pulled out a box covered in blue velvet. "Almost forgot. A *mea culpa*. From my brother."

Angie's hand froze, mid-reach. "Whatever it is, I don't want it."

"Tell me that when you've opened it."

No, she told herself. *Do not take that box. Do not give Milos that victory.* But the longer she gazed at it, the more curious she became about what might be inside. What exactly constituted an apology gift from a god? A voucher good for eternal life?

Angie sighed. Maybe it wasn't such a bad idea to find out what it was. If she didn't, she'd probably spend the rest of her life wondering. So she plucked it out of Jace's hand, opened it, and let out a shriek. Staring back at her were five tickets to tomorrow's Yankees game, the decisive seventh game of the American League Championship Series. And not just any tickets. Eight rows behind home plate. In other words, baseball gold.

Angie stood there trembling with frustration, knowing Jace's eyes were on her—and most likely, not just his. *Damn you, Milos. You've gone and given me the perfect gift.*

But it didn't mean she had to take it. She could hand the tickets back to Jace. Or give them to a charity to auction off. Or, and this could be way fun, take them upstairs and burn them, one by one, while eating Häagen-Dazs out of the carton.

Instead, she dropped the box into her purse. "Thank you, Jace. And uh ... thank him."

"I will." Jace didn't smile, but there was a hint of victory in his eyes. "So who you gonna take? Your mom? Your brother? That knuckle dragger you were with at Angelo's?"

"His name is Nick," she said, determined not to crack a smile.

"I know. And you're too good for him, even on your worst day."

"He's not so bad. Besides, all the good guys seem to be gay."

"Or engaged to red-haired succubi," he said, winking at her.

Just as Angie was about to protest, Jace pulled her into an embrace and kissed her on both cheeks. "See you around, huh?"

"You better." She kissed him back and started up the stairs.

A few seconds later, he called out to her. "Hey, Angie. If you take your mom, your brother, and Nick to the game, that leaves one ticket. Are you gonna ask your Ya-Ya?"

Angie grabbed hold of the railing, caught off guard. "I ... don't know."

"Well, you should," he said, not at all sounding like the impish Jace she'd spent the evening with. "And the first chance you get, you should ask her to fill you in on what she was trying to tell you the other night. *Ciao, bella.*"

Before Angie could catch her breath, Jace was halfway down the street, disappearing into the shadows.

———

"You did what?!" Milos shouted.

"Chill, brother. You rocked her world," Jace replied. "You should've seen the look on her face when she opened that box."

A second later, Milos had his brother up against a wall, his fist poised two inches from his cheery little face. "Dammit, Jace, how could you go meddling in my life like that? Angie doesn't need any reminders of me. She needs to forget about me and move on."

"Seriously?" With the utmost calm, Jace wrapped a hand around Milos's outstretched fist and squeezed so hard that Milos felt his eyes bulging out of the sockets.

Milos tried to brave the pain, determined not to give his brother the satisfaction of knowing how much he was hurting him. But eventually his body started to go numb and he realized he was about to pass out. "All right, stop!"

"Not until you listen to me." Despite his exertions, Jace hadn't broken a sweat. "You may think you know everything, but you've got your head so far up your ass you can't see daylight. She's in love with you, Milos. I could tell in a heartbeat."

For a moment, Milos forgot all about the pain. "Really?"

"Really. And maybe she'll get over you and maybe she won't. But you have to ask yourself something. If she never sees you again, what would you rather her last memory be? That heinous scene at your house, or the delightfully appropriate farewell gift you gave her?"

Grunting in agony, Milos said, "But I didn't give it to her."

"I won't tell if *you* won't." With that, Jace let go of his hand and walked out the door.

As Milos stood there, rubbing his throbbing hand, he was struck by another kind of pain. The pain of knowing his brother was right.

Well, *half* right. The tickets were a nice gesture. But they were merely a stepping-stone to something Angie would never forget.

TWENTY-THREE

EVEN BEFORE THE REAL magic happened, being at Yankee Stadium that night was magical. As it always had been.

Other than Ya-Ya's rooftop deck, this was the place where Angie's happiest memories had been made. It didn't matter that this new incarnation of the stadium was only a few years old. In Angie's eyes, it was still the house that Ruth built. And she still got a chill every time she looked out onto that stretch of Kentucky bluegrass and thought about all the summer afternoons and fall evenings she'd spent here with her favorite people in the world. How many seat-of-the-pants moments had they witnessed? How many high-fives had they exchanged? How many Cokes and hot dogs had they sucked down? And how many times had they cheered their throats raw rooting for the likes of Don Mattingly, Roberto Kelly, Wade Boggs, Bernie Williams, and, eventually, a kid from Jersey by the name of Jeter?

She got her first taste of beer here at the age of nine, courtesy of her father. Had her first kiss, courtesy of Nick. Watched gleefully as Ya-Ya went toe-to-toe with an obnoxious Red Sox fan, threatening to rip the man's head off when he called Phil Rizzuto a yutz. Witnessed the miracle of her parents holding hands. And saw her father cry for the one and only time when the organist played "Somewhere Over the Rainbow" in tribute to Mickey Mantle the day he died of cancer. The memory of that moment still brought tears to her eyes, and she thanked God there was a place like this that seemed to bring out the deepest emotions in everybody she knew, allowing her to get to know them better.

And tonight promised to be unforgettable for its own reasons. First off, the seats were nothing short of orgasmic. From her vantage point just behind home plate, Angie was so close to the batters that she could see the sweat trickle down their cheeks as they squared off against a hostile pitcher or their eyes bulge out of their sockets as they barreled toward home. The weather was cooperating, too. It was one of those rare fall evenings when the sky was flooded with stars and the temperature was in the fifties. "Windbreaker weather," her father used to call it.

And sure, she wished her father could have been here to share this special evening, but she'd been resigned to that empty seat for years. Among the living, Ya-Ya had unfortunately begged off, claiming she wasn't up to it. This had come after a tearful reunion during which Angie had apologized for her behavior the night she got back from Greece and asked Ya-Ya to fill her in on whatever it was she wanted to tell her. But Ya-Ya had begged off on that, too, claiming it was a story that could only be told when she was up to snuff.

But there were just as many reasons to be exhilarated. The seats. The night. The fact that the Yankees were leading the Texas Rangers by three runs late in the game, meaning her Bronx Bombers were just a few outs away from playing in the World Series.

And those good vibes seemed to be rubbing off on everybody in Angie's party. Nick was chummy and generous, never failing to keep the beers coming. Granted, Angie wished he hadn't returned two texts from Sylvie and sent her a selfie of him lofting a beer, but on one level, it made her feel less guilty about never having told him about Milos.

As for her brother, Anthony, he couldn't stop thanking her for letting him use the extra ticket to bring his new girlfriend, a pretty paralegal named Kristin. "You've changed my life tonight, Ang," he said after Kristin scooted off to the ladies' room. "I think this one's a keeper."

Angie suppressed a chuckle. How many times had her brother said that about a girl? A hundred? And how many times had the relationship gone south? Ninety-nine and counting? Hard as it was to believe, her charming, handsome brother, who was occasionally mistaken for Adam Levine, was terminally unlucky in love. But who knew? Maybe tonight was going to change that.

So she gave him a pop on the shoulder. "I've got a hunch you're right, Anthony."

"Thanks, Ang." He kissed her on the cheek. "Did I ever I tell you you're the standard by which I judge all my women?"

Angie smiled. How could she not be flattered by a compliment like that?

But it was her mother who was proving to be the most pleasant surprise of the evening. Naturally, she'd been on Cloud Nine for the past few days, ecstatic that her daughter had finally "wised up" and reconciled with Nick. But it was more than that. Whether it was the night or the seats or her own special memories of this place, she was acting more like a girlfriend than a mother, something Angie had always regretted she couldn't have been more of when she was growing up. Her mother laughed and gossiped with her, kept the whining to a minimum, and rooted loudly for the Yankees, with none of her usual worries about who might be watching her.

At one point, when she noticed Angie gazing off into the distance, she leaned over and whispered in her ear. "Thinking about your dad?"

Angie nodded, half-expecting her to toss out a gem like, "Well, snap out of it!"

Instead, she smiled. "Me, too."

If that weren't enough of a WTF? moment, she took Angie's hand and squeezed it. They sat like that for half an inning, clutching tighter during tense moments on the field. Later, during a long pitching change, she even told Angie the story of her third date with her father, the date that had sealed the deal for them. As a kid, Angie had heard her father tell the story a hundred times—about how they got stuck on the Wonder Wheel at Coney Island for two hours and passed the time trying to guess each other's favorite movie. Each would give the other a clue, and the penalty for a wrong answer was a kiss. He'd guessed hers, *The Way We Were*, on the third clue, but it had taken her a whopping eleven to figure out that his was *The Great Escape*.

At least that was what Angie had believed all these years. But hearing her mother tell her side of the story for the first time led to a stunning revelation. "I knew it on the first clue."

Angie stared back at her, dumbstruck. "No way."

"If I'm lying, I'm buying."

"Then why didn't you tell him? Why'd you give him all those wrong answers?"

"What can I say?" her mother replied with a gleam in her eye. "It was cold that night and your father was a good kisser."

As usual, Yankee Stadium was waving its magic wand over everything.

And it was about to get better.

As Angie reached down for a handful of popcorn, she felt a tingle run through her body, as if she'd stuck her finger in a light socket. Slightly freaked, she sat up in her seat...

...to discover she wasn't in the stands anymore, but on the bench in the Yankees dugout. She let out a small, confused squeal and gazed around at the faces of players she'd been rooting for for years—and in some cases, crushing on. Brett Gardner. CC Sabathia. Jacoby Ellsbury. Carlos Beltrán. But if they were surprised to see her in their sacred quarters, they weren't showing it. In fact, none of them were even looking at her. They were either watching the action on the field or talking among themselves, as if having a woman in the dugout were the most ordinary thing in the world. Which meant it had to be a dream.

But if it was, when had Angie fallen asleep? In the middle of reaching for popcorn? That didn't make sense. Food never put her to sleep. Plus, in what dream had she ever been able to smell things? But right now, she was picking up the pungent scents of sweat, chewing tobacco, and Aqua Velva.

Nevertheless, she pinched herself on the arm.

And got an even bigger shock. She was wearing a baseball uniform. Navy blue and white pinstripes, just like the guys around her.

And then it hit her. This wasn't a dream. It was a dream come true. At this moment in time, she really was a member of the Yankees. A major league ballplayer on the cusp of the World Series. And there was only one person in the universe who could have engineered this miracle. The immortal she'd been cursing out for the past several days.

It was going to be a lot harder to hate him now.

"Damn you, Milos," she muttered under her breath. Then she said it through a giddy laugh—"Damn you, Milos!"—this time drawing a raised eyebrow from Mark Teixeira, who was heading past her toward the batter's box, clutching a Louisville Slugger.

Suddenly, Angie couldn't sit still any longer. And it wasn't just because she was trembling with excitement. She realized she had no way of knowing how long this miracle was going to last, so she didn't dare waste a second. Bounding off the bench, she chirped hello to a few of her teammates, who responded with perplexed nods. Then she walked up to the team manager, Joe Girardi, and slugged him on the shoulder. "Hey, boss."

He gave her his patented blank stare, then grunted out a "Save it for the game," which raised goose bumps up and down her arms. *He said, "Save it for the game." I'm gonna play in the game!*

Angie stepped up to the dugout railing and stared in wonder at the field, which looked like no major league ball field she'd ever seen, because she was viewing it at eye level for the first time. The grass was feverishly green, as if it were lit from underneath, and seemed to roll on forever. The sand around the infield looked so clean and pure it could have been culled from a Caribbean beach. And the fans packed into the outfield bleachers appeared to have been dotted on by a million tiny paintbrushes. The whole panorama looked so mythical, so holy, that she wouldn't have been surprised to see a priest on the mound stirring up the congregation.

Instead, there was a veteran pitcher named Tanner Scheppers who was determined to close the game in style for his Rangers. Angie held her breath as he fired off a wicked slider. Teixeira swung and missed, sending up a collective groan from the stands. And even though Angie felt badly for him, she couldn't help wondering how she'd do out there when it was her turn at bat.

Just when she thought the experience couldn't get any richer, she caught sight of Derek Jeter walking toward her. In person, he was taller than she'd imagined, towering over her by a good head and a half. His face was slightly less angular and his stubble more prominent. But it was his eyes that really got her. Deep set. Intense. The color of cocktail olives and just as intoxicating as the martinis they'd escaped from.

"Yo, Costianes," he said in that baritone twang of his.

It had been one thing to hear him say her name over the phone when she was on the island. But to have him call it out from mere inches away was downright dizzying. The only thing she could think to say back to him was, "Yo, Jeter."

Then, just like that, the wheels came off her fantasy. He looked at her as if she'd just insulted his mother, his sister, and every other woman in his family tree. Then he spat the words back at her. "'Yo, Jeter?!' Are you even here tonight?!"

In all the times she'd seen him interviewed on TV, Angie had never noticed the bulging vein that ran across his forehead like a lightning bolt. Possibly because she'd never seen him this pissed before. But why would he be pissed at her? Wasn't this supposed to be her moment?

Just as Angie was forming the word, "Huh?" her memory banks were uploaded with all the information relevant to this alternate reality. Yes, she was a Yankee, a third baseperson in her rookie season, the first and only woman in the majors and the next player coming up to bat. But sadly, for the past few games, she'd been in a hitting slump.

Worse yet, she'd made a costly error in the sixth inning of this game that had allowed the Rangers a run. A run that gave them a 4–3 lead in this, the bottom of the ninth inning. At present, the Yankees had runners on first and second with one out and Teixeira at the plate with two strikes.

The weight of it hit her like a steam shovel. She'd gone from a world in which her beloved Yankees had a comfortable lead to one that saw them on the verge of a loss that would spell the end of their season. And it was all because of her.

Gulp.

She stared remorsefully at her idol, wishing she could think of something better to say than, "I'm sorry, Derek."

It didn't seem to enchant *him* either. He blew out an angry breath —a growl, really—then gripped a hand on her shoulder. "Don't be sorry. Just get your head in the game."

"My head's in the game," Angie mumbled.

"Really? Then why the hell aren't you out there loosening up?!" By now, that bulging vein on his forehead was threatening to pop. "You're better than this, Ang. I wouldn't have fought to get you on this team if I didn't believe that. Don't make me look like an idiot."

With that, Jeter turned and headed for the railing. Before Angie could fully digest his words, her attention was drawn to the plate by the whir of a hard-thrown pitch. Teixeira swung hard and popped up to shallow right. The Rangers' outfielder tracked it down and grabbed it, leaving the runners where they stood.

Angie sighed. It was down to the final out. The Yankees' last shot at the World Series was riding on the shoulders of a female rookie from Queens who'd been hitting like a spaz.

It was a lot to absorb. Then again, so was the fact that her idol, one of the best players in the history of the game, had gone to the mat to get her onto this squad. Which meant at some point in the not-so-distant past, she hadn't just been good, she'd been great.

Angie took a long hit of the crisp October air, then blew it back out. *Screw it. I can do this.*

With that, she grabbed a bat, marched out of the dugout and onto the field …

… where she was greeted by a schizophrenic symphony of sounds. There was a burst of applause that sounded like a million erasers being clapped together; a breezy chorus of "Let's Get It Started," courtesy of the Yankees organist; a ferocious outpouring of boos and hisses; and a handful of X-rated catcalls. Clearly, at the moment, she had as many haters as fans.

But she wasn't going to let it get to her. She'd jeered plenty of batters in her time, and she wouldn't hesitate to call out a female slugger if she wasn't pulling her weight. So she took a few practice swings, trying to block out everything but the feel of that lumber slicing through the air. Then she squared her shoulders and stepped into the batter's box.

From the mound, Scheppers gave her a sneer that seemed to say *Prepare to die, bitch.*

Recalling it was the same look a certain deceased serpent had given her, Angie choked up on the bat and went into the unorthodox stance that had been her calling card since childhood. *Give me all you got, Scheppers, and I'll send it to the parking lot.*

Instead, he checked the runner at first—not once but three times. Angie cautioned herself to stay calm. After all, she'd been waiting for this moment all her life. Would another few seconds really kill her?

Finally, Scheppers went into his windup and released a sinking fastball. Angie stared it down as it cut through the air and veered toward the inside corner. Then she launched her hips and swung...

...for an agonizing strike.

The boos were drowning out the cheers now, and she distinctly heard the c-word. Which kind of sucked. Did they really think *that* was the way to motivate her?

Still, she shook it off and bore down, digging a hole in the batter's box with her right spike. Once again, the flame-throwing right-hander reared back and fired a rocket at her. The good news was that Angie made contact with this one. The bad news was that it was a screaming foul that shot into the Yankees dugout like a missile. She turned around just in time to see Jeter duck out of the way, then raise his head and stare murderously at her.

As the boos rained down like an angry thunderstorm, Angie stepped out of the box to get her head together. She was better than this, dammit. Sure, Scheppers was a solid closer, but she had no doubt she had the skills to square around on him. Hell, she'd hit two doubles and a triple off Yankee legend Ron Guidry at fantasy baseball camp when she was just fourteen. So what was she missing? What was the mental ingredient she needed to make history out there?

On one level, she knew it shouldn't bother her. This alternate reality wasn't going to last forever. In all likelihood, she'd be back in the stands in a few minutes, and nobody in her world would know that for one stitch in the fabric of time, a woman had worn the pinstripes. And brought shame to them.

But *she'd* know it. And she had no doubt that if she was responsible for the final out of the season, it would eat at her like a cancer for the rest of her Yankees-loving life. In all likelihood, she wouldn't be able to watch another second of another game without recalling how she'd choked during her one chance to shine. Which meant she'd never enjoy another Yankees game again.

And if that wasn't sufficient motivation, she didn't know what was. So she strode confidently back into the box and tapped the bat on home plate as if she owned it. Then she rolled the bat around to her back shoulder and nodded toward the mound. She felt twice as strong as she had a minute ago, twice as confident, and three times as photogenic.

Which Scheppers apparently sensed, because he'd saved his best for last. After a blink-and-you-miss-it windup, he fired a four-seam fastball at her, a ninety-three-mile-an-hour burner that had flummoxed some of the best hitters in the league.

But not this one. As Angie planted her back foot and launched into her swing, she was seized by that sensation every great hitter has experienced at least once. That moment when everything seems to go into slow motion and you can actually see the stitches on the ball and know which one you're going to hit. And when she connected with it, she felt the spirits of Ruth and Gehrig and DiMaggio and Mantle riding along with her.

She felt immortal, really.

The ball exploded into right field, moving so fast it was probably catching the attention of every air traffic controller at JFK. With a "Yes!" for the ages, Angie barreled toward first base, begging the ball to make her proud.

And it did. It shot all the way across the right field sky and past the warning track, where it ricocheted off the wall and hit the outfielder in the shoulder. He fell backward onto the dirt as the ball caromed into a tricky corner, allowing Angie to round first and head for second. As she sped across the blessed base path, the fielder struggled to his feet and scooped up the ball.

But he might as well have stayed on his ass. The runner on second had already scored and the runner on first was rounding third and hurtling toward home. By the time the relay man delivered the ball to the catcher, the winning run had crossed the plate.

As the crowd roared loud enough to drown out the boom of the fireworks lighting up the sky, Angie forgot about everything but the moment she was living. She'd done it. She'd won the game for the Yankees. Thanks to her, they were headed to the Fall Classic. And whether this alternate reality lasted for hours or seconds, it would live in her heart forever.

As tears streamed down her face, she raced toward the first-base line, where her teammates were waiting to swarm her.

———

There were tears in Milos's eyes, too, as he watched Angie from his perch on the mountaintop. He'd promised himself he wouldn't envisage her during her stint with the Yankees. After all, he couldn't control the outcome. And if she faltered, he'd never stop blaming himself. But in the end, his curiosity had gotten the better of him.

And now, as he watched her bask in her moment of triumph, Milos felt a rush of euphoria unlike any joy he'd ever felt for himself. She was the hero of her people. The Atalanta of her generation. He'd helped her realize the dream of a lifetime. Maybe it wouldn't make up for the pain he'd inflicted on her, but at the very least, it was something positive she'd always associate with him.

His chest swelled with pride as he watched her teammates raise her high over their heads while the crowd chanted "Angie! Angie!..." with the fervor of an army after a hard-won battle. Even that Jeter fellow was exalting her, no small feat for a man with such a colossal ego.

And the smile Angie had on her face—mercy, it was beautiful. Full of wonder and self-discovery. The smile of a woman who'd just realized that her gifts were extraordinary and her boundaries limitless.

And that was Milos's reward. To see her smile one more time.

Because one thing was for sure. When he dismissed this alternate universe, he'd never envisage her again. For the rest of her life. And not just because she deserved her privacy.

It was for him, too. It was just too hard to look at her, knowing she'd never be his again.

———

One of the many tidbits Angie would take from this experience was that the color of Derek Jeter's eyes changed with his moods. They were pale green when he was angry and a vivid steamed-asparagus shade when he was happy.

And at the moment, they were bordering on neon. "You kicked ass out there, Ang. Swung us right into the Series. I guess my pep talk did the trick, huh?"

Although Angie barely knew the guy, there was no way she was going to let him get away with such rot. "Actually, Derek, I *was* tempted to make you look like an idiot. But in the end, my mad skills wouldn't let me."

He let out a chuckle and wrapped her in a vice-like hug. And even though Angie was barely able to breathe, it felt like a slice of heaven. God, he was strong. With a musky, citrusy scent that would've had her on her knees if she weren't his teammate. *His World-Series-clinching teammate,* she happily reminded herself.

Sadly, he released her a few seconds later and waved over a pack of journalists he'd been holding at bay. "Go easy on her, guys. She bites back."

Just as Jeter was about to make his exit, Angie grabbed him by the forearm. "Derek, hold up. Do you know where my family's sitting?"

He stared at her, puzzled. "Uh, yeah ... where they always sit." He pointed out a section between home plate and the first base line, then took off for the locker room.

Suddenly, microphones were being thrust in Angie's face and questions were being thrown at her about her "miracle at-bat." She knew she should be lapping it up. She'd spent a good chunk of her fantasy life wondering what it would be like to be the object of all this love.

But at the moment, she had a more pressing agenda. "I'll be back in a minute, folks."

But nobody heard her. She tried waving her arms in front of her, but that only caused an uptick in the camera flashes. Finally, she put her hands in her mouth and blew out a deafening whistle she'd perfected on the playground. Thankfully, that did the trick.

"Look, I promise I'll answer all your questions. But there's something I need to do first."

Then she headed for the section of stands Jeter had pointed out. Maybe it was silly, but she had to know who was in her cheering section. Obviously, she'd come tonight as a spectator with her mother, her brother, his girlfriend, and Nick. But in this alternate reality, when she was actually playing for the Yankees, there was sure to be a larger group.

Before she spotted them, she heard them—a boisterous pack of bridge & tunnel people screaming out her name. Her mother was blowing kisses at her, wearing a full-length fur coat. Standing next to her was Anthony, whose date for the evening was either a dead ringer for Eva Longoria or actually was Eva. *Funny what having a ballplayer in the family can do for somebody's love life,* Angie mused. Ya-Ya was tapping her heart lovingly while dabbing her eyes with a handkerchief. Nick was one row back with his arm around her cousin Sylvie, which strangely, didn't bother Angie at all. There were also at least fifty other friends and relatives as well as a contingent from the church, headed by Father Kontos, decked out in a Yankees jacket with number 49 on it.

Which was Angie's number, and ironically, the age her father was when he died. She wondered if in some alternate version of the afterlife, he'd tuned in to the game and was doing fist-pumps over her victory. The thought of it put a smile on her face.

Then, just as quickly, Angie's smile wavered. There was someone else she'd hoped to see here. One other fan she wished she could see smiling down at her.

Milos.

She knew it was crazy to think he'd be here. She'd made it brutally clear on the island she never wanted to see him again. And even though he'd engineered this miracle, he probably wouldn't want to risk spoiling it for her by showing his face. And that wasn't even the biggest risk he'd be taking. There was also the wrath of Zeus and

Electra to consider. Angie wouldn't put it past either of them to incinerate the whole damn borough to teach him a lesson.

And even if Milos *had* decided to come, there was no guarantee he'd be sitting with her family. Sure, Ya-Ya would be thrilled to see him, but how would she pass him off? "Everybody, say hello to my chiropractor, Aristotle."

Suddenly, Angie wanted to kick herself. *Dammit, why am I even thinking about him? Why can't I just enjoy this moment and forget him?*

But the fact was, she couldn't. She really, really wanted to see him. And not just to thank him for doing this amazing thing for her. It ran deeper than that. How far, she didn't know. All she knew was there was an ache in her heart that was dimming this shining moment just as surely as if somebody had draped a shroud over the stadium.

Then something hit her like a fastball to the temple. Something Jace had said about the widow at the fountain. "Sometimes all it takes is one little thing to break down the walls you've built around yourself and make you realize you really do love the son of a bitch."

Suddenly, Angie couldn't hear the crowd anymore. Or see the flashes of all the camera phones taking pictures of her. The only thing she was aware of was the question swirling around her head. *Is it true? Am I in love with the son of a bitch?*

She pored over the events of the past few days. She'd left the island hurt and angry, refusing to buy Milos's explanation of why he hadn't told her about Electra. In Angie's eyes, he was a scheming horndog, so anything he said was sure to be a lie. And any budding feelings she had for him were buried under the weight of all that deceit.

But over the past few days, Ya-Ya and Jace had chipped away at her anger, forcing her to reexamine his behavior and realize that while he may have handled things badly, he wasn't the scoundrel she'd pegged him to be.

On the heels of all that had come this miracle in the Bronx. The thoughtful prick had put her in a position to claim the one thing she wanted almost as much as true love. And she'd claimed it in style. She'd had an RBI double that would be a fixture on the highlight reels for years. She'd been hugged by Derek Jeter. Heard her name chanted by fifty thousand people in the stands and millions more at home.

And yet, the moment wasn't shining nearly as brightly as it should because Milos wasn't here to share it with her. The whole world was celebrating her. But without Milos, it felt hollow. Incomplete. Because she wanted to see the pride in his eyes. Hear him tell her she'd done good. Have him put his arms around her and hold her tighter than Jeter had.

And yeah. Feel his lips on hers again.

She let out a grumble. *Yep, I'm in love with the son of a bitch.*

A crush of voices jolted Angie back to the reality of this alternate reality. She turned around to find that the reporters were lurking a few inches away. And their numbers had grown, along with their urgent need for copy.

"Angie, how does it feel to be the first woman to lead her team into the World Series?"

"What do you think you've added to the debate about whether men are better athletes than women?"

"Who are you going to be celebrating with tonight?"

As the questions kept piling up, one on top of each other, Angie felt like she was suffocating. She wanted to shout, "I'm love-screwed!" but she couldn't get her mouth to work. She wanted to run, but her legs refused to cooperate.

Then mercifully, she felt that stray voltage sensation that had sent her down this rabbit hole. Two blinks later, she was back in the stands, her heroics unknown to everyone around her. And the Yankees were clinging to the same comfortable lead they'd had before this whole thing began.

Nothing had changed.

Yet everything had.

TWENTY-FOUR

IT DIDN'T WORRY ANGIE that Ya-Ya didn't answer her phone when she called her from the stadium. She figured her grandmother was either watching the game on TV with the sound cranked up or she'd gone to bed early and muted the ringer. Either way, Angie was determined to see her. So the minute Sinatra finished singing "New York, New York" to cement the victory, Angie broke it to her group that she'd be parting ways with them in Midtown so she could continue on to Brooklyn to check on Ya-Ya.

"So you're just gonna let Nick fend for himself tonight?" her mother said. "That's not the way you keep a man, honey."

Angie rolled her eyes. She knew her mother's transformation into a gal pal couldn't last forever, but did it have to end so soon? "Mom, I'm sure Nick understands."

"That's what they say, and then they stray."

Angie couldn't help but chuckle at that little gem. Where did her mother get these things, in some primer for terminally bitter women?

Thankfully, Nick was a trooper. He gave her a smile that seemed to say, "I feel your pain" and popped her on the shoulder. "Give Ya-Ya my best, will ya, Ang? I'll make sure your mother gets home unmolested."

"The story of my life," her mother replied, now fully back to *woe-is-me* mode.

Turning a deaf ear to the whining, Angie pulled Nick in for a hug. "Thanks a bunch."

He gave her a kiss on the lips, nearly causing her to cringe from the duplicity she was shoveling. *Here he is, being all lovey-dovey, and I'm going over to Ya-Ya's to talk about the man I really love. Oh yeah, I'm dirt.*

The subway ride downtown was less than celebratory, as if Angie's planned detour had killed everybody's victory buzz. Her brother and Kristin were sitting across the aisle, quietly arguing about something to do with his lack of chivalry. Nick was busy texting. *Probably arranging a booty call with Sylvie,* Angie mused. And her mother was dozing next to her, waking up at every lurching stop to give her a withering stare.

After the others left to take the transfer to Queens, Angie tried to reach Ya-Ya one more time, but got her voicemail. By now, Angie was sure her grandmother had retired for the night. She considered heading home and returning to see her first thing in the morning. But she was pretty sure Ya-Ya wouldn't mind being awakened, especially when she told her what she had to tell her.

Still, Angie figured, it wouldn't hurt to sweeten the deal. So when she got off the train in Park Slope, she stopped at Starbucks for two tall coffees, fetched a bottle of Kahlua from the liquor store, and picked up a few choice desserts at the Cocoa Bar. Thank goodness New York was open at all hours for people with cravings.

She first sensed that something was wrong when she walked up outside the townhouse and saw that the lights were blazing on both floors. Ya-Ya was in no way a miser, but as a child of the Depression, she'd always been careful about pinching pennies wherever she could. And keeping lights on in a room you weren't using was a big no-no for her.

Things went from bad to worse when Angie entered the building. Ya-Ya's front door was not only ajar, but the doorframe was splintered, as if somebody had forced their way in. Angie groaned. This didn't look good at all.

Pushing the door open, she called out to her. "Ya-Ya, are you all right? Ya-Ya?"

But there was no response. And when Angie edged in further, she noticed that one of the dining room chairs was tipped over, as if there'd been a struggle. Now she was really scared. Something bad had happened to her grandmother. And while she realized the smart thing to do was call the police and wait outside till they arrived, she couldn't imagine just hanging around while Ya-Ya was possibly lying somewhere, hurting. Danger be damned, Angie was gonna find her.

So she grabbed a fireplace poker and ventured up the stairs to the master bedroom. But there was no one there, and nothing seemed amiss. The bed hadn't even been slept in.

Dammit, where are you, Ya-Ya? Please be okay.

A check of the other rooms failed to turn up any sign of her. The only place Angie hadn't looked was the rooftop deck. Could something have happened to Ya-Ya up there, in her haven? Although Angie couldn't imagine fate being so cruel, she also realized there weren't many other options, short of Ya-Ya having been kidnapped,

God forbid. So she made her way down the hallway toward the spiral staircase that led to the roof.

Just as she reached for the railing, a voice called out faintly from downstairs. "Hello. Is anyone there?"

Angie felt a rush of hope. Was that Ya-Ya? Was she okay after all?

"I'm up here!" Angie shouted as she bounded down the stairs.

Then, just as quickly, her hopes sank. The woman in the living room wrapped in a housecoat wasn't Ya-Ya, but her next-door neighbor, Mrs. Hapgood.

"Oh, Angie, it's you," she said, tilting her glasses for a better look. "I thought it might be the handyman."

Angie stared at her blankly. "Handyman?"

Mrs. Hapgood nodded. "The paramedics said the door was locked when they got here, so they had to force their way in."

A chill passed through Angie's body and settled around her heart. "Paramedics? What happened?"

The old woman stiffened. "I'm so sorry, I thought you knew. Angie, I'm afraid your grandmother had a heart attack. They rushed her to Methodist."

————

Whether it was adrenaline or fear or equal shots of both, Angie made the ten-block sprint to the hospital in five minutes. All the way there, she was mumbling the Lord's Prayer, promising God all kinds of things in exchange for a few more years with her Ya-Ya. She also sent up a prayer to the gods of Olympus on the off-chance they felt they owed her something after the mess with Milos.

While waiting for someone to assist her at the front desk, she left voicemails for her mother and Anthony, making an effort to sound far calmer than she felt. When she finally got her turn with the receptionist, she had a hard time getting out the words, "I'm here to see Georgia Costianes," fearful the man would check his records and give her that hopeless shake of the head she'd seen so many times in the movies. Thankfully, he directed her to the cardiac ICU.

Too tense to wait for the elevator, Angie sprinted up four flights of stairs, quietly thanking her body for tackling all the exertions she'd demanded of it over the past few hours. She emerged in a corridor that was bustling with activity despite the late hour—doctors consulting with anxious family members, nurses rushing to respond to call buttons, patients tottering along with IVs on wheels.

But they might as well have been invisible. Angie's eyes were drawn to a thirtyish-looking man leaning against a doorway in a polo shirt and khakis. He was handsome in a sturdy kind of way, with wavy blonde hair, chiseled cheekbones, and green eyes that would've been hypnotic if they weren't narrowed with concern.

Although Angie was sure she'd never seen him before, the family resemblance was unmistakable.

"Excuse me," she called out. "You're from Elysium, aren't you?"

The moment the man saw her, his eyes softened in recognition. "Hello, Angie."

"Apollo?" she ventured.

Much to Angie's surprise, he rushed over and enveloped her in a hug, which made her even more nervous about what might have happened to Ya-Ya. In a trembling voice, she asked him the question that was ripping at her heart. "Is she—?"

Apollo gently cupped his hands on her shoulders. "She's going to be all right."

"Really?" She was blinking back tears now.

"Yes, my dear. Our beautiful Georgia is going to pull through."

Angie collapsed into his arms, muttering an endless string of "Thank Gods." Apollo was so quiet that after a moment Angie wondered if she'd offended him by invoking the name of another deity. But when she looked up at him, she saw there were tears in his eyes, too. At that moment, she knew beyond a shadow of a doubt that he still loved her grandmother. Which meant this had to have been hellish for him, too.

So she tightened her grip on him as if he weren't a stranger at all, but somebody she'd known all her life. And as they held on to each other, amid the life and death of the fourth floor, it occurred to her that if somebody was looking at them now, they'd have a hard time telling who was comforting whom.

All of a sudden, the fatigue Angie had been holding at bay for the past hour kicked in, turning her legs to jelly. Apollo caught her in mid-slump and guided her over to a bench. Then he produced a bottle of water out of thin air and sat down beside her.

"Thanks." She drained half the bottle in a single gulp.

"Would you like something to eat? Sandwich? Cookie?"

Angie smiled and shook her head. There was something oddly sweet about a five-thousand-year-old god offering to get her a cookie. She wondered if he was being nice to her on account of Ya-Ya or if he was just built that way.

Regardless, she had more pressing matters on her mind. "When can I see her?"

"Soon. They just need to complete the angioplasty and get her stabilized."

Angie lowered her head. She hated to hear those words associated with her grandmother, who'd always seemed invincible. But it was better than the alternative.

"What about you?" Angie asked him. "Have *you* seen her?"

Apollo nodded. "Earlier this evening, I sensed she was in danger, so I envisaged her. When I saw what had happened, I left Elysium and arrived just as the paramedics were taking her out of the ambulance. I pushed my way through and took her hand. A few breaths later, her eyes fluttered open and she squeezed back. And her grip was strong, Angie. So strong." He paused, as if reliving that auspicious moment. "Shortly after that, the doctors determined she had a partial blockage in the left coronary artery and took the necessary steps, but I knew right then she was going to come through."

"Could you have … healed her?"

"Yes, but I knew that was something she wouldn't have wanted. She made that clear to me a long time ago. Such a headstrong girl."

A smile that seemed to ache with longing spread across Apollo's face. How odd, Angie thought, that this legendary god, who'd seen and done so many extraordinary things over the centuries, was utterly sprung on her grandmother. So why hadn't they seen each other in years?

Before Angie could press the issue, Apollo turned his head away. When she saw that his shoulders were heaving, she pulled a Nathan's Famous napkin out of her pocket and handed it to him.

"You're a good girl, Angelica. Thank you."

Angie drew in a breath. Very few people called her Angelica and lived to tell about it. But there was someone a long time ago who'd gotten away with it because he had a movie-star smile and gave her a silver dollar every time he saw her.

She touched him on the forearm. "I can't believe I didn't recognize you. I used to see you at Ya-Ya's when I was little, didn't I?"

When Apollo turned back to her, his eyes were still moist, but he was smiling. And he was holding a silver dollar that glistened as he flipped it into her hand. "In all fairness, we told you my name was Mr. Cavanaugh. But you insisted on calling me something else."

"Mister Pitt," Angie chuckled. "Because I thought you looked like Brad Pitt."

A wealth of happy memories came flooding back to her. Playing hide and seek with Apollo and her father amid the potted plants on Ya-Ya's rooftop. Tossing a baseball and occasionally delighting in having her father and Apollo toss *her* back and forth. And sometimes just listening spellbound, as Apollo told her the stories of Pegasus and Medusa and the Twelve Labors of Heracles. *No wonder the stories were so colorful,* Angie thought. *They were pages from his family album.*

But a few months after her father's death, he stopped coming around. Angie couldn't remember whether anybody back then had told her why, she just remembered she was sad about it. Even though he was a grownup and she was just a kid, she felt like she'd lost a friend. Ya-Ya had a few other boyfriends after that, but none of them measured up to Mister Pitt.

Now here he was, sixteen years later, seemingly stricken by the possibility of losing her grandmother. And once again, the question was on Angie's lips. "What happened, Apollo? Why did you and Ya-Ya stop seeing each other?"

Suddenly, Apollo didn't look thirty anymore, but old and tired and beaten down by a thousand regrets. He didn't respond at first. He seemed to be weighing his answer, a habit he shared with Milos. But while she'd called Milos out on it, she decided to hold her tongue with Apollo in deference to his age and résumé.

After another moment, he spoke. "That's for your grandmother to tell you, if she sees fit. But I *will* tell you the decision wasn't mine. If I had my say, I never would have left her side."

Although Angie felt for Apollo, she also wanted to shake him by the shoulders. If it wasn't his decision, whose was it? Zeus's? And if Zeus had prevented his own son from getting tight with a mortal, what chance did she have with Milos? Dammit, didn't he realize how much this informed her future?

Then it hit her that he probably didn't give a rat's tush about Milos and her. He was, after all, a member of the Council, the prickly group that had conspired to join Milos and Electra in politically motivated matrimony and sicced a serpent on *her* to make sure she didn't get too cozy. Sure, he was all heart and hugs now, but if she made another play for Milos, who was to say he wouldn't order the sun to scorch her with a death ray?

Her musings were cut short by the arrival of a middle-aged woman in scrubs. "I'm Doctor Solomon. Are you Georgia Costianes's grandchildren?"

"Yes," Apollo replied, clearly opting to keep things simple.

"Your grandmother came through the procedure very well," Dr. Solomon declared. "She's resting, but I thought you might want to look in on her for some peace of mind."

As Angie released the breath she'd been holding, Apollo extended his hand toward Dr. Solomon. "Thank you, Doctor. That's very kind of you."

"It's my pleasure," she said, subtly indicating her interest in him by holding on to his hand long after the handshake was over.

But tonight would not be the doctor's lucky night. As Angie looked on, amused, Apollo gently shook himself free. "So, shall we have a look at Grandmother?"

Angie couldn't help smiling. How many women, mortal and otherwise, had thrown themselves at Apollo through the centuries? Millions? And how many had he scored with? Millions, minus a few uggos? But by all indications, his heart belonged to a now-elderly lady from Brooklyn whose biggest claim to fame was that she tended a good garden.

The guy had taste, that was for sure.

As Angie followed Apollo and the spurned surgeon into the ICU, she told herself that all that mattered now was that Ya-Ya was okay. And she'd do whatever she could to help her grandmother make a full recovery. Then one day, when Ya-Ya was strong enough, they'd have their talk. And if it was too late for her and Milos, well, she'd have to live with it.

A sigh welled up from deep inside her. *Is it selfish of me to pray for an overnight recovery?*

TWENTY-FIVE

THE FIRST THING THAT went through Angie's mind when she saw the woman in the ICU was that someone had made a mistake. There was no way this could be her grandmother. Lying flat on her back in a dreary hospital gown, stripped of makeup and hooked up to a network of monitors, the woman looked feeble and spent, as if whatever fire had once burned inside her had been reduced to a single flickering flame. And Angie had just seen her two days ago, and she'd been as vital and rosy-cheeked as someone half her age. This woman looked like she could be carried away by the slightest breeze.

"Georgia, I have Angie with me." Apollo's words left little doubt that the woman in question really was her grandmother. Angie shuddered. What did that say about how precarious the health of someone Ya-Ya's age was, and how easy it would be to lose her?

Trying hard to hold back the tears, Angie leaned over and took her hand. "I love you, Ya-Ya."

"Love you, too," she murmured through an oxygen mask. Then her eyes fluttered open, giving Angie a sliver of hope. Despite Ya-Ya's depleted state, her eyes were as blue as they'd ever been, like a crystal-clear lake tucked into the mountains. And when Ya-Ya worked her mouth into a smile, Angie felt her spirits rising again. Her grandmother was still in there fighting. She was going to pull through. She had to.

For the next few days, Angie pretty much camped out at the hospital. Even though Ya-Ya slept a good deal of the time, Angie kept a vigil beside her bed, often reading aloud from a selection of fiction, both noble and trashy. Apollo was often in the chair next to her, and at one point, he augmented her reading of *The Great Gatsby* by reciting the dialogue of Jay, Nick, and Tom without even looking at the pages. And although they never discussed anything of substance, his presence was reassuring—like that of a favorite uncle.

The only time he made himself scarce was when her family stopped by, so as not to arouse any suspicion as to how he might be connected to her or Ya-Ya. As a bonus, he always returned from his wanderings with one or another of Angie's favorite comfort foods— from McNuggets to cupcakes. He was so caring and unassuming that sometimes it was hard to believe he was the same Apollo who'd slain legendary giants and directed the arrow that killed Achilles. One day, over a beer, she'd have to ask him about that, as well as his take on her relationship with Milos. But for the time being, she was determined to stay focused on Ya-Ya's recovery.

And day by day, her grandmother was coming around. At first it was little things, like sleeping less and sitting up in bed. Then Ya-Ya began walking around the hallway, initially on Apollo's arm, then fully on her own. The color came back to her cheeks, she was able to talk without getting winded, and that familiar laugh rang out more and more. By the third day, Angie felt confident enough about

Ya-Ya's recovery to fill her in on the dramatic events at the Yankees game that had led to her change of heart about Milos. That seemed to do more for Ya-Ya than anything else had.

Maybe too much. After wrapping Angie in a hug, Ya-Ya informed her that at one o'clock the following afternoon, she intended to have her long-awaited talk with her.

"Ya-Ya, it's too soon. You heard the doctors. You're supposed to avoid stress."

Ya-Ya waved a dismissive hand in the air. "Do you know what's really stressing me out? The thought that I could leave this Earth before I have the chance to tell you all the secrets I've been holding inside. You'll understand your life a lot better, I promise. You'll also come to realize you do have a future with Milos."

It was impossible not to be persuaded by that notion. Still, Angie knew she'd never forgive herself if the disclosure of such emotionally charged information sent her grandmother's health into a tailspin. So she told Ya-Ya she'd do it on one condition: that Apollo be available to administer his healing powers if anything unforeseen happened to her. Although Ya-Ya balked at first, she eventually gave in, playfully chiding Angie for inheriting her bullheadedness.

So it was on an unseasonably warm October afternoon four days after the heart attack that Angie pulled up a chair beside Ya-Ya's bed and steeled herself for an onslaught, as Apollo stationed himself outside the door, ready to step in if needed.

At the moment, Ya-Ya looked like the picture of health. She was wearing her favorite kimono, a royal blue number with delicate Japanese lettering she'd once joked made her look like a high-class madam. And her hair and makeup were red-carpet worthy, thanks to a candy striper with mad skills Ya-Ya had enlisted with the promise of a home-cooked Greek feast after she was released from the hospital.

Angie, on the other hand, was pretty sure she resembled an extra from *The Walking Dead*. She'd spent the previous night tossing and turning, wondering what manner of bombshells Ya-Ya would be dropping on her. Would they make her sad? Angry? Give her the answers she needed about Milos? She was worried about Ya-Ya, too. What if something happened to her that Apollo was unable to reverse? And even if Ya-Ya got through her confessions unscathed, would their relationship be the same, or forever altered?

With all that uncertainty swirling around in her head, it came as no surprise to Angie that her hands were trembling as she poured Ya-Ya a cup of doctor-approved green tea.

"Thank you, my dear," Ya-Ya said, taking a sip. "If it's all right with you, we'll dispense with the small talk and get to the meat of the matter."

Angie nodded, feeling the butterflies take flight in her stomach.

Ya-Ya took a long look around the room, as if the ghosts of her past were tucked away in the shadows. Then she leaned forward and gently took Angie's face in her hands. "My angel, I love you more than anyone in this world, and that includes the extraordinary gentleman out in the hall. And if I've made a mistake by keeping these things from you for so long, please know I did it because I thought I was protecting you."

Angie offered her an encouraging smile, no easy feat. Then, for the first of what Angie figured would be hundreds of times, she cast a glance at the blood pressure monitor behind the bed. *124 over 85.* So far, so good.

Ya-Ya smiled coyly. "Am I still alive?"

"Yes, Ya-Ya, you're still alive." *God love her,* Angie thought. *Even when she's barely out of the shadow of death's door, she doesn't miss a trick.*

After another sip of tea, Ya-Ya fluffed up the pillows behind her and raised herself to a sitting position. "It's funny. I've told you this story so many times in my head. But now that it's finally showtime, I don't remember any of the words I was going to use, let alone the path I was planning to take. So I suppose I'll just start at the beginning and muddle my way through. Do you remember the story I told you about the furlough your grandfather and I had during the war?"

"Of course," Angie replied. Really, how could she forget? It was one of the most achingly romantic stories she'd ever heard. A young Army lieutenant stationed in London joining his wife, a proud member of the Women's Army Corps, for a two-day leave in Ireland to celebrate their first wedding anniversary. Less than a week later, he'd be killed in combat. But his grieving widow would soon discover that their passionate reunion had produced a lasting treasure of their love. She was pregnant with his son, who was, of course, Angie's father.

Ya-Ya rested her hand on Angie's. "Well, I'm afraid the story wasn't entirely accurate. Zachary did meet me in Belfast, just as I told you. But whether it was the horrors he'd witnessed in the war or something deeper, the weekend was anything but romantic. There was an awkwardness between us, as if we didn't know each other anymore. I can still remember taking a lonely walk along the banks of the Lagan, passing couples holding hands, as Zach holed up in the room—getting his head straight, as he put it. At the end of the weekend, when it was time to go back to our bases, I felt like we weren't just saying goodbye to each other, but to our marriage as well."

319

Two minutes into their talk, Angie was already shaking her head in disbelief. This was light years from the story she'd grown up with, a story that had formed the basis of her belief in the enduring power of love.

Which begged the question, "Did you love him?"

Ya-Ya's mouth twitched into something shy of a smile. "He was a good man, and I have no doubt that he loved *me.* But I think I married him to make everybody else happy. Him. My parents. His parents. I thought if I really worked at it, I could grow to love him. Imagine that. Turning something as wondrous as love into a homework assignment."

Sadly, Angie *could* imagine it. She'd been doing it for years with Nick, under the disapproving eye of her grandmother. Until today, though, she'd figured Ya-Ya's lack of enthusiasm for Nick was about wanting her granddaughter to have the best of everything. But now, it appeared that it might have been about keeping Angie from making the same mistake *she* had.

Ya-Ya set her empty cup down and reached for the teapot. But Angie intercepted it, concerned that she'd overexert herself by hoisting something so heavy.

Which didn't sit well with Ya-Ya. "I'm not helpless."

"I know that. Heck, you're the one doing all the heavy lifting with these revelations of yours. I'm just sitting here like a lump."

Ya-Ya's face softened. "If you really want to be of service, pop some brandy into those cups."

"Silly me," Angie chuckled. "Leaving my flask at home."

That struck Ya-Ya as funny, too, and for a moment, it felt like old times. The two of them making each other laugh and soaking up one another's company. Then the IV beeped, reminding Angie these were critical times and critical things were being said.

It seemed to resonate with Ya-Ya, too. She took a moment to compose herself, then picked up where she'd left off. "Regardless of how I may or may not have felt about Zachary, I was devastated when they told me he was gone. All that goodness, all that potential, cut short in an instant." She paused to wipe a tear from her eye. "The funeral was in Macedonia, where Zachary was born. His father believed a good Greek should return his body to the homeland to fortify the soil no matter where he settled in the world. I don't remember much about the service, other than that it was cold and rainy with a biting wind, and a flock of seagulls kept circling overhead, squawking their brains out. The next day, I took a bus to Piraeus to meet a military vessel that was supposed to drop me back at my base. But the ship was delayed, so I spent the afternoon wandering around the docks, trying not to feel so disconnected from everything around me. Eventually, I stumbled upon Pier Four, Slip 1212 and that perky little fishing boat. And before that son of a bitch Mathias could bark out the fare, I was handing him fifty drachma."

Angie's eyes narrowed in surprise. "Wait a minute. You just happened to find the *Harmonia*? You hadn't heard of it?"

"Not a whisper. But something drew me there, and deep down in my heart I knew I had to climb aboard and let it take me wherever it was going. And the minute I saw that island in the distance, all the hopelessness I was feeling faded away, and I allowed myself to surrender to the beauty of the place—and, of course, one of its inhabitants."

Angie felt a tug on the heartstrings. "Was Apollo waiting for you at the dock?"

"No. I got off the boat and started walking. And even though the island was foreign to me, I wasn't afraid. I just knew I belonged there. I first saw him when I was walking up the path to that bistro of theirs. He literally took my breath away. He was the handsomest man I'd ever seen. But there was a sadness about him, too; the kind of thing that makes a girl hope to God that she's the one to love it out of him. And if he was expecting me, he didn't show it. He just stood there staring at me all goo-goo-eyed as I stared back at him, like those two kids in *West Side Story*.

Ya-Ya looked off into the distance, no doubt reliving that extraordinary moment. When Angie noticed that her eyes were misting up, she reached over and squeezed her hand. "It must have been so romantic."

"It was," Ya-Ya said, squeezing back. "For three days and nights, we never left each other's side. The world knows Apollo as cerebral and unemotional, but he was nothing like that with me. He was sensitive and intuitive and delightfully naughty—everything I'd ever wanted in a lover. But it wasn't just about sex. We talked for hours on end, opening up to each other about our lives, our hopes, our secrets." She chuckled. "Obviously, his were a bit more dramatic than mine."

"What was it like, finding out he was a god?"

Ya-Ya smiled. "A little strange at first. But from the moment we met, there was a chemistry between us that seemed to melt away our differences, even the fact that one of us had been around since the Iron Age. I wanted to stay with him so badly, but I knew I had to get back to my base. Plus, my family would've been frantic if I just disappeared off the face of the Earth. So he arranged for my passage, and we said our goodbyes at the dock. He took my hands in his and promised me it would be forever, if that was what I wanted. Imagine that, the god of the sun telling me the ball was in my court. And even though we stopped seeing each other a number of years ago, he was right about it being forever."

Ya-Ya took a deep breath that seemed to fill her with resolve, then looked Angie in the eye. "He's your grandfather, you know."

Angie gaped at her grandmother, unable to get her mouth working. What she'd just heard was unimaginable. All these years, she'd believed her grandfather was a long-gone war hero she only knew from a faded photograph on Ya-Ya's mantle. But now, to be told that man wasn't her grandfather at all. That she was actually descended from a legendary god who was not only alive, but always would be ...

Well, it was crazy. Preposterous. Hell, if she saw it played out in a movie, she'd stand up and scream, "Oh, please!" at the screen. Things like this didn't happen in the real world.

Then again, up until two weeks ago, she also hadn't traveled to a mythical island, made love with a god, or fought off a serpent, either.

As she ran it all through her head, she was vaguely aware of a nurse coming into the room, changing Ya-Ya's IV and departing. A moment or so later, she felt Ya-Ya's hand on her shoulder. "Are you all right, sweetie? I know it's a shock."

Like getting hit by a beer truck, Angie thought.

"What can I do to help you?" Ya-Ya asked her. "Do you have any questions for me?"

Angie had about a thousand, but one of them elbowed its way to the front. "Does Milos know?"

Ya-Ya nodded. "He was the first person Apollo confided in."

That cleared up a big mystery: Why Milos was convinced there was a future for them. She wasn't just some random mortal. She was the love grandchild of his favorite relative.

Which led to a sticky question. "If Apollo is my ... *grandfather*, doesn't that mean Milos and I are related?"

Apparently, Ya-Ya found the question amusing, because she started to chuckle. But she stopped when she saw the worry in Angie's eyes. "Technically. But considering Apollo is thousands of years older than Milos, I don't think you have to worry about it being incestuous."

Maybe not, Angie thought. But maybe it didn't matter anyway. "I assume Zeus knows about this."

"He does." The response seemed tempered.

"But obviously, he doesn't approve."

"Yet."

Angie wanted to press the issue, ask Ya-Ya what the hell *that* meant. But she was suddenly struck by how utterly surreal this whole thing was. The man she was in love with was a god; her grandfather was a god; and the major obstacle to her happiness was the freakin' king of the gods, who also happened to be her great grandfather.

The word was out of her mouth before she knew it. "Wow." Then she said it again. "Wow."

Ya-Ya beamed. "I still say that sometimes. Wow."

Ya-Ya's words, however ordinary on the surface, hit home with Angie, reminding her that years ago, her grandmother had been in the same place that *she* was now. Faced with a mountain of impossible truths and searching for a way to make peace with them. "How did it feel, Ya-Ya? To know you were carrying the child of a god?"

Ya-Ya took a moment to collect her thoughts. "Exhilarating. Scary. And then there was the guilt."

Angie regarded her quizzically. "Guilt?"

"You have to remember I was eighteen years old, and times were different. I considered myself a modern-thinking person, but the fact of the matter was I'd had a love affair with another man before Zach's body was even cold. As much as I loved Apollo, I couldn't seem to let go of the feeling that I'd let Zach down."

"How?"

Ya-Ya shrugged. "It was a lot of things, really. I felt I'd dishonored his memory. That I hadn't fought hard enough to make things work when we were in Belfast. And mostly, that I hadn't been capable of loving him the way he deserved to be loved."

Angie couldn't believe she was hearing these things from Ya-Ya, who'd always seemed certain about everything she did. Who never seemed to look back. Who hadn't even expressed such dark feelings when her own son died tragically. Then again, maybe the experience had helped mold her into the woman she was today.

"So what did you do? Did you tell anyone about it?"

"Not a soul. As far as our parents and everyone else knew, the child I was carrying was Zachary's. And until the day they died, that was what they believed." Her eyes moved away from Angie, toward the floor. "And maybe that was a sin, too, but it helped them through their grief. Oh, how they doted on that sweet little boy."

Ya-Ya let out a heavy sigh, and her eyes grew moist.

Angie felt like she was on the verge of tears, too, but she forced herself to stay strong for her grandmother, who rarely needed comforting. "You didn't sin, Ya-Ya. You yourself said it brought you back to life. Plus, if you'd told them what really happened, they would've had you committed."

Ya-Ya smiled, but her tears told a different story. As she dabbed her eyes with her handkerchief, Angie stole a look at the blood pressure monitor. *136 over 91.*

Angie directed Ya-Ya's attention to the monitor. "I think we need to get Apollo in here."

"No!" Ya-Ya insisted. "I have to get this out."

"Really? Even if reliving these painful memories is gonna kill you?"

The remark earned a glare from Ya-Ya. "It's not going to kill me." Then, apparently deciding she'd been too harsh, she lightened things up. "And even if it does, I'm sure Apollo can work with it. He's quite gifted that way."

That got both of them chuckling again, easing the tension. And lo and behold, when Angie looked at the monitor again, Ya-Ya's blood pressure had dropped into slightly safer territory.

Angie was about to inform her of that when she discovered Ya-Ya was once again reaching for the teapot.

"Hey!" Angie shouted.

But this time, Ya-Ya gently slapped her hand away.

What a stubborn, frustrating, eccentric, extraordinary woman, Angie thought. *Will I ever have anybody in my life who loves me this much?*

After refilling their cups, Ya-Ya cleared her throat for Round Two. "Angie, I know you're familiar with Greek mythology. Lord knows, I've been pounding it into your head since you were a toddler."

Angie smiled wistfully. Those little lessons were among her favorite moments from childhood. While other kids were hearing lame stories about Jack and Jill trudging up some hill, she was being schooled on the fall of Troy and the three-headed hound who guards the gates of the Underworld.

Ya-Ya continued. "Do you remember what the stories said about beings like Heracles? Children who were produced by the union of a god and a mortal?"

"Yeah, they're demigods. Half mortal, half—" Angie's hand flew up to her mouth. She knew where her grandmother was going with this, and it was mind-blowing. "Oh my God. My father was a demigod!"

Ya-Ya smiled expectantly. "Not just your father..."

The minute the implication sunk in, Angie surprised both of them by bursting out laughing. "Me? Come on, that's impossible. I'm as human as they come. I mean, look at me."

Ya-Ya's expression remained sober. "I *am* looking at you, and I assure you it's the truth. You're a demigoddess, Angie. You have powers you're not even aware of."

Once again, Angie felt the foundation of her life shifting underneath her. If she accepted Ya-Ya's assertion that Apollo was her grandfather, then it followed that she was a demigoddess. A second-generation demigoddess, but a demigoddess, nonetheless. Still, it seemed too bizarre to be true.

So she threw down the gauntlet. "Name one of those powers."

"All right," Ya-Ya replied gamely. "After you were hit by that beer truck, do you remember how quickly all those broken bones healed? What was it, four weeks, without a trace of pain? I think it's safe to say a full-out mortal would still be popping the Vicodin."

Angie couldn't exactly argue. The doctors, her friends, even her physical therapist had marveled at how quickly she'd recovered. Hell, one of them had implied she'd never walk again, let alone swing a bat. But a few weeks later, she'd hit dinger after dinger while zipping around the bases.

Still, *her*? A demigoddess? "Yeah, but—"

Ya-Ya wouldn't let her finish the sentence. "Have you ever had a cold or any other illness that lasted more than a day or so? I can't recall. And do you remember the time you sliced your finger open cutting an apple?"

Angie remembered the blood, that was for sure. Gallons of it, all over her mother's clean linoleum. And when her mother inspected her finger and discovered it was slashed down to the bone, she wrapped it in a dishtowel and hustled her out to the car. But as it happened, the emergency was short-lived. "By the time we got to the doctor's office, it had closed up."

Ya-Ya held her arms out as if to say, *Voila!*

"But ... I'm lousy in math and, well ... generously proportioned."

Ya-Ya smiled. "Not every demigod is the same. It's not like you're produced in a factory. You all have your own qualities and quirks. From what I've been told, Heracles had a crippling fear of rodents."

Angie once again found herself laughing. Little old Angie Costianes from Astoria, a member of the same species as the mighty Heracles?

Ya-Ya was unamused. "What's so funny now?"

"I'm sorry, but you mentioned Heracles. And yeah, maybe he jumped up on chairs when he saw mice, but otherwise, the man was a rock star. He could beat the crap out of anybody—monsters, entire armies, even gods. And didn't he once hold the sky up for his buddy Atlas? Unless I'm missing something, all I seem to be able to do is heal fast. I must be the lamest superhero in the world."

"Correct me if I'm wrong, but you did tell me you killed a serpent, didn't you?"

"Yeah, but I had a weapon. A can of hairspray and a lit candle."

Ya-Ya rolled her eyes. "Some weapon. "I'm sure anybody could kill a ferocious monster with a spritz of extra hold."

Angie flashed back to that pivotal moment in Milos's bedroom when she lashed out at her meager weapon for emitting such a tiny flame, and it turned into a blowtorch. At the time, she'd attributed it to luck. But was it more than that? Had she commanded the flame?

Ya-Ya saw the uncertainty on her face and seized on it. "Trust me, Angie. Once you accept the reality of who you are, you'll discover there's a whole world of magic at your disposal. But there is one other power you've already demonstrated, however 'lame' you may say it is. Do you remember the trick you did with the flowers in my garden the other day?"

Angie frowned. "Yeah, but those were from Elysium."

"Nope. Picked 'em up at the Greenmarket." Ya-Ya swept her hand across the room, indicating an assortment of *get well* arrangements. "And if you don't believe me, give these babies a spin. They can't all be from Elysium, can they?"

Angie took a long look at the flowers, feeling a wave of giddy anticipation coming over her. Then she rose from her chair, took a couple of practice breaths and proceeded to huff and puff her way down the line. Amazingly, the arrangements morphed through a more dizzying array of colors than the flowers on Elysium had. Bright reds, eye-popping yellows, and a fierce shade of lavender that would have done Lady Gaga proud. As she stared at her handiwork, she felt her jaw dropping like a runaway elevator.

Ya-Ya flashed a victorious smile. "Now, do you believe me?"

All of a sudden, Angie felt dizzy, as if the world she'd known was evaporating before her eyes. She was exhilarated. Overwhelmed. And a little scared. All her life, she'd felt there was something special about her, despite the fair-to-middling trappings. But now, to find out that she wasn't just special, she was one rung below immortal...

Once again, the only word she could summon was, "Wow."

As Angie stood there, dumbfounded, Ya-Ya rose out of bed, lovingly placed her hands on her shoulders and kissed her on both cheeks. "You don't know how long I've been looking forward to this day, my angel. You're about to discover all the amazing things you're capable of."

Angie gazed into the eyes of the woman whose love had given her so much of the strength and confidence she had. "Other than you recovering, there's only one thing I want."

"And you'll have him," Ya-Ya replied. "I'm not saying it'll be easy, but I know that between the two of you, you'll make it happen. True love always wins out."

Angie felt her confidence waver. "Does it? What about you and Apollo?"

Ya-Ya sat down on the edge of the bed and sighed, as if she'd been dreading the question. "Did you ask *him* about it?"

"All he told me was it wasn't his decision. It was Zeus's, right?"

Ya-Ya took in a deep breath, then slowly released it. "No. It was mine."

Angie felt her heart stop. "What? No."

"It's a long story, and I'm in need of a nap." Ya-Ya slipped under the covers. "I'll explain it all tomorrow. And not to alarm you, but there are several other things you need to know."

"About me?"

"About you. Your brother."

"Oh my God, he's a demigod, too, isn't he?"

Ya-Ya nodded. "And one day soon, I'll have to have this conversation with him. Oh, what a handful he's going to be when he finds out." Her smile evaporated. "I also have some things to tell you about your father."

Angie felt a chill. "His ... suicide?"

From the heaviness of Ya-Ya's nod, Angie knew not to press the issue. Her grandmother clearly needed a break from all this drama. And her blood pressure was up a bit, too. *128 over 86.*

Feeling a little weary herself, Angie grabbed her purse and kissed Ya-Ya on the forehead. "You get some sleep. I'm gonna grab a cup of coffee. And maybe a bear claw."

As Angie started away, Ya-Ya reached out and took her hand. "One more thing. You know Apollo is outside. Knowing what you know about him now, I'm thinking it might be awkward for you to see him so soon. Shall I call out to him, ask him to disappear down the hall for a moment?"

Angie pondered the question. She definitely had some trepidation, but nothing she couldn't deal with. "No, it's fine. I want to see him."

A smile spread across Ya-Ya's face. "You don't know how eager he is to welcome you to the family."

Angie regarded her, puzzled. "Come on, this can't be that big a deal for him. He's had other grandchildren, hasn't he?"

"A fair number. But none of them have been as special to him as you. I don't want to toot my own horn, but I seem to be the love of his life."

Which was both touching and frustrating. "And yet, you're not together."

Ya-Ya faked a yawn. "Tired. So tired."

But Angie wasn't having it. "Just one question, Sleeping Beauty, and I'll leave you to the luxury of your hospital bed." Angie knelt down on the floor so she could be eye to eye with her grandmother. "Is there any chance you might get back together with him?"

For a moment, there was a girlish glint in Ya-Ya's eyes. But sadly, it disappeared. "Come on, it would be silly. He still looks like a college student and always will. And I'm old, and I'm only going to get older."

Angie stared pointedly at her. "And yet, here he is."

And there was that glint again. "Yes, here he is."

Angie smiled. There was hope in Ya-Ya's tone. Maybe, just maybe, she could find a way to bring her and Apollo back together. An image flashed into Angie's head. The four of them sharing a table at The Ambrosia. She and Milos and Ya-Ya and Apollo. Clinking glasses and laughing and enjoying a picture-perfect day. The thought of her grandmother and her sharing that kind of happiness was beyond any storybook ending Angie could imagine.

Realizing she was on the verge of tears, Angie leaned over and gave her beloved Ya-Ya a kiss on the cheek. "Love you, Ya-Ya. Sweet dreams."

"Love you, too, my little demigoddess."

Angie chuckled to herself. How strange that sounded. But maybe in time, she'd get used to it. After all, Kate Middleton had found a way to warm up to "Duchess." She blew Ya-Ya a kiss and stepped out into the hallway.

It didn't take long to find Apollo. He was sitting on a bench a few feet from the door. And although his midnight blue dress shirt and pleated grey pants were pressed to perfection, his face was creased with worry.

The minute he saw her, he bolted to his feet. "Is everything all right?"

"No worries. She just needs a nap."

Then, without a hint of warning, Angie was crying, overwhelmed by everything she'd heard in the past hour. And one thing in particular.

Apollo was at her side in a heartbeat, regarding her with loving concern. "Angie, are you all right?"

She looked into his eyes and noticed for the first time they were the same color as hers. "Yes . . . Grandpa."

TWENTY-SIX

IT TOOK EVERY OUNCE of self-control Angie could muster not to swing by Rosa's Pizza on the way home and pick up a large Sicilian with double meat. Instead, she settled for two slices with pepperoni and meatballs and washed them down with half a bottle of pinot grigio. And when the bottle kept on calling out to her, she took it across the hall and asked her neighbor to hold it for her overnight. Bad idea. Two hours later, while counting the cracks on her ceiling for the third time, she cursed herself for not finishing it off when she had the chance. At least it would've knocked her out, and a fitful night's sleep and a hangover were better than no sleep at all.

And really, how *could* she sleep? Twelve hours ago, everything she thought she knew about herself and the people she loved was put through a meat grinder. She couldn't deny it was exciting to find out she was a demigoddess. But it was no guarantee of happiness; otherwise her father would still be alive. And what was Ya-Ya going to tell her about his death? Was he unable to cope with being a demigod? Did he cross Zeus or some other bigwig? Up until today, those were the kind of things Angie would've figured he'd share with her. But now everything was up for grabs, including the close relationship she thought she'd had with her father.

Then there was the matter of Milos. On paper, Angie's semi-royal bloodline made it more likely the Council of Gods would be okay with her. It wasn't all that uncommon in Greek mythology for gods to settle down with demigoddesses. But in her case, Zeus and the others were aware that Milos loved her and were still forcing him to marry Electra, a full-blooded goddess and the Oracle's choice for the future. So why did Ya-Ya still think Angie had a shot with him? Was there some detail she hadn't told her that would turn the tide in her favor?

And what was Apollo's take on it? Although he seemed to care about her, Angie wasn't aware of him ever having gone to bat for her. Was he afraid of the wrath of Big Daddy, or was he just plain old-school about mixed marriages?

"God, I wish I could turn my brain off," Angie muttered to herself.

Rolling over onto her stomach, she flipped the pillow over so she could lay her head on the cool side. While that gave her some relief, what she really needed was Milos beside her. Even for a heavyset girl, a queen-size bed could be a damn empty place. She thought back to the night she'd spent with him on the island. Not only had the sex been amazing, but the intimacy afterward had been like nothing she'd ever experienced. As far as she was concerned, there was nothing in the world that could compare with the joy of spending long hours under the sheets with somebody whose mind was as much of a turn-on as his body.

But Milos wasn't here. He was five thousand miles away. And unlike some of her friends, Angie couldn't close her eyes and pretend a pillow or a vibrator was the man she loved. She wondered what he was doing now. Was he alone like she was? Was he unhappily sharing a bed with Electra, or had he come to terms with the hand he'd been dealt? Was the awesome gift he'd given her at the Yankees game a way of telling her he loved her and understood her like nobody else, or was it a parting gift?

Suddenly, she'd had her fill of questions that hung in the air without answers. Wrestling herself to a sitting position, she called out to him. "Milos, I know I told you I never wanted to see you again, but I was wrong. It hasn't even been a week, and I'm missing you like crazy. And if you're watching me now, could you give me a sign? Flick the lights on and off. Flush the toilet. Whatever. Just let me know I'm not alone in this. 'Cause right now, I'm feeling pretty lost."

Angie gave it a minute, but the room remained undisturbed, other than the usual white noise of her upstairs neighbors screwing or fighting or both. With a defeated sigh, she settled back into bed and covered her head with the cool side of the pillow. If sleep came at all, it would be fitful and dreamless.

But sleep didn't come. Nor did any reassurance from Milos. A few hours later, Angie was dragging herself down the hospital hallway toward Ya-Ya's room. She knew her grandmother had physical therapy this morning, but she was hoping they could work in a chat beforehand. She still had so many questions for her, and she knew Ya-Ya had things to tell her, not the least of which was what had sent her father off that bridge.

The minute Angie peeked inside the room, she forgot all about herself and soaked up the tender scene that was unfolding. Apollo was sitting on the edge of the bed feeding Ya-Ya from a bowl of chocolate pudding. A casual observer would have seen it as a devoted grandson caring for his grandmother. But Angie could see the spark in their eyes and the almost sensual way Apollo guided the spoon into Ya-Ya's mouth and she licked off the pudding. What made it especially sweet was the fact that Ya-Ya had been feeding herself since the morning after her heart attack.

After observing them for another moment, Angie cleared her throat. "Good morning, kids."

From the startled expressions on their faces, it was as if Angie had caught them in the sack. But soon enough they were all smiles, like the loving grandparents they were. *Loving grandparents*, Angie thought. A magical development, but one that was going to take some getting used to.

Ya-Ya greeted her with a hug, looking even healthier than she had the day before. "Good morning, sweetie. Did you sleep all right?"

Angie couldn't resist. "Did *you?*"

Through flushed cheeks, Ya-Ya replied, "Sorry to disappoint you, my dear, but I fell asleep around seven thirty and slept straight through till morning."

To which Apollo added, "I can confirm that. I sat here all night holding her hand."

Ya-Ya's eyes widened in surprise, as if this was the first she knew of Apollo's vigil. But soon enough, she had a glow on her face that made her look twenty years younger. Apollo gazed at her longingly, as if his heart depended on her to beat.

If it's the last thing I do, Angie thought, *I'm going to get these two back together.*

Feeling the heat of two pairs of eyes on her, Ya-Ya shifted into business mode. "Angie, I've asked Apollo to take you on a field trip this morning. That is, if you're up to it."

"Sure. Where to?"

"The Brooklyn Bridge."

Angie winced, just as she did every time she heard those words. For a good two years after her father's death, she couldn't even look at the thing—no easy feat considering how prominent it was in the New York landscape. Every time it came into view, she turned her head away, which didn't exactly endear her to her fellow pedestrians when she bumped into them. She also made a point of never riding or walking across it, even if it meant going out of her way.

Then she went through a period of seeking it out. Walking along the pedestrian level and getting as close as she could to the spot where her father had jumped, then staring up at it as if it were a puzzle that could be solved if she put every last brain cell into it. But the answers never came, and she finally told herself that unless she planned to leave Manhattan or gouge her eyes out, she was going to have to make her peace with it. Still, the little girl in her couldn't stop hating it for taking her daddy away.

And right now, the little girl had the floor. "What am I gonna see there, Ya-Ya? It's not like I don't know how he died."

Ya-Ya patted the bed, encouraging Angie to sit beside her. When she did, Ya-Ya kissed her on the cheek. "Believe me, sweetie, I know how painful it is. And if it's easier for you, we can talk it through right here. But I think it would help you to see it for yourself. I know it helped *me*."

Angie stared back at her, confused. "See what?"

Just as Ya-Ya was about to answer, Apollo raised a finger to indicate this one was his. "Angie, I have the ability to not only transport you to a place, but to a specific point in time as well."

He let the statement hang in the air, giving Angie time to grasp the implication.

It only took her a moment. "Why the hell would I want to see that?"

Ya-Ya stared at her purposefully. "Angie, what have I told you, time and again, when you've asked me why your father did what he did?"

"That there are things in life we can't hope to understand until the universe gives us the tools."

"Well today, the universe is giving you the tools."

Whether it was Ya-Ya's words or the wise look that accompanied them, Angie felt a flicker of hope. For half her life, she'd been aching to find out what had sent her father off that bridge. And now her grandmother was telling her her wish was about to be granted. Although the little girl in Angie wanted nothing to do with this junket, the grown woman with a thirst for closure figured she'd never get a chance like this again.

So she took a deep breath and declared, "I'm in."

When she drew back from the hug Ya-Ya had wrapped her in, Angie noticed that Apollo was holding his hand out. Her eyes fell on it warily. "What, you're gonna fly us there?"

"In a sense. We're going to journey through the fabric of time and space. Sixteen years, two months, eleven days, and three and a quarter hours at a physical distance of one point two miles. It should take us approximately forty-six seconds."

Angie took a moment to process that itinerary, then asked him, "And how's all that time-tripping gonna feel?"

"For the most part, pleasant. Not unlike riding downhill on a roller coaster. Although you might want to keep your eyes closed.

I've been told the fast-moving images can bring on nausea in neo-phytes like yourself."

Great, Angie thought. *I'm going to be puking and crying. Perfect way to impress my new grandfather.*

Still, the rewards outweighed any potential embarrassment. So Angie rose to her feet and took Apollo's hand, which was large and sturdy—a five-fingered life preserver, she hoped.

He tightened his grip. "Ready?"

"No, but why let a little abject terror stop me?"

He laughed, but it sounded forced and nervous. Angie had a feeling he wasn't just worried about how she'd handle the journey, but what she was going to see when she got there.

The last thing she heard was Ya-Ya's voice. "Don't worry, Angie. You're in good ha—"

Ya-Ya was cut off mid-sentence, along with every other sound in the hospital. It was the deepest silence Angie had ever experienced, as if somebody had hit the mute button on the whole world. A moment later, she was leisurely bobbing through time and space, feeling like an astronaut in one of those zero gravity chambers. Occasionally, she sensed bright lights in front of her, but she kept her eyes sealed tight. The bagel she'd scarfed on the way to the hospital was making some noise in her stomach, and she wasn't about to let it spoil the party.

"Are you all right?" Apollo asked her, his voice echoing across the void.

"Hanging in there."

"Hold on. We're about to pick up speed."

He wasn't exaggerating. Within seconds, Angie felt a blast of cold air on her face that was so strong her mouth was forced back into a smile. But that was nothing compared to the sensation of plunging downward at breakneck speed. She couldn't believe Apollo had compared it to riding a roller coaster. It was more like what it must feel like to be shoved out of an airplane at thirty thousand feet. The only thing that kept her from screaming her lungs out was the relative security of his hand wrapped around hers. She clung fiercely, thinking if he were a mortal, the back of his hand would be bleeding from the prick of her fingernails.

"We'll be at our destination shortly," he said in the self-assured cadence of someone who knew he couldn't die.

"Hope so," she managed through the rictus her face had become.

"And even though it will feel like we're physically there, we're nothing more than observers. Think of it as being inserted into the celluloid of an old movie. Nothing can hurt you. Nor can you effect change on anything around you."

In other words, I can't save him, Angie thought.

A moment later, their wild ride began decelerating to a saner speed. At the same time, Angie started to make out the sounds of a New York commute. Faint at first, then building to a boisterous crescendo. The whoosh of speeding cars and trucks. Horns honking, occasionally accompanied by four-letter threats. Stereos blaring everything from hip-hop to Christian talk radio.

It was all so distinctively familiar that when Apollo said, "We're here," she almost zinged him with a "Gee, ya think?"

Instead, she opened her eyes and let out a "Whoa!" She was standing next to Apollo on the lower ledge of the massive suspension bridge as traffic hurtled a few feet below them. The shock of finding herself in such a precarious spot combined with the rumble of the road under her feet almost sent her tumbling to the asphalt. Fortunately, Apollo had already put an arm around her, so she merely floundered for a second before getting her bearings.

"Remember, there's nothing to fear," he said, raising his voice to be heard over the hubbub. "Even if you did happen to fall, you wouldn't get hurt."

"Yeah, right," she retorted. "Other than the stroke it would scare me into."

Wrapping her free arm around a girder for added security, Angie took in her surroundings. As opposed to the sunny fall morning they'd left behind, this was a chilly winter day with thick, greyish clouds blanketing the sky, a recipe for a snowstorm if ever there were one.

Still, at first glance, she didn't see any obvious signs that they'd gone back sixteen years in time. "Apollo, this all looks pretty contemporary. Are you sure your time machine's up to snuff?"

"I'm disappointed in you, Angelica," he said through a smile. "I thought you were a car aficionado. What *don't* you see on the roadway?"

Embracing the challenge, Angie focused on the cars whizzing past her. After a minute or so, she realized she hadn't seen a single Prius. Which made sense, considering the popular hybrid hadn't even hit the market in 2000. She also didn't see any Chevy Volts, PT Cruisers, or those hideous Scions that were now polluting the landscape.

"Got it, professor," she said. "No hybrids, Cruisers, yada yada."

"Very good. You'll also notice a difference in the skyline."

As Angie looked across the bridge at Manhattan, she felt her heart catch in her throat. The Twin Towers of the World Trade Center were gleaming proudly. It was hard to look at them, knowing that in less than a year they'd come down in a tsunami of dust and stolen dreams.

Turning to Apollo, she confessed, "After all this time, I still end up crying every time I think about that day."

He nodded sadly. "Of all the evils mankind has perpetrated over the centuries, nothing compares to that which is done in the service of his gods."

Angie didn't know how to respond, considering the author of those words was one of those gods, so she clutched his hand a little tighter. They stood there for a moment before she remembered what this field trip was about. "What time is it?"

Apollo gazed up at the sun and stated, "Twelve-thirty-seven p.m., Eastern Standard Time."

"He should be on the bridge now," she said, courtesy of the police report she'd studied.

"He is."

Angie followed Apollo's outstretched hand to the far end of the bridge and drew in a breath. There it was, coming toward them, her father's pride and joy. A vintage 1965 Ford F-100 pickup truck in a bold shade of orange she'd once dubbed "Daddy's jack o' lantern." As a girl, she loved that truck almost as much as he did, especially when the two of them washed and waxed it on Saturday afternoons while singing along to Bon Jovi, Springsteen, Heart—whoever won the honor of being their CD *du jour*.

The last time she saw it was the day her father died. He dropped her off at school, and as she blew him a kiss, he did his trademark triple tap on the horn and took off in a Day-Glo blur. Later that day, long after the terrible news, the tow yard called her mother to tell her she could pick it up anytime. "Keep it," she said. "That thing is cursed." And for one of the few times in Angie's life, she agreed with her mother.

And now it was that day all over again. The accursed pickup truck was thundering toward her, taking her daddy on the last ride of his life. Her heart swelled with sadness when it drew close enough for her to see him behind the wheel. He looked desperate. Haunted. And was he talking to himself? She knew he wasn't on a Bluetooth. Those vile things weren't around yet.

"Are you all right?" Apollo asked her.

"Yeah." But really, she wasn't. She was seeing her father for the first time in sixteen years. He wasn't a picture on her dresser or an image in an old video. He was alive and breathing. So close she could practically reach out and touch him, or run a hand across the stubble on his cheeks. What she couldn't do was save him.

And his time was running out. He'd reached the midpoint of the bridge. If the police report was accurate, he was about to …

And he did. Without so much as a peek in the rearview mirror, he cranked the steering wheel to the right, sending the truck lurching across two lanes of traffic as the cars around him swerved to avoid him. Amazingly, he got all the way over to the right before a white Camry smashed into his bumper, shoving both vehicles forward another ten feet.

As Angie watched the Camry's airbag explode in a fury of white powder, she quietly uttered the driver's name, a name she'd committed to memory a long time ago. "John Nannicola."

She also remembered where he lived (Jamaica, Queens) and what he did for a living (life insurance). She'd even called him a few months after the accident, pressing him for anything he could remember about her father's demeanor that day. All he said before slamming the phone down was that he hoped her father was burning in hell. "Thanks to that crazy son of a bitch, my back will never be the same."

In fact, as Angie watched, Nannicola stumbled out of his car, pressed a hand against his lower back and grimaced. Then he spotted her father getting out of the truck and unleashed a torrent of anger. "Hey, asshole! What the hell is wrong with you? I'm talking to you, man!"

Her father didn't even turn around, another detail Angie knew by heart. As Angie watched helplessly, he raced over to the side of the bridge and climbed onto the lower ledge, just a few feet from where she was standing with Apollo.

It was all playing out according to script, the moment that had haunted her all her life. Why had Ya-Ya been so bloody eager for her to see this? There wasn't going to be any surprise revelation. No new plot development that changed what she'd believed all these years. Her father was going to commit suicide. And she couldn't do anything to stop him.

But she couldn't just stand there either. Not giving a damn whether Apollo was right about her being impervious to harm, Angie leapt off the railing and barreled toward him.

"Don't do it, Daddy! Please!"

"He can't hear you!" Apollo shouted after her.

Indeed, her father kept right on climbing. Moving like a gymnast, he swung himself up to the middle ledge and set his sights on a towering latticework of girders and steel cables, above which was the top ledge of the Brooklyn Bridge, also known as the suicider's swan dive.

Angie let out a sigh. That was where he'd be leaping from at twelve-forty-one p.m. on this frigid afternoon. And he was well on his way up, meaning she didn't stand a chance of reaching him in time. And what did it matter anyway? He couldn't hear her.

Still, something inside her wouldn't allow her to stand by. With a determined grunt, she boosted herself onto the lowest ledge. Then, using a horizontal cable as a foothold, she climbed to the middle ledge. That was the easy part. The top ledge was at least twenty feet above her, and the only way to reach it was to either wrap her arms and legs around one arm of an X-shaped girder and slither up like a possum or do what her father was doing: scale a vertical girder with ultra-narrow toeholds spaced more than three feet apart.

Praying her jungle gym skills could be coaxed out of retirement, Angie grabbed the girder with both hands and raised her right leg at an impossible angle that nevertheless enabled her to maneuver her foot into the groove. Then she tried to lift her other leg. But she couldn't seem to guide it into the toehold without looking down at it. And when she did, she lost her balance and fell ass-first onto the steel ledge. Although she didn't feel any pain, she was burning with frustration for losing precious time.

Doing her best to shake it off, Angie rushed back to the girder and started over. This time, she managed to get both feet into the groove. But when she tried to climb to the next rung, she discovered her feet were stuck. *Dammit!* And in struggling to work them out, she lost her grip on the girder and pitched backward, dangling by one foot for a moment before wrenching it free and tumbling back to the ledge.

Now she wasn't just frustrated, she was pissed. Royally pissed. Which, she realized, was exactly what she'd been feeling back on Elysium when her makeshift blowtorch failed her. And what had she done then? She'd let her rage explode to the surface, inadvertently triggering a torrent of power. The question was, could she do it on command?

Closing her eyes and placing her fingers on her temples for reasons she didn't fully understand, Angie tried to imagine the anger inside her as a fluid she could coalesce at will. She pictured it flowing from various parts of her body to her lungs, filling them like lava. Her concentration only wavered for a moment, when she allowed herself to wonder whether this was the most lunatic thing she'd ever done. But she brushed the thought aside and focused even more aggressively until she could actually feel the anger coursing through her limbs and down her windpipe. Moments later, she felt an intense pressure coming from her chest, coupled with the sensation that she couldn't quite catch her breath. But she held out, feeding her anger until it felt like she was either going to suffocate or her ribs were going to burst.

Then she let out a mother of a breath. "I WILL DO THIS, DAMMIT!"

Suddenly, she felt a ginormous surge of energy, as if she were a power tool that had just been plugged into a socket. *Yes!* she thought, *superpowers in the house!* Not knowing how long they'd last, she got right to climbing. This time, she was able to coordinate her hands and feet with minimal slippage. In a matter of seconds, she was storming up the ladder, feeling like Spider-Man on speed. Better yet, she'd closed the gap between her and her father and was only a foot or two behind him when he reached the top rung.

Now there was the matter of getting from there to the horizontal girder that formed the top shelf of the bridge. Since the climbing girder was under its wide overhang, reaching it meant making a move that, to Angie, seemed impossible. But her father didn't hesitate.

Jamming both feet securely into the toehold, he took his hands off the girder and swung the top half of his body out—backward, no less!—and grabbed the top girder. Then he freed his legs from the toehold and hoisted his body onto the girder in one colossal pull-up.

Angie couldn't believe what she was seeing. Her father had always been athletic, but she'd never witnessed him performing such superhuman feats. Clearly, he'd chosen to keep his demigod-ness under wraps.

As Angie watched her father scramble to his feet, she wondered if it was even worth trying to replicate his maneuver. He was up there now. What was he gonna do, other than jump?

Then she heard him murmuring something. And when she realized what it was, she had to choke back the tears.

"Our Father, who art in Heaven. Hallowed be thy name ..."

As poignant as it was, it also meant she had the length of a prayer to get to him. Jamming her feet into the toeholds, she said a quick prayer of her own before swinging her arms out toward the girder. Unfortunately, since she was six inches shorter than he was, she couldn't quite reach it. So she inched her feet out from the toehold and tried again. Now her fingertips were touching the girder, but she still needed a smidge more body length to get a grip. Wiggling her feet ever so slightly, she stretched her arms back ... farther ... farther ...

Until her hands were touching ... grasping ...

Suddenly, her feet slipped out of the toeholds. She desperately tried to lock her hands around the girder, but her left hand slipped off and she teetered in the air for a moment, feeling her right arm stretching out of its socket as it bore the weight of her entire body.

But the fight wasn't out of her yet. "Oh hell, no! I am *not* gonna come this close and fail!"

Once again summoning up that feral brew of anger and power, Angie began pulling herself up by one arm. All one hundred and sixty pounds of her. And even though it didn't hurt per se, it took every ounce of strength and concentration. At one point, her right arm was trembling so badly from the strain that she thought it might part company with the rest of her body, sending her hurtling to the road.

Thankfully, it held out, and she was eventually able to gain enough leverage to raise her left arm up beside it. Then she boosted her whole body onto the girder in a gymnastic tour de force that called to mind a pommel horse routine she'd done in high school gym class. Perfect timing, too, as her father was finishing his prayer.

"For thine is the kingdom, the power and the glory, forever and ever ..."

"Amen," she said in tandem with him, trying not to look down at the East River a hundred feet below. Then she rushed over to him and pleaded, "Don't leave me, Daddy. Whatever it is, we can talk it through."

She reached out to touch him, fully expecting her hand to go through him. But she actually felt the soft cotton of his shirt and the warmth of his shoulder underneath. She drew in a breath at the wonder and sadness of it.

Then things got even spookier. Still facing away from Angie, her father said, "I won't let you down, Sugarplum."

Angie was so stunned she almost fell off the girder. "You can hear me?"

But he didn't respond. He took a deep breath, then stepped over to the edge of the girder and launched himself off the bridge.

"Noooo!" she cried out.

But her scream was cut short by the impossible sight before her eyes.

Her father wasn't plummeting toward the river, he was moving across the sky.

It can't be, Angie thought. What she was witnessing defied logic and gravity. Then again, her father was a demigod. As she watched, enthralled, he continued gliding through the air until he was a good twenty feet away. Was this what Ya-Ya had wanted her to see? But what did it mean? If he wasn't trying to commit suicide, what was he doing?

The next thing Angie knew, Apollo was beside her, answering the question before she could ask it. "He's trying to get to *you*."

Now she was even more confused. "Why?"

"Remember, it was the *you* of sixteen years ago. You never knew it, but you were in danger that day. Your father learned of it just as he started driving across the bridge. So he pulled over and tried to fly to your rescue. But for reasons I'll never understand, his powers failed him."

Apollo didn't have to say another word. It was happening before their eyes. Angie's father began losing momentum, slowing to a crawl and losing altitude. He struggled mightily to rise in the air, but it was no use. Like an airliner that had lost all its engines, he began plunging headfirst toward the East River. Just as he was about to hit the water, Apollo grabbed Angie by the shoulders and spun her away.

As Angie stood there, overcome with emotions, Apollo uttered two sentences that would stay with her forever. "Your father didn't kill himself, Angelica. He loved you with all his heart."

From somewhere deep inside her, Angie let out a wail. It was as if someone had opened the doors of the cell she'd been imprisoned in all these years. She felt free, fifty pounds lighter and possessed of a whole new understanding of her father. He hadn't left her, he'd sacrificed his life to try to save hers.

"He really did love me," she said as the tears started to fall.

"As much as any father ever loved a daughter."

But sadly, one thing hadn't changed. "I'll never stop missing him."

"Nor will I," Apollo replied, his voice wavering.

And then it hit her. She'd been so caught up in herself that she'd forgotten a sad, simple truth. "My God, Apollo, he was your son."

Apollo managed a nod. "And even though he didn't succeed in his mission, I will always be proud of my brave boy."

Angie tried to get out the words, "Me, too," but they were lost in her sobs. Then Apollo wrapped his arms around her and she felt his body heaving along with hers.

As they consoled each other, Angie remembered something he'd told her a few minutes earlier. A statement that was aching for detail. "You said I was in danger that day, but obviously my father never got to me. Who stepped in, Apollo? Was it you?"

"No, Angie. It was Milos."

TWENTY-SEVEN

"IT WAS MILOS."

By her own estimation, Angie had repeated those words a hundred times since Apollo first uttered them this afternoon. And now she was winging her way across the Atlantic in the hopes of busting up a royal wedding and laying claim to her rescuer. It all felt so symmetrical. So poetic. As if the tale of Angie and Milos had been written hundreds of years ago by some starving but hopeful bard, and this was the sweepingly romantic, against-all-odds third act.

You saved my life, Milos, she thought. *Now I'm going to save yours.*

But first, she'd have to survive a ten-hour flight in a filled-to-the-gills coach section, which was already scheming to dampen her spirits.

"We're all out of cheeseburgers," the flight attendant coolly informed her. "But we have plenty of chicken Caesar salads. Interested?"

After cursing herself for getting to the airport too late to grab something at the Sbarro counter, Angie nodded halfheartedly. "And throw in a bag of M&Ms. You're not out of those, are you?"

"No worries." The flight attendant, whose nametag identified her as "Madison," gave Angie one of those Barbie-doll smiles that managed to be both sunny and insincere. Then she plucked the ATM card out of Angie's hand with her pale pink French tips and ran it through her shiny little machine, all the while humming something vaguely Beyoncé.

God, I miss Jace! Angie thought. *And everything else about first class.*

In truth, she'd had a chance to go first class. Ya-Ya had tried to spring for her airfare, arguing that a demigoddess on a crusade deserves to travel in style. Apollo had stepped up to the plate, too, hinting at some godly hocus-pocus that could get her there in under a minute. But after this morning's time travel experience, Angie figured she'd had enough freaky forms of transportation to last a lifetime. More importantly, she wanted to make this quest on her own terms. And that meant with her own bank account, measly as it was.

So she politely turned both of them down and bought herself a one-way economy seat, which at fifteen hundred bucks would be making her credit card company happy for months. She'd considered getting a round-trip ticket, which was only three hundred dollars more. But since there was no guarantee she'd live past tomorrow, she decided to hang on to her assets for the sake of her heirs—a giggle if ever there was one.

The only thing she asked of Ya-Ya and Apollo was to refrain from telling Milos about her mission. She couldn't quite articulate it, but her gut told her it was best that he not know she was coming until they were face to face.

And oh, what a face to be face to face with. The minute Apollo told her it was Milos who'd saved her life that day, Angie knew she had to make this trip. Granted, finding out she was a demigoddess

353

and granddaughter of a legendary god had helped coax her along. And learning the truth about her father's death had been even bigger. Not only had it rewired some of the self-pitying circuits in her brain, it had filled her with a sense of responsibility. A feeling that she owed it to her brave, beautiful daddy to lead an extraordinary life.

And how better to do that than to risk everything to be with the man she loved, who also happened to be the reason she was alive today.

Apollo had told her the whole story after whisking her back to Ya-Ya's hospital room. It had kicked off twenty years ago, when Poseidon fell out with the other gods over how to engineer their return to dominance. As Poseidon prepared to leave Elysium and set up shop elsewhere with a sprinkling of supporters, he ordered Milos and Jace to join him. Apparently, it didn't matter to him that he'd been a lousy father who hadn't lifted a finger to raise them. In Poseidon's eyes, blood was blood, and their duty was to follow him even if they didn't agree with his philosophy. Jace went along with him, thinking it might be a way to finally earn his love and respect. But Milos refused, which filled Poseidon with a rage that festered over the years, along with a need to punish him.

At this point in the telling of the story, Apollo cast a wary glance at Ya-Ya, knowing he was getting into heavy territory.

"It's all right," Ya-Ya assured him. "Angie's strong. She needs to know everything."

"Right," Angie added, trying to smile away her apprehensiveness. "No more secrets."

Apollo nodded dutifully and continued. "For a long time, Poseidon watched Milos from afar, trying to determine the form his revenge was going to take. Then he began to notice how attached he was becoming to you, in spite of the fact that he hadn't even met you. And as that attachment blossomed into love, the answer became clear to him. He'd do away with you and," Apollo hesitated ever so briefly, "send your head to Milos with his regards."

Angie shuddered. "So this major league god was going to punish his son by killing an innocent girl from Queens?"

"Welcome to our world," Apollo replied, his voice thick with shame. "And on that dark day in December, Poseidon dispatched two of his minions, both of them demigods, to accost you on your way home from school. Fortunately for all of us, Jace couldn't abide such madness and returned to Elysium to warn his brother."

Angie's eyes flew wide open. "Oh my God. I owe my life to Jace, too."

"You do, although he'd never take credit for it. Ever since that day, he's been trying to convince his brother that his loyalties will never again shift back to his father. I wish I could say that fence has been mended, but Milos can be mercilessly stubborn."

Angie took all this in, then asked Apollo a question that had been eating at her since their trip to the bridge. "But how did my father find out about the plot?"

Apollo flinched, as if he'd been hoping the question would never come up. Then he took a deep breath and unburdened himself. "I felt it was my duty as a father to tell him what was about to transpire. Even though I had no idea how things would go, I assured him we'd sent someone to your school and no harm would come to you. But clearly, he read the fear in my voice and decided to try to get to you himself. It's a decision I will regret for the rest of my days."

There was a pause in the story as Ya-Ya got out of bed, put her arms around Apollo, and wept with him over their loss. Angie wiped away her own tears, hoping her father was in a place where he could look down on all of them and see how much he was loved.

After composing himself, Apollo told Angie how Milos had confronted the demigods as they waited for her outside her school. It was a bloody battle that played out on the streets and in the sewers, but ultimately Milos killed them both and sent their heads back to his father with *his* regards.

"Wow," Angie heard herself saying.

"Wow, indeed," Apollo replied. "And a few hours later, he saved your life again."

For a moment, Angie stared at him, clueless. Then a rush of clarity hit her, and a sixteen-year-old mystery was solved. "He was there when I fell off the roof!"

Apollo nodded. "He told me he couldn't leave without making sure you were going to be all right. He watched you throw all those things off the roof that reminded you of your father, and he intercepted some of them, thinking you might want them one day."

"And then he caught *me*," Angie declared, "when the sound of the door banging open scared me off the roof. One minute I was hanging in the air, and the next minute I was safe and sound. And to think, I called him a stalker."

Apollo chuckled, then forged ahead. "After Milos returned to Elysium, we agreed there was a strong chance Poseidon would try to harm you again, so I persuaded Zeus to have a summit with him. Zeus warned Poseidon that whatever his differences were with his son or anyone else on Elysium, he could no longer take them out on the world at large, unless he fancied the idea of banishment to Tartarus."

Apollo's face turned dark. "Of course, Poseidon demanded something in return. A private audience with his son."

Angie gasped. "The scars on Milos's back."

"A souvenir of two weeks of torture at the hands of Poseidon. It was beyond savage, even by *our* standards. As you may have learned by now, most of our wounds eventually heal. But Milos endured it all because of his love for you. I can honestly tell you in all these years, that love has never wavered."

As Angie sat there, feeling her love for Milos wash over her in wave after wave, she decided her first order of business after being reunited with him would be to plant kisses on each and every one of those scars.

"Okay, I've got your salad and your M&Ms," Madison declared. "Did you say Diet Coke?"

Blasphemy! Angie almost shouted. Instead, she coolly corrected her. "*Regular* Coke."

"Regular Coke?" The look on Madison's face indicated she was petrified by all those empty calories. But she poured the demon beverage anyway. "I assume you want the whole can."

"You assume right, Madison," Angie replied with a sunny smile of her own.

Sure, a part of her wanted a glass of wine. And maybe a mojito. The past few days had been a blitzkrieg of revelations, and the next twenty-four hours looked to be equally explosive. Which was why Angie knew she had to give United a pass on their seven-dollar mini-bottles. It was essential that she be at her most clearheaded for the challenges ahead. And afterward, if all went well, she'd break her booze-fast by sharing a glass of champagne with Milos. And after they made love, another one.

She checked her watch. The flight had been in the air for a little over an hour, which meant she wouldn't be touching down in Athens for another nine hours, around three p.m. local time. According to Apollo, Milos was scheduled to marry Electra at eight o'clock that evening. So from the moment Angie got off the plane, she'd have to haul ass and pray for a bucketful of miracles if she had any hope of getting to him before the wedding.

And then what? Would Milos stand up to his superiors and refuse to marry Electra, or would he tell her it was too dangerous and insist she leave? And even if Milos tried to ditch the wedding, would they let him? And what might they do to *her,* the wedding crasher? Would they respect her bloodline and leave her alone, or would they sic a whole nest of serpents on her?

There were a thousand ways this mission could go wrong and only a handful it could go right. And *wrong* could mean more variations of dead than a *Final Destination* movie. Without a doubt, this was the most foolhardy thing Angie had ever done.

And she'd never felt more alive.

She popped a handful of M&Ms into her mouth and chased them with a swallow of Coke. She couldn't deny she was a little scared. But didn't professional athletes say they always got butterflies before the big game? Granted, this game could be a death match, but the bottom line was that life without Milos was a sad proposition. It was like being served hamburger all your life, then suddenly being treated to filet mignon, only to have it pulled after one meal and replaced by hamburger till the day you croaked. How could you ever look at that bland little patty again without pining over the loss of that brief period of deliciousness in your life?

Not that she was equating Nick with ground chuck, but Milos was the love of her life. The Romeo to her Juliet, the Lancelot to her Guinevere, the Jack to her Rose. Nobody else would ever come close.

So if she didn't at least try to get with Milos, she'd either be alone forever or end up settling for someone who didn't ring her bell. And that wouldn't be fair to him *or* her—especially her.

And if she failed? Well, she'd still be a winner, because she'd put it all out there for love. And really, how many women could say they'd gone toe to toe with the almighty Zeus to get what they wanted?

On one level, Angie was thankful to Nick. She never could have lived with herself if she'd left for Elysium without leveling with him about her feelings. So a few hours earlier, she'd called him and asked him to meet her at a pub near the hospital. She had no intention of getting into specifics about her trip. Hell, all that stuff about gods and monsters would give him an aneurysm. But she figured she at least had to let him know she was going there to meet the man she loved. And that, sadly, she'd never feel that way about him.

Sitting there waiting for Nick to arrive, Angie felt sick to her stomach about having to let the poor guy down for the second time in two months.

But then an amazing thing happened. He let *her* down.

"Ang, I know what you're gonna say," Nick declared over a pitcher of beer and a bowl of popcorn. "You want to make this thing between us exclusive again, maybe even dust off those wedding plans. But I gotta say, I'm not feeling it."

Angie practically kissed him right there on the spot, but she managed to keep her emotions in check. "What are you saying, Nick?"

"I'm saying I want to play the field. Keep seeing your cousin, maybe some other women." He drained his beer. "All this time, it's just been us. And that's been nice in a lot of ways, but I want to make sure I haven't missed out on something, I don't know ... better."

Angie didn't know whether Nick was sincere or trying to save face. Maybe he'd recognized that heavy look in her eyes from the last time she'd broken up with him and decided to beat her to the punch. Either way, it didn't matter. The deed was done, and he'd come through with his pride intact. So she gave him a hug and finished her beer, hoping she'd always have him in her life. The way she saw it, people who know you, who really know you, need to be kept close and treasured, even if they don't make your heart sing the way you sometimes wish they could.

Angie's train of thought was derailed by an announcement that crackled over the PA system. "Ladies and gentlemen, the captain has turned on the seat belt sign, indicating we're approaching some turbulence. Please return to your seats and make sure your seatbelts are fastened."

What was even more priceless than Madison's tired drone was the blasé look on her face. Clearly, it would be no big deal to her if her passengers got tossed around the cabin like tennis shoes in a dryer. Still, Angie beamed at her as she passed by, pretending to inspect her belt.

Then the plane *did* take a bounce. A big one that felt like being on an elevator when the cable snapped and sent it plummeting ten stories. Food and drinks went flying, passengers screamed and Madison was caught unprepared. As Angie watched with morbid fascination, the willowy brunette shot up five feet in the air, hit her head on the ceiling with a thunk, then pitched forward into the lap of an elderly gentlemen who stared slack-jawed at her nearly naked tush. Needless to say, she'd picked the wrong day to wear a thong.

A split second later, no doubt feeling the weight of a hundred pairs of eyes on her, Madison wrestled her skirt down over her thighs and rose to her feet. Then she scanned the sea of faces and seemed to settle on Angie, as if the whole thing were *her* doing.

Don't look at me, Angie was tempted to say. *It's not my fault you're bare-assed.*

Thankfully, over the next few minutes, both Madison and the turbulence settled down. For her own sake, Angie hoped they'd passed through the worst of it. What crappy irony it would be to be flying across the world to claim your soulmate only to have it rendered null and void by temperamental jet streams.

A moment later, Angie was sipping what was left of her Coke and thinking about her last conversation with Ya-Ya, which, like everything else these past few days, had surprised the stuffing out of her, and at the same time, inspired her.

After sharing a goodbye hug with Nick, she'd headed back to the hospital to find Ya-Ya alone in her room, doing a Sudoku puzzle. Ya-Ya seemed happy to hear how well things had gone with Nick and smiled when Angie passed along his declaration that she'd always be his favorite Ya-Ya. "I like that boy a lot more when I don't have to think of him as family," Ya-Ya declared.

"Me, too." Angie plopped down on the edge of the bed. "So where's Apollo? He hasn't gone back to Elysium, has he?"

Ya-Ya shook her head. "He thought you and I might need a little alone time. Don't worry. He'll be back before you leave for the airport."

Then she burst into tears, catching Angie off guard. "What is it, Ya-Ya? What's wrong?"

For a moment, Ya-Ya didn't respond. Then she grumbled something to herself and took a swat at the mattress. "Dammit, I promised myself I wouldn't do that!"

Under the circumstances, it probably wasn't a good idea to chuckle, but Angie couldn't help it. "Tears. Anger. If you were a little younger, I'd say your monthly visitor has arrived. What's bugging you, Ya-Ya?"

That seemed to lighten her mood. "Well, for one, I touched up my makeup a minute ago, and now I must look a fright."

"Let me take a look." Angie tilted her head toward Ya-Ya and faked a gasp. "Ooo, that *is* grisly. Let me see what I can do."

Pulling a Kleenex out of her pocket, Angie dabbed at the mascara that was running down Ya-Ya's cheek. Then she stepped over to the bedside dresser in search of the makeup kit.

"Bottom drawer," Ya-Ya called out.

As Angie retrieved the makeup, she heard Ya-Ya clear her throat. "Angie, I've wanted you to be with Milos ever since I can remember. And I'm so proud of you for taking this brave step and going after him. But at the same time, I'm worried sick. I don't want to lose you, sweetie."

Angie fought off the tug she felt on her heartstrings. "Okay, first off, no more tears. Unless you enjoy looking like a raccoon."

Ya-Ya smiled. "I'll do my best."

"You'd better." Angie set to work fixing Ya-Ya's mascara, hoping she could keep her own tear ducts dry. "Ya-Ya, I'd love to tell you I'm gonna get through this thing unscathed, but we both know I can't make that promise. What I will promise you is that I'll fight for it like I've never fought for anything in my life."

Ya-Ya gave her a squeeze on the forearm. "I know you will, sweetie. I'm just an old fool for flapping my mouth."

Angie smiled. "Speaking of which, those lips of yours need a little TLC, too." She took out a tube of L'Oreal and traced it over her grandmother's elegant mouth. "Now, I need you to promise *me* something."

"Anything," Ya-Ya said through rose taffeta lips.

Angie set the lipstick down. "Promise me that no matter what happens, you'll go on with your life, knowing I was doing something I believed in. And you and Apollo won't blame yourselves."

Ya-Ya sighed. "You mean like we did when your father died?"

This was news. "Both of you? I thought it was just Apollo who felt that way."

Ya-Ya took one of those long, deep breaths that seemed designed to build up a store of energy for a draining revelation. "You asked me why I stopped seeing Apollo. I can assure you he was never anything less than a loving partner. And no, I didn't blame him for your father's decision to take what he'd told him about Poseidon and try to get to you first. I stopped seeing him because I couldn't get over my own guilt."

Now Angie was really confused. "Over what? You knew Daddy hadn't killed himself."

"It may sound crazy to you, but your father's death resurrected all the guilt I'd been feeling when I was pregnant with him. No matter how hard I tried, I couldn't shake the feeling that it was my penance for dishonoring Zack's memory. That I was being punished for being intimate with another man so soon after he died. So I told Apollo I couldn't see him anymore, couldn't bear the pain. And he didn't fight it, really, because at the time he was beating himself up for his own reasons. He also agreed to respect my decision to keep the truth from you."

How sad, Angie thought, that two people who loved each other so much had guilted themselves into breaking up at a time when they needed each other the most. Then another cylinder clicked into place in her head. "*That* was why you didn't tell me for so long! You didn't want to lose me like you lost Daddy."

Ya-Ya nodded. "I thought if you never found out about it, you could lead a normal life. A safe life. And it pained me to do that, especially to keep you in the dark about how your father really died. But I told myself I was protecting you. I thought it would be too much for you to handle at such a young age. Not just about your ancestry, but the fact that there were people out there who wanted to kill you. I kept thinking, 'One day, I'll tell her.' But with every year that passed, I found myself loving you more, and I couldn't imagine my life without you in it. I was selfish, Angie. And I'm so sorry for that."

Angie didn't know how to respond, probably couldn't have put two words together if she tried. So she wrapped her arms around her grandmother and held her close enough to feel the beating of her heart. *Please let that beautiful heart of hers keep beating for a long, long time,* Angie begged through her sobs.

After a moment, Angie noticed something odd. "Ya-Ya, you're not crying."

"You ordered me not to."

That got both of them laughing. And after applying a Kleenex to her own leaky eyes, Angie asked her, "So what made you change your mind about telling me?"

Ya-Ya smiled faintly. "Believe me, from the minute you got engaged to Nick, I grappled with it every day. But it wasn't till the day of your wedding that I realized the time had come. When you ran down that aisle, I was so inspired by the strength you demonstrated, strength I never had at your age. I couldn't be sure what you were thinking, but I figured it had finally sunk in that you needed more.

And then, of course, you were struck by that beer truck. And I wondered if in trying to protect you, I was doing just the opposite. That you could be destroyed by *not* having your heart satisfied just as easily as you could by mixing it up with the gods. At the very least, I knew I had to give you the chance to see for yourself. And if you decided it was for you, we'd take it from there."

Angie felt a calmness settle over her. "And the rest, they say, is history."

Ya-Ya reached out and caressed her cheek. "My angel, I want you to have everything you deserve. Everything I was afraid to take for myself. And maybe that's what this whole saga has been about, starting with my first trip to Elysium. Maybe it was laying the foundation for this magical union between you and Milos."

"Maybe. But maybe it was also opening the door again for you and Apollo."

Ya-Ya didn't say a word. But a moment later, when Apollo appeared in the doorway, the sparkle in her eyes spoke volumes. And Angie gave herself a pat on the back for helping Ya-Ya fix her makeup, because it didn't take a genius to figure out who she was trying to look good for.

Angie almost said her goodbyes then and there. Her flight was only four hours away, and she still had to stop by her apartment and toss some things into a suitcase. But there was something she was aching to ask Apollo, something she'd put off far too long. "So tell me, Apollo, where are you on this Milos and me thing? Do you want us to be together, or is it all about the Oracle?"

For the second time that day, Apollo flinched. Obviously, in his corner of the world, people didn't put things to him so bluntly. Then a smile spread across his face. "Angelica, I would like nothing more than for Milos to have the benefit of your wisdom and beauty for the rest of your days. And now that I know it's what you and Georgia want, I will do everything in my power to help you make it a reality. I warn you, it won't be easy, but such things are not without precedent."

"What, like once every thousand years?" she quipped.

Angie wasn't prepared for the somber look Apollo gave her. "Not quite."

He must have picked up on the subtle slump in her shoulders, because he stepped up to her and took both of her hands in his. "I've watched you grow up, Angie. And I can honestly say I've never seen a demigoddess exhibit the raw powers you have without a whit of instruction. Not a second-generation demigoddess. Not even first generation."

Although that gave Angie a ripple of hope, she couldn't help pointing out the obvious. "But I'm going up against the heavy-weights."

"Not all of them. I'll be there for you, and I suspect I won't be alone. But never underestimate the fact that you have love on your side. With all the fire and fury in both of our worlds, there is still no stronger weapon."

And now, as she winged her way across the Atlantic, Angie played that statement over and over, hoping it would prove true for her tomorrow.

Now, if she could just do something about the turbulence. It had picked up again a few minutes ago, making it feel like they were lurching down a dirt road in a car with four flat tires. This time, Madison hadn't even bothered to make an announcement. She'd ducked into an empty seat near the back of the plane and strapped herself in. Apparently, she didn't want to run the risk of exposing the goods again.

Then the plane took a bounce that caused several overhead bins to pop open, including the one across the aisle from Angie. At first, only a duffel bag slid out and plopped harmlessly to the floor.

Then the plane pitched even more violently, and suddenly a guitar case was flying at her like a fiberglass missile.

Before the word "Shit!" was out of her mouth, Angie was bent all the way forward, covering her head with her hands.

No doubt about it, this was gonna hurt.

But then a second passed, and another one, and there was still no impact. Nor did Angie hear the crash of the guitar case landing elsewhere. Just a few "Oh my Gods!" from the passengers around her. What the hell was going on?

She slowly raised her head and turned toward the aisle. And practically lost it.

There was Madison, inches away, clutching the errant instrument. But that was impossible. There was no way she could've covered twenty rows in two seconds.

Angie stared up at her, her face a question mark. "How did you ..?"

Madison gave her a scathing look. "When my brother asked me to do this stupid favor for him, I had no idea you'd be flying coach."

For just a moment, Madison's near-bulimic face and cropped brown hair shimmered away in favor of the features of a dazzling blond with stormy blue eyes, full lips and full everything else.

The name sprang out of Angie's mouth just as quickly. "Aphrodite?"

She nodded brusquely, then crouched down in the aisle so they were eye to eye. "All I can say is you'd better kick ass tomorrow. I'd hate to think I went through all this for nothing."

TWENTY-EIGHT

"Are you ready, dearest?" Electra asked him.

Milos smiled back at the woman who would be his wife in less than an hour. He had to admit, Electra looked beautiful this evening. Her long red hair was embellished with a sprinkling of curls that gave her an almost girlish quality, a word he never thought he'd associate with the capricious daughter of Hades. Furthering that look was the light touch with which she'd applied her makeup, which served to enhance her features rather than make headlines of them. She wore a simple crown of white orchids that matched her knee-length tunic, the official garment for this ceremonial event. Her only affectation was a pink sash she'd cinched around her waist to spotlight a figure that had put many a siren to shame.

"Yes, dearest, I am," Milos replied. And really, he was.

They were standing on a mesa about a hundred yards from where the wedding was about to take place—atop the highest summit on Elysium at the crest of the waterfalls. Accompanying them were Eddie and Chrissie, who in a few moments would fly them to the summit to begin things. The horses had been groomed so beautifully that Milos could practically see his reflection in their coats. And around each of their necks was a wreath of white roses.

The entrance had been Electra's idea. "It'll be like something out of a royal wedding," she'd boasted. "The two most beautiful people in the universe descending from the sky on two magnificent horses." Milos hadn't bothered to remind her that only a week earlier she'd called those horses "foul, putrid creatures who should be hustled off to a dog food factory." He knew this was her way of atoning for her treatment of Angie. Plus, it was a good idea.

And while Milos would never forget how cruel she'd been to Angie, he'd largely forgiven her. It would've been one thing if Electra's behavior had been purely malicious. But when she broke down and confessed it was prompted by romantic jealousy, it opened his eyes to the fact that there was a heart beating inside that porcelain exterior. And while he couldn't say he loved *her,* he was finding her more and more enjoyable to be around. She was intelligent, passionate, and witty—when she wasn't using humor as a weapon. Maybe there really was hope for them beyond their role as the face of the family.

And that wasn't something to be sneezed at, either. Of all the younger gods on Elysium, the Oracle of Chaos had prophesized that he would be the one to steer the family into the future, the only stipulation being that he had to do it alongside Electra. Was that such a high price to pay for the honor of being their vanguard?

Milos gazed over at the mountaintop where they were all gathered: Zeus. Hera. Apollo. Aphrodite. Jason. The ancient and the not so ancient, eagerly awaiting the arrival of the betrothed couple, knowing this union was the first step toward leading mankind again, after nearly seventeen hundred years of waiting. And Milos felt a kinship with them he hadn't felt in a long time. *The blood of the mighty runs through my veins. I really do belong in their midst.*

An assertion Electra was only too happy to back up. "Uh, Milos? You know how Zeus hates to be kept waiting."

He turned around to find that she'd climbed astride Chrissie and was pointing to Eddie. Maybe it was the mood Milos was in, but something about the insistent look on her face made him want to toy with her. "Far be it from me to inconvenience Zeus on *our* special day."

Electra laughed, further raising Milos's hopes about their future. He gave her a smile, then jogged over to Eddie, who was sunning himself in the tall grass a few yards away. "The time has come, my friend. Duty calls."

If the stallion heard him, he didn't show any sign of it. He was staring off into space, as if his mind had gone on a journey and left his body behind.

Slightly unnerved, Milos waved a carrot under his nose. "Come on, Eddie. Perk up."

Eddie gave the carrot a halfhearted snuffle, then turned away again. This was beyond peculiar. Eddie had never turned down a carrot in his life. They were as precious to him as pizza was to Angie.

"Is something wrong with him?" Electra called out.

"I don't know." Milos stroked the horse's muzzle. "Eddie, are you feeling all right?"

Still, the horse didn't respond. And it wasn't like he was sleeping. Eddie always slept with his head down and his bottom lip drooping, as his eyes fluttered open and shut in tandem with his dreams. This was unprecedented behavior for Milos's companion of twenty-two years, and it worried him.

"Maybe he's just nervous about the ceremony," Electra offered.

"Maybe so." In fact, Electra might have hit it on the head. Eddie had never enjoyed performing for crowds, which was essentially what was being asked of him tonight. Once again, Electra was exceeding Milos's expectations.

Now, if he could just bring Eddie out of his funk. Rising up on his tiptoes, Milos gazed reassuringly into his eyes. "It'll be all right, my friend. Just a jaunt through the sky, and you'll be free to roam as you please. Maybe you and Chrissie can frolic in the tide pool. You've always enjoyed that."

Thankfully, that seemed to do the trick. Eddie's eyes snapped into focus, and his shoulders squared as if he were priming himself for the task ahead.

"Good to have you back, Eddie," Milos said, patting him on the head. Then Milos stepped alongside the stallion, rested his arms on his back and prepared to mount him. But just as Milos swung his leg around, Eddie shook him off with a seismic spasm that sent him skittering across the mesa. Then Eddie broke into a gallop, fluttered his wings, and flew away.

"Eddie! Where are you going?!" Milos shouted.

The stallion didn't even look back. He continued soaring through the sky in the opposite direction of the ceremony, as Milos stared after him in disbelief.

"Forget him, Milos. Come on!"

Milos turned to find Electra waving him over, urging him to join her astride Chrissie. He hesitated for a moment, then realized he didn't have a choice. The ceremony was about to begin, and his own mode of transportation had taken a powder. Milos rushed over and climbed on behind Electra, shaking off the fact that she hadn't offered to slide into the passenger position. After all, she probably didn't realize what a spectacle they'd make—the groom arriving under the thumb of his bride.

Thankfully, Chrissie showed no sign of following her mate's lead. On Electra's command, she trotted across the mesa with a grace borne out of decades of service, broke into a canter, and lifted them effortlessly into the sky.

"As usual, the female proves to be the reliable one," Electra declared. "What got into Eddie?"

"I don't know. He's never done anything like that before."

Electra reached back and squeezed Milos on the thigh. "Just so you don't go following him."

He smiled. "Not a chance."

As Milos wrapped his arms around Electra's waist, he wished he felt something. Some small stirring of desire. Then again, how could he, with the mystery of Eddie's departure weighing on him? That was it. It had to be.

Still, as they soared over the canyon, Milos found himself thinking about another horseback ride he'd taken. How every nerve ending in his body had come to life when he'd wrapped his arms around Angie and boosted her onto Eddie's back. How magnificently she'd ridden, on the ground and in the sky. And how for a few precious moments, it had felt like the sun was shining on them and them alone.

It was unlikely anyone would ever touch his heart the way Angie had. But this universe of his was a dangerous place, even for a demigoddess like her. She deserved to live a long, happy life, free of punishing gods, vengeful monsters, and a lover who wasn't worthy of her.

Well, maybe he'd been worthy on one occasion: the day he'd saved her life. He was glad Apollo had told her about it when he was in New York. Milos knew it shouldn't matter at this point, but there was something satisfying in surmising that Angie thought better of him now. At the very least, she had to realize his interest in her was a longstanding thing, not the whim of a creature hungry for a conquest. And maybe that would help her put things in perspective and realize that the magical things that had happened between them were heartfelt and real.

Milos couldn't deny there was a part of him that wished he could have envisaged her to see the look on her face when Apollo told her about his heroics. Did she break out in a smile? Did a tear run down her cheek? Was she still thinking about him now?

But he knew he'd never have those answers. He'd made a vow after the Yankees game never to envisage her again, and he intended to keep it. From now on, the less he knew about her, the better. Wherever she was, whatever she was doing, and whoever she was doing it with, was her business and hers alone.

"Marvelous light show, huh?" Electra remarked.

"Light show?"

"Uh, yeah..."

As Electra pointed ahead of them, Milos's eyes went wide. He couldn't believe he'd been so preoccupied that he'd failed to notice that the darkening skies were lit up like the Fourth of July over Manhattan. But this was no fireworks show. It was a dramatic fusion of astral phenomena in celebration of the pending nuptials, courtesy of Zeus. There were multicolored meteor showers that rained down like popcorn sprinkled out of a sack. Volleys of booming thunder followed by lightning that hurtled across the sky in white-hot zigzags. Puffy cumulus clouds that appeared and disappeared to their own particular rhythm. Even the Northern Lights had been imported for the occasion, painting the sky in impressionist dabs of azure, chartreuse, and violet.

"It *is* marvelous," Milos said. "As are *you*."

He leaned forward and kissed Electra on the cheek, feeling good about himself. If a new language or a musical instrument could be mastered, why not the capacity to love another being?

Moments later, Chrissie began her descent, affording them a view of another spectacle—a squint-worthy sea of white, courtesy of hundreds of deities in ceremonial tunics. Most of them were smiling warmly, although a few seemed amused by the seating arrangement on the horse.

"I see she's already shown you who's boss!" Athena called out.

That prompted a swell of good-natured chuckling, compelling Milos to put on a smile to show them he was a good sport. A moment later, the assembled raised their arms high in the air and waved pink rockroses at them to ensure their eternal happiness. Then Hera summoned a gust of wind that lifted the flowers out of their hands and carried them to the sky in a long, flowing chain that swirled around Electra and him, faster and faster, until it was nothing more than a pastel blur.

"Don't you just love being celebrated?" Electra purred.

"Absolutely," Milos replied. It was a lie, but this was no time to dim her enthusiasm.

"Think about it, Milos. Pretty soon, we're going to be more famous than Brad and Angelina."

"Mmm. Can't wait."

Fortunately, the conversation was cut short by their landing on the mountaintop. As Chrissie galloped across the meadow, the roses pulled out of their spiral and arranged themselves into a footpath that led to a gleaming archway carved out of a single diamond. Crafted thousands of years ago by Gaea, goddess of the Earth, for Zeus and Hera's wedding, it remained underground most of the time, unearthing itself for only the most important occasions, then burrowing its way back down afterward. And while Milos's ego wasn't as well fed as Electra's, he couldn't deny he felt a swell of pride knowing this was only the third time in his life the archway had appeared.

When Chrissie slowed to a canter, Milos leapt off and lowered Electra to the ground. Much applause and whooping followed, especially when she kissed him. "Admit it," she said. "These are the most delicious lips you've ever tasted."

Before Milos could respond, a hand gripped him by the shoulder and spun him around in one deft motion. And there was Zeus, his steel blue eyes sparkling with a warmth that would be comforting to someone who didn't know him better. "Good evening, young bridegroom," he enthused, sweeping him into a hug and kissing him on both cheeks.

"Good evening, Your Sovereignty," Milos replied.

Zeus followed suit with Electra, although the hug seemed to linger. Then he stepped back and gazed at them as if they were a pair of Ferraris. "I've waited centuries for the Oracle to prophesize this union. Are you ready to embrace your destinies?"

"I sprung out of the womb ready," Electra said.

That provoked a chuckle from Zeus, along with another lingering hug. *Is Hera not watching this?* Milos wondered, realizing he himself didn't feel an ounce of jealousy. He couldn't decide whether that should make him feel good or bad.

Eventually, Zeus broke the hug and turned to him. "And you, young master? Do you feel the weight of the ages bearing down on you?"

"On the contrary, I feel them lifting me up, emboldening me with their wisdom."

"Well spoken," Zeus replied, sounding surprised. "If I do say so myself, it's a beautiful evening for a wedding."

Zeus embellished his canvas by pointing a finger at the sky and filling it with constellations, as if it were no more than a computer application. Then he added a full moon that was so enormous it made the tunics glow brighter, prompting several guests to put on their sunglasses.

"How about that?" Zeus remarked. "I've saved on the electrical bill as well."

Milos's forced chuckle was drowned out by a near-deafening roar of laughter from the assembled. *Zounds,* he thought. *What sycophants we are!*

At least Jace wasn't laughing. He was giving Milos a look that seemed to say, "Hey, we tried." As for Apollo, he was his usual hard-to-read self. Although he was laughing, he seemed distracted, occasionally staring off into the distance. *Did he and Eddie drink from the same trough today?* Milos wondered.

As the laughter tapered off, Zeus vanished in a flash of light and reappeared under the archway. Then he held out his arms in a gesture that suggested supreme benevolence, but really meant he was tired of the small talk and ready to get things rolling. As if on cue, the other deities took their places on either side of the rockrose pathway.

"My friends," Zeus said, taking a long pause to gaze beatifically over the crowd, "we gather here this evening to witness the marriage of Electra, the daughter of Hades, and Milos, nominally the son of Poseidon, but really, an individual I like to think of as my own son."

The abrasive cough that followed must have come from Ares, Milos decided.

Ever so briefly, Zeus's eyes narrowed in anger. But he regained his composure and continued. "One day, mankind will see this wedding as the dawn of a remarkable new era of happiness and prosperity. But tonight, it is simply the melding of two hearts into a whole that shall not be torn asunder. By anyone." He cast a cautionary glance at the crowd, then motioned for the bride and groom to come forward.

As the orchestra struck up a processional by Vivaldi, a flock of seagulls flew overhead, their caws in perfect harmony with the music. This was the one element of the ceremony Milos had arranged, and he was proud of his gulls, especially considering they were still mourning the death of their leader. A renegade part of him wished their droppings would find their way down to Zeus, but he knew that would only ensure their annihilation—and probably his own.

Electra squeezed his hand. "This is it, dearest."

Milos squeezed back. "Yes, it is." As he gazed into Electra's eyes, he reminded himself that none of this was her doing. She'd been born into this arrangement just as he had. For all he knew, her heart had endeavored to make her fall in love with him to make it more palatable. Perhaps in time, his heart would do the same favor for him.

But first things first. He spoke *Now, darling,* into Electra's head, prompting them to lead off in unison, right foot first, as she'd had them rehearse over and over this week. As Milos walked down the aisle alongside his bride, he took in the faces of deities he'd known all his life. Friends. Mentors. Confidantes. Enemies. How many of them were happy for him? How many envied him? And how many hated him?

A few feet from the altar, Electra leaned over and whispered in his ear. "That horse of yours is a fool. Does he have any idea what he's missing?"

Although Milos smiled, he felt a pang of discomfort, as if an arrow had glanced off his head. But for the life of him, he couldn't figure out why her words had prompted such a reaction.

As they stepped up to the altar, Zeus dimmed the moon and most of the astral phenomena, so the only light that shone on them came from the stars twinkling overhead. Then he placed his hands over theirs and recited vows that were as old as the archway above them. "Chaos, Gaia, Uranus, Pontus, Eros, and Tartarus, we humbly call you forth and ask you to bless this union. For you are the void that reminds us we came from nothingness, the earth that sustains us, the heavens we gaze upon, the sea that protects us, the love we crave, and the abyss to which we condemn our enemies. We are your servants, now and forever, and nothing is possible without you."

After a few more stanzas, Zeus paused for the groom's response. But even though Milos knew his vows by heart, he couldn't get them out. Something had occurred to him. Something that was as illuminating as it was disturbing.

Earlier tonight, when Eddie flew off, Electra had asked him what was wrong with the stallion. He'd told her he didn't know; that Eddie had never done anything like that before.

But that wasn't true. Eddie had disrespected him on one other occasion: the day of Angie's departure. Although the stallion had responded to Milos's summons to take her to the dock, he'd touched down on the lawn wearing a look of contempt. And if that wasn't peculiar enough, he'd snorted at Milos. And why? Because the woman Eddie had fallen in love with just as surely as Milos had was walking out of his life, and Eddie was savvy enough to know who was to blame.

Eddie had been chilly to him the rest of that day. Then, coaxed along by an earnest apology and a slew of carrots, he'd come around. And things had gone back to the way they'd always been.

Until today. The day of Milos's wedding. To Angie's nemesis.

Was it any wonder that Electra's remark about Eddie had gotten his head throbbing? It had been trying to alert him to something that should have been obvious. Eddie knew exactly what he was missing—the spectacle of his master entering into a loveless marriage rather than fight for what he really wanted. Eddie had bolted because he was ashamed of him. So ashamed that he couldn't bear to witness this travesty.

I must be the most pathetic sap in the universe, Milos thought. *It took the simplest of creatures to point out something that should have been obvious to someone of my so-called intellect.*

"Milos, are you all right?" Electra was staring at him, obviously worried.

He managed a nod.

While Zeus still had a smile on his face, his lower lip was twitching. "Shall I repeat that last stanza?"

"Yes," Milos sputtered. "Sorry."

How could he have deluded himself like that? Convinced himself he could live with Electra for the rest of his days? Maybe even love her? And that together, they could lead the world as a united front? Sure, they were on their best behavior now. But in a month or so, they'd be at each other's throats. Him, because every time he looked at her, he'd resent her for not being Angie. And her, because she was too vain to accept the fact that she'd never be the love of his life. From there, it would only be a matter of time before the legendary brawls Zeus and Hera had engaged in over the centuries would be considered child's play compared to what they put each other through.

But what could he do about it? The wheels weren't merely in motion, they were spinning toward the finish line. Even if he managed to escape the island and get to New York, there was no guarantee Angie would take him back. And what if she did? Was there any place in the universe where they'd be safe from the wrath of Zeus?

I might as well face it. I'm trapped. Destined to spend eternity in a loveless marriage doing the bidding of everyone but myself.

"Milos?" Once again, he became aware of his name being invoked. A moment later, Electra cupped a hand over her mouth and whispered in his ear. "I shall do so in their honor."

He managed a smile, then ran the vow through his head a few times. Finally, he squared his shoulders and spoke.

"I can't do this."

The crowd gasped, but so did Milos. He couldn't believe the words had come out of his mouth. He'd been fully prepared to go through with this wedding and live with the consequences. But apparently, his conscience had had other ideas.

While Electra stared at him numbly, Zeus was seething. "Can't. Do. What?"

Milos sucked in a breath. It wasn't too late to turn things around. To come up with an innocent explanation for his words and spare himself a one-way trip to Tartarus.

As Milos stood there, suffocating from the pressure, he was acutely aware of everything around him. Electra digging her nails into his palm. Zeus's anger coming off him in white-hot waves. The crowd murmuring in confusion. And for some reason, the sound of wings fluttering overhead. Had his gulls come back?

"Milos!"

He wasn't sure who'd spoken this time, but he knew he couldn't hold things up any longer. Fortunately, at that moment, the clouds inside his head cleared, leaving his answer illuminated as if by a ray of sunshine. And this time, he was in full command of what he was about to say.

"My apologies to all of you. But I can't go through with this wedding."

The gasps were even louder this time, sharing the air with Electra's wounded wail.

He turned to Zeus, fully expecting him to be reaching for his throat. Instead, he was staring past him at something in the distance. Something that seemed to deepen his anger.

When Zeus turned back to him, his eyes were on fire. "You foolish boy. Do you have any idea how far you're about to fall?"

Milos whipped his head around to find out what Zeus had been looking at. And when he saw it, he couldn't help himself. He broke out in a smile.

Eddie was coming back. But not alone.

On his back was Angie.

TWENTY-NINE

For just a moment, as she studied the collection of angry, beautiful faces staring up at her, Angie felt like putting the brakes on Eddie and hauling ass back to New York.

Am I out of my mind? This isn't just any wedding party. These are the freakin' gods of Olympus. A group that makes the Sopranos look like Teletubbies. And I'm coming here to upend their sacred ritual. Do I really want to die tonight?

Then she saw Milos's face, full of joy and surprise. And looking so damn kissable.

"Angie!" he shouted. God, how she'd missed the sound of his voice, especially when it was calling her name so lovingly.

All the way here, she'd worried that he'd be less than happy to see her. After all, the last time they were together, she told him she never wanted to see him again. And now she had the nerve to try to bust up his wedding—in front of an audience of gods, no less.

But his ear-to-ear smile seemed to be saying something else entirely: *I want this, too, Angie. And together, we just might pull it off.*

So she put her fears on the back burner and pressed her heels against Eddie's sides. "Take us down, sport."

Eddie pulled off such a smooth landing that Angie could have been holding a topped-off glass of champagne and not spilled a drop. Then Eddie lowered his belly to the ground in his now-familiar gesture of idol worship. Angie kissed him on the forehead, kissed him again to buy some time, then marched toward her destiny.

And as she did, it occurred to her that the folks who were staring at her might be gods, but they were also family. So she gave them a big Rose Parade Queen wave and—unsure of the protocol for these things—a curtsy. "Hello everybody, I'm Angie. But I'm guessing you know that already."

That managed to make a few of them smile. Jace, natch. Apollo, every bit the proud grandpa, minus the looking-like-a-grandpa part. She even got a curt "Hello" from Aphrodite, who'd changed out of her flight attendant garb into the same toga they were all wearing, although she'd accessorized hers with more jewelry than a Tiffany's window.

But there was only outrage on the face of the George Clooney lookalike who had a stranglehold on Milos, presumably to keep him from running to her. Figuring this had to be the poobah himself, Angie decided it would be prudent to keep a safe distance.

"What is she doing here, Milos?" Zeus shouted. "How dare you conspire against us!"

Milo stole another look at her, then addressed Zeus with so much confidence that Angie wanted to high-five him right there on the spot. "Your Sovereignty, I assure you I had no idea Angie was coming. That said, I've never been happier to see anyone in my life. Hello, Angie."

"Back atcha, Milos," she took great pleasure in saying.

Which was anything but music to Electra's ears. "How would you like those to be your last words, girlfriend?"

Electra took a menacing step toward her, but Milos grabbed hold of her with his free arm and spoke to her with far more tenderness than she deserved. "Electra, I know I've hurt you, and for that I'm truly sorry. But you're a woman of great passion. You deserve a man who can return that passion and see nothing but you when he closes his eyes. You know I'm not that man."

"But you *can* be," Angie heard her whisper. "I can make you love me."

Milos shook his head. "No, you can't."

"Silence!" Zeus might have been king of the *Greek* gods, but the look he was giving Milos was pure Old Testament. "How dare you presume to dictate the terms of your life? You are our scion. You will do as we say. And don't insult my intelligence by telling me this rendezvous wasn't planned."

"It wasn't," Milos replied, steady as a rock. "I made my decision to back out of this marriage without even a hint Angie was coming."

Angie couldn't believe her ears. "Hold up. You already backed out?"

The smile that lit Milos's face was the proudest Angie had ever seen. "A moment before you arrived."

Any lingering doubts Angie had about Milos's feelings were washed away. He'd backed out before she got there, which meant he wanted to be with her as much as she wanted to be with him. Not only that, he was willing to take the same risks that she was to achieve that end.

Now, if she could only keep Zeus from obliterating the two of them, they might have a shot at happily ever after. "He's telling the truth, Your Holiness," she declared. "He had no idea I was coming."

Zeus flicked a dismissive hand in her direction, as if he were brushing away a mosquito. Then he continued his assault on her prince. "Really, Milos, you're asking me to believe this woman came here on her own? That without your knowledge or assistance, she conjured up the *Harmonia*, boarded it, then telepathically summoned Eddie to the docks?"

"Remarkable, isn't she?" Milos replied with a gleam in his eye.

Zeus frowned. "Remarkable or not, she can witness the ceremony along with the others." He picked out a face in the crowd. "Is that acceptable to you, brother?"

"She can juggle swords at the damn thing as long as the Oracle is honored and my daughter ends the day a bride," replied Hades, whose arched eyebrows and simpering smile reminded Angie of Alan Rickman.

Electra didn't say a word. She merely raised her head in that superior way of hers that was so infuriating.

"Have I not made myself clear?" Milos retorted. "I will not marry Electra!"

With an enraged growl, Zeus took Milos by the shoulders and shook him like a snow globe. "How dare you defy me? Don't you realize I can end this folly in a heartbeat?"

Milos didn't so much as flinch. "You made that abundantly clear at the Conclave with those snuff films of yours. And when you didn't think that was enough to send me scurrying to the altar, you sicced a Gaileoñtos on Angie. And I'm ashamed of myself for not making more of it at the time, because it was petty and heartless—everything you claim to be above now."

Angie snuck a peek at the assembled. Were they as worried as she was that things were about to go ghetto? As she'd suspected, every face was grim and anxious—with the exception of Aphrodite, who chose that moment to freshen her lipstick. And where was Apollo in this? Could he be counted on to step forward if she and Milos needed him?

Which was likely to be soon, judging from the way Zeus was staring a hole through Milos. "I'll tell you how much I've evolved, young master. A generation ago, I would have sent you to the darkest corner of Tartarus and disemboweled your lady friend. But today, I'll merely reiterate that I had nothing to do with that serpent."

"Then who sent it?" Milos demanded. Shaking himself free of Zeus's grasp, he spun around and faced the others. "Was it you, Ares?"

Angie followed his gaze to a curly haired specimen with a brooding sexuality. "Trust me, cousin. If I'd set out to kill your paramour, I wouldn't have failed."

Milos then turned to Electra. "And you? You still maintain you had nothing to do with it?"

"Please," Electra scoffed. "Why would I let a serpent do what I would've taken far more pleasure doing myself?"

Just when Angie figured she and Milos were never going to find out who'd unleashed the serpent, a voice called out from the crowd. "It was I."

The voice belonged to Apollo.

Angie felt like she'd been punched in the gut. Her own grandfather had tried to kill her? The same man who, only a few hours ago, declared his eternal devotion to her and all but begged her to make her stand? Had that all been a lie? Had he been setting a trap?

Milos seemed equally confused. "Apollo, you'd better explain yourself."

"And I shall." Apollo broke from a cluster of wedding guests and approached Angie. "I'm sorry, my dear. I should have told you in New York."

Zeus raised an eyebrow. "You were in New York? When?"

For some reason, the more time Angie spent with this crowd, the more fearless she was becoming. "Sorry, Your Excellency, one question at a time. And I think we'd all agree that the one about why he sicced a serpent on me is the biggie. Grandpa, you were saying?"

"Grandpa?" Zeus fumed. "Apollo, you told her?!"

Ignoring his father, Apollo put a consoling hand on Angie's shoulder. She almost slapped it away, but resisted the impulse. "Angie, please know I never would have let the serpent do you any harm," he said. "But over the years, I've sensed the greatness of which you're capable. And I thought it was time certain others witnessed it as well."

He stared pointedly at Zeus, who groaned. "Apollo, how many times must I tell you to stop foisting that agenda on me? This Angie woman cannot marry Milos. The Oracle of Chaos clearly states—"

"And how many times have the Oracles failed us, Father? Shall I enumerate?"

"And shall I remind you who leads us?"

They stared at each other with such malice that Angie figured the thunderbolts and fireballs couldn't be far behind. So she took a stab at deflecting the tension by asking Apollo the question that was dogging her. "Okay, I get it. You wanted to show everybody I was strong enough to hang with all of you. But you gotta admit, sending Silas the Serpent after me was a pretty extreme way of doing it."

"We're a pretty extreme people," Apollo said by way of apology.

Angie thought about it for a minute and found herself smiling. "Can't argue with that."

Apparently, neither could Zeus. "How about that, Apollo? You and I finally agree on something. Now, unless you want me to give this interloper a personal demonstration of just how extreme we can be, I suggest you step back so we can proceed with the ceremony."

Electra turned to Angie with a triumphant smile. "Such a pity. You traveled all this way for nothing. Milos is mine, and there's nothing you can do about it."

Before Angie could respond, Milos's voice boomed across the mountaintop. "I will say it one last time! I will not marry Electra, today or any other day." He held out his hand in Angie's direction as if they should take this moment to make a break for it.

Now it was Angie's turn to gloat. Turning Electra's words around on her, she said, "Such a pity. Milos loves *me,* and there's nothing you can do about it."

But Zeus had another agenda in mind. He loosed a theatrical sigh and said, "I'm disappointed in all of you. Such limited imagination you display. Apollo put our uninvited guest against a Gaileoñtos to test her mettle, yet I can think of a skirmish I'd find far more entertaining." He paused to allow a devious grin to twist his features. "Let us test our new friend against Electra."

Angie thought the bottom might drop out of her stomach.

"Absolutely not," Milos shot back at him. "Angie isn't some gladiator who's here for your entertainment."

Zeus chuckled. "Please. One way or another, you're all here for my entertainment. But what if I told you it might lead me to reconsider things?"

Milos eyed him dubiously. "What are you saying? Spell it out."

"Oh, but that would spoil the fun. How about we just stand back and see how events play out?"

"Out of the question." Milos strode toward Angie and grasped her hand. "I love this woman with every fiber of my being, but I'd rather live without her than see her risk her life on the off chance you'd sanction our union."

That prompted a catty laugh from Electra. "Seriously, Milos, do you really think I'd go so far as to kill the girl? I'd just toy with her for a bit, for everyone's amusement. Help her lose some of that tonnage."

Angie felt the blood boiling in her veins. And maybe her judgment was clouded by the fact that she'd gone twelve hours on nothing but a bag of M&Ms and a sad little salad, but it felt like she had no choice but to accept Zeus's challenge. Sure, chances were astronomically high that she'd regret it forever. But what if it were possible for her to wipe that Cruella de Vil grin off Electra's face and claim Milos in the process?

So she called out to Zeus. "Hold up, Your Supremacy. Do I have a say in this?"

From the way Zeus's eyebrow was twitching, he was either amused or ready to turn her into a salt lick. "Normally, no. In fact, the sound of your voice wouldn't even register with me. But to prove how magnanimous I am, I'll hear you out."

"Thank you." Angie turned to Milos. "I really appreciate you having my back. But if there's even a chance that I can prove I deserve to be with you by going toe to toe with Bridezilla, then I'm Rocky Balboa, Muhammad Ali, and Maggie Fitzgerald all rolled into one."

"But Angie, you have no idea how she—"

Zeus cut him off. "You heard her. She's in. Let the games begin."

"I'll make you proud," Angie promised Milos, even though she was lying through her teeth. In mere minutes, she could be reduced to dog meat.

Her bravado earned a faint smile from Milos. "I know you will."

At that moment, Angie yearned to wrap her arms around Milos and tell him she loved him. After all, it might be her last chance. But she knew it would only infuriate Electra, who didn't need any more ammunition than she already had. So she gave him a thumbs-up and headed toward the open patch of grass where her opponent was standing with her lips pursed, all superior-like. Feeling a surge of ass-whupping adrenaline, Angie pulled off her earrings and tossed them to the ground.

It was on.

As the two of them stared each other down, the crowd started buzzing like it was opening day in the Bronx. Some of the onlookers were even placing bets, which had to mean they thought it would be a real contest. For a few seconds, Angie allowed herself to wonder how many of them were betting on her and what the odds were. But she forced it out of her head. She might be a demigoddess with nifty raw powers, but Electra was a full-fledged goddess with a nasty streak as long as the Hudson. She'd need to put every ounce of focus into this battle.

And Angie's instincts told her that meant landing the first punch. So the minute she was close enough to Electra to smell her skeezy perfume, she went into her crouch. Then she raised her arms and made a few quick head bobs as she danced toward her opponent. Back home in Astoria, her right hook was legendary. She was about to put it to bone-crunching use in a whole nuther arena.

But just as Angie moved in for the strike, Electra casually waved an arm in her direction. Before Angie could register what was happening, she was scuttling backward across the mesa, propelled by a powerful blast of wind. She tried flailing her arms to slow her momentum, but it was no use. The wind was as merciless as the demon redhead who'd conjured it.

"Damn you, Electra!" she shouted, her voice lost in the maelstrom.

A moment later, Angie felt herself being lifted off the ground. Three feet. Ten feet. And the higher she flew, the more violently the wind corkscrewed her body, like a rag doll in a hurricane. Soon, she was flying backward over the river, whose waters grew more and more turbulent as they approached the waterfall. Angie knew she should be terrified, but she was too busy clenching her fists in frustration.

Then, abruptly, the wind stopped, just in time to send her plummeting into the river. She hit bottom, got her bearings, and swam for the surface, sputtering when her head cleared the water. But although she made a frenzied attempt to swim to shore, she was no match for the current. It carried her relentlessly toward the waterfall, mocking her every attempt to resist. She could swear the last thing she heard before she was swept over was the catcall, "Buh-bye, bitch!"

She could guess where that came from.

Then came the drop, all forty stories of it. Infinitely scarier than the plunge she'd experienced time-traveling with Apollo. Like being yanked straight effing down by the strongest pair of hands in the world. The water was assaulting her from all sides. Pounding at her head like a thousand fists. Gushing into her nose, her mouth, her ears. And whipping her limbs around so violently she was afraid they'd be ripped from her body.

To make matters worse, she was shooting down the falls head-first on her back, with no way of knowing what was coming up. She didn't know how deep the tide pool was, but she had a sneaking suspicion that if she didn't reorient herself PDQ, she'd either slam her head on the bottom or smash against the rocks along the shore.

She tried to spin herself around, but it was hopeless. The current was too strong and too fast, bearing down on her from all sides. There had to be a way she could manage it, but how? How could she beat a swirling column of water at its own game?

Then a crazy thought crept into her head. What if she weren't a doomed demigoddess shooting down a waterfall, but a ballerina about to execute a pirouette? All it would take was one little spin on her toe shoes, and she'd be golden. And it wasn't the crushing water she'd be battling, but that vile dance instructor who'd told her she was too fat for ballet. Summoning up a store of resolve, Angie pictured herself, the dance studio, and the vile Miss Madeline, right down to the fake beauty mark she never put in the same place twice. Suddenly, the resistance that had been thwarting her eased up, allowing her to pull her arms and legs close to her body and spin herself around.

And not a moment too soon. Angie got her bearings just in time to see she was only a few body lengths from the base of the falls. She managed to suck in a breath and stretch her arms over her head a split second before she plunged into the tide pool. Then down she went, deeper and deeper, past schools of Day-Glo fish who regarded her with territorial disdain. Inches from the bottom, she flipped her body around to allow her feet to touch down and push off. Then she clawed her way to the surface, resisting the overwhelming urge to gasp for air.

Just when it felt like her lungs were going to explode, Angie burst out of the water and took in a massive gulp of air. Then another and another, until she was coughing and her eyes were streaming and her body felt like one giant bruise. Still, she managed to tread water until she regulated her breathing and shook what seemed like gallons of water out of her ears.

Then she swam to the far end of the tide pool, wrapped her arms around a rock, and burst into tears. She wasn't just shaken; she was shattered. Sure, she'd survived, but what did it matter? Electra had made a fool of her, giving Zeus every reason to stick to his guns and force Milos to marry the bitch goddess after all.

Her sobs were interrupted by a splash on the other side of the pool. If this was Electra coming to finish her off, she wouldn't get much resistance. As much as Angie wanted to get back at the shrew, she was running on empty. On the bright side, her decision to opt for a one-way ticket was looking smarter by the minute.

But the head that bobbed to the surface didn't belong to Electra.

"Milos!" Although her voice was suffering from the effects of her trip down the falls, Angie was pretty sure no one had ever rasped a word with such enthusiasm.

For a moment, Milos just stared at her, his blue eyes dancing with relief. Then he swam closer and wrapped an arm around her shoulder, sending it straight to shoulder heaven. "Angie, are you all right? Is anything broken?"

She smiled. "Just my belief in the concept of a fair fight."

That got a rueful chuckle out of him. It wasn't the booming laugh that had charmed her during their one and only day together, but it still managed to make her heart ping.

Ditto for the next thing that came out of Milos's mouth. "Regardless of how it turned out, I couldn't be prouder of you, darling."

There was that word again. *Darling.* Coming off those beautiful lips of his. No doubt about it, Angie loved this man. Heck, she'd flown halfway around the world to be with him. And while she'd never expected their first moment alone to take place in a tide pool at the bottom of a waterfall, she'd take it any way it was offered.

So she put her arms around him and whispered in his ear. "I've missed you."

"I've missed you, too," he said. "Every second of every day."

It was a perfect moment. Two lovers reunited against a mountain of odds, quietly clinging to each other as the water rose and fell around them in a lulling rhythm.

But like all perfect moments, it had to come to an end. Gently disentangling himself from her, Milos rose out of the water. "If you're up to it, I'll summon the horses."

"What for?"

"I think it might be prudent to go back to my house and give ourselves some distance from the others. I don't want you to ever have to see Electra again. Or Zeus, for that matter. "

Angie stepped out of the water after him. "Milos, there's nothing I'd rather do than go back to your place. Pour some vino. Reacquaint ourselves with that guest bedroom of yours. But how much time would we be buying?"

He shrugged. "I don't know, a few hours?"

Angie took a deep breath. It felt like her whole life had been leading up to this moment. "I'm going back up there."

"What are you talking about?"

"I have unfinished business with Electra. I have to do my best to stuff her so we can be together. Otherwise, there's no reason for me to have come here."

As Milos stared at her, long and hard, Angie saw colors in his eyes she'd never seen before. She also saw a kaleidoscope of emotions—fear, amazement, pride, hope, to name a few.

Finally, he spoke. "Angie, you're remarkable. The fact that you took the risk you did coming here means more to me than you'll ever know. But I can't let you go back up there. As tough as you are, you're never going to vanquish Electra. She's too strong, too conniving, and too bloody jealous. It doesn't matter anyway. I have no intention of marrying her, regardless of Zeus or any other member of the Council. In fact, maybe we should leave the island right now. The horses can take us far away from here."

"How far, Milos? All the way to the moon? Seriously, is there anywhere we can go that they won't come looking for us?"

He turned away for a moment, no doubt trying to come up with an answer that might give them some hope. When he didn't find it, he took a different tack. "Why don't I talk to Apollo? Now that I know for certain he's on our side, he may be able to help us."

"Maybe he can. But that's not going to stop me from doing what I have to. Remember, I'm a Greek girl from Queens. That's how I roll."

Milos shook his head as if he couldn't believe what he was hearing.

"I'm a scrapper, Milos. Always have been. Whether it was the big kids in elementary school trying to scam me for lunch money or the black girls on the subway who thought the chubby white chick with braces was an easy mark, I've always felt the need to prove myself. Truth be told, it gets me off. But the one thing I have never fought for was a man. I know it had something to do with my father and how I thought he'd died. But the bigger reason was that I never met a man who was worth fighting for. Until the day you laughed your way into my head and busted up my wedding."

He smiled. "Had I known something that simple would provoke you to leave that man, I would have gotten into your head years ago. Still, I hate the idea of you fighting for me. It should be me fighting for you."

"You've done that, remember? You saved my life twice in one day. Isn't it time for some payback?"

He nodded, but his brow was furrowed.

"Milos, I know I'm not invincible. But I will not allow Electra or anybody else to think she's more deserving of you than I am. I may die trying, but I won't rest till I give it one more shot."

Milos smiled faintly, then stared off into the distance for a solid hour. Or maybe it just felt like an hour because she was finally beside him again and eager to spend every last second for the rest of her life looking at his face.

When he turned back toward her, he wore a grudging smile. "We'll go up there together. A united front."

Angie let out the breath she'd been holding. "Thank you."

"All right, I'll get the horses, and we'll—"

She put her fingers to his lips. "Uh, Milos. I'm taking the elevator."

"Elevator?"

She nodded in the direction of the waterfall. Then she raised her eyes to gaze all the way to the top, recalling the first time she stood at the foot of the Empire State Building and stared up a hundred and two stories into the smoggy New York sky. She was even dizzier this time.

Milos was looking at her as if she were dizzy in another way. "That's impossible. It took Jace and me years to master it, and we're ... full-blooded."

"Yeah, but I've got something going for me that the two of you didn't."

"What?"

She kissed him on the lips. At first he seemed to hold back, possibly concerned that he'd sap whatever strength she had. Then he gave in, kissing her back with such passion that it sent a rush of purpose through her body and made her feel as powerful as a recently crowned demigoddess with no on-the-job training can feel.

Then at last, she said the three words she'd been holding inside for days. "I love you."

"I love you more," he replied. His eyes were ringed with tears.

So were hers. "Doubtful."

And when Milos took her in his arms and kissed her again, Angie felt like she'd come halfway around the world only to come home. A part of her wanted to stay with him in this oasis forever. Find a cool patch of grass and make love till their bodies were spent. But she knew that unless she took care of Electra—if that were even possible—she and Milos would never be granted the peace they deserved.

So she released herself from his embrace and took a good, long look at him. Yep, definitely worth fighting for, especially with that damp toga clinging to him in all the right places. "So, before I go, do you have any pointers for me?"

He smiled. "Just one. Wrap your arms around me and hitch a ride to the top."

"Seriously."

He mulled it over, then said, "I used to think the key to conquering the falls was to focus every muscle and brain cell on the task at hand. And every time I did that, I failed. I'd get a quarter of the way up and find that I couldn't muster another stroke. Then one day, I decided to think about everything *but* the climb. To concentrate on pieces of music I loved. My favorite stories from the glory days of the Olympians. The way I saw my future playing out. The next thing I knew, I was cresting the top."

"That's all it took?"

"It's all inside you, Angie. The power. The magic. The well-wishes of those who've come before you. Allow all that to work for you, and you might make the impossible happen."

"I'll keep that in mind." She gave him a pop on the shoulder, then stepped to the edge of the shore. "Give me a head start, will you?"

With that, Angie dove into the tide pool. When she was about a third of the way across, she realized she'd forgotten to caution Milos about something. She spun around, treading water, and spotted him a few yards back. "From here on in, don't help me, Milos. I have to tame this beast on my own. And if, God forbid, something happens to me, scatter my ashes on the island. Can you imagine what it would do to Electra to know she was inhaling me every day?"

When Milos let out that laugh she loved so much, it was like somebody had injected Red Bull into her veins. She felt stronger and infinitely more determined. Which was good, because the current was picking up. Big whitecaps were surging toward her one after another. So she did what her father taught her when they went body surfing on the Jersey Shore. She timed her dives so she was plunging through the face of each wave just before it broke. Her pace was slow, but as long as she kept moving forward, she knew she'd make it…

That is, until she drew near the base of the falls and was catapulted back by the force of the pounding water hitting the tide pool. After catching her breath, she took another shot, swimming underwater this time. But she only hit the same punishing impediment.

"Remember what I told you!" Milos called out from somewhere behind her.

Milos was right. The power was inside her. It was time to disconnect from this hellish task and let her instincts take the wheel.

This time, as Angie swam toward the falls, she pictured Ya-Ya's rooftop garden, taking a mental inventory of all the plants that grew there. Queen Anne roses, daylilies, Blue Star junipers, periwinkle, lavender, snow peas, tomatoes, eggplant, arugula… Somewhere in the middle of the herb garden, she couldn't take the suspense any longer. She opened her eyes to see where she was…

… and let out a squeal. She had to be fifty feet up the waterfall.

Sadly, that was as far as she got. Having broken her concentration, she started sliding back down—plummeting, actually—catching sight of a blurry Milos on her way to the bottom.

Seconds after she surfaced, he was treading water next to her. She didn't let him get a word out. "I'm okay. I could be better, though." Then she put her arms around him and kissed him on the lips. He responded by gently sliding his tongue inside her mouth, a move she ardently endorsed. Soon their tongues were engaged in an erotic ballet that might have led to all sorts of pleasures if she hadn't broken the kiss and headed back toward the falls.

This time, she focused on her favorite songs. "Thunder Road," "American Girl," "Beautiful Day," "One," "Mr. Jones," "Barracuda," "A

Dustland Fairytale," "Single Ladies," "I and Love and You," "Girl on Fire," "Blow Me One Last Kiss..."

Then she segued into her favorite movies. *Field of Dreams, The Natural, Bull Durham, Ghost, Groundhog Day, Step Up, The Great Escape, Gladiator...*

If Hollywood made a movie out of *her* story, who would play her? Drew Barrymore, Nia Vardalos, Melissa McCarthy, Drea de Matteo, Beyoncé...

Who would play Milos? Channing Tatum, Channing Tatum, Channing Tatum.

What did she remember about Milos's naked body? How round his butt cheeks were, with dimples that looked like they'd been carved out by an ice cream scooper. How hairless his chest was, except for a jet-black patch of curls between his pecs. How soft his skin was, everywhere. How those four scars ran diagonally across his back like a team of lightning bolts...

What were her most cherished memories of her father? Horseback riding with him in Prospect Park. Waking up on Saturday mornings to find the Kit Kat bar and *People* magazine on her nightstand that he'd picked up for her during his morning jog. Dancing with him in the kitchen to "Ain't Too Proud to Beg." Feeling loved by him every minute he was alive...

During these mental journeys, Angie was vaguely aware of the sensation of water falling on her as if she were in the shower, but little else. Eventually, though, she started to pick up a sound that had nothing to do with the waterfall. At first, she thought it was in her head, but eventually she realized it was coming from outside her. Determined not to let it break her concentration, she rattled off a list of all the places she'd made love followed by an accounting of every time she'd had an orgasm, right up to those two glorious times with Milos.

Soon, the sound grew so loud it was impossible to ignore. It reminded her of the din of an exhilarated stadium when the home team scored a grand slam. But it wasn't baseball fans who were cheering her. It was gods and goddesses. Not all of them, to be sure, but a fair contingent. She might have even heard Apollo call her name. And the ovation kept getting louder, competing with the roar of the water. That had to mean she was close to the top, didn't it?

Unable to resist, Angie opened her eyes a slit, but couldn't make out anything past the water cascading down her face. So she tempted fate by opening them a tad wider and taking a peek above her. Sure enough, she was only a few yards from the top. She could see it, framed against a blanket of stars. The end of her journey.

Then, once again, she felt herself slipping. Cursing herself for not learning her lesson the first time around, she ramped up her stroke, but kept right on sliding. Then she closed her eyes and tried to conjure up a new list of favorites, but her mind was a blank. As her descent picked up speed, she felt her heart sink, too. Was she about to lose Milos for good? Would it be her legacy to have conquered all but five feet of a five-hundred-foot waterfall, only to be sent packing because there was too much *demi* in her and not enough *goddess*?

"NO!" she shouted at the top of her waterlogged lungs. "THAT IS *NOT* GONNA HAPPEN!"

Fully conscious of what she was doing but more determined than she'd ever been in her life, Angie launched a full-scale attack on the falls. Pumping her arms. Thrusting her legs. Spitting out mouthful after mouthful of water. Stroke after Heraclean stroke. The power wasn't just inside her now, it was flowing from every pore of her body. The raw strength. The magic.

It didn't hurt that she had a super-fine man bringing up the rear.

Fortified by the cheers of her Greek chorus, Angie crested the falls and proceeded to swim up the river, having her way with a current that had never before been bested by such an underdog.

They were still cheering when Angie swam to the shore and climbed out of the water. And although every inch of her body was begging for mercy, she had one more item on her to-do list. She marched up to Electra, whose superior smile couldn't hide the fact that she was trembling with shock, and delivered a right hook to her chin. And whether it was the adrenaline, the anger, or the otherworldly forces Angie was finding ever easier to summon, the blow sent Electra staggering to the ground.

But Bridezilla still wasn't ready to raise the white flag of surrender. Wrestling herself to her feet, Electra set her face like flint and started toward her. This time, Angie didn't even have to touch her. A fury of power ignited in her chest, surged to the top of her shoulder, then all the way down to her fingertips. And with a galvanic wave of her hand, she sent Electra hurtling through the air and landing twenty feet away with a demoralized thud.

Then and only then did Angie allow her body to absorb what it had been through. She dropped to her knees and fell forward until her face was smooshed against the cool grass and she was taking greedy gulps of the crisp island air.

Not thirty seconds later, a pair of men's sandals parked themselves next to her. Recognizing them as Bruno Maglis, Angie raised her head to acknowledge Zeus. "Hey, Your Highness. You don't mind if I don't get up just yet, do you?"

His laugh wasn't as appealing as Milos's, but it seemed good-natured enough. So did his grin when he crouched next to her. "I must say, your grandfather's stubborn blood does seem to flow through your veins."

Before Angie could respond, a sopping-wet Milos appeared beside Zeus and gazed at her with such admiration that she could have sprung to her feet in a second if it meant being in his arms. But she didn't have to move a muscle. Milos grabbed her around the waist, then hoisted her to her feet and kissed her with lips that were as replenishing as a beer on a hot summer day. She devoted every ounce of energy in her depleted body to kissing him back, not at all concerned that they were snubbing the king of the gods. In fact, the kiss might have gone on for hours if Zeus hadn't stepped in and pried them apart.

At first, there was a glint of something unpleasant in Zeus's eyes. But he shook it off. "There's a strength about you, Angie. Not only of body, but mind and spirit and soul. Apollo, is it true she's never had any training?"

"Not a bit, Father," he said. His pride in her couldn't be mistaken.

"And Milos?" Zeus continued. "How much guidance did you give her along the way?"

"Just one piece of advice. She forbade me to assist her any further."

"Forbade you?"

"That's how she is, Your Sovereignty. Determined to sink or swim on her own, so to speak."

"Really?"

Angie could hardly believe it, but Zeus seemed utterly charmed. Meanwhile, the other gods had moved in closer, apparently sensing that something momentous was about to happen. And even though there were scowls mixed in with the smiles, Angie was in love with the whole damn lot of them.

Zeus nodded at a striking brunette with short, wavy tresses and eyes that looked like they didn't suffer fools with much gladness. As the woman stepped up beside Zeus, his eyes found Angie again. "Allow me to introduce my daughter, Athena. A week ago, she made an appeal on your behalf, proposing that I allow you to remain in Milos's life. I was convinced that the only way he could move forward and embrace the critical duties required of him was to cut you out like a cancer. It appears I may have been wrong. For that, I apologize to both of you."

"Thank you, Your Omnipotence," Angie said, trying not to sound as giddy as she felt.

She turned to Milos, expecting him to be similarly stoked, but he was oddly expressionless. "What are you getting at?" he asked Zeus.

"Yes, by all means, illuminate us, brother." The prickly tone belonged to Hades, who stalked up to them with an arm around Electra, who was doing her best not to look like the poster child for the Agony of Defeat. "Because I'd hate to think you're about to jeopardize the delicate balance that has defined our relationship since the day our mother shat us out."

Zeus regarded Hades with obvious scorn. "And I'd hate to think you intended to disrespect me, our mother, and the rest of our family in one ill-chosen sentence."

"My apologies." Hades made a dramatic show of bowing his head. "Please continue."

Zeus turned back to Angie. "The point I'm trying to make is that I believe you could be good for Milos. I have no objection to you remaining here as long as you like."

Before Angie could ask the obvious question, Milos did it for her. "Remaining here as what?"

"Why, your mistress, of course," Zeus replied.

For a good ten seconds, neither Angie nor Milos said a word. She, because she felt like she'd been sucker-punched. And Milos, she suspected, because he'd seen this coming.

When Milos did speak, he practically spat the words. "My mistress?"

Zeus narrowed his eyes. "Surely, you didn't think I'd give you permission to marry her. She may be special, but she's not the chosen one."

"She is in *my* eyes."

"What you see through your eyes is of no concern to me. And what difference does it make? You can still have your little intrigues. Profess your love for one another a hundred times a day. But Electra will be your spouse. Now and forever."

Athena lay a hand on Milos's shoulder. "Everything can't be exactly as you wish it to be, cousin. You have responsibilities. Destiny awaits you. But what my father offers you is a reasonable compromise. It's remarkable, really. I can count on one hand the number of times he's compromised over the ages."

As Angie waited for Milos to say something, anything, she wondered how she'd feel if he agreed. Disappointed? Sad? Yes, to both. But what would she do? Go along with it? Content herself with the fact that she'd still play a role in Milos's life, which was almost more than she'd dared hope for when she arrived on Elysium?

Almost imperceptibly, she shook her head. As much as she loved Milos and had fought so hard to be with him, the answer was ...

"No." She and Milos said it at the same time. Soulmates all the way. She reached for his hand just as he reached for hers.

"No?" Zeus's tone was calm, but there was a storm brewing in his eyes.

Milos squeezed Angie's hand tightly as he addressed Zeus. "Your Sovereignty, for a hundred and six years, I've respected you. I've proudly learned at your feet. And until recently, I've followed your dictates, even when I disagreed with them. But if you tell me I can't marry Angie, we'll leave this island. And you can pursue us to the ends of Earth, but I won't change my mind."

For a moment, it looked like Zeus was going to pop off and slug him. Instead, he directed his anger at Angie. "Tell me, Angie Costianes. How does it feel to know you've seduced this man away from the role for which he's been preparing since long before you appeared on this Earth?"

Angie considered the question, then broke into a smile. "First off, I'm flattered. I mean, Milos must really love me to be willing to sacrifice something that's meant so much to him for so long. Not that I'm not worth it, but my last boyfriend would barely give up a subway seat for me. But just the same, I'm sad."

Zeus blew out a breath. "Really? How is that?"

"Because I know he'd kick butt as your go-to guy. And it seems to me that with all the brainpower you have around here, you should be able to find a solution that works for everybody. You're the gods of Olympus, for chrissakes."

"You know nothing!" Zeus's voice boomed across the landscape as if it were miked.

At that moment, Aphrodite strode confidently toward Zeus. "Daddy, allow me to suggest that we revisit the Oracle's declaration. Perhaps there *is* a better way to go forward."

From somewhere deep in the crowd, Ares spoke out. "For the first time in centuries, I'm in full agreement with Aphrodite. Cut Milos loose. There are far better leaders among us."

Angie had a strong hunch that Ares had himself at the top of that list. But if Zeus's scowl was any indication, the possibility had been raised and rebuffed ad nauseam over the years.

And, according to Aphrodite, it wasn't even relevant. "As usual, Ares, you've missed my point. I was suggesting that Milos be permitted to marry Angie."

Ares chortled. "You grow more doltish by the day. Why don't we just pluck two mortals from the general population to lead us? Like, say, Paris Hilton and that gloved fellow?"

"Michael Jackson is dead, genius," Aphrodite deadpanned. "Just like your chances of being our leader."

Clearly at the end of his rope, Zeus made a swirling motion with his hand, conjuring a blinding vortex of dust and debris that induced a hundred coughing fits. When it eventually cleared, Aphrodite and Ares had disappeared from the mountaintop. Angie knew gods couldn't be killed, but she suspected they'd been shipped off to some hellish detention camp.

With a self-satisfied smirk, Zeus glanced over the stunned faces of his family. "Who else would like to step forward and piss on the traditions that have guided us since the beginning?"

"I have something to say."

At that moment, the most beautiful woman Angie had ever seen emerged from the crowd. It wasn't just that she was physically spectacular, although she had the kind of looks that would turn heads in a morgue. But it also seemed there was a light shining from inside her that radiated strength and truth.

From the way Zeus winced, Angie had no doubt this was Hera, his better half of several thousand years. Aside from wondering how the poor woman had survived such a sentence, Angie was desperate to know where she stood with regard to her love affair with Milos. Angie's every instinct told her Hera's opinion would be critical.

Hera certainly started out with a bang. Stepping up beside Angie, she wrapped her in a hug and kissed her on both cheeks. "Welcome to Elysium, Angie. I've followed Milos's interest in you for years, and it pleases me to have the opportunity to meet you face to face."

"Thanks, Hera. I'm a big fan," Angie said, kissing her back. "I've been reading about you ever since I was in third grade. In my mind, you're right up there with Oprah."

"Delightful," Zeus grumbled. "A mutual admiration society. Could there be any doubt as to where my spouse stands on the subject?"

Hera tsk-tsked him. "Oh, ye of little faith. I'm as fervent a believer in the Oracle as you are, Zeus. Under no circumstances do I believe it should be subverted."

"Really?" Zeus looked positively jazzed. "Well, huzzah to that!"

Angie, on the other hand, was beside herself. If the goddess of love and marriage couldn't find some wriggle room in this situation, what hope did she and Milos have?

Milos looked to be similarly thunderstruck. "Hera, with all due respect—"

Hera held out her palm to silence him, smiling but steadfast. Then she turned to Zeus. "That said, I believe we've gravely misinterpreted the Oracle."

Zeus narrowed his eyes at her. "You cannot be serious."

"Oh, but I can. May I continue?"

"Not on my account. I have no interest in hearing the ravings of a madwoman."

If Zeus had been mortal, the look Hera gave him would have imploded him on the spot. But sadly, he was indestructible, so after a brief stare-down, he nodded grudgingly, as if to say, *Fine. Proceed with this inane line of thinking.*

"What did the Oracle say, Zeus?" Hera asked him.

The king of the gods cleared his throat and quoted with reverence. "'The chosen ones shall hail from the twelve-hundredth generation of offspring born to Hades and Poseidon. As the Twelve led them in the glory days, so shall the twelve hundredth lead them back to glory.'"

"Exactly." Hera smiled, satisfied. "Now, as we all know, Electra was the only child born to Hades in the twelve-hundredth generation. Therefore, she is undoubtedly the one we've been waiting for all these centuries."

Electra strayed back into consciousness. "Thank you, Hera. I've always believed you have superior judgment."

Hera gave her a perfunctory smile and pressed forward. "On the other hand, the twelve hundredth generation of Poseidon's sire produced two children. Both of them sons."

As the significance of those words set in, every head on the mountain turned to Jace. Except Angie's. She focused her gaze on Milos, hoping to get some indication as to how he felt about this bombshell. But he, too, was staring at his brother. Poker-faced.

At first, Jace looked like the proverbial deer in the headlights. Then, ever so gradually, a smile found its way onto his face. "Me? The chosen one? Sweet."

Not in Zeus's eyes. "I'm sorry, Hera, but that's the most ludicrous thing I've ever heard. Jason isn't a leader. He's been frivolous and distracted his whole life."

The smile on Hera's face indicated she'd expected him to have that reaction. "And in the past few weeks, Milos, the one we unanimously agreed was our vanguard, has defied us at every turn, found a way around our dictates, and today, the day of his wedding, has thrice refused to marry Electra. And did I mention how distracted he's been?"

Zeus wagged a finger in Angie's direction. "It's because of her! She's been his ruination."

"No, she's been his salvation," Hera replied. "And more importantly, *ours.* If not for Angie, our misinterpretation of the Oracle might have proven disastrous."

As Angie ping-ponged between the two of them, she couldn't help wondering where Hera really stood. Was this truly what she believed about the Oracle, or was the goddess of love and marriage taking this stand to allow Milos to be with the woman he loved? Either way, Hera had just earned herself a ginormous gift basket…

… *if* Milos could live with this seismic shift in his life. Unfortunately, he hadn't given any indication as to where his head was. And the longer he stayed silent, the more Angie worried.

She squeezed his arm. "Are you okay?"

He nodded, but it wasn't exactly reassuring.

Meanwhile, Zeus looked bereft. "But we've been grooming Milos. For half a century."

"And we'll groom Jason," Hera replied. "Nothing against Milos, but I believe Jace is possessed of an even keener intellect. And perhaps more importantly for the world we're about to reinhabit, he has a crafty side."

That seemed to resonate with Zeus. He shifted his attention to Athena. "And you, loyal daughter? Where do you stand?"

She took a studied moment, then said, "Father, you've always maintained that the couple who step forward will be our instruments. Intelligent and committed, yes, but beings whose primary purpose will be to carry out our orders and look good doing it. I can't conceive of a more charismatic combination than Jason and Electra. Can you imagine the reaction they'll get in America?"

Zeus cupped a hand over his chin. "You're serious about this, aren't you?"

"Have you ever known me to jest?" Father and daughter shared a chuckle, then she took his hands in hers. "Truly, based on everything I've witnessed in the past few weeks, I believe Hera has saved the day."

Angie could see the wheels turning in Zeus's head as he shifted his gaze back and forth between the two brothers and the two women he respected most in the universe.

But there was one woman who wasn't convinced. Undraping herself from her father's arm, Electra marched up to the royal couple. "This is a travesty! Reinterpreting the Oracle in the eleventh hour just to accommodate Milos's childish obsession is a horrendous mistake. We have no evidence whatsoever that Jace would be able to take on these responsibilities."

"Trust me," Zeus replied coolly. "We can make him into the man we want him to be."

Hera chuckled. "Is that your curmudgeonly way of saying you sanction this redressed interpretation of the Oracle?"

Zeus turned to his spouse and smiled for the first time since she stepped out of the crowd. And when Hera gently brushed a hand across his cheek, it struck Angie that these two legendary figures were just a couple of kids in love.

A moment later, Zeus broke free from the allure of Hera's eyes and addressed the crowd. "In accordance with the Oracle of Chaos, a wedding between the chosen two—Electra, daughter of Hades, and Jason, son of Poseidon—will commence in ten minutes time."

Jace wrapped an arm around Electra. "We're gonna have ourselves some fun."

That seemed to warm her up a degree or two. "You know something? We are." Then she turned to Angie, resurrecting that haughty smile of hers. "Don't get too cozy, girlfriend. You think you can keep Milos happy in that dreary little world of yours? Think again."

Angie flinched. Wasn't it just like Electra to zero in on her deepest fears? Of course, Angie wasn't about to let her know that. "He only needs one thing to keep him happy, girlfriend. Me."

"Right," Electra retorted. "Keep telling yourself that."

Although Angie waved Electra off, she was growing more and more uneasy about Milos's silence. He didn't look at all happy about the fact that he was no longer their golden boy. Once again, she glanced over at him to find that he was locked in a private exchange with Jace, whose smile had dimmed, making her wonder whether he wasn't as gung ho about this arrangement as he'd indicated. If she had to guess what he was saying to Milos, she'd bet it was something like, "Are we square now, brother? Am I forgiven?"

As for Milos, it was as if he were seeing his brother for the first time. There were tears in his eyes when he put his arms around Jace and kissed him on the cheek.

A part of Angie was thrilled. It appeared that Milos and Jace had finally put the past behind them. And she and Milos had been granted the freedom to be together. But had it come at too high a price?

Then the price grew steeper. Taking a tentative step toward Zeus, Hades said, "Do I have your permission to speak, brother?"

"You're asking my permission now?" Zeus grinned. "I believe the delicate balance of our relationship is shifting favorably. By all means, speak your mind."

Hades wrapped one arm around Electra and the other around Jace. "This was a stunning turn of events, but a fortuitous one, I believe. I proudly embrace Jason as my son-in-law. However, to expect my daughter to stay here and focus on the crucial duties expected of her while the half-breed who stole her bridegroom frolics around the island like a sea nymph is unfair to Electra and a danger to all of us."

Zeus seemed downright giddy with anticipation. "What do you propose, Hades?"

"That we banish the pair of them."

Of all the gasps that went up from the crowd, none was louder than Angie's. She turned to Apollo for an assist, but he was already marching toward Zeus. "Father, this is ridiculous. There has to be another way."

"Maybe in *your* kingdom, but not in mine. And might I remind you it was your seed that created this mess."

Then Zeus turned to his wife. "Hera, I know you're frothing with objections, but hear me out. Your observances on the Oracle were astute, but you failed to anticipate the fallout of such a shift. As queen of the gods, how would you feel about sharing the island with one of my paramours? If memory serves, you turned several of them into livestock."

Hera glared at him. "Only the ones who weren't already four-legged."

Zeus threw his hands in the air. "Do you see why this cannot work?!"

The two of them locked eyes for a good five minutes. Angie figured she'd never know whether threats were made, old wounds were opened, bargains were struck, or all of the above.

All she knew was in the end, Hera let out a sigh. "Milos, Angie, wherever the Fates take you, I wish you happiness."

His authority restored, Zeus fixed his eyes on Milos. "Summon your horses and have them fly you off the island. Your time here is finished. You will never see your homeland again. From this day forward, you are as dead to us as if you'd been devoured by Cerberus. Enjoy your life as a mortal, because that's essentially what you'll be."

Angie felt her heart break for Milos. It would be hard enough for *her* never to see Jace or Apollo again. Just looking at them now, staring helplessly at her, brought tears to her eyes. But Milos had known the people on this island all his life. They were his friends, his family. Could he live with such a cruel pronouncement?

Suddenly, Milos's lips were on hers, engaging her in a kiss that sent her heart soaring all the way to the heavens and back.

When their lips parted, Milos turned to Zeus, his face flushed with passion. "Then I suppose it's time for my new life to begin."

A moment later, the two of them were riding the horses across the Aegean.

THIRTY

THEY STAYED IN ATHENS that night, getting a room at a decent enough hotel down the street from the Grande Bretagne. They'd paid for it on Angie's credit card because Milos didn't have any money, having never needed it before this evening. He'd offered to do some hocus pocus to land them a five-star suite for free, but they both decided it wasn't the best way to launch their new life together. The next morning, they'd be flying to New York, commercially not equinely, with tickets paid for by Ya-Ya because Angie's credit card had maxed out with the room.

Ya-Ya spent the first few minutes of their phone call weeping with joy over the fact that Angie was not only safe but reunited with Milos, free of the obstacles that had threatened their happiness. Ya-Ya didn't seem at all surprised to hear she'd swum up a waterfall and walloped a full-fledged goddess. "Didn't I tell you you were special? Before long, you'll be scaling Everest with Milos on your back."

The only sad moment came when Angie told her about Milos's estrangement from his family. Ya-Ya struggled to find something encouraging to say, but it was obvious that she, too, saw it as a tough situation to turn around. And when Angie said she hoped it wouldn't prevent *her* from rekindling things with Apollo, Ya-Ya was noncommittal, declaring they should focus instead on "you and your soulmate, sweetie."

On that note, Ya-Ya insisted on hosting a cocktail party to introduce Milos to his new family upon their return from Athens the following evening. Angie hoped Milos would see a soothing symmetry in the fact that he'd traded one Elysium for another. The guest list would be small, just the three of them, plus her mom and brother. They were still clueless about everything that had transpired from Angie's first trip to Greece till now, so Ya-Ya pledged to have plenty of ouzo on hand to help them deal with the bombshells that would be dropped on them. "Of course, as soon as your mother sees the gorgeous man her daughter has landed, she may not hear another word the rest of the evening."

The minute she got off the phone, Angie wrapped her arms around Milos and pulled him onto the bed. Their lovemaking was every bit as passionate as that first night, but slower and more tender, because they knew they had all the time in the world. And as satisfying as that first time was, tonight was better. In the week they'd been apart, their longing for each other had only grown, and it seemed to Angie that Milos's body had become even more tantalizing, every little rise and fall a turn-on. And whether or not it had something to do with her having learned she was a demigoddess in the interim, she could honestly say she'd never worn a lover out the way she wore Milos out that evening. When he fell back on the bed beside her, his body damp with sweat and his eyes glassy, Angie felt a strange kinship with Aphrodite.

Afterward, they spent a long time lying there face to face. Sometimes touching. Sometimes holding hands. Sometimes just drinking each other in. And in those rare moments when they did speak, it was about nothing of any importance. There was a whole new world on the horizon for them, and he seemed to be in as little a hurry as she was to chart a course. As far as Angie was concerned, they could stay here—in this bed, in this room, in this moment—for the rest of their lives.

Angie had no idea what time she fell asleep, but she awoke the next morning as the first rays of light were tiptoeing into the room. After a discreet yawn, she reached across the bed to discover an empty spot where her soulmate had once lain. Thankfully, it didn't take long to find him. He was standing on the balcony, staring out at the Aegean, as naked as David and twice as sculpted.

But Angie's libido disappeared when she got a good look at his face.

It was creased with sorrow.

Climbing out of bed, she padded up beside him and placed her hands on his shoulders. He flinched, as if she'd pulled him out of a deep meditation. But when he saw it was her, his frown quickly morphed into a smile.

She kissed him first on the chest, then the lips. "Good morning, darling."

"Good morning, darling," he said, playing with one of the long curls dangling in front of her face. "Did you sleep well?"

She smiled. "Like a demigoddess who's just mastered the waterfall workout. You?"

He stretched his arms, flexing more muscles than she could count. "Wonderful, actually. I have you. What else could I want?"

She could have left it at that, grabbed his hand and led him back to the bed. But she couldn't get past the look she'd seen on his face a moment ago. "Level with me, Milos. Are you having any regrets about what happened back there?"

He hesitated for the briefest of moments, then smiled wistfully. "Will I miss Elysium and all those I love? Naturally. Will I miss having the opportunity to help lead them toward a new tomorrow? Of course I will. But if those sacrifices were necessary to ensure that we can be together, then I don't have a single regret."

Even as Milos leaned over and kissed her, Angie knew he was lying. She always knew when he was lying, and this time was more obvious than all the other times put together. It was in his eyes, which seemed willfully focused on her. It was in his touch, more tentative than usual. Even his lips were a beat behind.

It wasn't like she blamed him. She'd feel the same way if everything she'd known all her life had been taken away. Nor did she have qualms about how he felt about her. There was no doubt in her mind that he loved her completely. But it didn't mean his heart wasn't hurting because he couldn't have it all. And what would happen to that pain over time? Would it gradually fade away or would it fester inside him, threatening to tear apart this love they'd fought so hard for?

Well, Angie wasn't about to find out.

If it was the last thing she did, she was going to get it back for him. All of it.

But not without taking her place at his side.

EPILOGUE

It was all falling into place. And for that, he had his brothers to thank. Fools, both of them. One so blindly obsessed with his daughter's advancement that he was willing to accept any arrangement that would have her eating up the spotlight. And the other? What could be said about Zeus? Despite all his bluster, he was still under the thumb of his spouse. How else to explain how easily he gave in to Hera's dubious interpretation of the Oracle?

Not that it mattered. Neither interpretation would have gotten them what they wanted. Little did they know the Oracle was in his pocket, and always had been.

Soon, his son would be at his side, along with the demigoddess, whose gifts were revealing themselves to be more and more remarkable every day. To think he'd once tried to have her killed. But even *he* couldn't have imagined how deliciously full circle everything would come. And now, his every instinct told him that the three of them, along with the forces he'd assembled—both within and without Elysium—could easily vanquish his kin and take the true step forward into the world.

Of course, his son would fight it. He wouldn't respect him if he didn't. But Milos would give in. For the sake of the demigoddess, if for no other reason. Because while Elysium had been kicking up its heels last night celebrating the union the idiots thought would resurrect them, he himself had been trawling the Underworld. And with a combination of bribery and brutality, he'd come away with the perfect bargaining chip.

Poseidon laughed softly as he eyed his human treasure, whose glare hadn't softened despite his return to Mother Earth. "It appears you'll be seeing your Sugarplum soon. I can't wait to show you off to her, and to everyone else."

With a surge of satisfaction, Poseidon rose to his feet to take in the view from his hidden lair in the mountains of Crete. There was nothing he liked more than imagining that remarkable day, not so far off now. "Just you wait, dead man. Just you wait and see what an extraordinary family we'll make."

END OF BOOK ONE

ABOUT THE AUTHOR

Bill Fuller (Los Angeles, CA) is a television writer and producer. As a producer, his credits include *Hope & Faith*, *For Your Love*, and *Living Single*. Before becoming a producer, he was executive story editor on the long-running series *Night Court* and story editor for *Newhart*, as well as a writer for numerous other television series for Lifetime, Paramount, USA, NBC Universal, HBO, Disney, and others.